T
CALLISTA ALIGNMENT

STEVE GAY

ISBN: 978-1-8382177-2-3

United Kingdom, 2024 Rook Abbey Press

For Helen

“An outstanding SF series debut that explores what it means to be human.”

– Kirkus Reviews (starred review)

Prologue

NO ONE REMEMBERS THE moment they were born, but I do.

It was true at least the second time, Kali thought, lifetimes later and further from Earth than could ever be imagined. When she'd awoken in that dark womb, that capsule, a new life had begun. She'd stopped being who she was and started to become who she was destined to be.

In those first moments, she'd been consumed by panic, enveloped in blackness, and imprisoned inside her own paralysed body. Slowly her eyes had adjusted to a glimmer of light and her breath had returned, coughs and splutters first, then the terrified shrieks of a trapped animal. Her mind took its time to come back to her. It started with fragments of memory, random moments plucked from the past. She'd laid them out like a trail of crumbs. The farm, the sea, the library in the town. Leaving Devon, with the flags lowered for Churchill, and travelling to Africa. Writing to Mr. Dunstone, and then, someone coming with the news of his passing. She'd been with the children at Berseba, left them under a tree to read the telegram in the cool of the stock cupboard. *Then, a sudden shape, a dark movement, something engulfing me.*

A point of light appeared, red and blinking; it became characters, hieroglyphs dancing above her. Then the whole capsule seized a breath, gasped like someone released from the brink of suffocation. The lights subsided, became a constant red line stretching down to her feet, fine at first, then widening, opening.

Beyond the capsule, there was nothing but grey metal, a dimly lit corridor marked at intervals with strange symbols. A sweet draught arrived from somewhere and instinctively, she drew a breath. There was sensation coming back to her limbs now, fingers tingling, hands and feet cramping painfully, as if her blood was rediscovering abandoned pathways.

The roof to the cell had gone completely now, and when she looked up it was to a vaulted bulkhead and a row of windows, circular portholes rimmed in shining metal, and beyond them, the night sky. Beneath the floor a low rumbling started, like a mill-wheel grinding grain, vibrations growing and spreading, as if the walls, the floor, the whole corridor was awakening. It was as if she was aboard one of the steamers at Southampton docks, trapped in its hold as it prepared to cast off from the Ocean Terminal. She reached out to push herself into a sitting position, shouted again, and listened as her voice echoed along the corridor.

'Help! Help me! Please!'

There were more sounds now, something hissing like a garden hose, the squealing of metal in long-awaited motion. For the first time, the thought occurred to her that there was danger in being found, and she was afraid. Things of dark imagining were coming, drawn by the sound of her voice. A scream rose within her and she clamped it tight between her teeth. Further down the corridor, doors were opening in succession. There were indistinct murmurings, words being spoken, footsteps approaching.

1

Arrival

THE BODY LAY FACE up in the downpour, rain guttering along the ridges of its forehead. Dalatin Els-na regarded it from a distance, repulsed by the veins raised from its face, the swollen blue lips, the opaque blue eyes. He backed away, retreated to the cover of the pod station.

It could have been him, he thought. Perhaps if he'd been locked out a little earlier, he'd have encountered the assassin, met his end on this desolate street, far from his home world. And if he'd left the pod system where he'd intended, he wouldn't have been here at all; he'd be sipping cahcana at the Ancona hotel.

Els-na appealed to the station to admit him. 'This is an emergency!' he said. 'I know you're closed but someone's been murdered here, shot full of elemist by the look of it. You can't leave me standing here!' The station responded with an advisory that the body would be toxic and shouldn't be touched, but the doors remained closed.

The rain eased to a drizzle, and through a veil of clouds, three moons cast their light on the street. Across an empty lot, the twisted lattice of the old skytram emerged from the mist, a landmark that stood between the Commonwealth's glittering capital and the economic wasteland known as the Derelict Zone. There, the world of people dissolved, and the streets were abandoned to the depredations of wild creatures. He'd done business in more dangerous places, than Freeport, he told himself, systems where the rule of law was faint and distant, where murders like this were commonplace. This, after all, was the Commonwealth's great capital, the largest metropolis on Antaris and hub of the greatest civilisation ever known. This, more than anywhere was a place of order and enlightenment.

As if to confirm the point, a police detachment appeared at the end of the street, marching in perfect formation. Three of the officers went to the body and crouched around it, while another came over to the station to speak to him. For an android, it was very reasonable, Els-na thought, speaking to him in a civil tone, listening patiently. Once it had reviewed the record of what Els-na had seen, it offered to escort him from the area, set him on the right path for Ancona.

They walked side by side, the street darkening as they left the station behind, and their way lit only by the faint glow of kerb lamps. Els-na drew his coat closer around him, asked about the murder, whether an elemist shooting was common in the city.

'No more than most,' the officer said, then after a few paces added, 'Until recently.'

They turned into the next street, then into another, the glittering towers of the financial district rising ahead of them, transports coming and going from their skydocks trailing threads of silver. The street ended where the podway cut across it, and the officer stopped in front of a warmly lit underpass.

'Straight through from here and you'll see Ancona from the exit.'

The rain came down in a stronger burst. Els-na thanked the officer and hurried below ground. He strode out along the passage, ignoring a razorbird that burst from a ventilation pipe and hissed at him as he passed.

'Stop!' A voice echoed from the shadows of a side tunnel, bringing him to an abrupt halt. He spun around and peered into the shadows. It was a high voice, a curious voice, one that didn't belong to a person, but one of the feral humans that infested the Derelict Zone. This one was typically pitiful. It was less than six units tall and draped in rags, its hair a filthy mass, and its limbs fragile compared to his own. Quite why wild things were tolerated in the capital, Els-na had never been able to fathom, why the Derelict Zone had been given up to them, why they were allowed to stray beyond its boundary. He turned away from it, decided not to respond.

'Stop!' the human said, again, its voice now a dry rasp. 'Warm coat!'

'Away with you!' Els-na said. 'Off you go, now! Away!'

The human came into the light, and Els-na could see it more clearly now. It was holding a pistol at its side. The muzzle of the weapon was shaking, a row of amber lights indicating that it was still unprimed. A human attempting to use a pistol stretched credulity, but perhaps this one had seen the murder at the pod station and picked up the discarded weapon. Perhaps it had gathered its purpose, even if it couldn't understand how it worked.

'Warm coat!' the human repeated, and now it raised the gun and pointed it at him.

Els-na realised he had to act quickly, take back the initiative somehow. Whether domestic or industrial, the conditioned responses of humans were the same in every world. They understood authority, respected strength and confidence. He took a step forward and raised his voice. 'Away with you! Do you hear me, boy? Away now!'

The human appeared to waver. Its voice became quieter, but its words were still bold. 'Coat now,' it said. 'You die!'

Els-na stamped his foot and shouted with the full force of his voice. 'Put that gun down, I tell you!' he bellowed.

The human retreated a step, its hand shaking as Els-na started forward. It raised the pistol higher and closed one eye. Els-na lunged, but it was too late. The lights on the barrel went to blue and there was a blinding flash of elemist from the muzzle.

He hit the ground hard. The walls of the underpass reeled, and the floor moved in waves beneath him. There was hardly a trace of the toxin on his coat, but he knew it was already doing its work within him. He could feel it worming its way under his skin, chilling his bowels, starting its relentless journey to his brain. The effect would be fatal unless he was treated quickly, and even then, the odds were against him. The location of the nearest remedial post scrolled across his vision, followed by a message, telling him to go there without delay. It was a short distance on foot, just beyond the underpass, but it might as well have been the other side of the city. He forced himself to make the attempt anyway, to fight the freezing tide and push himself from the ground, but the most he could manage was to prop his shoulder against the wall.

There was a shuffling sound over to his side and he turned, hoping to see another late-night traveller. It was the feral again. It hadn't run off but stood watching what it had done.

'Alright, boy,' Els-na said. 'An accident. Just get help. Understand? Go to the remedial post! I'll give you anything, just... please!'

The human came forward and stared down at him, the gun still aimed. It glanced at the status display on the barrel, then lowered the weapon. 'I save,' it said. 'Stay here.'

'Save! Yes – good boy. Go to the remedial post! Quickly!'

The human crouched down beside him, pointed to the power cell bulging on the side of the weapon. 'Save *gun*,' it said. 'Stay for coat.'

Henik Varkesen shifted his position slowly, keeping his eyes on the feral humans in the plaza below. He slid another layer of packing card between himself and the floor of his balcony, tried to massage away the ache in his back. There had been a time when he had sat there more comfortably, a time when the balcony wasn't a naturalist's hide, but rather a place where people were happy to be seen. Then, it had looked across a vista of gleaming urban prosperity, and his guests were attentive to his stories of curious fauna, and adventures in wild and distant systems.

If anyone had told him back then, that Midsummer Plaza would become a wilderness itself, he would have considered it absurd. But no one had seen the hard times coming or expected such a cruel toll. For the commercial zone, the decline had been catastrophic. At the quays, the manufactories, the warehouses, workers were no longer economical to keep. The androids went into storage and the humans were just abandoned, left to fend for themselves. They turned feral, stripping the zone of anything that could be used, traded, or eaten, fighting to the death over a patchwork of territories that had once been business parks and shopping streets. Now, there was no need to travel off-world to study wild things; their behaviour could be observed within the city limits.

Henik adjusted his imager in anticipation of a coming drama. He had it focused on a feral tribe he called the 'Midsummer Clan.' They were searching the gutters of a conveyor opposite, sitting on each other's shoulders, and passing down fallen fruit. The display of peaceful co-operation was unlikely to last for long. It would be disrupted at some point by a dispute, or perhaps the intrusion of a rival clan. On this occasion, it was the latter.

He had seen the scenario unfold before. A scrub rodent or goad would venture into the plaza, hunted by ferals from an adjacent territory. The more aggressive members of the Midsummer Clan would rush forward, shouting and hurling stones, and would be met with a similar display from their rivals. Sometimes there would be injuries, but normally the interlopers would retreat, accepting the clan's possession of the square.

This time, it was a boark that was being pursued. A rare prize, it bolted from underneath the old skytram, a hunting party from the docklands desperately trying to stop it leaving their territory. Below Henik's balcony, the Midsummer Clan reacted as expected, grabbing anything that might be used as a projectile, and vocalising loudly to warn the intruders away. In the middle of the group stood the striking female he had named 'Alka.' The undisputed leader, she stood as tall as the males. Her overalls were worn knotted at the waist and her hair was drawn up into a wiry crest that stretched from her forehead down to the nape of her neck. In one hand, she held a blue javelin, and the other she used to signal to her clan members, dispersing them to concealed positions under the porticos at the edge of the plaza. Now, as she advanced alone, the boark burst through the encircling dockers and headed straight across the square at her.

The animal lowered its head and charged, squealing its

anger with every stride. It was no longer trying to escape but had selected a target. Alka stopped walking and stood quite still, showing no sign of indecision. The boark thundered at her, legs blurring beneath its squat body. She waited until the animal had closed to less than a hundred units, then drew the javelin back until the tip rested against her cheek. She settled into a low stance, knees flexed and ready, as the moments stretched and the distance compressed. Henik raised himself, sucked a breath, willed Alka to throw the javelin. Then just when it seemed she had left it too late, she snapped her arm forward and launched it with a high-pitched shriek and the full force of her body. It hit the boark square on the forehead and its legs crumpled mid-stride, the energy of its charge carrying it forward until it tumbled to a halt at her feet.

Alka stared at it for a moment, then wrenched the javelin from the animal's skull. She squatted to examine the prize, ignoring the dockland clan, who were already sprinting across the square to claim it. She took no notice when the flanks of the Midsummer Clan rushed from under the porticos and fell upon them with alloy bats from the old sports shop in the mall. It wasn't until the last moment that she heard the approaching footsteps, raised her head to see that one of the dockers hadn't been intercepted. He threw himself at her wide-eyed, and she reacted instantly, planting the javelin's tail deep into the dead animal, then pulling its point down to meet the attacker as he leapt. Henik had to look away, the need to spare himself the sight of a kill, something he rarely felt with other creatures. When he looked back, the docker had been speared cleanly through the throat and Alka was bracing the javelin against his momentum. Henik closed his eyes, erased the moment from his imager, marked for suppression the memory of another life lost in a conflict no one considered a priority to resolve.

Alka stood looking at the body for some time. She didn't appear to notice the enemy fleeing in disarray and didn't join her clan as it gathered around its prize. Instead, she pulled her fallen adversary aside, laid his body out in the shade of a tree. It wasn't until the boark had been bound to a pole and hoisted onto shoulders, that she turned away and followed her clan back towards the mall.

They filed past Henik's balcony, some of them leaping and spinning, calling to each other in high-pitched voices. Alka walked behind them in silence. She paused for a moment as if she'd heard something, then returned to the body and crouched to take something from it. She came back with an object, examining it as she walked, stabbing at it cautiously. Henik realised a moment too late that it was a pod token, too late to stop his own device responding to the request for a journey share. It emitted a muted tone, and displayed the location of its pair on a schematic map. Down in the plaza Alka continued walking, brought the token close to her face and studied it intently. Then as she passed beneath Henik's balcony, she lifted her head and stared at his position.

Henik didn't move until the Midsummer Clan was out of sight. Only then did he creep from the balcony into his apartment, re-entering the civilised world with the closing of a door. Not that there was much left there of his former life; the apartment was unsellable, everything of value and most of the furnishings moved to his new home in the centre of Freeport. It was a bare place now, but with the subject of his studies close at hand, he still found he could work better here than anywhere else. He sat and reviewed the day's observations, marking and filing them carefully, then sat back and looked at the plain walls and empty spaces. He stood up and went to the adjoining room, once a bedchamber, then wandered through the rest of the apartment, lingering in doorways, trying to remember how it had once been.

He went to the washroom to clean his hands and wondered how he'd ever been persuaded to make a mirror of the entire wall. His age was showing he thought, perhaps less in his body though, than on his face, which was beginning to crease heavily along his cranial ridges and cheekbones. It didn't matter, he thought; he'd never been handsome in the first place and his only interest these days was his work. It seemed a remote possibility that he'd find someone to share his life now, someone who would understand him, who would accept his controversial views on humans, his insistence that they should be considered fully cognitive, one of the advanced species of the cosmos.

The pod token had been unexpected though, quite curious, the more he thought about it. It was an attractive object to a human, he supposed, with its flashing lights and display. Or perhaps Alka had taken it as a battle trophy, the spoils of another small victory. Could she possibly have grasped what it was showing her, understood that it was connected to another token? It seemed unlikely. But then, she had looked up at the balcony so pointedly, stared at it. Could that really have been just a coincidence?

A vibration started in his skull. He walked back to the balcony room and slumped into an old recliner. 'Accept,' he said.

An ethereal figure materialised in front of him, the host of someone he recognised from long ago. 'Henik. I'm sorry to call you unannounced. It's been such a long time since our Compulsory Service, but I hope you…'

'Yan Feyrsten! It's good to hear from you! I always wondered if you'd decided to stay in the service, but then I heard you'd come back to Antaris. I meant to look you up, but...'

'Well, I did stay on for a while, but I was always more an academic than a military type. What about you? I keep seeing you being interviewed. Quite the celebrity you are, these days.'

'It pays the bills. Costs me in other ways, though. I get my share of hate.'

'Well, times are tough and you're still pressing for animal rights.'

'For humans. Only humans.'

Yan's host shifted uncomfortably, turned to look around the room. 'Well, actually, it's a human I'm calling about,' he said, a movement along his cranial ridges, betraying his discomfort. 'I think I've made a big mistake, Henik, and I could really use some advice.'

'What sort of mistake?'

'Well, I bought a human a few days ago and it's been really difficult. It's not taking to its new environment. You know, it's making a fuss about everything, hates being touched, hardly sleeps. I'm exhausted.'

Henik sighed. 'I'm sorry, but I've got to be honest with you, I really don't approve of the buying and keeping of humans. I know that sounds strange to most people but...'

'Please, Henik, I don't know what to do! She's not eating, and she won't take instructions. I've gone by the protocols, but it's no use. I was thinking about trying to take her back to the store, but then I saw you interviewed last night, so...'

'What do you mean "by the protocols"? What protocols?'

'*The Human Handbook.* I heard it was the best. It's the one everyone seems to use, anyway.'

'Sig Norvik. The gods' breath, Yan, you're reading Sig

Norvik! Look, he's great at the promotional stuff, I'll give him that, but not as a serious anthrozoologist. Just don't tell me you've adopted his "Assured Consequence" method.'

'Well…' Yan studied the floor, and his image lost some of its sharpness.

'You have, haven't you?'

'It seemed to make sense. I wasn't getting compliance.'

'So, you hit her.'

'Well, not exactly, but…'

'Look, you're an old friend Yan, but I really don't know what to say to you. I study humans in wild settings. It isn't my thing to work with companion animals. I don't find them interesting when they've been bred for domestic life.'

'But that's just it. This one *is* wild. She's just arrived on a transport.'

'What? Arrived from *where*? You can't just bring a feral human into your home! There are laws against it for good reason. Who knows what you could be spreading!'

'But she's not a feral! She's off-world. The transport came from Earth.'

'That's what they told you? Believe me, Yan, she hasn't come from Earth. The war in that quadrant cut off the trafficking several generations ago.'

'It was an old transport – really old. It was picked up interstellar, shot full of holes and drifting. The cargo was mainly minerals, but there were a few humans in suspension. She was the only one still alive.'

Henik stared at the hologram, the moisture suddenly gone from his mouth and his mind racing through the implications. Yan had no idea, Henik thought, not the slightest understanding of what he'd just said.

'Will you help me, Henik? Please. I really think you'd find her interesting.'

'Let's get this straight. You're seriously telling me that you've got a *natural*?'

'Well, if that's the term. Very natural I'd say. Is that bad?'

'Look, I doubt very much that you're right. But if you are, if you've really been told the truth, then you've got the only natural human we've had on Antaris in living memory.'

'Then you'll come?'

'I'm on my way. In the meantime, don't speak to anyone else about this. And mind your security.'

The day was draining from Midsummer Plaza when Torsta Jai spotted the body. It was lying out in the open, unclaimed and left to the elements. She approached it cautiously, turned full circle, holding her pistol in plain view and scanning doorways and alcoves for any sign of movement. The shadows were encroaching fast, clawing their way across the square, and with them came danger, the dark places bringing boldness to the feral tribes.

Satisfied that she was alone, Torsta detached the pistol from her palm, the lost connection prompting a warning message in her skull. She suppressed it, kept her attention drawn to the residential tower that dominated the far aspect of the plaza. It was a forlorn hulk of a building, weather-stained and left to decay, though when it was new, its cladding had shone so brightly in the solus that the crowds walked by, shielding their eyes. She'd considered buying one of the units; she could still see it, up near the top, on the morning side, with a view right out to the sea. It was affordable then, at the peak of her career, but in the end, she'd decided it was overpriced.

And now it was unoccupied like all the others, all except the unit owned by Henik Varkesen. There, the windows would sometimes glow at night, and from time to time she'd see him on the balcony making his observations of the feral tribes. She'd retreat then and stay hidden. She wondered sometimes what he made of her fall from grace, whether he remembered his part in it with satisfaction, or whether it played on his mind, perhaps even troubled him. She had no doubt what he would think about her change of occupation though, and that he'd bring unwelcome attention to her activities if he saw what she was doing.

Torsta took a black body sack from inside her jacket, unfolded it on the ground, and opened it from end to end. She worked a pair of protective gloves over her hands, tugging them into place over her cuffs, then took the body by the front of its coat, and lifted it into place. She walked to the pod station at the far corner of the square with the sack slung over her shoulder, turning to walk backwards every few steps, and keeping her guard up until she was safely underground and the station had brought a pod sliding to a halt in front of her.

Once she was inside, she dropped the sack on the floor and opened it to examine the body. She scanned the face, repeated it to make sure there was no mistake, then stood up, took a step away, stared at it. *Its Trajan. The gods' teeth, its Trajan!*

Of all the ferals in the Derelict Zone, the hundreds of them, thousands perhaps, this was the one with the biggest prize on its head. Trajan had ruled the dockland tribe for nearly a year, defeating its rivals and extending its territory from the transport terminals and the cargo port, right up to the gateway of Freeport's financial district. Under his leadership they'd become a menace to commuters, begging for food and harassing anyone that strayed from the beaten track. There had even been speculation about a feral connection to a number of murders recently, four off-worlders gunned down on the edge of the Derelict Zone, their bodies stripped of clothing. It seemed fanciful to most people that a human could use an advanced weapon, that it would attack a being so much more powerful than itself, but Torsta knew better; she'd seen how they could work together, how as a group they became so much more daring than any individual. Perhaps that was understood within the security service too, or perhaps it was just responding to media pressure, but the bounty on Trajan's head had been increased, unofficially as usual and only for those who needed to know, then doubled if a connection to the murders could be established. This small animal was a payday, the biggest of the year by far, and if it still wasn't much of a living, it would be enough to get by on, for quite some time.

That was all that mattered these days to Torsta. She had little use for honour anymore; that only counted when you had a position in society, when you had a respectable career, and when living comfortably was something you took for granted. Those times were gone, the public recognition, the friends in high places. Her crime, her downfall, had dismantled the achievements of a lifetime, washed away her principles, and reduced her to bounty hunting. Now the dark places of the metropolis were where she belonged, and her trade was in human flesh.

Trajan didn't look like much, Torsta thought, his face hollow-cheeked, and his eyes dull. But his coat was highly unusual, neither the corporate overall of a working animal nor one of the rough drapes ferals often made for themselves. This coat was fashioned from a woven cloth that appeared to have been cut from an up-market business coat. It was crudely reinforced with leather on the shoulders and elbows, but inside there were immaculately tailored pockets. It was evidence, but not conclusive, not enough to win the double bounty. There would need to be more.

One of the pockets had some weight to it, and the familiar shape of a pistol. Torsta pulled it out and studied it. It was a hopelessly outdated device, but that made it all the more dangerous. It wouldn't be security coded to its owner, so it could be lethal in the hands of anyone who found it, perhaps even a human. Torsta weighed it in her hand, felt the elemist gel shifting inside, but there were no lights on the display, and she couldn't get it to boot up and show its target log.

She placed the pistol on the floor, turned to search the other pockets, just as the pod swung into a sharp turn. The pistol skidded away and clattered against the door of the pod. For an instant, its charging light blinked, and a thought occurred to Torsta. She went to retrieve it, squatted against the bulkhead while she looked for the release catch on the grip. The charging cell dropped neatly into her palm, a standard specification still in common use. She drew her own pistol and swapped its cell into the old weapon. At first, the pistol was reluctant to respond to the new power source, but with a little coaxing from the heel of her hand, its display flickered into life. First, it laboured through an advert for an armourer on the other side of Freeport, then followed it with a public warning about a shooting range that had been prosecuted for offering human targets to off-world thrill-seekers. Finally, the weapon gave her what she'd been waiting for. 'Last Target' it said, then displayed the image of a man Torsta recognised immediately from the news feeds, an off-worlder who'd been found in an underground passage near Greengate Station.

Torsta slumped into a seat, let the pod's motion lull her as it careened through the darkness. It was tempting to take the two trophies in together, she thought, the pistol and the body, each of them validating the other. But she knew only too well how things worked in the security apparatus, and that placed more trust in the system than it deserved, particularly with an election approaching, and everyone seeking an advantage. Better to hold something in reserve, she thought, let Trajan's imprint on the weapon do the talking, and hold onto the body to raise the stakes. Or maybe she could go to the two rival political parties, split the package, and contrive two paydays.

She was still weighing how each course of action might play out when the pod called her attention with a soft vibration in her skull. It announced its destination, began to decelerate for its approach to Carnival Square. She told it to pause just beyond the security perimeter and sat looking at Trajan's face, juggling the risks and possibilities. It occurred to her that if there was proof that the ferals were now a violent threat, that they were killing people in the capital's financial district, it might force the Government's hand. If it decided to clear out the Derelict Zone, she'd be out of business. She turned the pistol over slowly in her hand and stared at it, hoped for inspiration. Then she noticed the raised impressions underneath the trigger guard. She ran her thumb over the grooves and the owner's details appeared in her vision.

Sela Leone. Now, isn't that interesting?

Torsta got to her feet, pushed the weapon into her belt. 'Redirection, pod,' she said. 'The Pet Warehouse at the Interstellar Terminal.'

***

The air in Midsummer Mall was heavy with wood smoke. It drifted along the main boulevard in clouds, bringing with it the fatty aromas of grilled boark. It rose through the trees to the tiered arcades, lifting spirits and bringing to Alka's struggling clan a brief sense of optimism. In the stairwells and on the bridges, women wrapped in their most colourful scraps chatted noisily, children ran laughing along the balconies, and down below, for once light of heart, men traded insults by the fire.

Further along the concourse, the smoke was interfering with the central display, reducing its holographic images to a weak dance. Alka moved from the shade of a bekan tree to improve her view. She scowled at two youths who were wrestling with the boark's head, chasing each other around the fountain that stood in front of the old veterinary clinic.

'Quiet!' she bellowed. though she understood almost nothing of the commentary. It was the graphic scenes flickering over the concourse that demanded her attention, that numbed her lips and chilled her blood. On the streets of some tropical town, humans were rioting. In this faraway place, buildings were ablaze and the giant people were hurrying towards waiting transports, some burdened by their possessions, others with children crying fearfully in their arms. Further back, the news drones had positioned themselves over a swelling mob. It surged through the streets like a river in flood, a chanting melee of field workers, waving sticks and tools.

Two guardsmen drew in on hoverbikes to cover the withdrawal. They held station on the road to the transport terminal, gunning their motors in a display of strength, sending up clouds of dust to engulf the advancing crowd. If it was meant to deter, its effect was the opposite. The humans reacted furiously, hurling stones and roof tiles, anything that came to hand, until suddenly, with all restraint gone, they charged. One of the bikes was struck by a chunk of masonry. It lost power and sank to the ground, the rider desperately trying to restart it. He had no chance. The mob was on him in an instant, dragging him from his machine and clubbing him mercilessly.

Alka turned away. She went to sit on the edge of the fountain, staring into its light-dappled water as she often did when she needed to collect her thoughts. One of the older males left his place by the fires and wandered over, chewing at a rib bone. He picked his teeth with a fingernail as he spoke. 'What does it all mean, Chief?'

Alka brushed her palm across the surface of the water and watched the spreading ripples. 'Trouble,' she said. 'It's somewhere else, across the sea, I think, but the People won't stand for it. We're already grit in their eye, Kit, and it will only take something like this…'

'We'll fight. We're the Unowned.'

She studied his face, the broad forehead, the skin of his cheeks weathered to a deep patina. There were times when she longed for things to be that easy, to have no responsibility for the sick and vulnerable amongst them. Then the choice would be a simple one, to fight, or to run. 'They can take us back whenever they want,' she said. 'Or wipe us out. They've left us alone because it suits them, Kit, but it won't last forever.'

He teased his beard through his fingertips, glanced away towards the grand arch of the mall's entrance, through the doors to the plaza beyond. 'Is that why that people has been spying on us, Chief?'

'He's been watching us since the cool season. I climbed up there and couldn't find much, just pictures and some speaking on a display device.' She looked back into the fountain. 'I call him, Plain. And I think he calls me, Alka.'

'Alka. It's a solid name. It sounds honest.'

She was suddenly aware of a constriction in her throat and swallowed it away to speak. 'I've never had a name before,' she said.

'What? You must have been called something, before this, Chief.'

'When I worked in the forest, we were called by our function. It was all that was allowed. My job – "cutter," and then a number.'

'So, we'll call you Alka, now?'

She smiled and prodded him in the chest. 'Perhaps, but "Chief" in front of the others. And that people, he's harmless, I think. But I'll go up there and check again.'

She left him and walked down to the entrance. The plaza was deserted now, the solus gone for the day, leaving only a light glow between the surrounding buildings. Across the square, the body of the Docker had gone too. If his clan had dared to come for him in daylight, it wouldn't be long before they were pressing their boundary closer to the mall, threatening the fragile encampment she presumed to call a citadel.

She studied the tall block of dwellings in front of her. A thick vine was strangling the façade, invading balconies, robing one side of the building in green. She had used it to reach each of the abandoned units at one time or another. Some nights she'd climb right to the roof and there, far above the Derelict Zone, she'd sit entranced, staring at the shimmering carpet of civilisation that butted against her world. Inside the block, most of the dwellings were tidy, some still furnished, as if their owners still hoped to return. They were spacious and comfortable quarters, but isolating spaces, designed to divide people one from another, separating their lives and their loyalties. Somehow, that suited them, but it wasn't right for humans; she'd sooner sleep in the mall, next to her fountain.

But how much longer could that continue? In some other land, field workers were fighting the People in the streets, and here the Dockers were provoking them without a thought for the consequences. *And all the time, the war of the clans goes on, the bloodshed, the killing, and no hope in sight.* She turned to look back up the boulevard, to where her clan was eating contentedly on a set of benches in front of the old veterinary clinic. As always, her eyes were drawn upwards to its haunting mural, the pale human girl that towered above the concourse on one of the supporting pillars, a cloak billowing around her and gold mosaic glistening in her hair.

2

Natural

KALI EASED HERSELF OUT of bed, trying not to put pressure on the bruise on the back of her thigh. She scowled at the translucent container by the wall, squatted over it to relieve herself, then returned to her foetal position on the bed, pulling the blanket around herself, like a cocoon. She tried to conjure a vision of her childhood, the beach below the farm, the warm pebbles, and the hush and rattle of the waves, but each time a picture formed in her mind, the clouds came over and the wind came at her in chilly gusts.

Three days it had been and there were no tears left to cry, three days of terrifying disorientation, three days of being prodded and restrained and scolded. Only now was she beginning to think rationally, coming to terms with a new reality. She thought of home, the farmhouse with its thick stone walls and its warm range, the sound of the tractor coming and going in the yard. Her father would know she'd disappeared. He'd sent the telegram about Mr. Dunstone, and would have heard in reply that she'd also gone. Lost in Africa. They'd go on with their lives never knowing anything more, everyone just wondering.

She wasn't sure how long she'd been asleep, but it was dark outside, and again the view through the window confounded her. The night before there had been two moons, smooth discs of similar size, one yellowish, and the other a striking shade of green. But if that wasn't disconcerting enough, they were now joined by a larger one, which was about to eclipse them both. Its surface prickled with the orange sparks of volcanic activity as if it was angry at its captivity. If there could be any doubt that this was a different world, the evidence wasn't hard to find.

But there was no doubt. Everything around her was alien, from the scale and vibrancy of the foliage outside her window to the grey vehicles moving over the distant hills, dancing on spears of blue light. And across the billowing lilac fields, three green towers drifted in defiance of gravity, colossal blocks of plant life, trailing tendrils of mist, they moved over the landscape, melting one by one into the distance, only for another to appear on the opposite horizon to take its place.

Inside the house there was more strangeness, rooms with shifting walls and curling ceilings, curiously moulded furnishings, and bizarre decorative objects. And there were unfathomable devices wherever she looked, things that winked and chirped, most of which she wasn't permitted to touch. None were so strange as their owner, though. Yan was a giant of a man, if that was what he could be called. She judged that he was at least eight feet tall, his body slim and muscular, his skin, smooth as a mannequin's, holding the exotic scents of cinnamon and sandalwood. The first time she set eyes on him, she'd recoiled at the coloured ridges along his skull and the pale yellow of his irises, but his face no longer shocked her. It was his hands that triggered a squeamish reaction when she saw them in motion. Not only did Yan have opposable thumbs like a human, but the last finger on each hand moved in the same way, folding around objects, manipulating them in a way that looked impossibly dexterous.

The hands came at her in her dreams, twisting her flesh, tearing it into morsels then raising them to his lips. In the light of day, her conscious mind comforted her with thin assurances, but her sleep belonged to fairytale horrors, giants in the sky, hideous laughter, and the grinding of bones.

That she was at Yan's whim and mercy was no delusion, though. He'd made no attempt to communicate his intentions, taken no steps to reassure her, or make her comfortable, made no effort to explain her circumstances. Yet somehow, his manner didn't seem predatory, his movements were calm, uncertain even, his speech deliberate, and there was something in his insistence on names and introductions that held a glimmer of hope. *Farmers' rule: Don't name the geese, or the pigs, only what you won't be eating.*

'Yan,' the first alien word she had learned, was obviously the giant being's name, and he used a word that sounded like 'Kali' to name her, urging her to repeat it over and over. At first, she tried telling him her real name, looking him in the eye and saying 'Emily.' It didn't seem to register, however firmly she said it, so eventually she relented and said, 'Kali.' Immediately there was a change of colour along the ridges on his head, but if it signified approval, it didn't show much in his facial expression. Perhaps there had been a slight nod, a movement of his mouth, but if she imagined it to be a smile, it was an economical one.

So, now she was Kali. She could live with that, but it was clear her status wasn't that of an equal. *Then what am I? Food: probably not. Slave: he expects no work. Something... else: no indication of that.* But a prisoner she most certainly was. She looked at the bracelet on her wrist. It was attached to the wall by some invisible bond that allowed her to walk only a few feet from the bed. It appeared a fragile thing, almost delicate, but it resisted all efforts to break free. For most of the time she'd been captive in Yan's home, she'd either been attached to some immovable object, or to an identical bracelet on his own wrist. It was as if he thought that given half a chance she would bolt for the door. It was beyond her why he'd think she would try to escape when, quite obviously, there was nowhere to run, but it was probably also the reason he didn't allow her any clothing. Clothes, washing and food, the most basic components of human life were things Yan was determined to control. Each of them, each element of independence had turned into a battle of wills, and they were battles she was losing.

Denying her clothes had been the main cause of conflict between them. It seemed to be a ground rule even when they had first met at the warehouse. It might have been because she had lashed out at him as soon as he came close, but the sheet was unceremoniously pulled from her grasp when she tried to bring it with her. She'd tried again at Yan's house, covering herself with a blanket or a towel whenever she got the opportunity but each time it had become a tug of war she couldn't win. 'No, Kali,' he would say calmly, followed by a complex range of noises, some of which seemed to originate inside his forehead, and caused the air around her to stir and prickle.

'No, Yan,' she replied, with as much firmness as she could muster, but to no avail. She was no match for his strength, and within a moment she was naked again.

She sat up and leaned her back against the wall. The volcanic moon had covered one of the others already and within a few minutes it would block the light from its twin. She wondered why covering her body was her top priority when she was constantly hungry and struggling to eat the dried food she was given. *I can't think clearly without clothes. I can't function. He has to understand that!*

She twisted to examine her bruise again. She wasn't quite sure how it happened, but one moment they were wrestling over the towel, and the next she was tumbling over the furniture. It was a hard landing on the floor, and then Yan was lifting her up again, setting her on a chair. The ridges on his head faded from bright red. 'Give, Kali,' he said quietly, reaching out to hold the towel between his fingers. 'Give.' This time she had unwrapped the towel herself and dropped it on the floor. It was a fine balance. She had to keep pushing for clothes but if it meant collecting bruises, she wasn't sure she could keep it up. *But there's no alternative. There can be no surrender.*

She took a deep breath and shouted, 'Yan! Yan! Give!'

Henik pulled off his boots and pushed them aside with his foot. He took a step into the lobby of Yan's home, took in the polished ironstone floors, the sumptuous drapery pooling in the corners, walls framed with camphorwood arches, and deep ceiling vaults, sculpted into shadows by hidden lighting.

'Nice,' he said. 'You're living comfortably these days, Trooper Feyrsten.'

Yan didn't look like someone who lived in comfort. He was dressed as if he was used to putting on the first thing that came to hand, doing so repeatedly until habit had robbed him of any choice in the matter. He was barefoot and wore a plain tunic with all the colour of the mudflats, and slung over that, a house robe, its sash left to trail on the floor.

'It's my parents' place,' he said, then sensing that his clothes were receiving attention, he smoothed his robe, gathered the sash by winding it around his hand. 'It used to be, anyway. They went to the gods last year. So, I came here from the coast, better than selling it, I thought.'

Whether a continuation of his parents' habits, or his own lifestyle, the house had none of Yan's personal disorder. There wasn't anything out of place, nothing that suggested casual living. 'And you aren't here very much?' Henik said.

'Most of the time, actually. My students are off for the recess, so I work here in my study.' He turned his head towards an annex where a desk and wall console shimmered through a verglas door.

'You teach...'

'Social History.'

'Of the Free Republic?'

'And the major Commonwealth systems. I'm at the National Academy. Usually though, I'm researching, so I'm here on my own.' He turned, observed the space around him for a few moments. 'Well, it's a big old place,' he said, quietly.

'And so, you got a companion animal,' said Henik. 'Where is she, then?' He took a few tentative steps into the house, half expecting something wild to launch itself at him, wielding a heavy object, as Alka might.

'Asleep – at least I hope she is.' Yan drew a wearied breath, 'Look, thanks for coming. I really hope you can help, but to be honest, after what you said, I'm even more worried.' He led Henik into a tastefully appointed reclining room, the centre of its floor sunk slightly lower than the area around it and clad with obsidian tiles in the style of the previous generation. On the far side of the room there was a low sea moss bench, straddled by an antique tray that was decorated with cavorting figures from antiquity. 'Take a seat,' he said. 'I've made some cahcana.' He stooped to lift the lid from a delicate enamelled pot, peered inside for what felt a very long time, then stirred it with a cupric spatula. Three times in one direction, three in the other. 'I don't suppose you approve of this. You know, the use of humans to…'

'Slavery in the Spice Islands, you mean – the plantations. You can call me a hypocrite where cahcana is concerned.'

Yan tapped the spatula on the side of the pot and poured the steaming liquid into two flasks. 'Slavery. I can see why you're making enemies if you go around referring to working animals that way.'

'I don't go out of my way to say it, but that's my view. If it gets me in trouble, so be it.'

Yan handed him a flask. 'Well, trouble's the last thing I want. So, when you said I should mind my security…'

Henik sank onto the bench, cupping the flask in his hands. 'Maybe I'm overreacting, but from what you told me it's just possible you've bought something very… special. The trader won't have realised what he sold you, but sooner or later he'll mention it to someone, who'll mention it to someone else. Then you'll be a target for every collector in the Free Republic, and believe me, some of them are people you wouldn't want to know.' He sipped his cahcana, held it in his mouth, let its vapours fill his head. 'We'll have to think about that,' he continued, 'but first, let's have some more of the background. You went to that animal warehouse over at the interstellar port, I suppose.'

'Two days ago. There were only males being offered around here, and I was looking for a female. I've already got one, so I thought that might work for them both.'

'You have another human?'

'Dill's been in the family for as long as I can remember. She works in the garden a bit, tends the orchard, although it's difficult to notice what she does.' Yan studied the surface of his drink as if he found something soothing about it. 'Not that I mind,' he said. 'It's just that she's getting old now; she's kind of reclusive and practically mute. Lives outside in the shed. I wanted a human for the inside, and didn't think it would be much trouble. Although, from what I've experienced with Kali...'

'Kali. And there was no mention that she was a natural?'

Yan sat down on the other end of the bench. 'I'd never heard the term until you used it, but they weren't covering up the fact that she was from Earth. They wanted her off their hands I think, so they offered me a deal. As long as I understood the risk.'

'That she wouldn't domesticate.'

'It was more the chance that she would catch something and die. She was looking very frail. It's quite a shock coming out of long-term suspension apparently, let alone adjusting to a new world. They thought she might have been out for two lifetimes or more.'

'Why suspension though?'

'It was a long time ago, so who knows. Perhaps they were sub-light for the locality and they intended to…'

'Well, we'll need to check her condition right away,' said Henik. 'I've brought my instruments and I can immunise against most things. Sounds like she was lucky if the others didn't survive de-suspension.'

'The transport had been caught in the war zone, so it wasn't in the best state. It probably didn't leave the quadrant in time to avoid the hostilities. You may know the history of it, a surprise attack by the Croesans on the Gilesse systems. It was full-on to start with.'

'It's still simmering now.'

'The transport had travelled out of the disputed zone when it was found. It was still out beyond the Outer Sequence, though, deep into frontierspace. Anyway, the hull had been breached and all the other cubicles had lost their seals.'

'Can't have been pretty.'

'Most of the humans died in the attack but apparently, a couple of them lived on for a while, roamed the ship. Probably not for very long. The jump drives were expended and most of the systems had powered down. You're right, Kali was very fortunate.'

'But as far as the warehouse was concerned you were buying damaged goods, or at least something they wouldn't guarantee. What made you take the risk?'

Yan's tone brightened. 'I felt… well, wait till you see her. I'm not sure what breed she is but…'

'Breed? If she's what you say, she won't have been bred. That's the whole point.'

'Well, I suppose. But anyway, she's quite something.'

'She'll be nothing if she doesn't thrive. We've got to get her settled before we can start work.'

'Work? You mean instruction?'

'Adaptation. I can help with that, but you need to understand that if Kali really is a natural, she's the answer to every anthrozoologist's prayers. She'll be untainted by selection or socialisation. She'll be able to unlock mysteries of human behaviour that have occupied the scientific community for as long as I can remember!'

Yan fidgeted in his seat. 'So, you want to study her, to experiment on her. I don't think I would be...'

'*With* her, experiment *with* her. She belongs to you of course, but if you let me work with her, I really think you'll both benefit from it.'

'I don't want her turned into a public curiosity. You've got to promise me that.'

'If anyone else gets hold of her, that would be the least of your worries. There are far worse outcomes, you know.' Henik reached over and poured himself another flask of cahcana, gave Yan time to absorb the implications. 'Does anyone else know about her?' he asked.

'No... well, yes, sort of. I did mention her to my brother this morning, but he's a busy man in Congress these days, and everything's about the election. No time for talking about everyday stuff.'

'Well, let's hope it stays that way. And let's hope we can get Kali to co-operate.'

Yan got to his feet, just as a high-pitched voice called from somewhere above. 'I suppose you'd better meet her then.'

By the time Yan had brought Kali down from her room, she'd said, 'Give' three times, and with increasing insistence. He'd decided not to react. Either she was mimicking the word without any understanding, or she was associating it with their quarrel over the towel. If it was the former, it wasn't a habit to encourage, and if the latter, it suggested that even after a rest, she was quite prepared to continue the dispute. Still, he'd brought the blanket from her bed and draped it over her shoulders, hoping it might make her more co-operative. *Just don't let her make a fool of you in front of Henik.*

Down in the reclining room, Henik was projecting *The Human Handbook*, its colourful diagrams fading away as it lost his attention. 'So, this is Kali,' he said, his voice low and calm. 'You'll see that I'm looking in your direction, not staring directly at her. Humans in the wild often take that as a sign of aggression or challenge. So, it's limited eye contact to start with. We don't want her to feel threatened.'

'You don't want to establish dominance straight away?'

'Trust me on this, Yan. It's a lot more complex than that "handbook" suggests. You can see already that she's not looking at me directly either. She's just snatching glances.'

'So, what do you think?'

'Unusual, to say the least, the pale skin, the copper-coloured hair. Doesn't look too unhealthy, all things considered. That's right, just let her go now, and switch off the bond. Those eyes!'

'Penetrating, aren't they? Feels like she can see right inside you. I keep wondering what she's thinking. Perhaps not very much, but when I try talking to her, you know, encouraging her, she stares at me as if…'

'As if she thinks you're condescending.'

'I know, it's a crazy thought.' Yan took a step back. 'Alright, the bond's off. Now, I've no idea what she'll do, so…'

'We'll just keep talking normally, body posture relaxed, and… she's slowly moving away from me.'

'Going to stand behind the recliner. She thinks she'll be out of sight.'

'She knows we can see her, but the barrier makes her feel more secure. Let her be for the moment. Just talk naturally.'

Kali didn't try to retreat any further; she just watched them over the back of the recliner. It wasn't much, but her calmness felt like progress and Yan was grateful for it. 'At least she's not being difficult,' Yan said. 'This is good.'

'Good,' said Kali, quietly, and shot him a glance.

'I think I've used that word with her before. You'll see she repeats things back.'

'Why don't you introduce us?'

'Introduce? Well, if you really think so.' He cleared his throat, waited until he had her attention. 'Kali, this is Henik,' he said. 'Can you say, "Henik"?'

She looked at him blankly for a few moments, and then her face creased at the forehead. Suddenly, her eyes widened, and she took hold of the recliner so fiercely that her knuckles stood out like pale marble.

'No!' she said. 'Yan! No Henik!'

Henik smiled. 'Well, that's clear enough. Maybe you're getting on better than you thought. Or at least you're the lesser of two evils.'

'You're not suggesting she thinks...'

'She's afraid I'm here to take her away. Even if you haven't got off to the best start, she prefers stability to uncertainty at this point. Now, can you see I'm smiling at her as I talk?'

'Grinning like an idiot, for some reason.'

'This is really important, Yan. The biggest difference between what I advocate and what's in that book is communicating with Kali on her own terms.'

'What does that mean – trying to copy human sounds?'

'No, not that. Anyone who's ever tried to mimic a human knows how difficult it is. Their palates have a completely different shape, and their larynx is more complex. They form sounds differently and across a greater range. But they still only have a fraction of our vocabulary because they can't communicate with their sinuses. Much of what we say is headspeak. It can never be comprehended by a human, or even heard, not to mention the way we manipulate data with cranial implants.'

'But they can hear what we vocalise?'

'They gain some understanding that way, but it's just the surface layer for us. So, we need to appreciate how they communicate, work at their level if we want more than a primitive interaction.'

'A conversation? You really think that's possible?'

'From what I've observed in the wild, I'm convinced of it. Humans make up for their deficit in part with fine movements of their bodies, their faces in particular. I've been studying it closely and if you want Kali to settle, you'll need to as well. They're highly communicative creatures, even if that challenges common preconceptions.'

His gaze went to Kali for a moment, and she didn't look away. He would discover, Yan thought, that dealing with Kali wouldn't be as straightforward as his scientific observations might have suggested.

'I've still got a place out at Midsummer Plaza,' Henik continued. 'There's a feral clan occupying the mall there and I've been studying them. According to what people would expect of humans, the strongest individuals should dominate, but it's not the case with the Midsummer Clan. A female leads them, including some much larger males, some of them nearly up to your shoulder. She shouldn't be able to do that, but she's an able communicator and that seems to be the decisive factor. She uses face and body movements to convey messages much more than the others.'

'And you think Kali will respond to that approach?'

'At some point in our evolution, we may also have communicated that way but we no longer need it. We're more static in our interactions now. That will confuse Kali, so it's why I am smiling at her. You think it's extreme, but she takes it as communication. She'll be reassured by it.'

'So, I should grin and move my body around when I speak to her. Then she'll stop playing up?'

'You've got to stop thinking about her in such simple

terms, Yan! The motions and expressions have to be correct and proportionate. You won't learn overnight.'

'But you can teach me?'

'If we let her, Kali will teach us both.'

Yan felt his insides slide. Whatever the logic in Henik's argument, he felt distinctly uncomfortable about where it was heading. 'I don't want to lose authority,' he said. 'I've heard you can never completely trust them.' Henik didn't reply. He turned, took a few steps away. Yan could sense the disappointment in his silence. 'I'm sorry,' he said. 'I just meant that…'

'I suppose you've been reading those baby-eating stories, have you? You've heard that if you turn your back…'

'Well, there was that priest last year. That was real enough.'

'So were the allegations against him from six of his novices. Maybe it really was his pet that caved his head in while he was sleeping. But if I had to live with the old turd, I'd have smashed him with that urn too.'

'Well… perhaps. Anyway, the point is that Kali needs to know she can't keep mucking me around.'

'Do you really think she doesn't understand the balance of power in this relationship? You're three or four times her size!'

Yan felt a knot of embarrassment forming in his chest. Standing quietly now, Kali was hardly a problem. 'I know!' he said. 'I know! I just don't know what to do! She's so demanding. I mean, she's got this thing about clothes, for example. I can't just give in.'

'Why not? Why not just give her what she wants?'

'Give!' said Kali brightly. She looked directly at Henik and smiled.

'Perhaps if she earns it with good behaviour, but it's the warm season, and in a natural environment, humans…'

'Forget that damned handbook, Yan! Listen to me – there's no one alive who's ever been to Earth, so just grasp what that means. There's only one standard for what's *natural* for humans, and Kali is it.' Henik drew his shirt over his head and held it out to her. 'Clothes,' he said. 'Henik gives Kali clothes.'

She let go of the recliner and came out from behind it, edged towards Henik a step at a time. She glanced back at Yan, then reached for the shirt. 'Clothes,' Henik said again, as she took it and began to put it on. 'Good! Well done, Kali.'

The shirt swamped her, falling almost to her ankles. She stood with her lips pursed, pulling at it, flapping the material. Then she turned to Yan and he felt her gaze weigh heavily on him. 'Clothes, Yan. Good!'

'That's told you,' said Henik. 'And can you see now, she's not just repeating what you say, she's learning words, manipulating phrases. This is impressive! I've known other humans build a vocabulary over time, but Kali has only just arrived and she's learning instinctively. I think there's even a rudimentary grasp of syntax!'

'Clothes,' said Kali again. 'Henik, give.' She had moved closer to him, extended her arm, with her finger pointed.

'That gesture shouldn't be too hard to figure,' said Henik. 'When they do that, they're directing attention along the vector of their arm. It's instinctive to them from infancy.'

She was standing in front of him now, touching his belt. Yan called to get her attention. 'Kali, say "Please".'

She looked back over her shoulder, chewing the side of her lip, then she prodded the belt again. 'Please Henik, give clothes.'

He unfastened his belt and gave it to her. She wrapped it around herself, drawing it tight and securing it with a knot. She was smiling at them freely now. 'Good!' she said, 'Well done!' She stretched her arms above her head and looked at the ceiling, vocalising a stream of unintelligible sounds.

'Say "Thank you" Kali.' Yan leaned forward and for a moment she drew away, as if she feared he would take the shirt from her. But when he extended his arm and pointed towards Henik, she understood immediately.

'Give Kali clothes,' she said. 'Well done, Henik. Thank you.'

'Extraordinary,' he said.

3

Trust and Fear

THE PET WAREHOUSE SMELT of animals, not of any species in particular but things that went with all beasts, the dried food and straw bedding, the musky staleness of urine and the chemicals used to mask it. The noises of animals echoed around the hollow building too, the competing calls and croaks and screeches rising and falling, as one creature triggered another.

The one that caught Torsta Jai's attention sat quietly. A furry thing with floppy ears, it occupied a cage in reception sucking the knuckle of its thumb, its unblinking eyes marbled with blue and gold. When Torsta came close, and tapped on the mesh, the animal turned away, tried to hide its face with its hands.

It seemed to Torsta that she'd been amongst animals all her life. She'd hunted them for food in a dozen different star systems, kept them from her camps with fire, driven them from their water holes. She'd fought them too, those beasts whose only use was to wield a cudgel. She'd shot and stabbed, and slashed her way through more animals, more species than she cared to remember. But she didn't understand them, she knew that, she didn't understand what caused a person to buy one either, to keep it as a companion, care for it as a family member even if it served no useful purpose. She understood even less what drew someone to work in a place like this, to spend their time tending to the needs of lesser beings, and consider it a privilege, a lifestyle choice.

The girl at the counter moved with a spring in her step, went about her duties with enthusiasm, and greeted Torsta with an unnatural cheerfulness. She wore a yellow tunic with the words 'The Pet Warehouse' emblazoned across the chest and a wide-brimmed hat in the style of a far-world explorer.

'Do you like our new arrival?' she said. 'That one's already sold, I'm afraid. If you're after one of those, you'll need to join a waiting list.'

Torsta turned back to the cage that had caught her attention and peered inside. The animal was rooting around now, pursuing a beetle with its long fingers. 'I've never seen a pog in the flesh before,' she said.

'Signa's a long haul for a trader. It's not even in Commonwealth spacetime, but that's the only place these little creatures are found, and they're fetching crazy prices at the moment. That one would have set you back ten thousand.'

'You could buy a transport for that. Or several humans.'

'Well, humans are alright, I suppose, but pogs make so much nicer companions. They're docile and affectionate. They have less intelligence than humans, so they can't do much, but that's an advantage for the up-market niche.'

Torsta tapped her fingers on the cage again. The creature gave a pitiful cry and shrank away. 'I expect the news from the Spice Islands will make them even more popular,' she said.

'We've already had some cancelled orders and returns. I had a customer this morning saying she didn't like the way her human was looking at her.'

Torsta left the cage and came to the counter. 'Well, it's a

human I've come about, one you might have had here a year ago. I need to talk to Sela.'

'He went home a while ago,' said the girl. 'We don't get much custom in the evenings.' She glanced at a holographic clock model of Antaris with its eight moons revolving in sedate ellipses. The planet glowed with the yellow and green colours of The Pet Warehouse and bore its logo above a display of the time and date. 'You'll have to come back tomorrow.'

'He'll talk to me,' said Torsta, evenly. 'Call him. Tell him it's Torsta Jai.' She held the girl with her eyes until she wavered.

'Well, I'll try, if you don't mind waiting a moment. Perhaps you could browse the pictures and tell me if you see what you're looking for. We've had over two hundred humans on the inventory in the last year.' The girl waved her hand over the counter and images of each human lifted from the surface. 'The first was this bald one, a corporate purchase, I think. And it runs all the way along to this copperhair female we sold a couple of days ago.' She prodded the hologram at the end of the line, and it shivered.

'Unusual appearance,' said Torsta. 'How much did it go for?'

'She was from Earth. They found her on a drifting transport way out beyond the Outer Sequence. Sela practically gave her away. She'll need expensive treatment, or she'll fall to her first bout of clearwater fever.'

Torsta leaned over the counter and studied the image of the human closely. She picked it up and placed it on the palm of her hand. It sat down, legs dangling over the edge of her finger, then looked around impassively. 'Earth, you say. That's the Sun system, I think. Further even than Signa, way further. Who bought it?'

'Just some guy.'

'A Freeporter?'

'Not for me to say.' The girl's forehead shifted to a warmer hue. She looked away, turned her attention back to the row of images on the counter. 'So, can you see the one you've come about?'

Torsta put the image of the Earth human back in its place, then scrolled along the line until she reached the early part of the year, and an image of a male of average size, with a thin beard and roaming blue eyes. 'There,' she said. 'This one.'

'Yes, I remember him,' said the girl. 'Miserable and bad-tempered. He would never have worked out in a domestic setting. Anyway, I came in one morning and he'd gone. Sela said he killed himself.'

The air began to shimmer beside the girl and the host of a heavy-set man appeared, the hideous colour of his shirt distracting from an ugly scar that intersected his cranial ridges. He sauntered around from behind the counter holding a grilling wand and accompanied by the sound of seafowl, until the girl made an adjustment and filtered it out.

'Life still tough is it, Sela?'

'I do what I can to get by. Didn't realise you'd been released, Torsta. How was life on *Bleak Penance*?' His lip curled in a vulgar display of amusement.

'You can imagine, I'm sure.'

Sela stared back, his eyes blank, as if his imagination was a muscle he rarely flexed. 'And now you're out early,' he said. 'Assault and battery in public service. Who would have thought it possible in this day and age? How many people did you bust up in that bar?'

'Only a few.'

'A Chief of Police who beats the shit out of anyone who

crosses her. So much for the "Peaceful Society" and all that crap.'

'None of us are peaceful when we reach our limit. Foolish to think otherwise.'

'And now they've forgiven you, so you can get back to hassling small businesses.'

'You were selling ferals, Sela. But you're presuming too much. They didn't reinstate me. I'm freelance these days.'

'And you make a living looking for lost pets.'

'Not quite,' said Torsta. 'We should talk privately.' The girl didn't need to be asked. She slid away from the counter and walked out into the warehouse with a bag of feed under her arm. Torsta watched her go, then turned her attention back to Sela. 'You had a human that killed itself,' she said. 'About a year back.'

Sela's host turned away, went through the motions of flipping something over on his grill. 'Doesn't happen often,' he said, 'Shame when it does, though. The record is on file.'

'How did it die?'

'Strangulation, as I recall.'

'And then it started a new life in the Derelict Zone.'

Sela's cranial ridges ran through a quick sequence of shades. He gave his grill a couple of prods, opened his mouth to say something, then appeared to think better of it. It was always that way with Sela. He had a cunning and duplicitous nature but lacked the composure to disguise it.

'Why did you lie about it?' said Torsta. 'I wouldn't have thought it was the first human to escape from here. And you can't be responsible for what it did afterwards – the *crimes*.'

Sela poked at his cooking again, his movements slower, more deliberate. It was as if his brain was telling his body to act naturally, so guaranteeing the opposite.

'Your human, reference 40/207 in your holodex. It's Trajan, one of the leading ferals. There's a price on his head.'

'As you say, I'm not accountable for it.'

'Except that you've falsified your records.'

'Oh, cut the crap, Torsta! Perhaps one of your arse-licks would've served me up with fine for that, but why would you give a shit now?'

'I hope my officers would've been more interested in your motivation for concealing the truth. Why would you do that?'

Sela sighed wearily, as if he thought the matter was now just a technical infringement, something he could bat away as a recording error. 'Look Torsta, just get to the point. Then I can tell you to piss off, and get back to my dinner.'

Torsta lifted the pistol into view and watched Sela's forehead respond with a livid blaze of colour. 'Trajan won't need this anymore,' she said. 'I've got his body outside in a bag. But the weapon is registered to you at this address, Sela. Its memory shows eight kills in the last year. Three of them are the faces we keep seeing on the news, the murdered off-worlders.'

The moons of the holographic clock chased each other around their orbits while Sela's grilling wand wavered. He stared at the gun as if it might provide him with some improbable explanation, but when he spoke, the arrogance had gone from his voice.

'What do you want?' he said.

'It's progress,' said Yan, 'but only by giving in to her. I can't always do that, Henik. I need her to accept instructions too.' Across the room, Kali was perched neatly on the arm of a recliner, her knees pulled up beneath Henik's shirt. She was watching their conversation closely, moving her lips when they used a word she recognised.

'Don't underestimate her. I came here more in hope than expectation, but what I've seen matches the story. This human isn't a feral or a working animal, one look at her hands tells you that. But she hasn't got the conditioned deference of a domestic either. She's trying to interact with us, one cognitive being to another.'

For some reason, Yan found Henik's appraisal disturbing. He felt a surge of apprehension as if he'd taken a wrong turn in the woods. 'Can we change that?' he said. 'Will she adapt?'

'Henik exhaled sharply. 'Will *you* adapt, Yan? That's what's concerning me most at the moment!' For a man who spent his time in patient observation, his frustration was bubbling close to the surface. 'I'm not sure you're getting this,' he continued. 'You're still talking about Kali as if she's like any other human you might have bought. You want her to be compliant, perhaps do some simple tasks, sit in quiet companionship.'

'You can still do your tests, though.'

'No, I can't. And to be really blunt, she would be wasted on you. If you want her to conform to standard expectations about how humans should behave, it would be really sad for you both, in my view. In fact, it would be a tragedy. You'd lose her personality, everything that she is. Is that really what you want?'

'Of course, not – I wouldn't want that at all! It's just that it's all so...'

'And from a scientific perspective, it would destroy what makes her a natural. We would lose the opportunity to properly understand the species.'

'But what's the alternative? I can't just turn my house into some zoology lab where she can do as she pleases and mess everything up.'

'I'm just saying we carry on as we've begun, and you take the word 'pet' out of your head. You have to think of this on a more co-operative basis. Trust me on this, Yan. Please.'

'Please,' said Kali.

Yan leaned back in his chair and watched her face. She didn't understand what they were saying, but her eyes darted back and forth between them as if she was desperate to discover the meaning of their conversation. Henik's argument made sense, but it meant he would need to treat her differently to every other human he'd ever encountered.

'I'll tell you what,' he said, eventually. 'Let's put your approach to the test. Let's see what happens when we want Kali to co-operate on something more challenging. You want to give her a medical check-up and shots? Let's see you do it without having to restrain her. I couldn't even cleanse her teeth this morning without a tantrum.'

'And that will convince you?'

Kali seemed to sense that the conversation had reached a crucial point. 'Yan?' she said, and smiled at him. 'Good?'

He sighed. 'Yes… good.' He got up and brought Henik's black medical case from the hall. Kali stared as it opened on the floor, revealing an array of shiny instruments, coloured vials in padded compartments, and a clutter of mundane clinical materials.

Henik held out his arm and made a hooking gesture with his fingers. 'Alka, that clan leader at Midsummer does this when she calls them all together. Kali, come here please.' She tilted her head and held him in her gaze for a moment, then slipped down from the arm of the recliner and went to stand in front of him. He motioned at the medical case. 'Trust me, Kali,' he said. 'Trust.'

'Trust,' she repeated, and Yan caught her glance in his direction. It was only for an instant and he couldn't imagine that she had any real understanding of the word, but somehow, he felt it was meant for him, that she knew he had set her a test.

Henik pointed to her mouth and without further ado she opened it wide, waiting patiently while he shone a light into it and palpated the glands around her neck. 'Human physiology has some broad similarities to our own,' he said. 'More complex in digestion and respiration and less efficient, reproductively quite effective, nervous system more…' He took a bacterial reading from Kali's palate, then pointed to her eyes and she allowed him to examine them as well. Finally, he scanned her forehead, checking the data for abnormalities. 'All fine,' he said. 'In need of nourishment, but we'll get to that. I would put her somewhere in her third decade. And she's co-operating, you'll notice.'

'Just wait till you get out that probe. They say that humans don't feel pain like we do, but…'

'But you are an educated man, and don't believe that,' muttered Henik. He took hold of Kali's hand and looked her in the eye. 'I'm going to inoculate you now. It will hurt a bit. Trust?' He reached into his case and brought out a polished cylinder, inserting an orange vial with a crisp click. The cylinder hissed in response and a sharp point of light extended from its end.'

'Good luck,' said Yan.

Kali looked at the light as it came towards her in Henik's hand, then she pushed up her sleeve and offered her arm. 'That's interesting,' said Henik. He put the cylinder to Kali's skin and sent its light spearing into her. She watched her flesh illuminate and didn't flinch. 'Unless you disagree, I'll install a tag as well, so she's on the central register in your name.' He took another device from his case. 'Just a dot in the heel of her hand, similar to the ones we all have, but with a locator. She'll be safer that way.'

'You mean against theft?'

'Well, yes. You'll have to take particular care with her.' He pressed the device into her hand. 'There we are,' he said. 'Finished. Well done.'

'Finished,' said Kali. 'Thank you, Henik.'

Suddenly, Yan felt outnumbered. He watched them smiling at each other and wanted to be on the same side as them, not fighting a rearguard action against mounting evidence. 'Alright, you win,' he said. 'I accept it. She made an effort to tolerate that, because you won her trust.'

'Payback for giving her something to wear.' Henik put his instruments away and sat staring into his bag for a few moments. When he spoke again his tone was quieter, almost as if he was talking to himself. 'There are a few old images of Earth in the Commonwealth Archives. Very few, and very old, collected by traders and pirates, several generations ago, at least. The images show humans living in thick forests, on small islands, desolate plains. Scattered tribes, still at the early stages of civilisation.' He raised his head and looked into Kali's eyes. 'You know, we suppose this species to be primitive in its natural habitat, but I'm sure Kali knew what I was doing. Somehow, she understands inoculation.'

A small crowd had assembled in the twilight to watch the spectacle outside a dilapidated house on one of Freeport's outer estates. Local beat officers had stationed themselves either side of the gate, and the owner was standing on the street, grim-faced and shaking, as a large transparent box was carried down her path towards the jaws of a waiting transport.

'Jus' look at it!' she said bitterly to a news reporter. 'Look at it! It got into my kitchen store. An' it had a sharp!'

Inside the box, a ragged human was making frantic attempts to escape, hurling himself repeatedly against the sides, his face obscured by a flying mass of hair and his body smeared with the filth of an urban wasteland. The box shifted unsteadily, and the androids at each corner paused at the gate to reposition their grip. The woman retreated a step, moved closer to the reporter.

'Knows it's a goner, that one. Won't be the last, though.' The woman gripped the rail of her fence and paused to draw a breath. 'There's children round here an' we're 'spected to put up with this?'

'Have any of your children been harmed by humans?'

'Not yet, but a girl in the block over yar, she were out playing and got threatened with a stick by two of 'em. And there's been those what have lost their pets. Humans they'll carry away with them, but other sorts, goads, dorgs, they'll butcher them in our own yards. I'm tellin' yer, we'll be next. She looked towards the horizon where the streetlights stopped in a clean line, the darkness beyond marking the abandoned expanse of the Derelict Zone. 'What's happening on them islands, it'll be here next. These vermin need proper sortin' else there'll be blood running down these lanes too.'

The reporter shifted his imager from the human to a close shot of the woman's face, then followed her gaze to the darkening skyline. 'And what do you think should be done?' he asked.

'Well, not this! Not waitin' till they wave a sharp at you, then putting 'em in a box, nice and gentle. There's got to be ways of getting rid. If you ask me, we'd be better off startin' again with androids than fearin' them filthy things.'

'So, there you have it from the people most affected,' announced the reporter, cutting back to a shot of the transport's closing doors. 'Real voices from the fringes of our city saying they've been abandoned by the Government, that they're afraid of the animals that hard times are bringing to their doors. This is Niko S'tana on the Marsh estate, reporting exclusively for The Georgi Factor.'

Santi Aspil adjusted the collar of her tunic and scrolled through her debating points one last time. Arcing around her, The Georgi Factor's simulated audience was responding to the Marsh Estate report with conservative shades. At her shoulder, Georgi Sivas was tugging at his cuffs while he waited for his cue light. As the report came to an end, he straightened in his seat and signaled the beginning of the debate with his trademark drumming of his fingers.

'Thank you for that, Niko,' he said, with a grave tone Santi had only ever heard him use in front of an audience. 'For those of you just joining us here on The Georgi Factor, I should update you on the developments in the Spice Islands today. We're hearing that the SI Government has lost control of one of their ten islands, which has been overrun by renegade humans. We've seen horrific acts of violence, hundreds of people killed, hostages taken. Chief Counsellor Haugen has promised our unwavering support in restoring order. He's assured those with loved ones holidaying there, that their safe return is his highest priority.'

In truth, that wasn't what Amund Haugen had said first. Only Santi had witnessed his initial reaction, the stream of obscenities, the frustration that a crisis overseas was threatening his slender lead in the final days of the election campaign. What he had said in public though, the calm and considered comments, Santi remembered verbatim. She'd composed the words herself.

Georgi swivelled in his chair, conjured a model of the Spice Islands on his news desk with a sweep of his arm. The volcanic archipelago rotated on a glittering sea, then faded into an image of the city of Freeport, with its familiar coastal features and iconic landmarks. 'The appalling events across the sea may seem very distant,' he said, 'but we have echoes of unrest much closer to home. Many are now urging strong action to deal with feral humans, and it's fast becoming the central issue of this election. Heritage candidates seem to be catching the public mood better than the Progress party, the latest projections showing the outcome too close to call.

'This evening on The Georgi Factor, we'll be asking how worried we should be about the humans among us, and we'll be hearing from a stellar panel of guests. On my right, please welcome Widdig Terreden of the Human Policy Unit, a campaigner for what he calls 'enlightened engagement.' For the Progressive Government, we have Counsellor for Internal Affairs, Santi Aspil, and for the opposing view, Heritage leader, Maarten Feyrsten, a man who may be just days away from becoming Chief Counsellor of the Free Republic of Antaris and its Commonwealth. Also, here tonight and well known to many of you with companion animals, is Sig Norvik, celebrated author of *The Human Handbook*. So, let's get to it, and if I may begin with you Widdig, tell us what you make of the scenes we've been witnessing in the Spice Islands.'

Widdig Terreden appeared to be taken off guard by the question. Santi knew him as a modest and gentle man, who was rarely in the public eye. Perhaps he'd been expecting Georgi to go to the politicians first, but he had to clear his throat before responding and he started nervously. 'Well, I believe… I think that most of us will be horrified. Could such events occur in a more advanced country such as our own? Yes, I'm afraid they could, but we must consider root causes, rather than leaping to poorly-considered solutions.' He was hitting his stride now, and Santi felt relieved on his behalf, even if his message was not entirely helpful. 'The fundamental issue,' he said, 'is that we've uprooted a species of cognitive beings and treated them very badly, holding them in captivity, breeding them for our own purposes, casting them aside to fend for themselves when it suits us. The humans on the Spice Islands are starving, for reasons that were entirely avoidable. And in our Republic, there are many destitute humans too. Unless we re-think this relationship, we are storing up terrible problems for ourselves.'

The holographic audience lit up in a range of opinion colours, quickly settling into a pattern that disagreed with Terreden's perspective. Santi could see a nerve twitching at the back of his neck.

Georgi stared at his data display, then froze the hologram with a casual flick of his fingers. 'Fifty-nine percent, against,' he said, turning his gaze on the Leader of the Opposition. I imagine you'll be pleased to see that, Maarten Feyrsten. It's only a small sample, but perhaps you see it as support for your position.'

Feyrsten launched into his opening comments with the assurance of a man entirely confident of his argument. 'Results like this may chime with our message, Georgi, but in times like these, I take no pleasure in them. Not when they show the extent to which people are living in fear, right in the heart of the wealthiest city in this or any other world. This Progressive Government has been entirely inept on the human question, and people are paying the price for its complacency.'

Feyrsten's attack came as no surprise to Santi. It was as direct and vigorous as she expected, and she had enough experience of him to know there would be no winning. She would fight back when her turn came, but there was something about Feyrsten's manner that always unsettled her. Perhaps it was his composure, the way he kept his hands loose and still, however strongly he made his point, that left her feeling that he had won, even when she made a better case. He had the air of a superior being, handsome, urbane, difficult to resist without appearing desperate.

'I am not anti-human, as some have been suggesting,' Feyrsten continued, sweeping his eyes around the virtual audience. 'Far from it. We have a human at home, and we're very fond of him. I know millions of other families feel the same way about their pets. I also recognise the importance of humans as productive units in our economy, driving our trade here on Antaris, and throughout the Commonwealth. That said, we simply can't ignore the risks that humans present to an orderly society when they aren't managed properly. We have a responsibility to act decisively, so people can feel safe in their homes.'

Santi knew she had to assert herself. If she didn't take Feyrsten on, his blend of guile and reason would give Heritage the high ground. She raised herself up in her seat, and without waiting to be asked, went straight to the deceit in Feyrsten's comments. 'Act decisively?' she said, her tone a bitter contrast to Feyrsten's smoothness. 'Let there be no illusions about what

Maarten means by that. He would mobilise the National Guard to tackle a few stray animals. How strong! How courageous! Perhaps he believes we should be setting elemist traps, culling humans across the country. Well, I am sure that would be popular with his most ardent supporters, but …'

'That really is unworthy of you, Santi,' countered Feyrsten, barely raising his voice. 'It's quite wrong of you to suggest that controlling feral numbers can't be done responsibly.'

Santi wasn't going to be put off. The graphics were showing she had scored with her opening attack, a slim majority of viewers sharing her concerns. She shifted her weight onto her elbows, locked eyes with her opponent, with all the intensity that had propelled her from provincial obscurity to a leading position in government. 'I'm afraid this is the sort of honeyed deception we've come to expect from Heritage,' she said. 'Voters won't be fooled by your assurances, Maarten. However, you look at it, the outcome of your policies would be the violent death of large numbers of humans. Your conscience might allow that, but it's not what our Peaceful Society should be about.'

Feyrsten came back effortlessly. 'If Santi still believes in the old Peaceful Society sentiment, then she hasn't been to the Marsh Estate,' he said. 'She hasn't spoken as I have, to our leaders of commerce, outraged that visitors from Commonwealth worlds are killed on our streets when they come here to do business. And frankly, she's out of touch with ordinary people too, as she'll discover when the votes are counted. These are hard times, and the public won't accept politicians who sit on their hands.'

Santi was stung by Feyrsten's remarks, and the graphics showed they had been effective with the audience too. When she spoke again, she found she was wrestling with herself as much as with her opponent, struggling to maintain an authoritative tone. 'I'll take no lectures from the party that presided over the causes of this situation,' she said. 'The public knows very well that there would be no feral humans, no Derelict Zone, but for the reckless economic policies of Maarten's party in the past. Now he's playing on the public's fear, blaming humans when they are just the symptom of a much deeper problem.'

Georgi seized the moment to intervene, lifting his voice to regain control of the debate. 'Strong stuff, from both sides! I was expecting a lively debate this evening and that's certainly what we're getting!' He turned his chair towards Sig Norvik, who was sitting quietly at the end of the table, with an air of relaxed detachment. 'If I could bring you in at this point, Sig. As a leading authority on humans, can you give us some insight into the behavioural issues at work here? What lessons should we be drawing?'

Norvik stroked his chin with his thumb and looked at each of the other panel members in turn, as if he was about to deliver the wisdom of the ages. There was no doubting his popularity, but he was far too smug for Santi's liking. In fact, there was something about him she found decidedly creepy, something artificial and self-regarding. 'Your viewers will have heard me say this before, Georgi,' he said. 'This isn't the fault of humans, it's bad owners who are to blame. That is what needs to be addressed. Widdig makes a fair case about the way humans have been treated, but his standard for what he considers cognitive is lower than mine. What I can say from many years of experience with this species, is that humans are animals that crave discipline. We shouldn't imagine that they are happy roaming the streets in the Derelict Zone, or that they enjoy going on the rampage in the Spice Islands. It's a cry for direction and order.'

Santi watched the colours flicker in the virtual audience. It appeared confused by what Norvik was saying. There was no requirement for him to favour one side of the argument or the other, but if he gave his support to either of the parties it would be a significant development in the campaign. Georgi seemed to sense that what Norvik said next might be crucial and pushed him for a further opinion. 'And how should that cry for help be answered?' he said.

'Well, I'm afraid that some humans have gone too far to be retrieved. Sad as that is, I do have some sympathy with Maarten's view. On the other hand, there are many ferals that simply need to be brought to heel so they can be valuable assets once again.'

'Do you think that people would be prepared to take a feral human back after what we've seen of their capacity for violence? Would that be wise?'

Norvik turned his head and stared into the audience. 'Certainly not where humans have strayed from a domestic setting. There's no going back once their natural cunning and depravity has come to the fore. But most will be industrial animals and I believe there's a fair chance of putting them back to work. With firm management and strict containment, they could once again play a productive role.'

'I would like to respond to that, if I may,' said Widdig Terreden, his tone as ever, mild and courteous. 'What worries me is that there will be owners out there who hear Sig's description of humans and take it as the excuse they need to abandon their pets in difficult economic times. It's only going to make the feral problem worse if people gain a false impression of human behaviour. Treated well, with dignity and respect, humans are loyal and obliging.'

'Well, I agree to an extent,' sniffed Norvik. 'I abhor the idea of humans being abandoned, and action should certainly be taken against irresponsible owners. I also agree that humans can be wonderful companions, but where we differ is on this question of dignity and respect. I don't think it's respectful to treat humans like third-class persons, rather than the very fine animals they are. It is a misplaced sentiment to project our feelings onto animals, to imagine how we might feel in their place. To personalise them.'

'But isn't that just empathy?' asked Georgi. 'And isn't empathy the foundation of respect?'

Santi suddenly found that Norvik was looking straight at her now, and when he replied, it was clear that he was giving Feyrsten his support rather than her. 'No Georgi, I think that *discipline* is the foundation of respect. It's not respectful to an animal to let it do as it wishes, knowing that it will lead it into confusion and conflict. This species needs clear boundaries. Humans must be treated with a very firm hand.'

A muted glow seeped under the door to Henik's Midsummer apartment. He stood outside in the corridor, staring at the gap. Listening. The soft rush of the bubble lift receded behind him as it slid back down to the pod system. Silence now, but if there were lights there was a being inside, something to trigger them with its presence.

He eased the door open, and the evening air breathed coolly on his face, bringing with it something of the sea. In the reclining room, coloured shadows moved on the ceiling, and there was a barely audible humming from the holoscreen. He edged his way forward until he could see the room reflected in the blackness of the balcony door, until he could see the intruder.

Alka was sitting with her elbows resting on her knees, engrossed by the recording he'd just made of her in the plaza. His cover was blown. He'd underestimated her, and now the game had changed. He could either retreat quietly and come back another time to retrieve his research, or he could engage with her and hope she didn't run off, or come at him with a weapon. *A risk, but this might be your only opportunity.*

He considered how he could reduce the chances of Alka reacting in shock, her instinct to fight or flee taking control. Facial expressions and gestures would be critical. His manner would need to be unthreatening, but without fear, his hands visible, his voice calm. He edged into view, leaning his shoulder casually against the wall.

Alka didn't seem to notice him to start with. She continued to stare at the display, watching the recording of the Midsummer Clan as they carried the boark away to the mall. Gradually though, her hand crept away from her side until it found the javelin propped against the arm of the sofa. Her fingers closed around it gently and then, when it was firmly in her grasp, she turned her head and looked at him. Henik wondered what depth of thought was occurring behind her dark eyes, whether her heart was hammering as fast as his own, and whether his apprehension was concealed half as well. Her gaze shifted over his body as if she was assessing his posture, determining his intent. Then, she relaxed her grip on the javelin, stood up slowly, and faced him.

At close quarters Alka looked younger than he'd expected. She was probably no more than thirty years old and in prime physical condition, easily the tallest female he'd seen. She carried herself with confidence too, her body relaxed at the joints and her face showing no sign of fear, or tension. Henik smiled cautiously, then spoke in a soft tone.

'I won't hurt you,' he said. 'It's fine – we're fine.'

She responded with a salvo of incomprehensible sounds, pointed at the display, spoke again, in a harsher tone. Then she took a step backwards, turned towards the balcony door.

Henik was desperate to keep her in the room, to continue the interaction. He stepped forward and reached out to disturb the display, scattering the image for a moment. 'Does this bother you?' he asked. 'You don't like me watching you?' Even if Alka wouldn't comprehend, it was clear that the image could hold her attention. He let it settle and refocus, then expanded it until the Docker she'd killed was filling the display, his holographic image projecting in front of the wall as if he'd been murdered in the room. 'Who is this?' he asked.

Alka was drawn to the image. She came away from the balcony doors and moved closer, until she stood in front of the display, barely an arm's length away, the images washing her face a cool shade of blue. When Henik looked back at the display he realised what had seized her attention. The image had changed, and an athletic woman in dark clothing was now standing over the body. She looked around the plaza for a moment, a pistol held at the ready and the plumes of hair along her cranial ridges fanning and rippling in the breeze. Henik recognised her and so it seemed, did Alka. She moved closer still and stabbed at the image with her finger.

'Torsta Jai,' she said.

4

Prodigy

NO ECLIPSE FOR YOU tonight, my friends.

Kali stood watching the moons through the curving window in her room, leaning as close to it as her bond bracelet would allow. Both moons appeared larger than Earth's familiar companion, although that might have been because they were closer. They were visibly faster too, chasing each other across the night sky. The paler moon held the eye more than its neighbour, its colour a more striking green, and its picture book contours arranged to form a benign smile, on a face of jade. *Is that smile for me? Will you be my guide in this place?*

Yan had come up from his work and was watching her from the doorway, shuffling his feet but saying nothing. After a while, he came over to the window and crouched to her level, raising his arm to the sky and sighting along it. 'Callista and Oberon,' he said. Then he pointed to some smaller discs of light that she hadn't noticed and said some more words with the practiced cadence of a list. After a moment of silence, he held up eight fingers which she took to be the number of moons orbiting this world.

'Eight moons,' she said, then formed a large circle with

her hands and made picking motions with her fingers. 'What about the big fiery one?'

Yan stared at her hands without grasping her meaning, then after a moment his forehead made a minor shift. 'Calderon,' he said. He led her away from the window and back to her bed, almost as if he was afraid to continue the exchange. She lifted her hand towards him and shook her bond bracelet so that it swirled around her wrist.

'Trust Kali?' she said and took hold of his sleeve. Yan exhaled heavily. He patted her gently on the head, drew his hand through her hair, then went to the door.

Patronised again. Different world, same story. Kali thought of the farm, nestling in the folds of the headland, and the birds flocking behind the plough. It was the cradle of her self-sufficiency, her mother lost to the sea since early memory, and her father, locked in his grief, avoiding her mention but expecting her shoes to be filled. He never allowed his daughter to handle the tractor by herself, even though she'd proved herself capable. Instead, she inherited responsibility for the kitchen garden and the geese. They became her disciples, following her around the yard, and even into the kitchen if she left the door open. There she would tell them stories of faraway places, and recite poems, sing to them while breakfast sizzled in the pan.

It was the same at the village school. She was put at the back where she could barely see the blackboard, until her intelligence became impossible for the teacher to ignore and he moved her forward. After two years she was teaching the younger children to read, only the girls though, instructing them while the boys were occupied with their science experiments. It was a responsibility she was proud of, though she could never explain how she learned to read herself. It felt somehow that she'd always been able to do it, that it needed no effort. Perhaps that was why her father had sent her to school, when her brothers, Lar and Den were kept on the farm well beyond the harvest.

Even Mr. Dunstone had condescended in the beginning. He'd paid her no attention in the street when she'd said good morning and barely acknowledged her presence when she picked up a book he'd dropped. It wasn't until Christmas Eve that she realised he was almost blind. She found him in the Post Office, desperately trying to write a letter on the little wooden desk in the corner and becoming more agitated with each attempt.

'I can write it for you, sir,' she said. He waved her away impatiently, but she stood there nevertheless, hands clasped behind her back until eventually he turned his head and squinted at her through his spectacles.

'What's your name, child?'

'Emily Coppen,' she said. 'I'm seven, and I can write anything.'

Mr. Dunstone pushed a sheet of paper in front of her. 'We'll see about that,' he said.

Well… we'll see about this too. Kali toyed with her bracelet, turning it round on her wrist. It was an attractive thing, a smooth ring with no obvious join, soft to the touch, and finely tooled with a swirling pattern. She would have been glad to wear it if its purpose had been merely decorative.

Still, it had been a day of progress even if it started out with a continuation of their battle of wills. First, there had been a skirmish in the bathroom. She'd tried to take the washing pad from Yan's hand, but he wouldn't yield even when she got angry and shouted at him. Eventually, she had to admit defeat and suffer the humiliation of being washed.

She decided to make her displeasure obvious by standing stiffly, her eyes fixed on the ceiling.

Then there was the ongoing problem with eating. She kept bringing her bowl to the kitchen table and each time, Yan would put it back on the floor, always in exactly the same position in the corner which was marked by a circle of red lights. Finally, as she went to pick the bowl up once more, he growled, 'Kali!'

She took a handful of the dried food and made an attempt at eating it, before deciding on a different policy. She went over to where he was sitting at the table and stood next to his chair looking up at him. 'This won't do, Yan', she said. 'I'm hungry enough to eat a horse and I need to try what you're eating.'

It was obvious that he didn't understand, even when she pointed at his food. He consulted an ethereal book he had floating over the table, then stooped to adjust her bracelet so that it was no longer attached to his wrist but dragged her slowly and firmly towards a new anchor point by her bowl. Then she was forced to sit on the floor, observing him while he finished his meal, and busied himself around the kitchen, pressing coloured lights on strange pieces of equipment. He didn't look in her direction again, and she began to wonder whether the book had told him not to.

Whether it was the issue with clothing, the dispute over washing, or the problem with food that had led to Henik's arrival, it was a timely intervention. She'd expected Yan to come up to her room angry that she was shouting for clothes again, but he seemed more relaxed than he'd been earlier. He crouched in front of her with those huge flexible hands resting on his knees, then reached out and stroked her hair. He turned her gently and examined her bruise, saying something under his breath that might have been an apology. He didn't even react when she pressed her case again. She must have said the word 'give,' several times as he took her downstairs, but he no longer seemed to mind.

At first, she thought that Yan had lost patience and was about to give her to the stranger. Instinctively it felt more of a risk than an opportunity, the fate of someone considered too troublesome to endure. It was soon apparent though, that Henik had a much better sense of how to communicate than Yan. In fact, he appeared to be instructing him. She couldn't understand their conversation, and much of it seemed to be conducted through clicks and vibrations in their skulls, but when they spoke aloud, she thought she could follow the gist of what Henik was saying, at least when he used hand gestures to emphasise his points. Still, she would have to maintain a healthy scepticism. There was something awkward and naïve about Yan that gave her a slight advantage, something that was almost endearing. But Henik was much more knowing. He exuded confidence and seemed to have an agenda as far as she was concerned. Whether it would be to her benefit remained to be seen, but for the moment the clothes were the deciding factor. They were a concession she needed to build on, so she had responded with co-operation and made sure that Yan noticed. Without that, Yan would never have left her in front of his three-dimensional television, and she would be none the wiser about this world. *Never mind the washing, it's the food I need, and that television thing. Bit by bit, I'll push the boundaries with them. Like I always do.*

It was late in the evening when Henik returned. He dropped his overnight bag heavily as if he hadn't the energy to carry it any further. 'Well,' he said, absently. 'Well.'

Yan led him into the kitchen and took a bottle and two goblets from a shelf. 'Looks like you could do with a drink.'

Henik sat on a stool in the corner and slumped against the wall. 'I went over to Midsummer for some things and had another human encounter. But more of that later. How's it been with Kali?'

'Not sure,' said Yan. 'I put her in front of the display with her bowl. Something for children, I thought, colourful and non-threatening to look at. I thought it might encourage her to eat. Then I left her and went off to do some work in the study.' He poured measures into both glasses feeling a sudden urge to drink them both.

'Giving her some space. I like that.' Henik took a glass and swirled the amber liquid in it. 'But I assume it didn't go well?'

'When I came back, she was watching a debate on The Georgi Factor. You know, Spice Islands, Derelict Zone, and all that. My brother was a guest, of course, arguing with the Counsellor for the Interior and…'

'I watched it,' said Henik, keeping his eyes on his glass. 'How do you think she did against him?'

'Santi Aspil? She did alright, I suppose, as well as anyone does against my brother. You can't trust any of them though, can you? They all let you down in the end. They all…' Yan noticed the colours shifting along Henik's ridges, turning to a stronger hue, and it triggered a memory of something he'd once read. 'Oh! I'm sorry. Didn't you once…? Weren't the two of you…?'

'Long time ago,' said Henik. 'I haven't seen Santi for a long time, but whenever she's on the news, I find myself watching.' He shifted on his stool, coughed into his hand. 'Anyway,' he said, 'Kali was watching the debate, you say, taking an interest in how people interact?'

'I'm afraid it was much more than that. Not only did she figure out how to access the news but… well, you'd better have a look.'

'Look at what?'

Yan led him across the hallway to the reclining room. 'I've left it exactly as it was,' he said. At first, Henik didn't appear to notice anything amiss, but then his eyes settled on the floor next to Kali's food bowl, where the nuggets of fibre and protein had been arranged carefully to form a word. *Human.*

Henik drew a breath. 'She did this herself?' he asked. 'You didn't show her the word first?' He sat down. 'I can't believe it. That's… that's…'

Yan could feel his skin reacting, flushing and prickling as it had when he first saw the word at his feet. It felt like a warning, and for a fleeting moment, he was a child again, threatened by the dark unknown, the storm rattling his bedroom window and Calderon's mythical dragons prowling outside with their fiery talons. 'Do you know what it means?' he said.

Henik crouched beside the bowl, stared at the word on the floor as if he didn't know what to say. 'Is it natural?' Yan prompted.

'Well, it means she's either an exceptional human, or that in their natural state, humans are more intelligent than I ever imagined. Perhaps it's both. How did she react to what she was seeing on the screen?'

'Completely absorbed by it. She was sitting very still, and didn't even notice I was in the room.' Yan stooped to gather up the food nuggets. 'Why do you think she did this?'

'She's trying to gain your respect, would be my guess. And she's telling you what she thinks of that pet food.'

'So, it's not about the Spice Islands then. I can't believe I'm saying this, but she's not making a political point?'

'She'll have seen there are other humans here, obviously, gathered something of their lives. And she paid enough attention to work out our word for her species, and how it's written. Kali wants us to know that.'

'Shit! I knew I shouldn't have left her alone!'

'Grace of the gods, man – what are you talking about? This is unprecedented! We're discovering things no one else knows!'

'But they're highly controversial things! I'm a historian, and I know how events can unfold!'

'We're both academics, Yan. We value truth! Do you really want to close your eyes to this opportunity?'

'I'm as curious as you are, excited too, but…'

'But what? Can't you see what she's doing? She's reaching out to you!'

An old picture-book image of the dragons of Calderon sharpened in Yan's mind, but now it had borrowed a name. 'My sister-in-law, Jocasta called me,' he said. 'She's heard about Kali from my brother and wants to visit. You don't know her, Henik, but I'm telling you, this situation is dangerous. We're walking on slippery rocks.'

The light had a different quality in this world, Kali thought. Things looked sharper, cleaner, and shadows seemed to move more quickly. She'd been awake since dawn and lay watching the light as it melted the stars, intensified until it fell from the roof lights in speckled buttresses. Now there were sounds coming up from downstairs, a clashing of metal from the kitchen and directly beneath her an assertive voice that sounded like the newsreader the night before. Then she heard Henik's voice, a distinctive rumble you could almost feel against your skin. He was back, and that meant she would need to perform for him again. *Alright, but I'll want concessions.*

It was Yan that came to get her. 'Good morning, Kali,' he said and pointed at the window.

'Good morning, Yan,' she said. She slid off the bed and reached for Henik's shirt. It was only then that she saw it had been replaced in the night by a new one, sealed in a translucent film. Yan pointed at her thigh and she let him examine the bruise again. 'Sorry,' he said quietly. He made an adjustment to her bracelet and she felt the bond dissolve, the bracelet falling loose around her wrist. He went back to the door and held it open. 'Come on, Kali,' he said. 'Wash.'

Kali sidled past him and through the door to the washroom. She stood stiffly in front of the sink again and looked at the ceiling. *Just grin and bear it. Battles in priority order.* But this time Yan had other ideas. He produced a yellow washing block like he had used the day before, and held it up for her to see.

'Kali,' he said. 'Trust?' His face loomed close, huge and heavy-browed, with that crocodile-ridged forehead. But there was uncertainty in his eyes, perhaps even insecurity. In his own way, she sensed that Yan was no more confident than she was. He placed the washing block in front of her, very deliberately, then drew away and went over to the shower, demonstrated its operation with a few motions of his hand, how the water could be made to dance and bubble. Then he walked to the door and with a brief glance over his shoulder, he left her.

She wasted no time inspecting the bathroom, however different it was to any she'd used before, with its seamless cladding and embedded lights and buttons. Instead, she luxuriated under the pulsating water, feeling relaxed for the first time in days. She cupped her hands, watched the water pool in frothy pinkness then raised it to her nose, detecting in it something mossy, like woodlands after the rain. Its scent penetrated her head, and she felt her mind clear as if suddenly it was ready to think, to consider, to plan.

She had decided not to dwell on what she'd seen on the news, but still, it had kept her awake in the night. She wasn't sure whether she felt reassured that there were so many other humans in this world or appalled that they were locked in such an unequal contest with these smooth-skinned giants. The implications were too much to fathom, but what she'd learned reinforced in her mind the need to build a relationship with Yan and Henik. *You've got to stand up for yourself, but you also need to win them over. They're all you've got.*

Henik and Yan were in the kitchen when she came downstairs. They must have heard her footsteps, she thought, but still, they reacted as if her appearance was a welcome surprise, the smiles coming to their faces as if they were using unfamiliar muscles. 'Good morning, Henik,' she said.

Henik pointed at her new clothes, the shirt a much smaller version of his own, and in a slate grey colour, pyjama trousers in a smooth fabric printed with strange creatures and trees. 'Clothes, Kali,' he said. 'Very nice!'

'Clothes. Yes, thank you,' she said. *Children's department probably, but could be worse.*

Yan presented her with a box, which parted magically in her hands. There were shoes inside, the sort she might have worn to the beach. They looked too large, but they contracted when she put them on, moulded themselves comfortably around her feet.

'Good,' she said. 'Well done!' She danced a little jig to amuse them, but they exchanged serious glances as if they imagined some hidden meaning in her antics.

'Food, Kali?' Yan looked across at Henik, then pointed at her metal bowl, which was now on the table. She approached it with optimism but found yet again that it was full of the dry bullets.

She pushed the bowl away and covered her face with her hands for a moment. 'Clothes good – thank you,' she said. 'Food, no good. No well done.'

She got down from the table and went to the cupboards beside Yan, watching him from the corner of her eye and expecting him to intervene at any moment. She opened them one by one with a wave of her hand, as she'd seen Yan doing, and still, he made no attempt to stop her. Henik said something to him in a stream of cranial clicking and they sat watching her going about her search until eventually she found a deep larder stocked with all manner of curious foodstuffs. Near the front there was a row of large bluish eggs, and further back a slab of meat that looked like pork but smelt stronger, more like game. *Right then. Let's see how far they'll let you go with this.*

Maarten Feyrsten's limousine swung through the gates and onto his estate, swept through the shadow-striped lawns and flowered terraces, and settled onto its haunches at the front portico. A thin human in a braided white jacket scurried out to meet him, bowing and skipping around him excitedly. He patted him on the shoulder. 'Alright, Juno – that'll do. Where's the mistress?'

'Garden. Nice drink.'

He marched through the house, over the lacquered floors, and through gauze curtains billowing from windows thrown open to the heat. From the veranda at the back, he looked over the formal garden, down to where a pool glinted in the afternoon sun. *Nice drink? Drunk more like.* He took a curving path through a dense avenue of fruit trees, then over manicured lawns to where his wife was reclining, a goblet swinging between her fingers. She didn't greet him as he approached, just turned her head wearily and adjusted her wide-brimmed hat.

'Bit early for that, Jocasta,' he said. 'I thought we decided...'

'Oh, here comes the high and mighty Opposition Leader. Give me a break, Maarten. Solus is out, and there's not a damn thing to do but smell the flowers! Just smell them – go on! No? Oh, of course not – there's another crisis! A crisis in some crappy corner of the planet. Let them rot, I say – or wipe them out.' She slurped at her drink. 'Yes, that's it, elemist the whole lot of them!'

There were times when Maarten found nothing attractive about Jocasta. Her behaviour had been a liability for years, but she'd always been able to turn on the charm when the occasion demanded. At home though, things were different. Even her beauty had lost its hold on him; increasingly he saw it as a veneer over a personality that had become grotesque in its self-regard and casual unkindness. Soon, there would need to be a change.

'The election is only two days away,' he said. 'With things as they are, we could be sitting in Check St. very soon. So yes, I *am* preoccupied with the thought that I might well be running the Free Republic, not to mention a vast Commonwealth of star systems... and I'm more than a little concerned by the thought of you as Lady Consort.'

Jocasta rattled her glossy nails against her goblet. 'There's not even a proper garden at Check St. I might not come, darling.'

'Believe me, if you don't do something about the drinking, Jocasta, I'll be keeping you as far away from there as I can.'

'Ooh, look at your ridges flare! You'll have to keep that under control, Maarten. They'll focus on that. You'll be glowing red in living rooms across the Republic.'

Maarten took a slow breath, then released it. 'Do you enjoy baiting me, Jocasta?'

'I'm staying away from the campaign, aren't I? Promised I would. I'm being good. Even called your little brother for you.'

'Yan – what did you do that for?'

'To find out how his new human is settling. Remember how difficult it was to break Juno in? I thought Yan would need some advice. You're so busy and he's so soppy.'

'He's hardly that, Jocasta, he's a highly-regarded academic. It's just that we see things differently.'

'He's full of permissive bollocks. You think having a hard-drinking lady by your side is bad? Better not let the press get their hooks into your namby brother when you're cleansing the streets of vermin.'

'For the last time, stop calling them that! I've told you, as soon as we start talking like we've been bitten by a crazed animal, the public will think twice about us. Look, there will have to be firm policies, but we need to keep the language moderate. So that's what you'll do, Jocasta, whether you're out in public, or just talking to your friends.'

'You're a bloody hypocrite, Maarten. When you're in, they'll find out what "standard training" for humans is all about. What's your brother going to say when the goons come knocking for his little human, drag her off for a behaviour implant?'

'It won't be like that. Our policy is for voluntary controls, and it's been thoroughly researched. Anyway, I thought you approved.'

'Oh, I do! I'm just not pretending it won't get brutal.' Jocasta examined the finish on her nails. 'I'm not concerned about public opinion.'

'Well, you just stay sober and that'll give me one less thing to think about.'

Jocasta stretched her arms wide slopping some of her drink onto the lawn. 'Sobriety is not really my forte dear. But I'll be looking in on Yan for you, just to… well, you know.'

'No, I don't know! Looking in to do what?'

She took a large gulp of her drink. 'To manage his expectations.'

5

Jocasta

HENIK PUSHED HIS PLATE away and sat watching Kali across the table. She in turn was observing Yan as he finished his breakfast. She was paying close attention to his face, searching his features, perhaps for traces of communication. How did she view him? Surely, she would see Yan as a captor, holding her prisoner, controlling her life. Yet, here she was, trying to engage with him, not so much eager to please as captive animals often were, but keen to communicate, perhaps even wanting to teach. Despite the capability deficit of her species, she wasn't discouraged; she still behaved with remarkable assurance. She was nothing if not bold.

Eventually, Kali reached out her hand and touched one of Yan's cranial ridges, which was shining with the enjoyment of his breakfast. 'Good,' she said. 'Food, well done?'

Yan turned his head toward her and smiled, emphasised his response with an awkward nod of the head. 'Yes, well done. It's very good.'

'Give me your thoughts,' said Henik, 'both from a practical and an academic perspective.'

Yan rolled his tongue around his mouth as if to capture

every last molecule of flavour. 'Bloody marvellous, that's what I think.'

'Bloody marvellous!' echoed Kali. She laughed.

'You rarely hear that,' said Henik. 'That sound is a spontaneous expression of human pleasure. But the practical point is that she will eat if you allow her what she is accustomed to, even if it lacks all the recommended nutrients. She's much happier with a full stomach, and what's more, if you let her loose in your kitchen you could eat very well too.'

'If this is what food is like on Earth, I'm on the wrong planet.'

'What we've just learned is that natural humans can be highly skilled at preparing food. So were we, at one time, but now we rely too often on intelligent devices to do it for us, or we just ingest protein constructors and nutrient tabs. We've lost a lot of the pleasure in food, except in the smart restaurants downtown, and those are mainly run by off-worlders.'

'She had me worried though, using my antique blade, and then the open pan, the high temperatures. I would have intervened but...'

'But you decided to trust her. We've all been brought up believing humans are inherently unreliable. But as a social historian, you know better than most that an oppressive regime doesn't allow confidence to flourish.'

'Oppressive? That's a strange word to use. You think higher life forms are being oppressive to lower ones?'

'The law of forest and field is necessarily oppressive. The only choice is to compete or to die. But there is another option for high-functioning species: co-operation. When we choose not to do that, we're being unreasonable. We should recognise humans as higher life forms, co-operate with them more. They're closer to people than they are to other species.'

'That's revolutionary stuff, Henik. Some of my students would love it, but my immediate concern is Kali. If she's not a companion animal, then what is she? How can she be anything else, and thrive in our society?'

'We're going to have to figure that out, and not just for her benefit.'

'Isn't it possible that Kali's just a one-off. You may be an expert on ferals, but I've met plenty of domestic humans in my time, and they're nothing like Kali.'

Henik held his frustration in check, reminding himself that he was expecting Yan to make a mental adjustment that had taken him years of observation. 'They're different to Kali, because that's the way we've made them,' he said.

'Code manipulation? That's just a conspiracy theory. You know it's prohibited for dependent species.'

'Even though it means they are burdened with preventable disease.'

'Then how can...?'

'Because we don't allow humans to breed independently. We've controlled their environment, who they have contact with. We want them docile around the house, and resilient but compliant in working environments. So, that's the way generations of humans have been selected.'

'But ferals aren't like that. Are you saying Kali has feral traits?'

'It's more the other way around. Humans that manage to sustain themselves in the wild are likely to be ones that have retained more of their natural characteristics. The independence and resourcefulness we see in Kali works to the advantage of a feral human. But anyway, it's about tendencies, not absolutes.'

'What about training? That must have an effect too.'

'Of course, it does, but the default characteristics are

inherited. We've imposed our preferences through generations of reproduction.'

'So, they've become what we think of them.'

'Precisely. Our expectations have become self-fulfilling. We don't know the true capabilities of the species because we haven't *wanted* to know.'

'But you do want to find out. You don't really expect people will listen, do you? You don't imagine they'll suddenly start thinking differently. Consider what it would mean.'

Henik looked at his plate, aware once again of the aromas that lingered in the air, speaking more powerfully of new possibilities than any words. 'You've seen the news,' he said. 'Change is coming. The question is whether we should play a part in shaping it.'

Yan slumped in his seat, closed his eyes. It was a lot to take in, the idea that he had in his custody a being of such scientific importance. He would be struggling with the responsibility of it, the knowledge that she was likely to bring trouble to his door.

Kali had been watching their discussion patiently, but now she took advantage of the pause. She slipped down from her chair and beckoned to them. 'Come,' she said, 'Come here.' She led them out of the kitchen, and over to the verglas door at the back of the reclining room. She pointed outside, where the garden was losing its morning jewels. The solus was raising a thin layer of mist, lifting it through the richly-coloured plants and sending it aloft in curling shapes.

They sat on the steps at the back of the house and watched her wander barefoot around the garden. Henik studied her behaviour, made careful notes and recordings, while Yan adjusted the resistance of her bond, allowed her to draw it out, to walk further down the mossy lawn, putting her nose to each species of flower in turn, caressing the blooms between her fingertips. She came to a small stone edifice that nestled amongst the spear palms, Shala the foam-robed goddess of tides with water trickling from an urn on her shoulder. Kali squatted in front of the shrine and washed her hands in the stone basin at its base.

'You're a man of the spirits, then?' said Henik.

'Lapsed,' said Yan. My mother was devoted to the Aquatic gods, but since she passed, I just haven't felt the same.'

Kali was sitting on the lawn now, rolling up the sleeves of her shirt. She craned her neck to the sky where violet clouds were sailing inland on a warm breeze, pushed back her copper hair and tilted her face to the solus.

There was movement in the bushes. She snapped her head round to look at Yan, then seemingly reassured, she turned back towards the disturbance.

'Dill,' said Yan, just loudly enough for Kali to hear.

A tiny olive-skinned human emerged from the bushes, almost entirely naked and with her hair twisted around a short stick at the back of her head. She edged forward onto the lawn, leading with her right foot in a crouching motion, ready to retreat at a moment's notice.

'How old is she?' asked Henik

'I've no idea. She's always looked old to me. I see her less and less though. I'll spot her from the window, but she usually makes herself scarce when I'm outside.'

Kali remained perfectly still as Dill approached, then when she had closed to within a few units, raised her hand gently and waved, gesturing at the lawn in front of her. Dill came forward again. She knelt on the moss in front of Kali and mumbled something, a brief sequence of sounds. Kali replied, echoing the pattern. Dill's eyes flew open, and as Kali continued to speak, she responded first with nods, then by placing her hands upon her chest and rocking backwards and forwards.

'I've never seen anyone speak to Dill this way,' said Yan. 'She was never able to communicate with other humans.'

Henik was entranced. He didn't reply for a while, and then he could only manage a whisper. 'I've often wondered whether there is more than one human language,' he said. 'It would make sense. If we have many on Antaris, so might they on Earth. Perhaps different language traditions have been handed down.'

'Language? I hadn't thought of their sounds that way. You think they're actually structured as languages?'

'Of course! You don't think Kali could grasp our language so intuitively if her own human sounds were just random, do you?'

'I suppose I've never really thought about it.'

'Hardly anyone does. That's part of the problem, and no one will fund the research. It's too contentious.'

Suddenly, Kali's voice changed. It rose sweetly in a pattern of tones and phrases that formed an undulating rhythm, a trilling chant that lifted and fell, immediately pleasing to the ear, and strangely stirring. 'Do you hear that?' whispered Yan. 'Listen! What... what *is* that?'

Dill was crying now, her head nodding as tears streamed down her face. She crawled forward to Kali and placed her head on her lap. Still, the sounds came from Kali's throat, rising like living things, seizing the very air around her, until finally they subsided, and she placed her hand gently on Dill's head. She looked back at Yan and called softly.

'Well done, Dill.'

***

At the back of the Café Republic, Santi Aspil watched a miniature version of herself strolling around on the table. She could recall every word of her speech the night before, as well as the answers she gave to questions. It had been a good performance she thought, with only one or two things she might have said differently. She glanced across the bar and caught the eye of the waiter, then brought the latest polling results into her vision. *Progress down another two points. It's slipping away from us.*

'You still think you're going to win?'

She looked up to see a familiar figure approaching her table. He stopped short and regarded her with his shoulders hunched, hands jammed into his pockets. 'Mind if I join you?'

Santi's throat felt warm. It was as if she had gulped a shot of mead, then chased it down with another. 'It's been a while, Henik,' she said, her voice struggling to find any volume. 'A lot more than a while.'

'You don't look any different to me,' he said. 'You've hardly aged.'

'Miracle of the gods, that would be! This campaign is aging me double-quick, I can tell you. I need to come in here for some sanity.'

Henik sunk slowly into a chair on the other side of the table. 'Are the polls right?'

Santi glanced around the café. A group in the opposite corner erupted suddenly in laughter, before settling back to earnest discussion. 'We'll push to the bitter end,' she said.

The waiter came to the table and placed two steaming flasks in front of them. 'Complimentary,' he said. He looked at Santi and her holographic miniature. 'You've got my vote.'

She closed down her image with the flat of her hand. 'Thank you,' she said. 'That's good to hear.' The waiter had the eager eyes of youth, she thought. He lingered a fraction longer than was necessary. 'Do you mind me asking what the deciding issue was for you?' she said.

'Well, I'm not too happy with you lot on some things, but it's the human crisis that does it for me.'

'So, you don't think Heritage has the right answers on that.'

'Their solutions are worse than the problem. I'm fine with sending troops off-world. I'm even fine with sending help to the Spice Islands, but I don't want them on the streets here in the Republic, shooting stray humans, or taking them off for destruction. Once you start that, where would it end?'

'Well said! I'm confident the majority will agree with you when they cast their votes tomorrow.' Santi watched as the waiter retreated. He went out into the solus to clear a table, glancing over his shoulder at her when he switched off its shading post. 'Did you hear that?' she said. He's more right than he knows. History is at a turning point.'

'People want change, though. They're tired of Haugen's leadership, tired of his government. The approval ratings are grim.'

Santi felt a spike of irritation. 'Thanks for telling me something I didn't know,' she said. Henik took a breath and dropped his gaze. 'Sorry,' she said.

'Your personal rating is one of the few bright spots though. You're well positioned to go for the leadership if the election goes against you.'

'I'm not even going to think about that. I'd rather be following Amund Haugen in government for all his faults, than leading a defeated party.' She watched Henik stirring his drink. He tapped his spatula a little too firmly on his flask and didn't look at her. There had been a time when she would have been more honest with him, when the trust between them had been unreserved.

'But you won't rule it out when the time comes,' he said,

Santi watched his face, the wide intelligent brows, the decency in his eyes. He was the same Henik she remembered, but public service had rubbed discretion into her pores, and she decided not to answer his point. 'What brings you into town?' she asked.

'I live here these days. I've got a little place behind the square, not far from your office, actually. You know there's a protest going on outside your building. You're taking a risk being out and about.'

'I'm waiting for it to die down. It doesn't worry me – I've seen it all before.' A memory came to her and she sighed.

'What?'

'I was a lot more scared when you took me to the Iota system. Sleeping under the stars, all around us things with claws.'

'They were probably more scared of us in reality. But I remember that herd of armoured bison. Couldn't believe it. We just sat there, and they came past, all day long. On and on, millions of them. I'll never forget that.'

'Do you only remember the good things? What about what happened afterwards, when we got back to our hopper to find it'd been caught by a dust demon? The motors were choked with that filthy red stuff. You didn't think that was so wonderful, a hundred leagues from the nearest settlement. You thought we were dead!'

'I seem to remember being quite calm about it.'

'Calm? You think you were calm?'

'And it turned out alright, didn't it?'

'What? You mean the fact that we were spotted by nomads with rotting teeth, and they crowded around us like we were their next meal?'

'I just remember how good they were. They hooked us up to their transport and used its drives to blow the sand out of ours. No drama. It was like they did it all the time.'

'We were bloody lucky, and you know it.' said Santi. 'Hey, are we arguing again already?'

Henik stared into space. 'Long time ago, wasn't it? We did some things, didn't we?'

'You were always pushing me, *daring* me.' Santi paused, feeling the air suddenly thin in her lungs. She wondered whether to change the subject, but it was the eve of the election, a day of endings and beginnings, so she just said what she'd been thinking. 'I loved you, Henik.'

'We were young. We didn't know what we had – at least I didn't. Always looking for the next adventure, always hurrying. Look at you now though, running the Free Republic!'

'I don't run the Republic.'

'Parts of it, you do. You run the things people care about most, these days.'

'Well, not for much longer, if the polls are right. You still care about those things too, from what I see. Social justice – humans specifically.'

'I've still got my place over at Midsummer, you know.'

'The Derelict Zone. I suppose you blame me for not being able to sell.'

'Course not. I still go there, you know.'

'Do you? Why?'

'To observe feral humans – to understand them. By the

way, I heard what Maarten Feyrsten said about you the other night, that you were "out of touch".'

Santi took a sip of her drink, watched Henik's eyes over the rim of her flask, suddenly uneasy about the turn in the conversation.

'Do you want to get back "in touch"?'

'What do you mean?'

'Visit the Derelict Zone with me.'

'Be serious!'

'I *am* serious! You're going to be kicking your heels while those protesters are outside your building, so put the time to use. Win or lose tonight, you'll find Midsummer enlightening. Come with me, Santi.' He touched the back of her hand. 'I *dare* you.'

Yan's heart sank when Jocasta's arrival was announced, her name invading the house, seizing control of the space, even before she'd left her transport. He knew she was bound to turn up before long, with her overbearing manner and unwelcome advice, but he'd hoped it wouldn't be quite so soon.

Kali turned away from the holoscreen. 'Henik?' she said brightly.

'No, it's not Henik – it's Jocasta. Please be good, Kali. *Please*.'

She looked at him hard, as if she could sense his anxiety. 'Be good,' she said.

Jocasta wasn't alone. Out on the street, a bodyguard stood stiffly beside her transport, a young man whose chiselled physique would be of more interest to her, Yan thought, than any experience of personal security he might have. But it was the human trailing behind Jocasta that would seize Kali's attention.

Juno was dressed in a bizarre parade ground uniform that matched the pink shades of Jocasta's outfit and he carried a cluster of shopping bags, each bearing the name of an exclusive boutique on Carnival St.

'It's good to see you, Jocasta,' Yan said. 'Nice of you to stop by.'

She flounced up to him and flung her arms around his neck. 'I know, my dear. It's such a testing time for you with your newcomer. But never fear, I'm here to help. It's all going to be *just* fine, so don't you worry about a thing! Now, where is the little darling? "Kali" isn't it? Funny name but you can change that, of course. Perhaps we should…'

'I chose "Kali" myself,' said Yan. 'She's got used to it.'

'Well, no matter, she won't be attending the salons in town very much, will she? A suburban name will be fine for everyday use and we can call her something more appropriate when she visits. "Kallista" perhaps. What do you think, Juno? Do you like "Kallista"?'

Juno's eyes widened and his mouth said the name without making a sound. He looked up at Jocasta, but she was already striding into the reclining room.

Kali was waiting in the middle of the room. She stood quite still, with her hands clasped behind her back, as Jocasta swept in.

'And here she is!' said Jocasta. 'Well, look at you, sweetie! Aren't you a pretty thing? Yan, haven't you taught her how to greet?'

Yan struggled for a response. As usual, Jocasta's self-assurance made him feel flat-footed.

'Goodness! Show her, Juno. Go on – greet!' The little human scurried forward and bent into a deep bow in front of Yan, then retreated in backward steps, without saying a word.

He stood to attention beside Jocasta, but kept stealing glances at Kali.

Jocasta cleared her throat, making it clear that she was expecting the greeting ritual to be reciprocated.

'Kali, this is Jocasta,' he said quickly. 'Please greet Jocasta.'

'Greet,' said Kali, and performed a tentative bow.

'Well, it's a start,' Jocasta sniffed. 'If you got her from that pet warehouse, she'll have no pedigree, so there's no way of knowing where she was bred and raised. You'll need to start from scratch. Just a little tip for you to be getting on with: never say "please" to a human. They must understand that they will do as they are told, whether it pleases them or not. And most of the time, it won't.' She turned to look at the holographic display. 'You've got her watching that thing? Oh, Yan! That won't do at all!'

Yan glanced at the display, and then at Kali. She'd been watching the news but had changed it while he was answering the door, and now there was an animated children's programme, with pastel creatures and squeaky voices. She met his gaze, with no trace of movement to her face. Then, just for an instant, one of her eyes closed.

'Now, where shall we start?' said Jocasta. 'You might get me a nice glass of something strong, darling, the larger the better, at this time of day. Meanwhile, I'll get this little thing looking presentable. What in all the gods' names have you got her wearing, Yan? I always say that if you can't dress them properly, you might as well leave them as nature intended. Of course, you couldn't bring them into town like that, these days.' She shuddered. 'Most vulgar!'

'Yes, but...'

'No buts. I have it all in hand, darling, so off you trot, before I die of thirst.'

Yan looked at Kali and tried to interpret her expression. She was biting her lip. He wasn't sure what it meant, but he didn't think it was positive. He went to the kitchen to get Jocasta her drink and brought it back as quickly as he could. By the time he returned though, his worst fears were being realised. Kali's clothes had been flung in the corner and she was wearing a garish shift in a fabric of huge contrasting squares. On her feet were glossy slippers in different primary colours, and Jocasta was in the process of securing a cone-shaped hat that seemed to be testing the limits of Kali's patience. She was standing with her jaw clenched and her eyes closed just as she had that first day in the bathroom. Her eyebrows were being drawn upwards as Jocasta tugged at her unruly mane and fed it through an opening in the hat.

'Now there!' said Jocasta. 'Isn't she a picture! This is absolutely on trend at the moment. You'll have to come walking with her in town. But I have to tell you, Yan, that I do detect some signs of insolence in her, which will have to be stamped out.'

'What insolence?' said Yan. He glanced at Kali just as Jocasta was turning away and saw her stick out her tongue, a gesture that needed no explanation.

'It's difficult to put your finger on it darling, but we females have a sense of these things, and this one does *not* have a submissive nature. I think I'll have to come back another time and work on her for you.' She stooped in front of Kali and brought her face close. 'Yes, we'll have to watch you, little minx, won't we?' She prodded Kali on the end of her nose. 'Or there's going to be trouble.'

'Trouble? What are you talking about, Jocasta?'

'Yan, darling! Oh, it's not your fault. I'm close to what's going on, and you don't talk to your brother much, but things are going to be changing in our Free Republic. Your brother will be Chief Counsellor when the election results are in tomorrow, and you'll be getting some media attention, I don't doubt.'

'Surely, no one will be interested in me. I'm just an academic.'

'Oh, not *you* dear – your Kali! Maarten will be clearing the vermin from our streets and restoring good order. Humans will need to conform to much higher standards of behaviour and anyone with a pet will have to be a responsible owner. The media will expect Maarten's family to be role models. They'll jump on any sign that you aren't upholding the Government's policy.'

'So, this is why…'

'Yes, dear boy! I want to help you both! Now, look at my Juno. He hasn't moved a muscle since we arrived. I'm sure he has his eye on Kali, but he's not made a sound. *Discipline*, that's what it takes, and then I'm sure she'll shape up too.' Jocasta moved behind Kali, straightening her shoulders with her bony hands. 'But we won't win any awards like that! There – that's better. Now chin up a fraction. Good girl!'

'Good,' said Kali, through clenched teeth.

'Thank you,' said Yan quickly. 'We'll have to work at it.' He turned to Kali. 'Thank Jocasta for the clothes.'

'Thank,' mumbled Kali.

'Thank you, *esteemed*,' she said. 'Now Yan, there are more clothes for her in those bags. I just couldn't resist them.' She tapped her cheekbone. 'And I've just sent you a present as well. *The Human Handbook* tells you everything you need to know about the species. Sig Norvik really is essential reading. I know him personally and I got him to inscribe it for you. Isn't that sweet of him, particularly when he has so much on his mind?

He'll be so busy after the election. So much influence and responsibility.'

'Well, I suppose he's a celebrity but…'

'Oh shh! Don't be so condescending! He's a man of insight and learning, a visionary in my view. And Maarten agrees, which is why he'll have a key role in the Government. I shouldn't really tell you, but I don't suppose there's any harm. Sig Norvik's going to be Counsellor for Human Affairs.'

Torsta Jai didn't like the Green Zone very much. It was out on the perimeter of Freeport, where the streets were sterile, and the verges maintained themselves to geometric perfection. The houses were identical at first glance with their sleek verglas facings, but above the roofline, they reached competitively towards the sky with their exquisitely sculpted spires. To someone like Torsta, it was all far too pleasant, too stifling. She felt conspicuous and thought carefully before parking her transport opposite Yan Feyrsten's house, wondered whether, in such a sleepy community, anyone would notice, or care much if they did. She took a cluster of beirfruit from a bag beside her and settled down to wait.

Intuition, that's what it was; whether to advance, or retreat, to speak, or remain silent. Sometimes there was no calculation about it, you could just feel where to go with an inquiry, sense when something was hidden, some truth left untold. Tempting as it was to use Trajan's gun to extract a quick profit, there was something about this Earth human that stirred Torsta's interest, something that suggested a much bigger prize. Of course, Sela had tried to make a deal out of it, sensing an opportunity he'd overlooked, but his predicament was far too obvious and he gave Torsta the information she wanted with only token resistance.

She decided to read Sela's file on the Earth human again, as well as the research she'd done on its owner, the brother of a man on the verge of becoming Chief Counsellor. The creature's data was unimpressive; it was a small and weak specimen, and it was easy to see why Sela wanted rid of it. The hair was a selling point of course, but only a fool would buy something so fragile without a warranty. Yan Feyrsten was no fool though. He had an impressive academic record and was highly regarded amongst his peers. He would know the human was from Earth, it was on the bill of sale, and if he'd done even the most basic research, he'd understand that he'd bought something unique, something scientists had been thinking about for generations.

A white limousine glided to a halt opposite, sinking to the ground with a gentle sigh. A well-groomed young man got out and straightened his jacket. The flex of his knees and the way he scanned the street were a giveaway. Torsta's transport caught his attention immediately, and he walked over to it to check its identification. Torsta raised the shields and waited, but the man didn't attempt a scan. He made a cursory tour of the vehicle, then walked back across the road and tapped on the limousine's flank.

The vehicle separated at the rear to allow a woman to dismount. She was dressed in a sharply tailored pink suit and had a human in matching colours by the scruff of the neck. Torsta recognised the cut of her hairlines immediately, the imperious way the woman carried herself, and not because she had any interest in the rich and famous, but because she had a long memory for unsavoury deeds. *Well, well! Jocasta Feyrsten. Come to see your brother-in-law's new purchase, have you?*

Torsta waited for her to disappear inside Yan Feyrsten's house, before taking a small pouch from her pocket. She opened the top and gave it a shake. Inside, a seething mass of black metal scrambled towards the light, a multitude of tiny insects wrestling madly with each other, their red eyes pulsing with minute bursts of electromagnetism and their legs and wings clashing in a barely audible fizz. Torsta opened the door of the transport and tipped them gently onto the road, watched them take to the air, swarm away on their mission. They crossed the street, headed for the eaves and window ledges and were soon lost from sight.

It didn't take long for the microbots to get inside the house and begin their espionage. Some quickly found their way into the reclining room, where the Earth human was the subject of the conversation. There was nothing in its appearance that differed from the file, although it did seem particularly alert and focused on the conversation, even if it couldn't understand what was being said.

Watching Jocasta with Yan Feyrsten was revealing as well. She hadn't changed. Her arrogance was just as he remembered, the act so practiced that it was now second nature. And Feyrsten's appeasement of her was amusing, the response Jocasta was accustomed to, the way people always behaved around her when they wanted to avoid conflict. What was obvious though, what was particularly noteworthy, was that neither of them seemed to understand what might unfold. Yan Feyrsten knew the human was a natural, and Jocasta had inside knowledge of the policy changes a Heritage government would bring. But neither would have an understanding of both factors, neither could grasp just how unstable the combination might be.

6

Mosaic

DEAR MR. DUNSTONE,

I'm sorry it has been so long since I have written. It's such a comfort to write to you now though, even if you are in the hereafter and I am goodness knows where.

I can say at least that I am at a desk once again, this one so peculiar that I can scarcely describe it, except to say that it captures my words as if possessed with a mind of its own! I would think it magical but for the strangeness of everything else in this world. Indeed, if a white rabbit were to come by with a pocket watch I would hardly be surprised!

You might say that's a frivolous thought under the circumstances, but I have resolved not to worry about my situation. You have taught me to face everything in life as an adventure, and this is even more so than Africa. Who would have thought when you put me on the steamer at Southampton, that the journey would lead me as far as this?

It must be said that for all my curiosity, I would never have had the courage to venture abroad, without your faith in me. Do you remember when curiosity first led me astray, Mr. Dunstone? It was the day of the Coronation and the bunting was strung over trestle tables all along Sheep St. You wondered why I was in the library when you found me there, but the papers held news about the conquest of Mount Everest, and I was engrossed. You told me I must be made for greater things than parties and farmyards. After that, it was nothing but your maps and globes, taking me, I suppose, by ways and means to the dear children in Berseba. It was the languages that did it though. I don't rightly know how that came to happen, but perhaps you will recall better than I. French first, I think it was. Yes, French I learned first, then Spanish, and all the others.

You should hear this language though! In some respects, it's quite straightforward, more regular than English and certainly more approachable than your blessed Greek! What makes it so tricky is that so much of it can't be spoken and that which can, has no written translation to work from. It has occurred to me that I should be the first to learn its symbols and translate it, after all, it can hardly be more cryptic than the Times crossword and we managed that most of the time! Perhaps that's why I am here, Mr. Dunstone for I have no doubt that it must be for some purpose.

I am not sure whether Yan knows my purpose, but I don't think it's what he intended. He certainly is a great lump, but quite sweet really, and so hesitant at times that I do wonder whether he is more lost than me. You should have seen him when Jocasta visited. He was desperate for her to leave, and so was I by the time she had me dressed up like a court jester. She is such a force that he could offer her no resistance.

I think I can appreciate Yan's reticence. My desk shows me many things about this world, and I have gathered that there's an election tonight. It seems likely that Yan's brother, Maarten will be Prime Minister. The dreaded Jocasta is his wife, so she is someone of influence. Unfortunately, she also has strict views on behaviour, particularly where human beings are concerned.

Oh yes, there are other humans here too, in fact, the giant people of this world are quite preoccupied with them, even if they often seem to treat them cruelly. I sense there will be conflict to come, so I must count myself lucky to have allies. Apart from Yan, there is Henik, who studies me, as if I am a scientific project. I have started to have some fun with him by pulling faces or behaving in ways he can't fathom. Then there's dear little Dill who lives in the garden. When we spoke, it was as if she'd hardly had a conversation in her whole life. She was born here I'm sure, for she has no notion of home, but her language is a sort of Spanish patois, and she was quite overcome to hear it spoken. I sang a folk song I learned when we put in at La Coruna and from her reaction, it was familiar. It seems that all has not been lost for humanity here.

I shall leave you, dear Mr. Dunstone, with an attempt at a sentence or two in this strange new language. I shall pretend you are still able to appraise it and are encouraging me to make further efforts…

Kali glanced at Yan while she puzzled with the last few words. He had sidled into the room while she was writing and had picked up the multi-coloured outfit his sister-in-law had brought her. He said something she didn't fully understand, but 'sorry' was a word she now knew, and it was followed shortly afterwards by 'Jocasta.'

'No sorry,' she said, and continued working, while he folded the garment and put it away on a shelf. Then he came over to the desk and knelt on the floor, so his face was at her level. He looked at the coverage of the election which was still displayed on one side and then at her make-believe letter, running his finger along the lines in search of something he might understand. Eventually, he came to where she was attempting to write in the intricate characters of his own language. He glanced at her, then drew the letter closer. 'I do more learn of this world,' it said. He started to correct what she'd written, then stopped, and read the final words aloud, 'Also be well done friend to Yan.'

His voice dropped to a whisper. 'Friend,' he repeated. The skin tone on his forehead shifted as the moments passed and the edges of his ridges softened. 'Well done, Kali,' he said quietly. 'And… thank you.'

'It's not quite what it was,' said Santi, gazing around Henik's Midsummer apartment. She'd only been there once or twice, but it still held memories, happy ones, even if their relationship had ended shortly after Henik bought the place.

She drew a line on a dusty shelf with her finger. 'I'd be concerned if you still lived here.'

Henik watched the dust fall from her finger as if he was noticing it for the first time. 'I do stay overnight from time to time.' he said. 'Well, I camp here, anyway.'

'Among the ferals.'

'I'm sure they get in from time to time, but there's nothing of much use to them, so I don't worry about it.'

'I remember when I first came here,' she said. The mall hadn't long opened and the whole area was beautiful. I was still a junior attorney. I was so impressed.'

'But not so impressed by *me*, at that point.' said Henik. His voice was soft, perhaps even regretful.

'Well, you were progressing faster than I was, that much was impressive. But we were drifting apart, weren't we?' She waved the balcony doors open and looked out at the immense canopy of Midsummer Mall, its curves and waves taking their inspiration from the turbulent waters of the estuary beyond. 'Still, it took a long time to get over you.'

'I was self-absorbed.'

'That's one way of putting it. I remember one time when we had dinner and you didn't even think to mention that you were off to some far-flung system the next day. You were a shit at times, Henik, even if you never meant to be.'

'Well, it turns out that you've done far better without me. I'm a nuisance to the establishment, these days. I would've held you back.' He came to stand beside her, leaning far out over the balcony with the wind flapping at his shirt as if he was searching for the lost thrill of youth. Ten stories below, the plaza was deserted, the solus beating down hard on it, and the shadows still short around the trees and sculptures. 'Remember what this used to be like?' he asked. 'The noise of the crowds, the life and vibrancy of the place?'

'I remember. People outnumbered humans ten to one, and you hardly even noticed the one. You know, Henik, people are always complaining to me that the ferals have taken over here. Sure, some have migrated from elsewhere or deserted domestic homes, but the truth is that most of them just stayed on after we pulled out.'

'And the result could've been predicted. Humans are shaped by their environment, just as we are, and this is a brutal place now. It may just look neglected, but what you see below is the front line of a battlefield. The group that holds this square, I call the Midsummer Clan. They've managed to keep hold of it for nearly three years now. They've been successful, relative to other feral groups, but it's cost them dearly. They've suffered, seen a lot of death.'

It had never been easy for Santi to find the right level of detachment in her role. Her instinct was to see injustices at an individual level, even if she'd learned to be pragmatic, to weigh her conscience against political realities. 'So, those who argue that humans' first instinct is violence might have a point.'

'I think if we were living in fear of starvation, we'd soon be fighting each other for territory too. More territory means more hunting, more foraging, more chance of surviving.'

'If they aren't killed in the process.'

'More of them fall to disease than conflict. And they lose their strongest, their leaders to bounty hunters.'

'Bounty hunters? What do you mean?'

Henik exhaled sharply. 'I suppose I'm relieved you don't know about it. But really, you should. There are people who'll pay well for the heads of notable ferals. Some have business interests to defend, but others are within the security apparatus, I gather.'

'I'm not having that! That must stop right now! I'm going to…' *I'm going to wake up tomorrow and clear out my office, ready for its new occupant.*

'Well, you may still win. But if you don't, someone else will be responsible for the problem.'

'From what I hear, it's Sig Norvik.'

'What? You're telling me Feyrsten's going to give your portfolio to that self-regarding…'

'I'm afraid so.'

'The gods' breath, Santi! This is going to be a disaster for humans everywhere! They won't go down without a fight, you know. Just look over there on the far side of the square.'

Down in the plaza, a jumbled line of materials formed a knotted sinew from one side to the other, ugly and threatening even in this bleak environment. 'The fortifications, are growing by the day. If it was just to keep out other clans, they would have built the barrier long ago. It's a futile effort of course.'

'How can the ferals know what may be coming?'

'Because they're not as stupid as people think. The public sees the docile ones being dragged along the streets, and they see the violence in the Spice Islands. What they don't see is the underlying level of capability.'

'That doesn't explain how they know.'

'Well, I'll give you an example. I found Alka in here…'

'Who's Alka?'

'She leads the Midsummer Clan. She was in here watching the holoscreen the other night. It was only my recordings, but she wasn't here by chance. Trust me, she has a sense of what might happen, and that barricade is the response. Look, there she is now.'

Across the plaza, a tall dark human had emerged. She was holding her pod pass and walking straight towards them. Henik took his own pass from his pocket and showed Santi. 'She knows I'm here.'

'Really? I can't believe…' Santi paused, suddenly unsure. 'Is this dangerous, Henik?'

He looked her in the eye. 'You used to like danger.'

'That was then. This is now.'

Alka didn't look at them until she was directly under the balcony, then she raised her head and shouted. When she saw Santi, she placed her hands on her hips and lifted her chin slightly. Then she beckoned to them.

'That means she wants us to come down.'

Santi felt her stomach lurch. 'Henik, we can't! Surely, you're not going to go down there?'

'Of course, I am.' He reached out and took her hand

tenderly, entwining his fingers with hers. 'You can stay here if you want, or we can do this together. Just like we used to.'

'Please, Henik. I mean, I know she's only small but…'

Henik came close to her now, their noses almost touching. His breath was hot on her face, and she could see her reflection in the ellipses of his pupils. 'I'll stay with you,' he said. 'There's always some risk, there always was. But doesn't it make you feel alive?'

Down in the plaza they found Alka squatting in the shade of a bronze sculpture. She stood up and loped over to them, squinting into the solus. 'Plain,' she said.

'Hello, Alka. This is my friend, Santi.'

Alka's mouth twitched at the corner. She put her hands on her hips again and regarded Santi warily. 'Santi Aspil,' she said.

Santi's stomach flipped again. She could feel the blood draining from her lips and fingers. *She knows me! She knows who I am!*

Alka seemed to sense Santi's unease and the corners of her mouth rose further until she was smiling. 'Return the expression,' said Henik. 'Treat it as a gift.' He pointed at the barricade. 'What's that all about, Alka?'

She nodded at it soberly, then took her fist and rapped it twice into the palm of her hand. She turned towards the mall, motioned for them to follow, and Santi was suddenly aware that her hand was holding onto Henik's. She wondered who had initiated the contact, but she felt better for it as they followed Alka across the plaza and into the mall. It was the first time she'd been there since its heyday, and the deterioration was obvious wherever she looked. The shops had been stripped of merchandise, and all along the concourse grit crackled under their footsteps. But the sheer scale of the place still impressed.

There was a time when it had been the largest mall on Antaris and her predecessor at the Department for the Interior had attended its opening, speaking of it as a 'glorious temple of commerce.' Hundreds of units above them, the verglas roof still rippled and gleamed, splitting the light into shafts of component colours. Over the years, the arcades had softened under a green cloak of climbing plants, some brown and dry, but most managing to thrive on secret water sources, winding their way across the bridges, spanning the thoroughfares, and cascading from balconies. The air was thick with moist perfume and all manner of winged creatures flitted, birds and bats and painted lizins, bringing the air alive with high-pitched chattering. Nature was reclaiming the space for itself and for all her rationality, Santi felt a part of her rejoicing.

'Look!' she said, attracting Henik's attention with a tug of his hand. 'Have you noticed they still have power here? There's some lighting in the shops and the fountain is still working.'

'And the screens. There's the answer to how they know what's happening in the world.'

Alka came to a halt in front of the fountain and called out, hands cupped around her mouth and her voice echoing, until human faces began to appear from doorways and over balconies. One by one the Midsummer ferals emerged onto the main boulevard, congregating slowly to form an arc around them. Santi counted about seventy in all, mainly males and most still wearing the overalls of their former occupations and corporate owners. They looked a surly crew, most slouching with hands in pockets, but respectful to Alka as she drew them forward to the fountain. The exception was a pair of twins with close-cropped blond hair. They stood off to the side, shoulders touching as they whispered to each other, their blue eyes darting between Alka and the rest of the group. Then, as if directed by a single mind, they switched their attention to Santi and stared at her for several moments until again, in a moment of unison, they looked away towards their leader. Santi gave Henik a nudge. 'I'd watch those two if I were her,' she said.

Alka stepped up onto the edge of the fountain and began to speak. Her voice echoed crisply around the mall, the pace measured at first, and emphasised by the sweeping movement of her arms. Soon the momentum increased, her words delivered more sharply and with the jabbing of her fingers, but then softening with emotion, her hands floating, caressing the air. Santi found she couldn't look away, that she was captured not just by the extraordinary sight of a human engaged in oratory, but by the sheer force of Alka's delivery.

The address finished on a crescendo that drew shouts of approval from the clan and the raising of hands towards the fountain as if it was a source of fortitude. Eventually, Alka stepped down. She took Santi's hand and led the way through her followers, towards an annex, where a flight of steps brought them up to a carpeted area in what had once been a department store. There were more humans there, but they were old and sick, lying in rows on stained mattresses. There were mothers too, cradling babies too weak to cry, their faces grey and hollow. Alka walked amongst the invalids, pointing at those who appeared most pitiful, drained of flesh and strength, eyes blank and without hope. She was speaking again now. She turned to look up at Henik and Santi, as if determined that they should understand what she was saying, and her voice was laden with sadness. Occasionally as they went from one invalid to another, her tone would become bitter and there might be a word spoken in their own language. But she preferred the fluency of her own tongue, trusted that the passion in her voice would serve more effectively than mere words.

From time to time, Alka's attention would leave them, and she would stoop to take hold of a hand, or crouch and whisper comfortingly to a child.

'Makes you think,' said Henik.

'What is it? What's the matter with them all?' asked Santi, her voice ringing hollow in her ears, as if someone else was asking the questions. *They're dying of course, that's what's the matter.*

'It's more than one thing,' said Henik. 'Those over there on their own have clearwater fever, I think. That's about sanitation, so there's no excuse for it in the richest city in the Commonwealth. Humans are at risk of all sorts of diseases that we no longer have. There's never been a compelling reason to develop resistant humans.'

'Too costly, I suppose,' said Santi. *When they are so replaceable.*

'Which tells you how little we value them. Some of these humans are just old and with no one to care for them. They have no value at all. Some civilisations just terminate them at a certain age.'

'Decca. I tried to discuss the practice with them once.'

'What we do on Antaris isn't much better. We just turn our backs on them, leave them to their fate. Look at those behind you. They're the ones who shame us most, wasting away from exposure to rare metals. We import the ore from the high-gravity systems to make the linings for stellar drives. And you can see the by-product of it, the sails of all those solus yachts, glittering by night out by Oberon. This is what it means. This is the cost of it all.'

Santi stared at a small group who were sitting quietly

together in a corner, their limbs thin as water canes, and their skin shining with perspiration. Their bodies looked as if they were about to crumble. 'I don't understand,' she said. 'There are strict regulations on toxic materials, severe penalties. I strengthened them only last year.'

The corporates flout the law all the time where human workers are concerned. There's little risk of prosecution because the humans can't speak up for themselves, and the profits far outweigh the penalties.'

Santi found herself struggling not to cry. She held her hand over her mouth to stifle the sobs that were pushing at her chest. Alka caught her eye, then drifted away, watched them from a distance.

A large male appeared in the doorway. He marched into the room shouting, his eyes wide and fierce. Alka moved fast to intercept him, barked an order and pushed him back towards the door. He argued, pointing at Henik and Santi over her shoulder. Alka shoved him hard in the chest, shouted in his face, shoved him again. At last, he retreated, smashing his fist into a wall panel, before storming off down the stairs. Alka stood staring at the floor for a moment, hands on her hips, then she breathed deeply and motioned them to follow her once again.

When they returned to the main boulevard the clan had disappeared. Alka led them back to the mall's entrance, walking with a rangy stride, past the fountain and down the tree-lined avenue. As they passed an old veterinary shop, she turned towards a giant mosaic mural of a human female. Her hand went to her chest as she walked, and she uttered a few soft words.

They stopped at the entrance to the mall, and she spoke again, first in her own tongue, then finally, looking at each of them in turn, making an attempt in theirs. 'I go,' she said.

'I want to say something to her,' said Santi.

'The best you can do is to speak simply, make motions with your hands if it feels right.'

Santi took a step forward. 'I've heard your message, Alka,' she said. She looked back down the boulevard, towards the first-floor annex. 'I will get you help, somehow.'

Alka held her for a moment with her dark eyes. 'Santi Aspil,' she said, and nodded. Then she strode away towards the fountain.

'Don't worry,' said Henik. 'She understood you, at an emotional level at least.' He watched Alka walk back down the arcaded boulevard. She made a small bow as she passed the towering mosaic and Henik found his gaze drawn upwards to its face, the pale skin, the penetrating eyes, the wild copper hair.

Henik and Santi left the pod station at the far end of Carnival Square and walked slowly through the centre of Freeport. The streets were quieter than usual, the shops closed, and the bars not yet in full swing. The skeleton bats were out early though, skimming over the ornamental pools, triggering the fountains as they went. From far away, a light breeze brought with it the intermittent rumble of bulk transports outbound from the Interstellar Terminal, and from a window nearby came the voice of a child, calling for its mother.

Santi had been keeping her own counsel since they left Midsummer, and now she walked with her head down, and her arms folded. She'd been shaken by what she'd witnessed, retreating into herself as she always used to when she was troubled. Henik remembered that about her, that conversation would be impossible until she'd processed the experience thoroughly. Then, as they passed the Department for the

Interior she raised her head, lifted her chin higher and higher. 'Somewhere up there,' she said. 'The one with the light on, probably. I guess it's still mine, just about.'

'I suppose you have things to do in there,' said Henik. It didn't feel right to mention work. Not when the afternoon had felt so much like the adventures of their youth and when standing under the Carnival St. lights, Santi looked so much like the person he once knew, the idealist, the champion of lost causes. She was still beautiful he thought, her face softer perhaps, but the fine ridges and prominent brow were still there, making her appear both strong and weary at the same time. Perhaps she was heavier now, in her maturity, but her posture was as compact and tidy as ever, and she carried her clothes well, no longer dismissing fashion, but every bit the well-dressed public figure.

In truth, Santi had always been more than Henik felt he deserved, and perhaps on some level it had weighed against them. There had been women since, but none had lasted or mattered, and he was always wary of their motivations once he was in the public eye. He never imagined that they were drawn to him by his appearance, but neither did they have Santi's disdain for such considerations. True, she had embraced presentation as a tool of her trade now, but underneath, she was still the same person that she was. Midsummer had shown him that, illuminated her compassion, her integrity. That was Santi. And perhaps it was why she'd never found anyone to spend her life with. *Plenty of men of thin principle in Freeport, plenty trading on their charm.*

Santi seemed in no hurry to go back to her desk, to face the consequences of the people's verdict. She stood staring at the building's famous geometric façade as if seeing it for the first time, with its verglas rippling in reflected light, and transports spearing through its upper tiers. Perhaps she was committing its contours to memory while a piece of it was still hers. She turned full circle, lifting her gaze higher still, up to the surrounding halo of lights, the forest of cloudpiercers with their suspended platforms and misted sky gardens, that formed the commercial hub of the greatest civilisation ever known.

'I'm not looking forward to tomorrow,' she said eventually.

'What are the timings?'

'Local votes will be in by dawn, and pre-voting from Commonwealth systems shortly afterwards. Then if it's close, they'll look at the proxies for orbital stations and vessels in transit. Final results by breakfast. Then, barring some miracle, the CC will resign with a balcony address, and we'll vacate mid-morning.' She sighed, then continued. 'Meanwhile, the media will lay siege to my door demanding explanations and wanting a reaction to Norvik's appointment. And I guess they'll be bound to ask if I'm going to challenge for the party leadership.' She shuddered as if struck by a sudden chill. 'You know, I don't want to go back in there now, Henik. Will you take me somewhere? Can we stay young this evening… tonight?'

It was after midnight before Santi wanted to speak about Midsummer. She got out of bed and wrapped a sheet around herself, went to sit at the window, and gazed down on Carnival Square. Henik brought her some hot cahcana.

'Can you see that?' he said. 'All eight moons visible at once tonight. I like sitting here, breathing the night air. I listen to the city when I can't sleep, and I watch the sky. But I've hardly ever seen the moons like this before. You can even make out Zante and Kelso on the horizon.'

'It's always Calderon that gets my attention,' said Santi. 'Look at it. It's so violent, so close. You can feel its madness from here.'

'Our gravity is pulling at it mercilessly, distorting it night and day.'

'That eruption a few years back. I remember how it had people running around the corridors at Check St. Scientists darting in and out of the CC's office.'

'And what came of it? A bulk transport lost, and some crops destroyed. Then back to normal.'

'But do you remember how it sent people flocking to worship the Astral gods? The temples were packed. And people still pay more attention than they did, myself included. I can't help thinking that one day it will just blow, right here over Freeport.' She pulled the bed sheet more closely around herself. 'Just imagine.'

Henik sipped at his drink. 'People have been saying that for as long as they've been watching the sky. "Someday". The experts say it's no more likely now than it has ever been.'

Santi exhaled slowly. 'But somehow when the moons are bright like this it feels like they're about to teach us a lesson.'

Henik decided it was time to change the subject. 'We have a more local eruption to worry about first,' he said.

'The Spice Islands, or the Derelict Zone?'

'They're not unconnected. There may be a wide sea between Freeport and the Spice Islands, but people here are still influenced. Humans are too.'

Santi put her feet up on the windowsill. 'You really think humans will take note of events on the other side of the planet?'

'Can you doubt it after what you saw today? Sig Norvik may deny their cognitive abilities, which will excuse whatever treatment is meted out to them, but you know better now. You've seen the raw feeling they experience, the way it can easily turn to aggression. You've also seen the extent of their restraint and compassion.'

'Yes, it was quite…'

'The way Alka spoke to her clan… It made me wonder if there's something in the way they communicate or the way they hear it, that holds more power than our more functional interactions, that pulls them together, holds individuals to a common cause.'

'There was a spiritual element too,' said Santi. 'Did you notice that? Alka had a reverence for that mural.'

'I've seen it once or twice in the past with humans. An act of worship is evidence that they can perceive non-tangible concepts, imagine mythical characters.'

'What mythical character is that mosaic?'

'I'm not sure, but I think it's supposed to be a representation of Callista. It's an obscure legend about a human, and the green moon.'

'So, she's looking to a mural for help, because she can't expect it from us. Because amongst all our riches, her clan is dying.'

'I suppose so. Perhaps.'

'I feel responsible. I know the economic crisis wasn't our doing, but I've been more focused on the problems of the voting public than the ferals, and they're more connected than I realised. I should have done more, and now I've lost my chance.' She leaned towards the window and searched the sky. 'Do you know that until recently I had one of those solus yachts myself? Toxic coating and all.'

Henik put his hand on her arm. Her flesh was warm despite the chill of the night. 'Compromise is what takes us forward, and you've done what you had to. Out of government you won't be so constrained.'

'I'll be able to say that public well-being is unsustainable if the cost is human misery.'

'And that economic recovery won't last unless we make humans part of the solution.'

'Maybe you should write my speeches,' said Santi. She raised her glass. 'Step into the spotlight, Henik Varkesen.'

'I might understand humans, but you have a grasp of the whole picture. You must lead.'

'Lead what? Awareness, reform?' Santi chuckled under her breath. 'Revolution?'

'Depends what happens next. Once the state starts poking its nose into every house and business that has a human, you won't just see barricades going up in Midsummer Plaza. They'll be down there in Carnival St. too.'

Santi cradled her flask in her hands and looked up at the boiling surface of Calderon. 'And we'll need to decide on which side to stand.'

Yan's brother looked as happy as he'd ever seen him, as he made his triumphant passage through the crowds on Check St. Not that it was easy to tell with Maarten. He had always been the least expressive member of the family, his facial tones shaded to neutral, and his behaviour always decorous. His wife more than made up for it, though. Jocasta walked at his side, her designer suit bright enough to strain the eyes, her gloved hands working the crowd tirelessly and her face turned in the direction of the media at every opportunity. Soon they would reach the door of their new residence, its former occupant having left at the rear not long before. There would be a speech proclaiming a new dawn, and then they would get down to business, setting people against each other and species against species.

Yan sometimes explained his relationship with his brother as being like a planet held in a distant orbit. He moved unnoticed around a brilliant source of light, and most of the time, that was the way he liked it. On the occasions when they spoke, they still got on well enough, and on Republic Day they would meet with family and friends and it would be as if the years had taken nothing from the closeness of their childhood. But they rarely talked politics. They both knew they were on different sides of the balance, and there was nothing to be gained from exposing their differences. Yan wasn't in any sense outspoken on current affairs, but it was in the nature of academic life to see the possibilities more than practical constraints. The world of business though, where Maarten's views were forged, was more invested in the way things were. It saw stability as reason enough to crush an unquantifiable risk.

Yan looked away from the display. Across the hall, his own unquantifiable risk was busy in the kitchen, babbling to herself in her own strange patois, then testing new phrases she was learning in the language of the Republic, changing the order of words and adopting comical tones as if she was imagining their application.

'Oh no!' she said suddenly, causing Yan to start. 'Is table by window please, for my friend!' She took a blade and attacked a large beabub tuber with it, chopping it into fine pieces while her voice softly trilled the sequence of sounds that had moved Dill to tears. 'Feyrsten – yes, is truth! Is table for brother to Chief Counsellor!'

'Henik Varkesen,' announced the lift. When it opened, he didn't step out immediately, and when he did emerge, his fingers were toying with a fallen leaf from one of the potted plants.

'Grim day for the Republic,' he said.

'Tell that to our protégé.'

'Good morning, Henik!' said Kali. She came to the

kitchen door and performed an elaborate bow. 'Greet,' she said, then laughed as she went back to her work.

'What in the gods' names was that?'

'Something Jocasta had her doing. I've told her not to, but she seems to find it amusing. Just as well that she does, because our new Lady Consort was at her most annoying yesterday. Kali took an instant dislike.'

'Henik be hungry?' asked Kali.

'It smells very good. What is it?'

'More bloody marvellous!' she said. 'You like. Fishy soup, I do make.'

Yan waited for Henik to enthuse about Kali's meteoric progress, but he made no comment. He just stood with his hands in his pockets and watched her closely.

'I got out my old school desk,' said Yan. 'She's been using it all the time, studying everything. We found a language course for off-worlders and she's consuming it with ease. She's even started writing!'

Henik folded his arms 'I didn't imagine she could do that,' he mumbled.

'Well, she can. She's so keen to learn. You tell her once, and she just remembers. I wish my students were like that.'

Henik shuffled a bit further into the house, glancing around as if it was his first visit. 'So, she's settling down well,' he said. 'That's... good.' He peered into the kitchen.

'She's thriving. Henik. I really appreciate what you've done for us. You've changed everything.'

'Well don't get too comfortable just yet, there are going to be changes.'

'I know. Sig Norvik will be the Counsellor for Human Affairs. Jocasta told me.'

'And here's Jocasta!' enthused Kali. 'Lady Consort be wearing blue, today. Crowd is loving!'

'I thought you said she didn't like her,' said Henik, quietly.

'That's another thing about humans – irony.'

Henik lowered his voice further. 'Well, let me show you something else you're not going to like.' He reached into his pocket and took out the leaf. 'Let's step outside.'

They walked to the end of the garden, Henik looking around suspiciously. 'Are you alright?' said Yan. 'You don't seem very pleased with Kali's progress. I thought that...'

'I'm sorry. I was saying as little as I could without it sounding too awkward.' He unfolded the leaf carefully and tipped its contents into Yan's palm. 'It's broken now, but I found it in the lift.'

Yan examined the microbot. If he had seen it around the house, he wouldn't have recognised it for what it was, but it was so tiny that he probably wouldn't have seen it at all. 'It's like we used in the National Guard,' he said, 'but so much smaller.'

'There won't be just one. These things hunt in swarms. You'll never find them all, and they can pick up cranial vibrations as easily as voice. You're being monitored. Your house is compromised.'

'But why?' Yan could feel the fear clawing at his throat as the answer came to him. 'Kali,' he said. He looked back at the house, through the kitchen window to where she was working. *Alone in the house for the first time, apart from an army of robots.*

'It's probably about your brother's security, or even your own. This sort of hardware is top-grade and fully intelligent. If you're not the Security Service you'd need to be well-connected to get it. Whoever's behind this, will have seen Kali, and unless they're off their game, they'll understand her significance.'

'I'll need to get them all cleared out.'

'That'll take too long, and this situation is too dangerous. You're close to the new Chief Counsellor, you're under serious surveillance, and you're in possession of something uniquely valuable.'

'I hear you,' said Yan. 'We're getting Kali out of here, right now.'

7

Gold

IN MIDSUMMER PLAZA THE barricade had been rising day by day, a bristling wall of materials that had been brought in a steady procession and now stretched right across the square, from the mall at one end to the pod station on the other. At the bottom, anchoring the construction were abandoned transports, dragged from the skytram's parking lot. On top of them were commercial appliances, then building materials and interior fittings from the shops. Now the clan was ferrying domestic furniture and soft materials that would be arranged along the battlement to absorb the impact of elemist pellets.

Alka dusted her hands and surveyed the morning's work from the top of the barricade. It would keep the Dockers away, but it wouldn't be much of a defence against the might of the giant people. Still, it felt good to be engaged in something constructive, and she hoped the effort would bind the clan more closely in the hard times that were coming. She shielded her eyes against the solus and scanned the square, wondering if anyone was watching the barrier going up, whether it would be a source of amusement, or if it might precipitate the reckoning she knew was coming.

Kit came out of the mall and came striding across the plaza, his swinging gait rocking him sideways with each step. He was carrying a small box in one hand and twisting his beard with the other. 'Chief!' he shouted as he drew nearer.

Alka climbed down from the barricade to meet him, glad that he was breaking the silence that had hung between them since she'd brought the two people into their midst. 'Barricade's unstable at that end,' she said. 'It'll need more support at the bottom.' She pointed at the box, which was brimming with cable connections and circuitry. 'That's not going to help much.'

Kit studied the barrier for a moment, his fingers still working at his beard. 'You really think all this will keep them out of our citadel?'

'It won't stop the People over-running us once they make their minds up, but it may deter them.' There was some truth in what she was saying, the possibility that showing themselves ready to fight might delay an assault, but it was more hope than belief. And it felt a hollow boast to call their home the Citadel, these days, persisting with it only to maintain morale. 'It will buy us time,' she said.

'Time for what? You're counting on Callista, I suppose.'

Alka looked up at the sky, the green disc of her favourite moon, ghostly pale in the morning light. *There you are, merciful one. I see you, and you see me.*

'I've watched how you pray at night,' continued Kit. 'You really think she's up there?'

'She will come. It's foretold. She is the Redeemer, and the time is approaching.'

'And if she doesn't come?'

'We all go to the stars in the end. In the meantime, I'm reaching out to those who can help.'

'That politician. You really believe...'

'She saw our pain. I know she felt it.'

'Chief, I don't want to argue with you. Without you, we wouldn't have held against the Dockers or any of the other clans. It would have been over long ago. I didn't mean to go against you, but...'

'I know. You don't need to say anything, Kit. It's hard, but there are moments when we must put our anger aside and find a different path. There's no sense starting a battle we can't win.'

Kit took a deep breath and shook the box he was carrying. 'Well, you're not going to like this, then.'

She took it from him and peered inside. 'What's all this crap?'

'It belongs to the twins. It was under their bed.'

Alka sighed. 'They've gone, haven't they? Did they say where?'

'They left in the night, but they were talking about joining the Chemical Clan.'

'What? That makes no sense. The Chemicals are tiny. You could count their number on your fingers. They've got much less chance than we have.'

'Perhaps the twins don't see it that way. I used to work with them over at the power plant.'

'What's that got to do with it?'

'They were always cunning little shits, but smart as you like. The company would send us to dig up the old transmission relays. The really ancient stuff was fibre, like in this box. It still worked well enough, and the twins could do all sorts of tricks with it. Even I understand what you can do with the bits and pieces in this box if you know how to configure an explosion trap.'

'But they've got no explosive material or toxins.'

'Some say the Chemicals have both. They've managed to brew some elemist.'

Alka felt the moisture disappearing from her mouth. 'We need to move fast,' she said. 'Call everyone together, Kit. I want two volunteers to come with me to the chemical works. We need to see if they'll parley.'

'I'm coming too.'

'No, I want you holding the Citadel. The clan needs you.'

'They need you too, Chief.'

'And I will return,' said Alka. She glanced again at the green moon. 'Callista watches over me.'

The Department for the Interior hummed with nervous energy as it awaited its new Counsellor. Work points were in motion, spaces re-configuring themselves to create a divided office, general domestic matters on one side, and control and management of humans on the other.

There was new signage as well, new titles, new faces. Sig Norvik was pleased to see his name and image rising from the floor when he arrived, rotating to greet him in the lobby with an air of calm assurance. It reached out as he approached, inviting him to establish his identity by pressing hands with himself.

A young clerk in a silver-grey suit was waiting for him on the twentieth level. 'Good day, esteemed. It is a privilege to be the first to welcome you. Please come this way to your office. I'm Alid, your administrative assistant. I'll meet your everyday needs.'

'Not all of them, I hope,' said Norvik dryly.

'All that are within scope, esteemed.'

'Ah! You're android.'

'But of course, esteemed. I am more economical than a person, more capable than a human, and I present less operational risk than either.'

Norvik followed Alid along the building's curving walkways. Officials left their work and lined their path, welcoming him with an acclaim that was more polite than enthusiastic. 'Alright, Alid. Tell me about the risks presented by humans,' said Norvik.

'Risk one: reliability – moderate to severe. Risk two: emotional disturbance – highly variable. Risk three: insubordination – modest with due mitigation. Risk four: security – severe to critical. Risk five...'

'That will do, Alid. That's quite satisfactory.' They arrived at the door of what had been Santi Aspil's office and walked in to the smell of cleaning fluid. Norvik was taken immediately by the panoramic view behind the desk. It reached in one direction as far as the Interstellar Terminal and the technology park, with its white buildings laid out on the landscape with laser precision. Flanking it was the woodland of the Green Zone, with the purple hills of the Near Interior rising behind in sleepy folds. On the other side, the view stretched out to the estuary. At its mouth the vast green curve of the algae and seagrass farms spread in a lattice of floating booms, conjuring from the flow of nutrients the food, the clothing, the substance of daily life for a million families. Beyond the farms, the Septentrional sea sparkled under a cloudless sky, its golden shores the last landfall between the Free Republic and the turmoil a thousand leagues away in the Spice Islands. Then, further along the coast, the Derelict Zone spread its tentacles right to the edge of the financial district. From this distance it looked benign enough, the roof of Midsummer Mall and the metalwork of the disused overland transport system glinting just as brightly as they had in better times. All of it, and much more besides was now within his remit, subject to his plans, relying on his unmatched expertise. Hundreds of millions of humans in the Republic, he thought, admirable and vile, disciplined and feral, loved and despised. All ripe for reform, an unruly forest ready for the torch.

'Your Heads of Staff are waiting to brief you,' said Alid. Shall I send them in, Counsellor?'

'And some refreshments please.'

'Yes esteemed, of course.'

Norvik met his new reports at the door and greeted them warmly, addressing the shorter of the two first. 'Good to see you again, Panos. I recall we debated sometime last year.' He turned to his colleague, a lean man whose eyes shone with intelligence. 'And you must be Vi'Shvni Faluavanati...'

'Please just call me, "Vish".'

Norvik pulled out a chair. 'Take a seat and let's get started. I know you'll want to give me a full briefing, but first I would like to check that we're of the same mind as far as basic principles are concerned. Now, I know you both worked for Santi. We did clash on policy as you know, but we shared a commitment to maintaining order and treating both our fellow citizens and their animals with good judgment. I'm sure I can count on you to be as supportive to me as you were to her.'

'That's our duty, Counsellor,' said Vish. 'We serve the duly elected Government.'

'Indeed, and it's good to hear you say so. Now, the way I see this is that we have two adjacent briefs for Human Affairs, both of which will be reforming ones.'

'Public Order, and Welfare,' said Panos.

'No, we'll be changing that setup. Welfare is implicit and needs no focus, so instead Human Affairs will be divided into Domestic and Commercial, with an emphasis on *public order* in both. Vish, will take Domestic and Panos you'll have the pleasure of Commercial.'

'So, the Derelict Zone is my patch, and Vish has the lawns and gardens of the Green Zone.'

'There are major challenges in each brief. Your feral problem is pressing Panos, but more straightforward to tackle. Domestic humans are a more subtle concern. People feel more strongly about a subject when it's sitting at their feet, so it will need careful handling.'

'Forgive me, Counsellor,' said Vish. 'I would like to understand the new policy line on domestics. Could you clarify your thinking?'

'Certainly,' said Norvik, rolling up the sleeves of his shirt. He was pleased to find his staff ready to listen and understand his agenda. 'We all recognise that ferals need to be dealt with decisively. They are having a noticeable economic impact, and if the situation is allowed to fester, their wild ways will spread like a contagion. But we must also protect what has not been infected, and the way to do that is to make sure that humans are properly controlled, that wayward behaviour is not allowed to take root. We know on the Marsh Estate that dealing firmly, harshly even, with minor infringements will reduce more serious crime, and so it is with the conduct of animals in the domestic setting. Now, are we all aligned on that?' He looked from one of them to the other until he received their confirmation.

'And what about process,' said Panos. 'Our approach will divide opinion. How do you see the consultation operating?'

'Consultation?'

Panos and Vish exchanged a glance. 'Well yes,

Counsellor,' said Vish. 'Normally we consult on the details for at least three cycles for major policy changes. Would I be right in thinking you want this done more quickly?'

There could be no room for doubt, Norvik thought. The moment had come to establish his authority. He brought the election results into view on the table in front of them in bright graphics. '*This* is your consultation. This Government has just won a strong mandate from the public, particularly on the human question. We have the answer we need already. You may think that unconventional, but we have a crisis on our hands and my brief from the Chief Counsellor is to travel light and move fast. That's what I intend to do, and it's what I expect you to do as well. I hope the pace won't be too much for you.'

Norvik paused to let his meaning sink in. Panos and Vish shifted slightly in their seats, but they kept any reservations to themselves, one of them staring at his hands, and the other pretending to study the election statistics. Norvik got to his feet, signalling the end of the meeting. 'Now, let's get going,' he said. 'I'm sure you've been giving this a lot of thought already, so let me have your proposals first thing in the morning when we reconvene. Thank you, both. That's all for now.'

Kali stood waiting in the hallway as Yan and Henik gathered what they needed. They moved around her briskly as if, for the first time since she'd arrived, they didn't consider her their priority. They hadn't told her why they were leaving, or where they were going, but it was clear they were in a hurry and she knew better than to press them with questions.

With so few possessions, it had taken her no time at all to prepare for whatever adventure was in store. The priority had to be her magic desk. She'd watched Yan setting it up, but reversing the process required intuition and an element of luck before a humming started somewhere inside. The desk began to fold like an origami model until it had turned itself into a tidy package.

Leaving Jocasta's gaudy outfit behind had been an easy decision, but it was only when she was checking around the room that she noticed the other shopping bags behind a chair. In one, she found a garment just as ridiculous as the one she'd been forced to wear, but when she opened the other, it appeared that Jocasta had been overcome by a bout of good taste. Nestled in an elaborate bed of packing was an exquisite coat in a soft crimson fabric. It had a large hood and wide sleeves, and it was lined with a fine gold satin material. On the back and sleeves, thread of the same colour had been used to embroider a bewildering array of stars, arranged in their constellations with careful symmetry. Kali had never seen such a beautiful coat, let alone been given one. She swung it on to her shoulders and turned in quick circles, watching the thread shimmer as the coat flared around her.

Yan was too busy to notice what she was wearing, and Kali decided to hold her tongue, in case she was not meant to have it. She hugged her desk to her chest and stood quietly, until finally, when they were all ready, Yan led them into the lift, and they descended into a network of passages beneath the street. Kali had been to a few underground stations in London, and wondered whether something similar was in store. There was a station beneath the street but it turned out to be a very disappointing one, nothing more than an austere room with a shelf to sit on, and an ethereal display that showed a train approaching. Almost as if it had responded to their presence, an egg-shaped vehicle emerged from a solid black circle on one wall, made an announcement, which included the word 'sorry,' then departed through another black circle on the opposite wall. When it had gone, Kali found she'd been gripping Yan's shirt. He studied her, his mouth drawing up to form a hesitant smile, and then they sat in silence watching for the next pod. Even though she was expecting its arrival, it still took her by surprise, entering the little station room from the opposite direction and greeting Yan by name. There was a graphic display flashing on the door, two figures that appeared to represent Yan and Henik, and in a different colour an oval shape which Kali presumed to mean an accompanying being or item of luggage.

It wasn't until the doors had closed behind them and they had settled into their seats that Kali asked where they were going.

'We must go to live in my house by the sea,' Yan said. 'You'll like it, and it will be safe there.'

'Not safe *here*?' asked Kali.

'People are watching us and listening. When they learn you're not from this world, you may be in danger.'

'Why is danger? Is well done with Yan and Henik.'

They looked at each other. 'It's difficult to explain,' said Yan. 'The Government wants humans to be… like Juno.'

Kali stared at the floor of the pod and thought about Yan's answer for a while. She thought about Jocasta and what she'd expected of her, and how Juno had behaved, how stiff and obedient he was. The thought of it made her shiver.

Yan began a conversation with Henik, an appraisal of her progress, from what she could understand, but much of it vibrating in their skulls and beyond comprehension.

She reached up and touched his forehead. 'You speak here, yes?'

'It's not possible for humans to hear it. But you're

speaking to us with your voice Kali, and you can write. Will you show Henik what you've done?'

She got down from her seat and opened the little origami desk, watched it unfold in front of him and ignite with a burst of colour and sound. She stood back and watched while Henik and Yan engaged in an intense conversation about the letter she'd written. First, they examined what she'd put in her own language, Henik bringing his face close to the text and marvelling at the structure and pattern of the words. But when they came to the sentences she'd written in their own language, he drew a sharp breath and became sombre. Yan continued to talk enthusiastically, pointing out words like "pride", but there was something about what she'd done that seemed to trouble Henik.

'You not be happy?' she asked.

'It's this new Government. If they know about your ability…'

'Understand,' she said. 'Be problem, maybe.'

It wasn't the first time the thought had occurred to her. The more she'd learned about this world, the clearer it had become that what she was doing, the learning of their language, the way she was behaving, was beyond what they expected of humans. It was special, they thought, *she* was special. That had resolved the immediate issues of her existence, her basic needs, the relationship she had with Yan, but not everyone would embrace it, not everyone would accept it.

Yan re-folded the desk, and they sat quietly as the pod sped under the city, each now absorbed in their own thoughts. Kali watched them from under the hood of her coat as they stared into space and she could detect no communication between them.

'Is she worth it?' they're thinking. 'Are we prepared for the consequences?'

She was suddenly aware of Henik looking at her. He'd noticed her coat, she thought, with its embroidered stars and gold lining. But it wasn't that. He reached out slowly and eased the hood back on her head, so that more of her hair tumbled from beneath it. Then she felt something new in his eyes, something unsettling. It was as if he was looking at someone he recognised.

Beyond the city limits the route out of Freeport ran flat and true for over thirty leagues. For a while Torsta's transport maintained a modest pace, constrained by the weight of traffic. Soon though, the suburbs gave way to pasture, then to woodland reserve, and the commuters fell behind. Now the flyway was hers alone, the forest rushing by in an endless green tunnel. After a while it began to rise above the trees and curve, the grey shapes of the hill country coming into view, sprawling across the landscape like sleeping beasts.

At the base of the hills, her transport turned onto a narrow route that twisted up a steep valley. It made another turn to crawl along a stony track that led to a high pass. At the top, it opened onto a secluded meadow overlooking a steep escarpment, a wild place where the wind whipped up from the valley behind, and the hills were flanked by barren scree slopes. The meadow responded to Torsta's arrival as if it had been waiting for her. The ground rose into a yawn, accepted her transport into its throat, then lowered it down a shaft of orange lights.

This was the place Torsta had called home since her release from *Bleak Penance*, exchanging a prison ship for this austere cavern space, one among many here, where the occupants had no names and came and went unnoticed. When the machinery had come to rest, Torsta stepped out of the transport onto the rough granite floor. The security system registered no intrusion, and everything appeared as she'd left it, her black hoverbike up on its trestle with its intake covers off for maintenance, her body armour hanging from a hook in the kitchen, and the remains of her last meal still on the table. She drew off her combat boots and cast them aside, then walked over to her bed and threw herself onto it.

There was something comforting about the cavern, not that Torsta would ever admit she needed comfort, even to herself. With the cliffside shutters open, the views along the valley were spectacular, but when they were closed, it felt as if the space had curled itself around her, intimate and unjudging. It was a place where nothing could reach her, a place where it was safe to remember.

Eighty people I've killed, at least that. Regulars, mercenaries, conscripts, civilians even, people just in the wrong place at the wrong time. There had been so many conflicts, vicious little disputes in colonial outposts, civil wars on vassal worlds, and frontier skirmishes between rival systems. *The orders I've given, the scale of the destruction, all in the service of the Republic. Twenty years of it, pushing you to your limit. Then when you finally lose control, let the rage loose, it's in downtown Freeport, in a fucking bar.*

She closed her eyes and tried to relax, to reduce her breathing to the minimum. *Bleak Penance. The cursed silence of it, ringing in your ears, roaring at you like a stellar drive. How long was it in that metal box? Long enough to change you, to twist your mind.*

Torsta slept without removing her clothes. Her first kill

came to her in the depth of the night as it often did. In a grey alley, a face came charging at her with wild eyes and sharpened teeth. Then she was diving for cover, rolling, firing, again and again, falling on her back with the alien soldier on top of her, ending him with a frantic stabbing of wet metal.

When she woke, the solus was pushing through the gaps in the shutters. She turned her pillow and stared at the roof of the cavern for a while, gathering her thoughts. She mumbled an order for breakfast, rolled out of bed to collect it from the dispenser in the kitchen, and stood there eating while she retrieved the data feed from the microbots at the Feyrsten place.

Most of the two hundred bots were still operational, almost all stationary, having reached places where they had become stuck, or where there was no movement to attract their attention. Only two were still in motion and in the presence of a warm-blooded organism.

Torsta went to the stronger of the two signals first, looking through the eyes of a bot that had made its way into the garden. There was a patch of sky in one corner of the feed, and the bot was crawling on a surface identified as human skin, until quite suddenly it appeared to be transported into the air and a human face came into view, elderly but with shining brown eyes. Then the view went dark again, and the data spiked with function alarms suggesting the bot was under attack from digestive enzymes.

There was no view at all from the last bot. The screen was dark, but the data showed no malfunction. It was close to a source of heat and in the presence of a natural fibre, amber or gold in colour. The co-ordinates didn't correspond to Yan Fernsten's house though, they weren't even in the Green Zone, but were at a location on the opposite side of the city, somewhere out on the coast. There were any number of ways the bot could have been transported so far from its release point, but rather than speculate about one stray unit, Torsta decided to run through the material from all the others. She ran a search for proximity life forms, then narrowed it to the human signal.

The bots had captured the Earth human working in the kitchen, left alone with sharp-edged instruments, and on the stairs, carrying a bag and a foldaway table. Finally, there was a shot taken from a high vantage point, showing it waiting in the hall as two men moved busily around it. One of them was Yan Feyrsten, but the other was unidentified. His back was turned but his voice sounded familiar. He was glancing around as if he might be expecting surveillance, urging Feyrsten to hurry and placing bags into the lift. For a moment he looked in the direction of the bot, and that was enough. *Henik Varkesen.* She knew what his archive file would contain even before it was retrieved. There would be a recording from The Georgi Factor, and she would be on it.

Only two years ago it was, but with all that had happened, it seemed like an eternity. This was the moment when it had all gone wrong, when her life had started to collapse. She'd been on the panel with Varkesen that evening, both of them invited to discuss a notorious incident where a human had been beaten to death by his owner in a crowded street. The public was shocked not only by the brutality but the fact that no one had intervened. There had been a street protest when the man was released, but there had been no evidence that the beating had been unprovoked, no evidence of a chargeable offence. It had fallen to Torsta, as Chief of Police to speak to the media, and in hindsight, she'd badly misjudged the debate. The discussion with Varkesen had been cordial enough beforehand.

They both held the view that what had happened to the human was unacceptable, although Varkesen was more concerned about the loss of life, while Torsta was thinking about the awful spectacle of it. Still, she'd gone onto the set thinking that the discussion would be a considered one, and they'd be broadly in agreement.

Georgi had other ideas, though. He turned first to Varkesen. 'We know where you stand on the way humans are treated,' he said, 'but surely this has shocked even you, perhaps not that we have some citizens who behave cruelly, even in front of children, but by the way the police have handled the matter.'

Varkesen looked in her direction before he began. They both knew in that instant that they were being cast as adversaries. The question was how much Varkesen cared to resist. He made a good start. 'The idea that this is merely a distasteful thing for children to witness is entirely the wrong perspective,' he said.

'It was the brutality, I was highlighting,' said Georgi.

'When a sentient, thinking being is murdered in our midst, simply because someone was annoyed with it. I think that…'

'Murder?' said Georgi. 'Well, that does seem to bring us to the heart of the matter. Chief Jai, are you condoning *murder* by releasing this individual?'

'That's not how the law defines murder,' Torsta said. 'Whatever people might think, murder must be one person on another – not a human, or any other animal species.'

'So, it doesn't matter if a human is brutally killed then,' said Georgi.

'That's not what I…'

Georgi turned back to Varkesen before Torsta could finish. 'Henik, the police are making a fair point, aren't they?

It's not for them to care about animals. They must uphold the law.'

'Then the law needs to be changed!' said Varkesen. 'I call on Chief Jai right now, to join me in demanding that murder should include the deliberate killing of humans, as well as people.'

Georgi sat back in his chair as the challenge was made, satisfaction rippling across his forehead. 'What do you say to that, Chief Jai? Will you argue for that reform?'

'The role of the police is enforcement of the law as it stands, not to advocate change for the benefit of animals. That's a matter for Congress.' The answer was correct, even if the tone might have been more sympathetic, but it was a fatal misstep.

'I see!' said Georgi. 'You're unwilling to protect humans from being brutally killed on our streets.'

'I am *not* unwilling to protect…'

'Well, if you aren't prepared to argue for change, then surely you are. So, I must put it to you again Chief Jai. Are you going to stand up for…?'

'Answer the bloody question!' A woman stood up in the virtual audience, and then suddenly others were following her lead. 'Answer!' they shouted. 'Stop ducking the question!'

'Shame on you!' came a shout from the back, and within moments others had added their voices, the shouts quickly becoming a chant – 'Shame! Shame! Shame!' until Georgi cut to a commercial break with Torsta's face the last to remain on screen.

She'd gone straight from the show to a bar in the Commonwealth Quarter. How she'd ended up there, she couldn't remember, and how many drinks she had was anyone's guess. The whole city was at her, her news feed alight with harsh comments and insults, flashing into her vision moment by moment. She approved of people beating their pets to death. She was a disgrace to her office. She should be dismissed from the police service, publicly degraded in honour. She deserved to be beaten to death herself. And then someone pulled her off her barstool and shouted it in her face. Spat in her drink. The rest was a blur, the ferocity of her reaction, the bodies flying, the blood and noise of it all.

Career over, life wrecked. All over a human.

Torsta often thought about whether she should blame Henik Varkesen for it. She wanted to. He'd put her in a difficult position and could easily have stepped in to put it right. But it wasn't Varkesen's responsibility to defend the police. She'd told herself that all the time she'd been on *Bleak Penance*, worked to rid herself of any bitterness. But it still returned at the mention of his name, that enduring sense of having been mugged.

Torsta took a deep breath and focused again on the display, where the microbot recording had ended with a shot of Varkesen getting into the lift. So, Henik Varkesen and Yan Feyrsten were leaving the house, travelling somewhere with the Earth Human. There was nothing strange in that, necessarily. Then she remembered the microbot that had gone astray, the one that had been transported out to the coast. She retrieved its data, then checked it against the recording, the three individuals standing in the hall: the professor, the naturalist, and a human in a red coat. *A coat with a gold lining.*

8

The Chemical Clan

THE CHEMICAL PLANT STOOD a few leagues along the coast from Midsummer Mall, its pipes and towers giving it an imposing presence it no longer deserved. With little there to sustain its occupants, it was a territory few coveted, and fewer considered worth a fight.

At the service entrance behind Midsummer Mall, Alka watched a wisp of steam rising from one of the plant's chimneys. Her attention shifted away to the blue waters behind, where pleasure craft danced on the waves, and fishing boats scoured the shallows for the shrils they landed further up the coast. The larger vessels had gone away with the hard times, although Alka still spotted them on the horizon from time to time and wondered where they were going, what cargo they might hold. There were times when she imagined herself attacking one, leading her clan up rope ladders, and taking possession of enough resources to last a lifetime. It would be a short life as a pirate though, one moment of triumph, and then extermination for them all.

She turned her gaze back to the land, to the arid territory that sloped down from the mall to the chemical plant on one side, and in the other direction the hard-baked and stony ground that stretched over to the docklands. The wind was coming off the hillside, laden with spice and morning dampness, promising more than the land could ever provide. Three leagues in each direction, it was a habitat of grassland, tumbled rocks, and scrub, barely able to sustain enough wildlife to feed one of the four clans that claimed it. *If we're still here next year, we must start planting. But somehow, we must get seed.*

She shielded her eyes with her hand and checked her markers were still flapping on their posts, following the course of a stream that cleaved its way down the hillside. She wondered again whether it had been wise to stake their claim. On the one hand, they'd managed to hold it by constant patrolling, but on the other, they were getting into skirmishes more frequently when they foraged further afield, picking up injuries that reduced their collective strength. Today, they would be travelling the full length of the disputed territory. There would be danger, but the policy would be the same as ever. *Avoidance if possible, but in confrontation, never a step backwards.* The security of the clan demanded a fierce reputation.

A shout from behind her caused Alka to turn. She watched two of the older members of the clan approaching, swinging their alloy bats as they came up the boulevard. *The cousins. Easy company, and reliable in a fight.*

Gallen, the older of the two, was a small man with watery eyes and a broken nose. What he lacked physically though, was outweighed by his work ethic and fearless optimism. Ice was no beauty either. He suffered in comparison to his more gregarious cousin, but those who took the trouble to know him were impressed by his persistence even when the odds were against them. He was one of those individuals who improved in tough situations.

'My elders,' said Alka. 'I am glad you're coming.'

Gallen shifted his bat from one shoulder to another. 'Had to be us, Chief,' he said. 'Kit says we're binding with the Chemicals in matrimony. You need the best-looking of us.'

'Prettiest derelicts of all, them Chemie girls,' said Ice.

Alka looked from one to the other then shook her head. 'You keep dreaming,' she said, then led them away down the hill.

If there had been less urgency, Alka would have chosen to go at sunset when they would have been less visible to other clans and less vulnerable to ambush. Instead, they set off in the heat of the day, following the coast road but keeping to the trees further up the slope. Alka had covered the tip of her javelin with dark tape so it wouldn't catch the light, and when they had to cross open ground, it was only after she had stopped and studied the hillside, using the scope she had taken in their winter campaign against the Squalids at the sewage works.

When they reached Chemical territory, she paused to brief the cousins, the three of them squatting in the shade of a tarberry tree. She brushed aside its fallen fruit, and used her javelin to draw in the dirt, outlining where they were and establishing a meeting point if they became separated.

'I've met Chemical Mike once before,' said Gallen. 'You'll know him because he's only got one eye, and he's got a toxic symbol inked on his chest.'

'And his neck,' said Ice, 'and his arms, and…'

'Alright, I get it.' said Alka. 'You're going to win the beauty contest, after all.'

Gallen squatted closer and lowered his voice. 'What's the plan then, Chief?'

'Haven't got one,' admitted Alka. 'So, you'll need to keep your wits about you, coz anything could happen. But be clear about this: you don't start anything unless I say.' She searched their faces for signs of dissent but found their expressions solid and unquestioning. 'There's not many of them, but who knows what the twins have told them, and they'll know we've come to take them back.'

'Only fair,' said Ice. 'They left without your blessing, challenged your authority.'

'There's more at stake than that. Anyway, enough talk. Time to go.'

They stepped out of the bushes and went down to the road, only a short distance from the perimeter fence of the works. Alka motioned for them to stop. The gates stood open in front of them, without a barrier or sentries. She watched the compound for signs of movement. A bird wheeled around one of the towers, and a feeble dust devil sprung up for a moment, then dissipated.

'They're inviting us into a trap,' she said, pulling a pillowcase from inside her overalls and holding it aloft, until the sea breeze filled it and it fluttered and snapped in her grip. She took a deep breath and shouted at the top of her voice. 'Parley! We of the Citadel ask for parley with the one called Chemical Mike, whose reputation is known to all clans!'

There was a scuffing sound behind them. 'Cover the rear,' said Alka and the cousins turned, while she forced herself to stand unflinching, her eyes fixed on the gateway. 'Parley!'

'Six of them,' whispered Gallen. 'They look green, and scrawny.'

There was a moaning of metal just inside the gateway, and a trap door rose from the dirt. A lumbering figure came up into the light, preceded by a hairless creature on a heavy fibre cord. It strained forward on four thick paws, its skin flapping loose with each step. It bared its teeth and swung its head, saliva dripping from the corners of its mouth. Alka tightened her grip on her javelin. 'Don't turn,' she said, 'but he's got a naked bear.'

The bear's master was no less repulsive. He wore tight leather breeches and was stripped to the waist, his tattooed belly overhanging his belt, almost as if to demonstrate his ability to take the lion's share of any meal. 'I see you!' he shouted. 'The one the People call "Alka". Saw you coming a long way back, approaching in stealth, like a bushdorg!'

'These are dangerous times to travel,' said Alka. 'Don't take our caution as a sign of disrespect.'

Chemical Mike looked at the bear and gave its leash a jerk, causing it to rise onto its hind legs and roar. 'You wouldn't have come if you'd seen one of these animals making a kill.'

'Your bear has my admiration, Chemical Mike. It's an impressive beast you have there. I would hate to spill its guts. It has more value to your clan than it would on our dinner table.'

This time it was Chemical Mike who roared. The laughter exploded from his throat, his face turning red and his belly moving like water slopping in a bucket. 'You've got some balls, Alka of the Citadel! "On your dinner table!" You are what they say of you! We will parley.' He fastened his bear to the perimeter fence and strode forward until he stood in front of her, no taller than she was, but wider in girth than any in the Midsummer Clan.

'I've heard about you,' said Chemical Mike. 'I heard that on the night of the winter solstice, you drowned Mo Squalid with your own hands, in a pot of his piss.'

'No,' said Alka slowly. 'It's not so.'

'Ah… I am disappointed. When I heard of it, I said to my brothers that the leader of the Citadels was someone to be reckoned with. I said…'

'I did it the day afterwards,' said Alka. 'The solstice is sacred to me.' She waited for Chemical Mike to laugh again, but this time he didn't. He looked at her hard, then took a step closer and spoke in a whisper.

'Sacred, you say. I heard also that you revere the Redeemer. I heard that she speaks to you.'

Alka nodded. 'I keep the old faith, even if others have deserted her.'

Chemical Mike's shoulders sagged. He gestured at the ground and they sat down in the dust of the road. Alka was surprised to see how flexible he was for someone of his stature. He sat cross-legged, folding himself into a bundle of flesh that seemed to shrink in front of her. She waited as he stared at his fingernails, then after a few moments of silence he raised his eyes. 'We are lost children,' he said. 'We posture. You have your fountain and luxuries like that fine pillowcase, and I have my beast and my body markings. I am in need… I need…'

'Redemption,' said Alka.

Chemical Mike lifted his head and looked up the hill to where Midsummer Mall stood overlooking the coastal plain. The lines on his forehead faded, his face gentling to a new train of thought. 'How did she first come to you? Tell me.'

Alka turned and followed his gaze. 'She speaks to me in the waters of the fountain. Her voice is distant, but it still soothes me, just as it did the first time. That wasn't at the Citadel, but in the forest where I laboured once, as a woodcutter. I fell one day with a tree branch pinning my arm. Two days and nights I lay there, seen only by the forest animals. On the second night, I took a knife to my arm to free myself, but I lacked the courage. I tried to cut, but the blood brought the wollven circling, until one breathed hot in my face and I cried out for the mother I've never known.'

She paused, suddenly feeling the need to catch her breath, her lips strangely numb, as if the telling still held some essence of the experience itself. 'Then the green moon took pity on me. It grew large, and she spoke, giving me strength and comfort. The beasts felt her presence too. They shrank away to their lairs, and I was kept safe till dawn. The corporation found me in the morning, and I was still filled with her spirit, and felt nothing when they flogged me for my carelessness.'

Mike's eyes glistened. 'I knew my mother,' he said. 'They dragged me from her one cold winter morning. Will you tell me more of the Redeemer? I must know her story.'

Alka looked behind her at Gallen and Ice. She cleared her throat, and Mike took that as a cue to call his clansmen to gather round. When they were all seated, she began.

'I will tell you, as it was told to me when I was small. Long ago it began, before our grandfathers' grandfathers were in this world, before the wollven ran in the forests, before the creatures of the air flew over the hills. Before then, the Great Spirit of the universe, who inhabits all things and knows all things, made a place more special and perfect than all the other worlds it had created. It called this place, "Terra" and ordained it as a sanctuary for all humans to live in peace.

'Sometimes, my dreams show me such a place,' said Mike.

'But we were not worthy of our special world,' continued Alka. 'And for our wicked ways, we were cast into the void to become slaves to the People. It brought sadness to the Great Spirit to do this, so it sent with us a guardian to watch us through our trials and to suffer with us. She is Callista, who lives in the most beautiful of our eight companions, and weeps for us with tears of moonlight.'

'Why won't she help us?' said Ice.

'She will come to redeem us, so we might show ourselves worthy of our true home. The Great Spirit decreed that we can return only when we have used our gift to spread hope and rise above our adversity.'

'What is this gift?' called a small voice from the back.

Alka exhaled slowly. 'Our gift… We hear its sound as the spirit that moves in everything. We hear it in the crashing waves, and when the trees stir in the wind. Sometimes we feel its vibrations in our throats and on our lips. We humans feel this above all other beings, but we no longer know its name.'

'How can that be Alka?' said Mike. 'Why do we not know the gift?'

'Because our happiness has been stolen by those who dominate us. We've been reduced to fighting amongst ourselves. I have killed many times so that my clan might live. But it gives me no satisfaction. I know my sins will keep me from the gift. She tells me so when I ask her to come for us.'

'When will she come? Does she tell you?'

'She will come at the Time of Times. We see the storm gathering, and Callista sees it too. She fears we won't know her when she comes. And so, she waits, until the night is so dark, and we have become so pitiful that we will open our hearts to her.'

'Doesn't she tell us to fight the giants who take our happiness?' said Gallen, and his question received mutterings of approval from the Chemicals.

Alka shook her head. 'She will not tell us what to do. But she watches us, and when she comes, all will be clear.'

Mike breathed a heavy sigh and looked at his ragged band.

'Alka of the Citadel. I don't hear the vibrations of our gift, and Callista doesn't come to me. But my heart is open, and if you will allow me, I'll come to your fountain and ask for her mercy. But I have nothing to offer in return. I have no elemist to give you.'

Alka picked up the pillowcase. She folded it into a triangle and handed it to Chemical Mike with both hands. 'Callista will hear anyone who comes to her,' she said. 'Our door will be open if you approach under this banner. But I have not come here for elemist, Mike. You may control it with your knowledge of essences, but I wouldn't have it amongst us at the Citadel.'

'Then why have you come?'

'My business is to find two brothers who've deserted us. We're told they came to join your clan.'

'They deceived us. They came last night and spoke of leaving the Citadel. Then at daybreak, we found they had gone, and they'd taken the small amount of elemist we had.'

Alka got to her feet and signaled for Gallen and Ice to do the same. 'Then we must leave you, Chemical Mike. I fear what the twins have in mind will bring the fury of the People upon us. Pass the word to detain them on sight, in the interest of all the unowned, whatever their clan.'

'And the Dockers?'

Alka turned towards the city, where the old docks sprawled between the sea and the inland waterway. Two lattice towers reached up a thousand units above them to the sky platforms, the intensity of their lights marking their location in all weather. Somehow, they still received vessels, sub-orbital traffic manoeuvring like insects around a carcass. But the sleek stellar transports stayed away, deterred perhaps by the chaos that reigned below. That was the Dockers' territory and their occupation of it was formidable. Alka was under no illusion that she could ever subdue them or be free from their incursions.

'It's time to put differences aside,' she said, eventually.

Mike wiped his bald head with his forearm. 'They're the only clan that matches the Citadels for size. A lot of blood has been shed between you.'

'Nevertheless, it must be done. Will you intercede for me?'

'If you will intercede for me with Callista.'

Alka nodded. 'The Time of Times is coming, Mike. I can feel it.'

'Look at her,' said Yan. 'I think she's happy.'

They sat in the sand below the beach house, watching Kali skipping in the surf, with the sky on fire behind her. 'I don't think I've seen a human behave like that.'

'There's an instinct for simple amusement among non-captive humans,' Henik said. 'Serves no obvious purpose, but it's... enchanting.'

'Wouldn't you like to feel what she's feeling, to know what it's like?'

Henik continued watching Kali as if he hadn't heard the question. She emerged from the waves soaking wet, her clothes sticking to her body, and her smile white as the foam. 'Yes,' he said, after a while. 'I would.'

She spun around and looked back up the beach to where they were sitting, then waved enthusiastically with both hands.

'What does that mean?' asked Yan.

'Whatever it is, we should reciprocate. There! She seems pleased that we've done it. Some sort of happy greeting, apparently.'

'And what about that sound she was making with Dill, that sort of high undulating sound. I keep thinking about it. Was that a type of greeting too, another happy thing?'

'I've never heard anything like it. It was extraordinary, like a ritual chant, but with a tonal pattern. Her vocal range goes much higher than ours, and she can use her voice more flexibly as well. I need to analyse it.'

'We don't understand humans very well, do we?'

'We *think* we do, but we really have little idea how they perceive the world around them. We can get closer to it if we can communicate better, and that's why Kali is such an important find. But what we saw, what we heard in the garden this morning, does make me wonder if we can ever truly know their minds. Consider this, Yan – we're struggling to take meaning from those sounds, but Dill responded immediately, instinctively. She needed no explanation. Perhaps all humans have that in them, and we just haven't.'

'Well, we both thought it was beautiful. We can try asking Kali to explain it, can't we?'

'Perhaps, if it happens again, but that seemed like a sensitive moment with Dill, so I think we should tread carefully around it for the moment.'

Kali was still splashing. A wave took her feet away, and she shrieked but still came up laughing.

'It's as if her contentment and the simplicity of the environment are connected,' said Yan. 'Yet she craves knowledge like no one I've ever met. It's like she can switch between advanced and primitive, have the best of both. Perhaps we could learn from that.'

'Well, hold that thought,' said Henik. He got up and brushed the sand from his legs. 'If we want her advanced skills with food, we're going to need a primitive burner pit. 'So, start digging, and I'll see if I can catch us something to eat.'

Kali didn't seem at all impressed by Henik's efforts to catch their supper. He'd set the drone float without difficulty but had caught no more than a small snarp. Kali glanced at it but showed little interest. She sat beside him just above the wet sand, with the solus smearing scarlet across the horizon and the waves chasing each other up to their toes.

'You've been fishing before?' he asked.

'I do live by sea,' she said. She looked out at the drone float, a hundred or so units out, its amber lights chattering with Henik's rod, then at the snarp lying between them on the sand. 'Is not good fish.'

'Are you hungry?' he asked.

Her face creased, and her lips moved as if she was searching for words. 'We do wait for longer,' she said. 'Big fish come.'

Henik instructed the rod to send the drone further out. He turned to Kali and found he was being observed. She had her arms wrapped around her knees, and the breeze was tugging gently at her hair.

'You think Yan be alonely?'

The insight in the question caught Henik off guard, and he found himself wondering at the thought process behind it. He noticed that Kali had lifted one of her eyebrows, a sign perhaps that she was waiting for an answer. 'Yes, perhaps he is lonely. Why do you...?'

'You think for *that* he do have me? Be friend for lonely?'

'I think he needed company. I'm pleased he has you, Kali.'

She stared at her feet, pushed her heels deep into the sand. 'I like Yan,' she said.

Henik watched her face. The muscles moved in a thousand different ways, shifting almost imperceptibly with each passing moment as if responding to her every thought and emotion. He wondered if the language of the human body might be almost as complex as the headspeak of people. A small indentation appeared above her nose in a way he'd noticed before when she was about to make an observation. She turned her head and looked directly at him again.

'You be clever person,' she said.

A compliment from a human was another unimaginable first, but this time it felt personal, something to treasure. 'Thank you,' he said.

'You science person, Henik?'

'Yes, I study nature. I learn about wild animals. I watch humans in particular.'

'And I do watch,' said Kali. 'Watch you, watch me.' She tapped the side of her nose. Whatever the gesture meant, the comment felt vaguely unsettling. Perhaps it was the knowingness of it, he thought. *Yan's loneliness. My work. She's considering what motivates us, what we may be thinking.*

He felt the touch of her hand on his arm. 'You think human be wild animal?'

He looked away, feeling embarrassed. He didn't want to lie to Kali when she was nothing if not honest herself, but the words deserted him. He had after all, studied humans for years, and however progressive his thoughts about them had become, he did still consider them animals, rather than people. *All except Kali, and Alka. All except the humans you've engaged on equal terms.* He met her gaze again, suddenly realising that his failure to answer would be taken as an answer in itself.

Kali's expression changed abruptly. Suddenly she was staring at him, eyes blazing, and her nostrils flared. She bared her teeth and snarled, hands hooked into claws as she launched herself at him. It wasn't until he'd scrambled backwards, raising his arms to ward off the attack, that she began to laugh. And then once she had started, it was as if she didn't know how to stop. She stood over him, with her hands on her knees and tears spotting her cheeks, and he found himself smiling back, grinning, not for any conscious reason, but because it felt the natural thing to do. Finally, Kali gave him a playful shove and sank down onto the sand again, still smiling broadly.

She made a clicking sound with her tongue. 'Wild animal,' she said.

Yan had the fire pit ready by the time they came back. He'd arranged blankets and cushions around it so they could sit watching the surf while the fish cooked. Henik and Kali had caught a large rockfish, gutting it in the surf and bringing it back up the beach in triumph. He watched her as she cut it into steaks, then wrapped them individually in leaves she'd picked from behind the house, pushing the remaining pieces onto sturdy reeds together with an assortment of wild fruits that grew amongst the dunes. It was done with such confidence, he thought, as if she'd done it so many times, that it never occurred to her that anyone else would take charge.

He brought out a jug and some cups and poured mead into each of them. 'Do you think Kali should have this?' he asked Henik.

'Yes,' she said and reached out to take a cup from his hand. She smelt it carefully, then rolled her eyes and put out her tongue.

'Only have a little,' Yan warned, lowering himself onto the sand. 'Now, tell me what you were talking about down there.'

'Henik do say I be animal. Be carefully. He think I do eat you!'

'That's not quite fair,' said Henik. 'It's just that we're still learning about humans. You are teaching us so much.'

Kali raised her shoulders and dropped them again. 'You be science person,' she said, 'I be teacher.'

Yan caught Henik's eye, not sure if he was understanding correctly. It had never crossed his mind that a human might have a professional occupation, in fact, any occupation beyond labouring. 'Are you saying that on Earth…'

'Earth? What Earth?'

'Your world. "Earth" we call it. Are you saying you were a teacher?'

Kali nodded. 'Teach children. Is well done. I do like very.'

'What did you teach them?'

'Read, write, number.' She made an expansive gesture with her arms and grinned. 'Teach languages!'

'That explains a lot,' said Henik, switching into rapid headspeak. 'She's a language teacher! I can hardly believe this, Yan. This is *so* important! It confirms that there is specialisation of occupation in natural human society! This is exactly the sort of question I hoped Kali might answer.'

'No!' said Kali sharply. She stood with her hands on her hips. 'Talk with mouth, thank you! Head talk be not for understand.'

'Sorry, Kali,' said Henik.

Yan nudged him with his foot. 'Definitely a teacher,' he said.

By the time they'd finished eating, Kali was on her third cup of mead, and she was feeling its effects. Her fingers and lips were numb, and she was finding it more difficult to speak. Not that she cared. The mead was having the most wondrous effect on her body. It rose in vapours from her throat into her head, until it seemed that gravity no longer had a hold on her. It sharpened her thoughts too, heightened her perceptions, wrapped them in a seductive sense of well-being.

Yan appeared to be feeling the effects too. He was staring up at the stars while he reclined on a pile of cushions like a giant sultan. She watched him, considered all that he was, and realised that she was growing quite fond of him. She felt easy in his company, understood his quiet sensitivity, his isolation. There was even something about being his property she almost liked. It provided some security in this alien world, even if it was quite absurd, abhorrent in fact, to any normal way of thinking.

As if he had read her mind, Yan rolled onto his side and looked at her with his muddy yellow eyes. 'Now you can speak some of our language, will you tell us about Earth? Is it very different?'

Henik stirred and sat up to hear her response. She wondered how she could ever answer such a question when it invited her to describe everything she knew, in a language she hardly knew at all. She imagined herself opening the door of the old farmhouse and looking out to where the undulating pastures formed a line against the sea, and the clouds billowed, soft and white as goose down. 'The sky in Earth be more blue,' she said, deciding to start with the basics. 'More strong, the wind. There be trees, animals, hills, sea. She smiled. 'Is… beautiful!'

'Are other animals clever like humans?'

She shook her head. 'Some animals with clever. But human be very more clever.'

Yan drew the outline of a house in the sand with his finger. 'Do humans build things?'

She got up unsteadily and went to crouch beside him, bracing herself against his shoulder. 'Well done, Yan! Is good house!' She looked up, and when she saw Henik watching her, she winked. He attempted the same, but didn't seem to be able to make his face do it. 'Earth house be more good,' she said. She drew a chimney with a plume of smoke, then a twisting path to the door, a fence, and a barn with a tractor, and finally a plane flying overhead. When she had finished, she sat back on her heels. Yan had called Henik over. They stood gazing at the picture and she could feel their head chatter stirring the air. Then it stopped, and Yan pointed at the picture of the plane.

'Is this a bird, or something else?'

'*Bird?* Is not *bird!* Is *transport!*' Kali held her arms out to her sides and made a whistling sound. Henik shuffled closer to the drawing and the head talk began again. It was obvious that she'd given them something to think about, so she decided to say no more.

Instead, the discussion was interrupted by the appearance of a distant light high above the sea. It pulsed red and moved towards them, growing with the passing moments. Kali watched it descend and approach the beach, the single point gradually splitting into several, then hundreds until the outline of the object became clear, expanding until it filled the whole sky above them. She scuttled close to Yan and held onto his arm as the giant object towered over them like an enormous ocean liner passing in the night. Yan appeared to be enjoying the spectacle, lying on his back and staring up as the vessel moved overhead. He said something that Kali assumed to be an explanation. The vocabulary was beyond her, but she felt reassured by the calmness of his voice, the warmth of his hand as it closed around hers.

9

Abduction

SANTI ASPIL WAS treating herself to some time with the morning news in her walled garden. With the trees in full bloom, her bench was shielded from the surrounding buildings, something she appreciated on this day, more than ever before. She was doing her best to avoid anything in the election coverage that discussed her party's defeat, the Progressives' shortcomings or prospects, and most particularly anything that mentioned her. Unfortunately, her name was everywhere.

Her comments on the results were getting a mixed review. Some were arguing that she should have said more on the human issue, and should have done more when she had the opportunity. Others were concerned that her light touch would be replaced with policies that would only inflame the situation.

Inevitably there was speculation about the leadership of the party too, and her name was very much in the frame, however much she had tried to deflect the questions. As usual, Niko S'tana had been the most persistent reporter. He'd cornered her as she left at the rear of the Department for the Interior, wasting no time to move on to the leadership story, even as the election results were still reverberating around the planet.

'Congressioner Aspil! Santi! Can you spare a moment please? What are your thoughts about your future?' He had been too close to ignore, his line of sight too direct.

'Perhaps later, Niko. At the moment, we're performing our duty to vacate and assist a smooth transition.'

'Have you a view on who should lead the Progress Party back from this defeat?'

'We have a leader already, as you well know, and as far as I'm aware, he isn't going anywhere.'

'We're hearing reports that Amund Haugen may be about to announce he's stepping down. Do you think that would be the right thing to do after this defeat?'

'We all share responsibility for that, and I think when the dust settles, we'll see that this wasn't a verdict on Amund's leadership. There needs to be a period of calm reflection. What Amund does is a matter for him to decide, but he continues to have my support.'

'So, you won't stand if there is a leadership contest?'

'It is far too early to be considering that.'

'But you wouldn't rule it out.'

'This morning I am doing my constitutional duty. It's as simple as that. Now, if you would excuse me. Thank you, Niko.'

There wasn't really much else she could have said under the circumstances, but it didn't stop the spin. The story was that she hadn't dismissed the possibility of a leadership challenge, and it broke almost immediately, with the headline, 'Aspil may seek Progressive leadership.' Then she had to go into hiding for the rest of the day.

A call vibrated in her skull, a familiar figure appearing in the side of her vision, pushing away the news reports to make space. 'Nice of you to call, Vish,' she said. 'Where are you?'

'I'm standing outside your door. I don't really want to be seen here so…'

'Come through. I'm out at the back. Bring a flask with you from the kitchen. I've got a pot of cahcana here.'

A few moments later he emerged from the back of the house, flask in hand, and made his way up the path. He was wearing his usual high-collared suit, and stooped awkwardly under branches as he came until he reached her retreat. She stood up and embraced him.

'How are you doing?' he asked.

'I'm tired. It's as if my body is calling time on me, after running full tilt these years in Government. I don't even want to think about the future.'

'Only natural, I suppose. After losing to that lot.'

The conversation hadn't started as Santi would have liked. She straightened in her seat and steadied her voice. 'I'm touched that you should come by so soon, Vish, but I'm sure you know it's a breach of protocol not to cut your ties. You should have a care that your new boss doesn't find out you came here.' She took the cup from his hand and poured him a drink, gently swirling the essence, then allowing it to settle and concentrate before handing it to him.

'I see you know the traditions of my homeland,' said Vish. 'Did I ever tell you I grew up climbing trees to pick cahcana?'

'You're a first-generation Spice Islander? I'm sorry, I should've known that.'

'Don't worry, I don't know much about your background either. It was always just work wasn't it, never time for what really matters. Glad I'm out of it.'

'What do you mean? Vish, you haven't done something stupid, have you?'

He perched on the arm of the bench. 'Probably, but I don't care. I told Norvik I couldn't go along with what he's intending. Actually, I used stronger language than that.'

'Because?'

'I was given a brief to reform domestic human affairs. Norvik gave me less than a day to come up with proposals to advance the Heritage policy. No public consultation. I worked all night but he hardly looked at my ideas before throwing them out.'

'What were you proposing?'

'Reduced ownership taxes after approved training, a bonus scheme for good conduct, and a campaign for responsible ownership. The approach was to be largely voluntary.'

'Far-reaching, though. It would have still led to protests. I suppose he thought your plans didn't go far enough.'

'He has no idea what he'll be unleashing.'

'You mean he's come up with something else already?'

'Compulsory training, with seizure and destruction of humans for non-compliance. Behaviour implants for humans that fall short of prescribed standards. Naturally, he'll provide the standards and the training courses based on his own expertise.'

'Surely, he knows there will be an inquiry. And how the public will react, we can only imagine.'

'He feels unassailable, Santi. He has Maarten Feyrsten's confidence, and the public see him as the authority on all things human.'

'But the public wasn't told what he was planning!'

'He expects some temporary resistance, but he seems determined to drive it through. Destroy a few pets, he said, and owners will be careful about protesting. Meanwhile, he'll divert attention with firm action in the Derelict Zone and some patriotic slogans to make anyone who disagrees look disloyal.'

'It'll be a disaster.' said Santi. 'How long before it all starts?'

'He wants to move quickly, while your party is in disarray and can't put up much resistance. But he needs a clear and present danger and unfortunately, from his perspective, the ferals are behaving themselves at the moment. I'm sure it's just co-incidence, but there have hardly been any incursions in the last few days. If I didn't know better, I'd think the ferals have been holding their breath through the crisis in the Spice Islands.'

Santi thought about Alka, standing on the fountain in Midsummer Mall, and the promise she'd made to her. It occurred to her that even in opposition, she still had a role to play in preventing conflict. Defeated or not, she still felt a responsibility for the human issue, a need to do something.

'Let's hope the ferals don't give Norvik the excuse he's looking for,' she said. 'He'd exterminate them all given the opportunity.'

'My concern is more how people are affected, than the ferals. I suppose I can say it freely now that I don't really like humans, whether they're under control or not.'

'But you care enough to resign.'

'The rights of citizens must be upheld, and for many of them there's nothing more emotive than the Government coming after their pet.'

Santi felt a vibration in her skull and a name appeared in the corner of her eye. 'I've got a call coming through, Vish. It's important, I'm afraid, but we can have lunch later if you like?'

He got to his feet. 'I'll go over to the Café Republic and you can come over afterwards.'

Santi watched him walk away, his place immediately filled by an image of the former Chief Counsellor.

'Hello, Santi. I hope I'm not disturbing you.'

'No, of course not, Amund. I was planning to call you. I'm really sorry about that interview I gave. I hope you know that I wasn't intending…'

'Don't worry, I know how it is, and actually, I'm calling to tell you that Nico S'tana was right. There have been a lot of people pushing and pulling me since the results came out, and I've decided it's time for me to step aside. I'm about to announce my resignation.'

Santi sighed. 'I can't say I'm surprised. But I'm sad. I'm worried about the future, Amund, I really am.'

'Then you need to do something about it. It's in your hands.'

'Well, I know my responsibilities but I think that's…'

'I'm going to put you forward as my successor, Santi.'

'Wh… what?'

'There won't be any other challengers, I can guarantee that. So, it's just a question of whether you have the stomach for it. Like I say, it's in your hands.'

Santi struggled for words. Her fingers played absent-mindedly with the flowers beside her, while her thoughts scrambled and raced. 'I'm flattered,' she said, 'But why me? I'm not the obvious choice to succeed you.'

'Yes, you are, and the fact you don't think so makes you all the more credible. You've never lost your social conscience. That's what we need at the moment, distance between ourselves and Heritage.'

'Many think I failed in my last role. Either they think I was too soft on the ferals, or that I didn't care enough about them.'

'Lick your wounds if you need to, but if you're expecting

the public to be reasonable, then you're fooling yourself. You kept the peace, and you stayed out of people's personal affairs. Your colleagues respect you, Santi.'

'I've been to the Derelict Zone, and I was ashamed. It's awful, and it was happening on my watch.'

'So, this is your opportunity to put it right. Look, I've got to go. Unless you're turning it down, I am going to announce you. You won't have much of a chance to change your mind after that, because the media will be all over you. *Are* you turning it down, Santi?'

'Amund, I really…'

'I'm gone in a moment, so you'd better stop me now if you really don't want this. Three… two… one…'

The hologram faded, leaving Santi staring into space. She took a deep breath and exhaled very slowly. *You must be out of your mind.*

'One of only four,' said Torsta Jai, the wind ripping the words from her mouth, throwing them from the headland, across the beach to where the breakers were advancing in foamy ranks. A league away, a row of beach houses nestled against the dunes, the morning solus striking low against their roofs. Inside one of them was Yan Feyrsten's human, still asleep probably, and somewhere nearby would be her coat, with a miniature passenger in its gold lining still faithfully sending its signal.

She studied the steep terrain behind the houses, decided to work her way across the dunes, close enough to identify the human's exact position. She looked down at her hoverbike, crouching on the sand at the base of the cliff. It was fast and agile but its propulsion unit was too loud to approach undetected.

There was a flicker of movement at the window of the nearest house. The front door opened, and a figure emerged. Henik Varkesen stood looking at the sea for a moment, then went down the steps and disappeared behind the house. A few moments later, he came into view again, labouring up a path between the dunes to where a transport was parked, half-obscured by the windswept grass. Varkesen disappeared behind it, and then after a few moments, it rose on a cloud of dust and moved off in the direction of Freeport.

It wasn't until the transport had disappeared from view, that Torsta realised someone else had come out of the house. It was the Earth human, striding down towards the sea with swinging arms, the lining of its coat flashing as the wind snapped at it.

Torsta was on her feet in an instant, sprinting back along the cliff to a place where a track wound its perilous way down to the beach. Halfway down, she vaulted over the handrail onto a scree slope and skidded through the shale until she tripped, then tumbled the rest of the way until she came to a halt beside her hoverbike.

The human was at the water's edge, standing in the waves and looking out to sea. Torsta kept the bike at low throttle until she had closed to within a few hundred units, until the sound of it gave her away. The human turned, stared in her direction for a moment, hair billowing in a cloud around its head. Then it ran.

Torsta changed course to make the interception, positioned herself more firmly in the saddle. The human was fast to begin with, racing across the wet beach with light steps, but nearer to the house, the sand deepened and its progress slowed. Torsta steered the bike to cut off the escape, forcing the human to skid to a halt a few paces from safety. It stood screaming at the beach house as Torsta shot past, hauling the machine back so fiercely that it reared up and blasted sand in all directions.

Yan Feyrsten stumbled out of the door into the sandstorm, then threw himself towards the steps. Torsta wrestled the bike into a tight turn as the human made another attempt to reach the house, launching itself forward, arms flailing and legs pumping at the sand. For a moment Torsta thought her opportunity had gone, but she banked the bike over on its side and got a hand to the human's coat. She gunned the throttle to keep the machine from stalling and dragged the human on board. The bike flashed a capsize warning and spun on its axis, making heavy contact with something on the steps. Over her shoulder, Torsta caught a glimpse of Feyrsten falling over the handrail, before the machine swung around again and demolished it.

The human wasn't going to give up easily. It squirmed and kicked and shouted Feyrsten's name. Torsta fought to hold it with one arm and keep control of the bike with the other, but it spun again, this time taking out a balcony support. The structure lurched forward and threatened to engulf them, but now at last the bike was stabilising, and Torsta could use her heels to back it away. She took it higher to subdue the human's struggles, then opened the throttle. And then they were away, curving out across the beach and over the sea, gathering speed, until the water frothed in their wake.

'You'll have to stand still for a moment!' said Henik. 'I can't examine you if you're pacing about.' He picked up his instruments and followed Yan out onto the deck. 'You've been out cold for some time so let's just check you out before we do anything else.' He pointed a scope at Yan's temple, glancing at the tilting structure around him while he considered the reading. 'I'm not sure we should be standing out here either.'

'You can see the tracks in the sand,' said Yan. 'There's Kali's footprints where she was trying to reach the house, and there are the blast marks from the hoverbike. I can't believe it, Henik! You warned me, and I can't *believe* I let it happen!'

'The police are on it, and blaming yourself isn't going to help. We both thought she'd be safe here.'

'But I released the bond on her bracelet – how stupid was that? I could have just extended it as far as the shore.'

'If the bond had been in place, she'd probably be dead now. When it reached its limit, that hoverbike would have been travelling at speed, and forty units or so off the ground. She wouldn't have survived that.'

'Is she going to survive anyway? The gods' breath, Henik, I never expected I'd become so attached to her. I can't lose her now, I just *can't!*'

Henik turned Yan's head and scanned the base of his neck. 'Looks like you're alright,' he said. 'No significant damage. Now, let's think this through. You say you didn't get a clear view of the attacker.'

'A woman, I think, but there was sand everywhere and I was focused on Kali. Maybe she knew that Kali's a natural. It wasn't as if she just snatched her as she passed. She pursued her right to my doorstep and pressed home the attack even when I got hold of the bike.'

'Which suggests she knew Kali was here. Either we were followed from the house, or some of those microbots came with us. It does seem probable that she knew what she was taking.'

'So, what do we do? I'm not just going to wait around for news.'

'As far as the police are concerned, I think we've said enough. Bearing in mind who you are, they'll take it seriously. They don't need to know Kali's origin, at least not yet, but there's a good chance they'll find out because the Pet Warehouse will be one of the first places they'll enquire.'

'I'm going to post a reward for her.'

'I'm not sure that's a good idea.'

'I want it out there, Henik! I won't mention Earth, but I want Kali's face known before she can be taken out of Freeport, or off-world. I'm not naive. I know what can happen. She'll end up as a plaything in a foreign shithole or sold for breeding… or even worse, that station orbiting Letna, the cult that believes human body parts have healing properties.'

Henik sat down at the top of the steps. He tilted his head to sight along the tracks in the sand. 'Unlikely,' he said. 'Over there, across the bay is the Derelict Zone, back door to the capital. If you wanted to take a human off-world illegally, you wouldn't be heading there. You'd go the other way, up the coast, the sub-orbital ports up there, and the sea harbours. Pevensy, Oldstation perhaps, that's where the trade happens. The standards are lower. They don't check every vessel, and you can find people who'll look the other way.'

'So, you think she's still in the city.'

'I'm saying this isn't about cults and body parts. It's about those microbots and political interests in Freeport, the Security Service perhaps. If Kali's in an official transport or a government building, it would explain why her locator isn't working.'

'That hoverbike was the type used by the military, but it

didn't look official. I still think it could be organised crime in Freeport.'

'Then you might want to swallow your pride and use your connections. Not your brother at the moment, but you should see if Jocasta can motivate the authorities to find her. In the meantime, there's another avenue I'm going to pursue. If this is what I think it is, I know someone who might be able to help.'

The mother was too delirious to notice that her baby had passed away in the night. Her breath was coming in short rasps, and the final sweats were upon her. Alka lifted the infant from her arms. She turned to an elderly nurse who was crouching nearby. 'How many is that now?'

'From the fever, seven. It will be eight by nightfall.'

'It will slow when the cooler weather returns,' said Alka. She knelt in front of a bowl and scooped a small handful of the water she had brought up from the fountain, trickling it onto the child's forehead. 'Go, little one. Go to Callista's mercy.'

There had been a time when Alka would cry at the passing of a child, but the tears no longer came. Somehow the battle for survival, and the knowledge that she had taken lives herself had steeled her for further losses. Some would be warriors, but others were innocents like this one, knowing nothing of the forces that shaped the world.

She walked down to the main boulevard and out to the back entrance, where Kit was engaged in conversation with Gallen. 'News has come up from the Chemicals,' he said. 'Mike's been at it all night. Seems he's more of a diplomat than he looks.'

'Tell me.'

'He's got the Squalids, what's left of them, and the Packers have agreed too. He's still working on the Constructors, but he's hopeful. And if they come, others will too – the Pharmas and the Scraps.'

'What about the Dockers?'

'Told him to fuck off. He thought it was progress, though.'

Alka glanced over at the docks. 'Because they didn't try to kill him?'

'Their new leader came out to speak to him, even if it was short. Mike thought the attitude was just for show. There was some arguing going on in the background.'

'So, they're unsettled now that Trajan has gone. Do we know the new leader's name?'

'Trajan.'

Alka shook her head. 'And this new Trajan, what's he…'

'She. Mike thinks she's trying to show her strength to you, says you should take her reply as a compliment.'

'I don't need compliments. I need peace and unity. We all do. What's the deal with the others?'

'They'll come at solset. The leaders will come forward alone, as you said. But they're expecting something from you, something to give them confidence it isn't a trap.'

'Fair,' said Alka. She paced slowly looking at her boots, avoiding the cracks in the tiles, as she always did. 'Alright,' she said eventually. 'When they arrive, they will lay down their weapons, as will we – in plain sight. We will all line up outside the barricade for them to observe. Then the clan leaders will enter the Citadel alone, each as vulnerable as the others. We'll talk under the Great Tree in the transept.'

Gallen shook his head. 'They want more than that, Chief.

They don't just want to talk to you. They're coming for the waters. They want Callista.'

'Tell them I will revere the Redeemer in their presence, and anyone who wishes to be anointed may receive her blessing. Tell them...' She stopped, suddenly aware of a howling sound coming from further down the hill, somewhere on the waterfront. A small craft was approaching the shore, drawing a white trail of turbulence behind it. It crossed onto the land without checking its speed and continued up the coast road, the howl of its drives growing louder, and a cloud of dust rising to announce its presence to anyone on the hillside.

'Hoverbike,' she said. 'Coming this way. Doesn't give a shit, so it's probably armed. Stay out of sight and no provocation, you hear?'

They ducked inside the mall and stood watching as the bike came up the valley, a large and powerful machine. The rider was leaning forward on the saddle, steering it with one hand while the other held something wrapped in crimson cloth. It came up past the mall, its drives quelling to a low whine as it slowed. The rider leaned to the right, and the machine banked lazily towards the plaza, sweeping through the trees and around the mall in a smooth arc.

For just an instant, Alka caught a glimpse of the rider's face, and her senses triggered to high alert. 'It's Torsta Jai!' she shouted. 'Come on – to the barrier! We're not losing anyone to her!'

She sprinted back through the mall, calling everyone to arms as she ran, passing the veterinary shop and its towering mosaic without a glance. By the time she emerged onto Midsummer Plaza, the hoverbike was entering the square at the far end. It had slowed to a walking pace and was now only a few units above the ground, drifting in towards the pod station.

'Onto the barricade!' she ordered. 'Stay hidden, but ready to attack on my word!'

The clan swarmed forward, climbing to their allotted positions along the battlement as they'd practiced. Alka took her own place in the centre, motioning to her left and right flanks to keep their heads down. *Torsta Jai. Torsta fucking Jai!*

The bike was hovering over the station forecourt now, but Torsta didn't seem to have it fully under control. Whatever was concealed under the crimson robe was struggling, and the machine was rocking and pitching as she tried to settle it for landing. It hit the ground with a heavy jolt, and she was thrown forward. Her hands went to brace herself, and in that moment the cargo slipped from her grip.

It fell to the ground, then stood up immediately and ran, a human girl, clothed in a hooded coat and shrieking for help. Torsta Jai leapt from the bike and lunged to stop her from running into the maze of alleys that led down to the docks. She grabbed at the crimson coat, but it swirled away from her as the girl made a sharp turn, and headed towards the barricade.

Alka's decision was instinctive. 'I go alone!' she shouted and vaulted over the battlement. In a couple of bounds, she was on the ground and sprinting towards the hooded girl. The distance between them hardly seemed to close in the passing of moments. Torsta Jai was closer, and she got to the girl first, diving to grab the back of her coat. Her hand caught hold of the hood and the girl was jerked backwards, her hair spilling out in all directions, a cascade of blazing red that framed the paleness of her face.

For a moment, their eyes met and Alka felt as though her chest had been hit with a mallet, the breath crushed from her lungs. The mosaic image floated in her vision, and her legs turned to pulp beneath her. She stumbled, recovered, then stumbled again, landing heavily on her elbows and knees, and when she looked up the horizon had tilted, fractured. Torsta Jai was still there though, dragging her prisoner towards the pod station. And the red-haired girl was still crying for help, holding out her arms imploringly.

Alka struggled to her feet, commanded her legs to drive her forward. The doors to the pod station slid open, and now the moments seemed to be on her side. The girl's eyes were urging her on, and she was crossing the plaza in rapid strides. She begged the doors to stay open a few moments longer, and even as they began to close, there remained the possibility of reaching them in time. She launched herself across the remaining distance to the doors and hit them at full speed, just as the gap between them disappeared.

From inside the pod station came a final muffled call for help, and then there was silence. Alka fell to her knees, and there was only one word screaming in her head, one word that filled the breath of her lungs: 'Callistaaaa!'

10

Café Republic

THE CROWDS IN CARNIVAL SQUARE drifted slowly, drawn by the mid-day heat from one pool of shade to another, pausing beside the fountain jets that soaked the tiles, and sent water trickling to the surrounding porticos through a web of open channels. Some people were with children and struggling to keep them from the fountains. Others had humans for company, allowing the young ones into the water where they played easily with the children. The more mature pets, they kept closer, permitting them only brief interactions, pulling them away to the boutiques, or securing them outside when they were prohibited.

Few humans attracted much attention, not even those whose purpose was precisely that, decked out in designer outfits to reflect their owners' wealth and taste. The twins were the exception. Not only were they identical, with white-blond hair and blue eyes, but the filthy state of their dungarees marked them as ferals. They walked briskly, aware that it was just a matter of time before they were detained for lack of supervision.

As they crossed the square, they caught the eye of a police

officer, who moved to intercept them. They glanced at each other and increased their pace, shifting their packs on their shoulders in unison, threading their way through the shoppers as they homed in on their target.

The Café Republic was buzzing with activity, its tables fully occupied inside, and under its shaders on the square. The twins walked through the doors unnoticed at first, but very quickly, the murmuring started, and people began to shuffle their chairs. There was a shout for a waiter, and he hurried towards them, waving furiously. They stood their ground, moved closer together, and held hands. Then as customers began getting to their feet around them, and as the shrieks and protests rang in their ears, they turned to each other and stood nose to nose. And that was it.

The café exploded in a burst of blue light, the twins' packs propelling their lethal combination of metal and elemist into every corner and beyond. The blast smashed through the ceiling and walls and blew the front of the building into deadly shrapnel, carrying the elemist across the square, the toxic metal scything into shoppers, and propelling blood and tissue high into the trees.

The sound of the explosion reverberated for a few moments while debris rained down, all over the plaza. Then as the fountains turned red, there was silence. For the time it took for a breath to be drawn, and held, there was not a sound. And then the screaming began. Anyone wounded knew they were going to die, they could feel the elemist working its way through their bodies, chilling their fluids, preventing the movement of oxygen. For some it took only moments, but those who had suffered lesser wounds would have longer to wait, and even minor abrasions would prove fatal when the victims overwhelmed the remedial posts.

There would be no help for those dying in the square. Sirens heralded the arrival of emergency services, but the medics held back from the trauma scene, where the slightest cut or scrape might add their names to the list of victims. They would stand helplessly behind the security cordons, ignoring the victims' pleas as they lay in the heat, under a clear blue sky.

The pod came to a halt in an artery not far from Carnival Square. Torsta Jai checked its status and found everything in order, then brought up a schematic of other pods in the system. They were all diverting away from the centre of Freeport or had stopped at a constant perimeter. An incident had occurred, disrupting the service over a wide area of the capital.

The human hadn't said anything since they'd entered the pod. It had stopped its shrieking noises and was sitting quietly on a seat opposite, confined in a sound-resistant sack. Torsta had opened the sack at the top, to allow the human to breathe more easily, and now it was watching her intently, its round eyes hardly blinking. Not that it mattered in the least; any primitive thoughts it might be having weren't of any consequence to the enterprise.

'Why you do take me?' it said, after a while. Torsta focused on the stationary lights on the schematic and didn't acknowledge that she'd heard it speak. *Ignore it. Just ignore.*

'Is not well done. I be with Yan Feyrsten. Why you do take?'

You are not impressed by this. Do not be impressed.

'We talk, yes? You do say why. Is not well done.'

Do not engage. Those eyes! Don't even look. It's just another animal.

'We talk. I not be animal, Chief Jai.'

Torsta snapped her head round to look at the human; she couldn't help it. 'How do you know my name, you little shit?'

'Not be angry. See Georgi Show. See Henik Varkesen and Torsta Jai.'

Oh, for fuck's sake – a human that watches the news! 'Shut up, now! No more speaking!'

The human was looking at her now with even greater intensity, not at all frightened by her annoyance. 'Why no speak?' she said. 'You do more violent – like in bar?'

'Shut up! Just shut your mouth, or I'll close that bag!'

The human was quiet again. It appeared to have got the message, finally. But then it spoke once more.

'Bar violent be mistake,' it said. 'This also mistake.'

Torsta reached forward and sealed up the sack, then checked to see if the system had updated the schematic. The pods were starting to move again, heading for stations away from the shopping district, and there was a voice announcement, something about a security incident in Carnival Square. An explosion. People were being kept out of the area, and the pod network was being evacuated.

She slumped back in her seat and waited for the pod to tell her where they would be going. On the seat opposite, the human was still and silent, its face out of sight. Somehow though, the eyes were still there. Even concealed inside the sack, she knew they were open and alert. And judging.

Santi's rental trunk seemed reluctant to get out of the pod at Midsummer Station. She shouted at it, then gave it a kick to hurry it along the quay. She'd forgotten that the lift under Henik's apartment was right at the other end, and by the time she'd reached it, she'd taken to swearing at the trunk for not keeping up. Then it wanted to scan inside the lift before it went in, murmuring nervously about the dangers of squeezing in together. '1012 Varkesen,' she said, and kicked the trunk again when it tried to respond. 'Not you, stupid.'

If she had sent the trunk on ahead it would have warned her. She would have been more composed when the lift opened and she saw Alka standing there, rather than jumping back with a shout of alarm.

'Santi Aspil,' said Alka. She looked into the lift for a moment. 'Plain?'

'Henik isn't here. I'm just bringing some nutrients and biofixes.' Alka looked her in the eye for a moment, then dragged the trunk across the landing and into the apartment, ignoring its frantic attempts to reverse. Santi wasn't expecting to be thanked, but she was surprised that Alka gave the trunk only cursory attention. Instead, she tugged at Santi's sleeve, drew her towards the reclining room.

'Come, Santi Aspil!'

The holoscreen was displaying a view of the plaza. It showed the barricade stretching across the image, a thorny mass of upturned furniture, and a log reference showing that the recording had only just been made. Alka pointed at the screen and began to talk in her own language. Her hands moved continuously as she spoke, and she looked earnestly from the image to Santi as if determined that her message would be understood. Then she walked up to the display and gestured at it to play the recording.

It didn't take long for Santi to realise the significance of what had occurred. She watched the Midsummer Clan running to the barricade, the hoverbike entering the plaza, then when the imager found the rider's face, they said Torsta Jai's name in unison.

Then came the attempted escape, the human running desperately towards the barricade in her crimson coat, and Alka racing out to meet her. Alka stopped the recording at the instant when Torsta Jai grabbed the human's hood, and her face was revealed. It expanded to fill the screen, the neat features, the disorderly copper hair, the piercing gaze. Santi didn't need to see Alka's reaction to know what it meant, the likeness was undeniable. It was as if the mosaic in the mall had been brought to life, the subject of Alka's reverence in flesh and blood, calling to her in the middle of Midsummer Plaza. 'You think it's *her*, don't you?' she said, softly.

The rest of the recording played out to its agonising conclusion, Alka left kneeling at the doors of the pod station, her energy spent as her goddess was dragged beneath the city. Santi reversed the recording until the human's face filled the screen again. 'The gods' mercy – you really think that's *her!*'

Alka went to the screen again, turned in the image so that it was superimposed on her face. 'Santi Aspil,' she said. 'Help Callista.'

Santi paced across the room, her mind running through the possibilities. She knew that Torsta Jai had been released from prison, she'd authorised it herself. Perhaps Torsta was doing freelance investigation. Perhaps she'd been assigned to find a runaway, one which just happened to look like a piece of artwork in a shopping mall. But abandoning a valuable hoverbike in the Derelict Zone suggested something more significant. *That's not an ordinary human as far as the ferals are concerned. And she's not ordinary to Torsta either.*

She felt a call coming through and looked across the room to where Alka was still staring at the screen. 'Henik,' she said, positioning his image so that he stood between them, his arms folded and his fingers teasing at the greying hair on his chin.

'Look, I'm really sorry to ask you this, Santi but I've got an urgent situation, and I need your help. I hate doing this, but it's very important, and if you could just speak to...'

'Hold on – just back up a moment. Tell me the problem. What's happened?'

'It's about a human, a special one. Her owner is an old friend of mine – he's Maarten Feyrsten's brother. I've been helping him with a human he bought a few days ago. She was stolen from outside his beach house this morning.'

Santi sank onto the sofa. 'I'm sorry to hear that, but isn't it a matter for the police? You've notified them, I assume?'

'Yes, of course. But this isn't just any pet, and it isn't any normal crime.'

'Well, I can understand if your friend feels close to...'

'It's not that Santi! Someone's had Yan Feyrsten's property under surveillance. He moved out to his beach house yesterday, then this morning a woman on a bike, swoops in and snatches the human off his doorstep, right in front of his nose.'

'A hoverbike?' said Santi, looking at the image pulsing in front of her. 'This human hasn't got copper-coloured hair and a crimson coat, has she?'

'Yes! You've seen her! Where?'

'At Midsummer. That's where I am now.'

'What? At my apartment?'

'Your equipment caught the human being dragged into the pod station by Torsta Jai.'

'Oh shit! Torsta's a bounty hunter these days!'

'Santi moved closer to Alka, who was squatting spellbound in front of the screen. 'And can you see who I have with me, here?'

'Alka. Has she seen...?'

'First-hand. She thinks the state has taken away her goddess. You saw that mosaic, Henik. Surely you noticed the resemblance to Yan Feyrsten's human?'

'Well, yes it had occurred to me, but I never imagined Alka would ever see her.'

'And now she'll have the ferals thinking that Yan Feyrsten's pet has come down from the heavens.'

Henik sat down heavily, hands covering his face 'Actually,' he said, 'that's exactly what's happened.'

There were new security gates at the entrance to Maarten Feyrsten's house, forbidding structures that bristled with the latest security measures. Yan only had to stand in front of them for their slatted design to contort into a reinforced barrier of sharp-edged plates. A holographic guard emerged from the bushes with an uncomfortable expression, almost as if it had been relieving itself in the undergrowth, a whimsical thought, that distracted Yan for no more than a moment before his fear returned in a surging wave of nausea.

'I'm here to see the Lady Consort,' he said, his voice sounding unsteady to his own ears.

'Have you an appointment, esteemed?' The guard stared blankly over Yan's shoulder, an outdated programme, trapped in a habit of rudeness.

'No, not exactly.'

'The Lady Consort only receives by appointment, esteemed.'

'I'm her brother-in-law. I'm Yan Feyrsten.'

'The Lady Consort is not to be disturbed, esteemed.'

'Look, this is urgent! I did call her, but she wasn't answering.'

The guard turned away abruptly and walked back into the bushes. Yan shouted for him to return, waved his hands frantically in front of the gate, hoping to stimulate a further response. He stood looking at the driveway, suddenly aware of his breath, surging hot and ragged through his throat. How many times had he driven up to the front porch? How often had he opened the door and walked in calling his brother's name? Now suddenly he was powerless, unable even to approach the house he knew so well. For a moment, he thought he was going to vomit, as he had on the journey from the beach, but this time his insides coiled into a different spasm, one that rose into his chest as a sob of desperation.

A small figure appeared from the side of the house and came down the driveway at a trot. It was Juno. 'So glad to see you!' said Yan, as he approached the gate. 'I'm here for the mistress.'

Juno bowed as the gates slid open. 'Greet,' he said and led Yan back up the driveway towards the house. He was dressed in a formal high-collared jacket, in spite of the heat, and a hat with blue tassels that swung as he walked. It occurred to Yan that before Kali's arrival, he would have paid scant attention to Juno. It certainly wouldn't have entered his head that he might have found his clothes irritating in the hot season. In fact, he wouldn't have imagined Juno having any thoughts on the matter, or on anything else. Now, everything was changing. Now he felt he should at least speak to him, as he was escorted around to the rear gardens.

'Nice day, Juno,' he said awkwardly.

Juno didn't respond, but Yan found himself watching the language of his body. His brows arched, and his eyes narrowed. Perhaps, it meant that Juno wanted to speak to him, but there was nothing in his expression that felt warm, or friendly.

Jocasta was lying under a large canopy beside her swimming pool. She was wearing a patterned wrap that showed off her flawless legs, and her face was obscured by a wide-brimmed hat. A small table was floating upside-down in the pool, and an empty bottle bobbed alongside. Juno hurried ahead to speak to her, bowing submissively as he reached her side. She grabbed him so fiercely that she spilled her drink, then released him as soon as she saw Yan approaching.

'Darling! How lovely of you to pay me a visit!'

'I'm sorry if I've come at a bad time,' he said, turning his head towards the telltale flotsam.

'Oh, that's nothing at all. Just your big brother being a bit dramatic. Wants me to live in dreary old Check St. and play the part full time. Don't you ever turn into a stiff like him. Decorum and all that crap.'

'I thought you were a stickler for…'

'I expect to be treated properly, of course, but I'm not going to stand on ceremony at the expense of having some fun! Style *and* enjoyment, that's the way, dear boy!' She reached out to pull a chair closer to the pool. 'Now, do sit down and enjoy the weather with me. At least someone has time for a social call these days!'

'Well, actually I have a problem, Jocasta. In fact, I'm worried sick about it and I thought…'

'Oh, my dear Yan! How awful! I'm a good listener, so you just spit it out. Whatever is troubling you?'

'It's Kali, she's…'

'Ah! I *knew* she might cause you trouble. Wilfulness, is it?'

'She's been kidnapped.'

Jocasta sat bolt upright. It was as if the phrase had sobered her in an instant, and her mind was now hungry for detail.

'It happened right in front of me,' continued Yan., 'At the

beach house. I know who did it, which is why I've come to you for help.'

'Good gracious! Who? How could I…?'

'It was Torsta Jai. She was caught later by an imager, dragging Kali into Midsummer pod station. You know Torsta Jai, don't you?'

'Me? Whatever makes you say that?'

'You told me once that you used to be members of the same club, the one on the waterfront, by the old seaport.'

'Oh, that was ages ago! I'm sorry, Yan, but I haven't seen Torsta Jai for years. And you know, after that nasty business she had… I simply *abhor* violence.'

'But you're well connected in Government circles, of course.'

'Yan, I'm so sorry. She was a pretty thing and I had high hopes for her, but I can't imagine what the Government could do that the police can't.'

'Torsta is still connected to the Department for the Interior, somehow. I'm sure of it.'

'Goodness! Surely not, darling.'

'I have it on good authority that she's operating as a bounty hunter in the Derelict Zone.'

'Oh, that old story! I don't believe there are bounty hunters, but if there are, I expect it would be the corporates who contract them. And with good reason, I should say.'

'Please, Jocasta, I implore you! Please just make a call to Carnival St. The department will talk to you! I'm sure someone there must know something!'

'Darling! I simply can't bear to see you like this. Of course, I'll do it! I had no idea you'd feel so strongly about a human. I'll go right to the top, dear boy. I'll do it now.' Jocasta turned away, pressed her fingers to her cheekbone, then held out her hands to examine her nails while she waited. 'How peculiar!' she said, after a few moments. 'I can't connect for some reason. Now, don't you worry, my dear. I'll keep trying until I get through, and we'll get to the bottom of this!'

Yan got to his feet. 'Thank you, Jocasta, I really appreciate it. Now, I'm afraid I must go. I really can't rest until...'

'Yes, yes. I quite understand,' said Jocasta, looking around the poolside. 'Now, where's Juno! I'll…'

'No, please. Don't worry. No standing on ceremonies, as you say. I'll see myself out.'

Juno was in the front garden when Yan came around the side of the house. For a moment, he thought it was a different human, one who stood more erect, shoulders back and feet firmly planted. The collar of his jacket was undone, and his hands were in motion as he talked to another human, who was leaning casually on a rake. For some reason, Yan decided to stay hidden from view and watch the interaction. Juno chattered forcefully, turning occasionally to look towards the house and emphasising what he was saying with chopping movements of his hands. Yan's stomach twisted as it had when he saw how Kali could understand the news and spell words. Now it was Juno. This wasn't the submissive animal he'd met before. This was something very different, an assertive being who used two distinct modes of behaviour. *Self-confident by nature, but he knows to put on an act when there are people around.*

By the time Henik arrived at Midsummer, Santi and Alka had unpacked the trunk. He found them standing in the kitchen, sorting the various nutrients and biofixes into piles. There wasn't a great deal of communication between the two of them. However articulate she was in her own tongue, Alka knew almost nothing of the language of people and Santi was trying to make herself understood with actions and gestures.

'It's heavy going,' she said. 'Explaining the different dosages and applications is almost impossible, but without this 'language of the body' as you call it, we wouldn't be able to communicate at all. I'm putting markings on the boxes which I hope she'll understand.'

'She'll make it work. We are all guilty of assuming the communication deficit equates to a lack of intelligence. But that's quite wrong. Humans are highly intuitive, and the fact that she's still standing there tells you she's taking it in.'

Alka hadn't even acknowledged Henik's arrival. She was staring intently at each box of tablets, mouthing words to herself. 'Plain,' she said after a while, but her eyes didn't move from her task.

Santi took a deep breath. 'So, this legend is more than just a mural in a shopping mall.'

'Until I saw Alka's little homage the other day, I thought it was something we'd made up back in antiquity, just a fable about humans. I didn't imagine they'd know it too, that their language could sustain it down the generations.' Henik looked over at Alka. 'But it seems she may know the story and that it's very important to her.'

'But *why?* Who is this goddess figure?'

'Well, the legend tells of the planet Earth as the place where the human species originated. That much is true, but the story also imagines a time when they can return there, when they have proved to the gods that they deserve the home of their ancestors. And in the meantime, they've been placed at our disposal. As we tell the story, they are under our protection, but I doubt that's how they will have handed it down.'

Santi lowered her voice. 'And Callista – I suppose the legend says that she will come to take them home?'

'I think it's more that she will show them how to become worthy of their place on Earth.'

'To start a revolution, in other words.'

'There are different types of revolution, but with almost as many humans as people in the Free Republic, we must hope that if and when it comes, it's a peaceful one.'

'And what about Yan Feyrsten's Earth human? You think she brings that closer?'

'It's the economic crisis that does that. Poverty, abuse, desperation. You've seen it among people in places like the Marsh Estate, and you've seen how much worse it is for humans in the Derelict Zone. But if the ferals are looking to their goddess for salvation, they'll invest their hopes and dreams in Kali, whether she wants it or not. She's a spark on dry moss.'

'Well, she may not be who they imagine, but you say she's different from all the others. What's so special about her?'

'Well, quite simply, Kali confounds all our preconceptions about humans. She certainly has me baffled, and I've been studying the species most of my life. She's only been here a few days, but she already has a better command of our language than any human I've ever encountered. Her thirst for knowledge is insatiable, she has considerable practical skills, and she grasps abstract concepts with ease. What's more, she has no appreciation of her status here, no acceptance of our superiority, our dominance. She just expects to be treated as an equal.'

Santi stared into space for a while. She drew a breath to speak, then stopped, her eyes flicking to Alka. 'An equal,' she said eventually. 'You think Kali is evidence that humans are capable of playing a more elevated role in our society, that they shouldn't be categorised with other animals? If that's so, then she challenges… well, pretty much everything.'

'Couldn't have put it better myself. You could say she's the winning card for the animal rights lobby.'

'How much of this does Yan Feyrsten know?'

'I've warned him, but at the moment, he's more worried that she'll fall into the hands of a criminal gang, or a cult.'

'I can't see that happening. Torsta was sent to *Bleak Penance* on my authority, but I'd worked with her before that. She's not someone you can ever really know, but she was always principled. She won't be dealing with criminals. She'll be looking elsewhere, trying to gain influence. She'll want Kali for leverage of some sort, and my guess is that it won't be long before she figures out this Callista legend. What does Yan make of it?'

'I haven't told him yet. Until now, it's just been an uncanny resemblance to a mural in the Derelict Zone.'

'Don't you think you should?'

Henik watched Alka delving into the box and pulling out more supplies. She was sorting the packs into piles now, tapping them in turn with her fingers as if she was counting. It occurred to him that the more he treated humans as if they were people, the more he noticed them behaving that way. It was as if his altered expectations created a new reality.

'Yan has enough to contend with,' he said. 'I'll tell him, but the priority is finding Kali.'

'And then what? Alka is keeping her head at the moment, because she thinks we can intervene. But if we do find her goddess, what would the ferals do with her as their inspiration?'

'And if we don't find her, if Torsta Jai takes Kali to the Government, they won't understand the implications, how volatile…'

The display in the reclining room suddenly burst into life, the still image of Kali replaced by the urgent tone of national news and a scene of chaos in the city centre. Simultaneously the announcement burst into Henik's head, over-riding everything else on his feed. 'We are interrupting to bring you breaking news of a major incident in central Freeport where there has been an explosion. There have been a great many casualties and considerable loss of life. Citizens are advised to stay well clear of the city centre while emergency services work to contain the situation. News is still coming through to us from the scene where according to reports, an elemist-based device detonated a few minutes ago at the Café Republic in Carnival Square.'

Henik felt a chill rippling his skin, as it always did at the mention of elemist. Alka drifted past him and stood in front of the display, her arms tightly folded. Then, when he looked at Santi, he saw her cranial ridges had paled.

'I was only just there,' she said. 'Oh, no! I left Vish there!' Her fingers went to her cheek and she closed her eyes as she tried to raise him. 'Come on! Come on! Oh shit, Henik, he's not responding!'

The news bulletin switched to a reporter on the scene. Sirens were wailing in the background, and he was being jostled by the crowd as he spoke. 'We're being kept well away from the square now, but you can just about see in the background, the tangle that was once one of the most popular places in central Freeport. The emergency services have cordoned off the whole area, and we're told they are attempting to save some people who are trapped higher up in the building. Sadly, there will be no hope for those who have suffered injury. Eyewitnesses report seeing a blue flash, characteristic of elemist munitions. Of those who weren't killed immediately, many are likely to have fatal wounds, the bombers' choice of explosive toxin ensuring that even minor injuries may add to the fatalities. No names have been released yet, but it's known that several public figures and government officials were regulars here. Amongst those, the former Counsellor for the Interior, Santi Aspil, is as yet unaccounted for.'

'Is there any indication yet who might be responsible?' said a voice from the studio.

'No group has claimed responsibility, but I spoke to a witness earlier. She told me that moments before the blast, she saw two identical ferals walk inside.'

'Ferals? Surely the suggestion isn't that a human could have been responsible.'

'That was indeed the implication. Humans wouldn't have the capability to plan this themselves, but some officials are suggesting this may be a reaction to the election result, some person or group using feral humans to execute an attack. Whilst we shouldn't jump to conclusions at this early stage, the police have issued an image of two individuals who are of interest.'

An image appeared on the screen, two blond humans in green dungarees, striding across Carnival Square. Henik recognised them immediately, and so did Alka. She dropped to her knees and stared at the display through the fingers of her hands.

11

Captive

'WHERE'S MY SPEECH?' ASKED Maarten Feyrsten as he strode past his aide in the corridor. She turned to follow him, dodging around plants and pedestals to march by his side while she explained the amendments she had made.

'We thought a call for national unity was important, Chief Counsellor. The policy proposals can follow, but we didn't want them to look rushed. The message is one of remaining calm, particularly with the unfortunate overreactions we're seeing.'

Feyrsten came to an abrupt halt. 'What overreactions?'

'The lynchings. You haven't heard, esteemed?'

'No, Gavi, I haven't bloody heard! I haven't been *briefed*! Delay the broadcast and get me Sig Norvik.'

By the time he had walked the length of the building and turned into his office, Sig Norvik's host was waiting in front of his desk. Feyrsten addressed him from the door.

'Are you going to tell me what's going on, Sig?' We've all just had a Crisis Group meeting, I'm about to speak to the nation, and I hear in a corridor that there have been lynchings! Didn't you think I might want to know about that? He went to stand behind his desk, used the side of his hand to sweep away an untidy display of crisis reports and graphic scenes from the Café Republic.

'The situation is very fluid, Chief Counsellor. We're being asked to speculate when our information is still sketchy. I haven't briefed you on the lynchings because information is only just coming through and I wanted to be clear about the position first. I understand the violence is ongoing.'

'Ongoing? You mean we have humans being killed on the streets, as we speak?'

'I'm sending you what we have, now. It's not pleasant.'

Feyrsten's desk began to play the record of a lynching in the city centre. It showed two humans cowering in a doorway as they were surrounded by a group of young men. A woman tried to intervene, but she was pushed aside, and the humans were dragged screaming into the street, where they were given a savage beating. If that hadn't killed them, they were certainly dead after they had been hoisted by their necks from a hovercrane and swung above the mob like hunting trophies.

'This was the first,' said Norvik, 'but there have been at least six other incidents, each using a crane in a similar way.'

'You need to get your shit together on this. We want the human population subdued, not inflamed.'

'That's understood, Chief Counsellor. We can't have people taking the law into their own hands. I'm liaising with the Chief of Police on the matter. However, he does seem reluctant to call a human curfew to get them off the streets, so…'

Feyrsten ignored Norvik's attempt to involve him in an inter-departmental dispute. 'A curfew isn't going to help where an animal is separated from its owner. Look, Sig, we want to see humans under proper control, but the fault here is with the perpetrators. We're already dealing with a terrible atrocity. I can see the death count rising as we speak. Infirmaries are battling to save lives, and the police are stretched to the limit. This sort of mindless retribution against animals is making everyone's job even harder.'

'Yes, I agree with you, but we also want to rid the streets of strays.'

Feyrsten was familiar with this style of passive challenge, and he found it dishonest. He knew from experience how it could be used to contrive a misunderstanding. He got to his feet slowly and stood leaning on his knuckles. 'Sig, I want you to hear me very clearly on this,' he said, lowering his voice a notch. 'We have been too permissive for too long, and you have my support in installing an orderly environment, but do not think that means a reign of terror, where any human who might have lost its owner or been abandoned can be seized by a mob and destroyed without due process. If we appear to be condoning that, even for a moment, we will find the public will turn on us. We will have lost the moral high ground. Now, do we understand one another?'

'Yes, Chief Counsellor – definitely. I didn't mean to suggest any approval of what's been happening.'

'I'm glad to hear it. Now, we're all having a rough day, so let's...'

There was a knock on the door and Feyrsten's aide put her head into the room. 'Sorry to disturb, esteemed, but we're ready to go with the speech when you are. And we've had confirmation on those feral suspects.'

Feyrsten turned back to Norvik. 'Are you getting this? The suspects have been confirmed.'

'Yes, Chief Counsellor, it's coming through here. I'm looking at a recording of the two little bastards walking into the Café Republic, just before the explosion.'

'Draft something into the speech, will you, Gavi? Progress is being made, but speculation is unhelpful. Appeal to civic duty, lawful behaviour and so forth. And Sig, I want to know who was behind this, and I want them in custody, so you better fix your difference with the police.

Santi had never liked Maarten Feyrsten. It wasn't just that his party wanted to dismantle four years of her work, nor even that his business success had come from exploiting the Commonwealth's vassal systems. Somehow, she also needed to know that he was a bad person. She saw arrogance in the way he walked, condescension in his patrician accent, and she looked for corruption in everything he did. She didn't like his clothes, or his affluent lifestyle, and the thought of anyone lying next to him in bed made her shudder. She felt her disdain for him right down to her working-class roots, held it with the memories of her childhood poverty in the backstreets of a provincial techtown.

Yet her brain told her it was all nonsense. It said to her that Feyrsten was an honest man who happened to hold different views, a man who played hard, but in his own way wanted what was best for the Republic. It chided her that disliking him was a merely a sign of her own insecurity. So, when his face appeared on Henik's display, she made herself see a man wrestling with a career-defining crisis, only a day after he'd been elected to the highest office in the Commonwealth. She saw a man with the weight of a nation on his shoulders, a man whose decisions in the coming days might shape a generation.

Henik watched the speech with her in silence. Once or twice, she thought he was about to make a comment, but he waited until Feyrsten had finished before he said anything. 'It was alright,' he said, 'but I think you could have done better. He was too smooth by half. There's no honour in the man.'

Santi went out onto the balcony and looked over the Derelict Zone, towards the city centre. Such a short distance from the fight for survival here was the wealth and comfort of Carnival Square. *Glamour, privilege, and now carnage.* 'No, he got it just right,' she said. 'Credit where it's due. He met the moment.'

'Everything he says, he judges politically, even when he isn't saying anything political.'

'Good grief, Henik! Sometimes I think if you were to smell flowers in Carnival Square, you'd ask where the funeral was.'

'Well, I would today.'

Santi felt her ridges colouring. 'I can't believe I just said that. Feyrsten can take on the mantle of a statesman as if he was born to it. But me...?'

'He's Chief Counsellor. It's his job.'

'That's the benchmark, if I am to challenge him for it.'

'What do you mean?' said Henik, sitting upright.

Santi looked away, thought for a moment. What she was about to say felt surreal. 'I'm going to be the next leader of the Progress Party, Henik. It's decided. It would have been all over the news by now if it wasn't for what's just happened.'

'I don't understand. You said you didn't want it.'

'Well, when it's offered to you on a plate, it feels like a different decision. Maybe it's this place that's done it to me. You've shown me that Midsummer is unfinished business. I just feel I've got to do it, Henik. This crisis is uncharted spacetime, and I can't just turn away.' She went to him and took his hand. 'I know it probably isn't what you were hoping, now that...'

'Do you know, Santi, there were times, when I'd be entertaining here, when people were clinking their goblets, and looking at my artifacts. I'd imagine you turning up out of the blue, the most welcome of gatecrashers. You've never been far from my thoughts, but I accepted that you'd chosen a different life. A few days ago, I'd have shouted out your name for party leader. But then, with the election result, with you out of office, it felt like everything might change. I thought we might have a second chance.'

'And you don't think it can work if I do this?'

'It doesn't sound like there's much "if" about it. Oh, I don't know, Santi. I can't change. I don't think any of us can. Circumstances have brought us together again, and perhaps they're just going to tear us apart the same way they did before.'

'Perhaps it's different this time.'

'Because we're older and wiser?'

'Well, I suppose we know the value of things more than we did, how easily things that matter can slip away. But I wasn't thinking of that.'

'Then what?'

'I was thinking, hoping I suppose, that the things each of us value most are now pulling us along the same path. A peaceful republic, a just society, a shared sense that history has reached a critical moment.'

Henik turned to look across the room to where the display had reverted to the image of Kali in Midsummer Plaza. 'Perhaps, you're right he said. Perhaps Callista is calling to *us* as well.'

***

The guide moved smoothly through the corridors of the Department for the Interior, walking through obstacles, but always warning Sig Norvik of their presence however conspicuous they were. It took him briskly down the stairs at the back of the old building, offering an occasional comment about its history, then directing his attention to the various city landmarks as they passed over a vertiginous glazed bridge to the new section of the building, transports passing beneath them far too close for Norvik's liking. They took a sharp turn, into a narrow corridor. At the end of it, struggling through a doorway with a bag under her arm, was a woman dressed entirely in black. 'You can leave me here,' he said to the guide, causing it to shimmer and dissolve.

When he entered the room, Torsta Jai was placing the bag on a bench. Behind it a granite wall appeared to have water pouring down its face, the trickling notes pretending that the problems of government could be addressed with serenity.

'It's been a while, Torsta.' he said. 'You're looking well.'

She took rather longer to answer than was comfortable. Norvik remembered that about her from the occasion they had met before, at a government reception when she was Chief of Police. It was as if she made a deliberate assessment of people before she spoke, and didn't find the silence uncomfortable.

'And you're looking like shit.' she said eventually. 'But if you weren't, on a day like this, you probably wouldn't be doing your job. Don't worry, this will be worth your while.'

'I think I'll be the judge of that. Why don't you start by getting it out of that laundry bag? Make sure it's standing first. Rule number one is that they don't sit in a person's presence unless instructed.'

Torsta released the closure at the top of the bag, and it dropped to the floor. The human was disorientated to start with, turning its head and squinting against the light. But then it composed itself. It stepped out of the sack, showing none of the fear that commonly drove human behaviour. Instead, it looked him in the eye, then thrust its hand at the granite wall, only to find that the water was a mirage.

'It's thirsty,' said Norvik. He took a flask from the table behind him and poured a cup of water. He held it out, waited for the human to come forward, then stooped to place it on the floor. 'Lesson two, Torsta. Never hand a human something they want. It gives them an inappropriate sense of their status. Always use the floor, so it requires an act of submission. Do you know what it's called?'

'Kali, I believe.'

At the sound of its name, the human drew a breath, as if it was about to speak. 'Drink, Kali,' Norvik said. It looked at the cup on the floor and swallowed hard, took a step toward it. Norvik moved forward too, so the cup was directly at his feet. 'Drink,' he repeated. There was eye contact for a moment, then the human reached out with its foot and gently kicked the cup over. It watched the water pool around his shoes, then stepped back, lifting its chin and fixing him with a steady gaze.

'Oh! Now that really *is* interesting!' said Norvik. He reached out and took a fistful of the human's hair, holding its head immobile and drawing it close. 'How fascinating! I'm tempted to believe you, Torsta. It has an unusual appearance, striking in fact, but it's that defiance that's so intriguing. It's in the eyes. Suggests a complete absence of training. And yet it isn't feral, otherwise it would have lunged at the water. There would have been no self-restraint, just the need to satisfy its thirst.' He let the human go, and it drew away, stared at him insolently. 'Well, well, a natural! A *natural*! I never thought I'd ever see such a thing. I almost wish I wasn't Counsellor for Human Affairs. I'd take this one as a personal project, the ultimate test for my methods. Maybe, I still could...'

'I haven't offered her to you yet,' said Torsta. She went over to pour another cup of water, placed it on the bench beside the human. 'And whatever battle of wills you want to have with her, she needs to be hydrated.'

'Preserving the merchandise now, are you? After dragging it across the city, sealed in a bag.'

'Necessary, for something so valuable.'

'Valuable? Alright, I'll bite. What's the price? Not credits, I'll bet.'

'The market value would do me nicely, but you're right – that's not it. I think you have a problem I can help you with.'

'Oh, you think? Just *one* problem?'

'Your police force doesn't like you. The Chief of Police may report to you in theory, but he's strong-willed. He's a friend of Santi Aspil's and you can't rely on him to enforce whatever reforms you have in mind. He'll drag his feet, frustrate you.'

'Well, if you think I'm going to give you back your old job, you can forget it. I sympathised with you at the time of your unfortunate incident Torsta, but things have moved on.'

'That's not what I want. But I do want to be recognised in a different capacity. I doubt if anyone's got around to telling you, but I've been working for the state anyway, as a bounty hunter. Off the record of course, and entirely deniable, but you have me to thank for removing a few notable ferals.'

'You don't say. Did Aspil know?'

'Doubt it. It's under national security, not this department.

But I want it official now. I want a team, resources, and a mandate to deal with the Derelict Zone.'

Norvik looked at Torsta's face. He admired its stillness, its neutral tones the epitome of Antarian composure. He imagined Torsta in that bar assault. The victims would never have seen it coming. 'Where would you get the people?' he said. 'How quickly could it be operational?'

'So, we're talking details now, are we?'

'Well, the idea has some merit, I'll give you that. But I'd be courting controversy to take you on. All in return for one human, however interesting.'

'It's not just interesting. You've seen a glimpse of its capabilities in the botclips I sent, and I've witnessed more first-hand. If this one's typical of natural humans, then your view of the species as non-cognitive looks very shaky. In the wrong hands, this human could call your whole agenda into question. You really don't want that sort of challenge, that social upheaval.'

'Neither do you. As a patriot.'

For a moment, Norvik wondered whether he'd touched a nerve. Torsta stood motionless and unblinking. 'I live for my own interests, these days,' she said.

Norvik suddenly felt tired. The pressures of the day were taking their toll, and his mind was reluctant to spar with Torsta when there was so much else to occupy it. He slumped into a chair. 'So, you'd give the human to the Progressives, would you? How public-spirited of you.'

'It was about to fall into their laps. I've already done you a favour bringing it here.'

'So, how did you come by your precious bargaining chip, then? Not legally, I'm guessing.'

'Possession is the gravitational force of law,' said Torsta.

'If you were to take it as a 'project,' your gain would be Henik Varkesen's loss.'

'It belongs to Varkesen?'

'He's been studying her, but she belongs to Yan Feyrsten.'

'Yan Feyrsten!' chirped the human. It was sitting with its back to the wall now, the water appearing to cascade over its body. 'I do speak with – yes?'

Norvik could feel the tension in his head turning to pain. He took a deep breath, and then another. 'Torsta,... *please* don't tell me you've gone and stolen this human from the Chief Counsellor's brother!'

'It's illegal to own a feral. Heritage has been promising to clamp down on it. It was in your manifesto.'

'But it's not a fucking *feral*! Anyone can see that!'

'If the legal definition of a feral doesn't already include natural humans, then it should. The disease risk is much greater. Perhaps it's just a matter of interpretation, a wording amendment at most.' Torsta's voice maintained a constant pitch and volume, betrayed no concern that she was playing for high stakes. She knew her position and was clear about her objective. It was easy to see why she'd thrived in the military.

'And it was alone on a beach at the time,' she continued. 'Unbonded, unsupervised. That's another thing Heritage promised voters it would tackle.'

Norvik stood up and paced slowly across the room, beginning to sense the opportunity, the way he could sell it. 'It's arguable, I suppose.'

'It's also arguable that you would be saving the Chief Counsellor a scandal. The media would love it if his brother's pet was a focus for the animal rights movement, particularly after what's just happened in Carnival Square.'

Norvik found himself standing in front of the little

human. It showed no inclination to get to its feet, no trace of deference in its manner. It just sat with its arms folded across its chest and looked him in the eye. 'Yan Feyrsten,' it said. 'I do speak with.'

'Does it always stare like that,' he asked. He'd never encountered such defiance in a human, but after the damaging exchange with Feyrsten about the lynchings, this untrained animal might serve him well, might allow him to regain the initiative with the Chief Counsellor. 'Let me think about this,' he said.

'I need an answer now, so here's one last morsel to help your thinking. I still have my connections, and one of them was the owner of the Café Republic. Varkesen was in there the day before the election. He was talking about feral humans – to Santi Aspil.'

'Alright, Torsta. Alright. You make a good case, and I think we can do something with this. But you'll have to start by getting that human somewhere secure. I'm not going to have it in custody if there is any question of it being stolen property.'

'I have something in mind,' said Torsta. 'Just temporarily, while you make sure the law is on our side. But you'll need to arrange a transport for me.' She took hold of the human's coat and pulled it to its feet. 'And I look forward to hearing you announce my feral task force.'

A security officer had been sent to wait for Torsta at the rear entrance to the building. 'Esteemed,' he said, standing a little taller as she approached.

She stopped short of the door and took Kali by the front of her coat. She lifted her off the ground, brought her face so close that she could see her reflection in her eyes. 'Now, I know you can understand me, so just listen very carefully. We're getting into a transport outside and I'm warning you. Don't try running. Don't try *anything*.'

At first glance, the narrow lane outside was entirely quiet, a canyon of austere government buildings, clad in verglas and ironstone, without any of the shops and bars that made the main street so vibrant. A sleek limousine rested close by, but it wasn't until Torsta was halfway down the steps to it that she saw the media scrum. They were huddled around a doorway on the opposite side, a haze of micro-drones buzzing around them.

'Let's go, man!' shouted Torsta. 'Get that transport open!' She tucked Kali under her arm and ran with her down the steps. It was too late to avoid detection. The media drones switched their attention to the transport and made straight for it. Torsta lowered her head and charged at the vehicle. It slid apart and she propelled Kali inside, barking more instructions at the security officer. 'Get us out of here! Windows and roof cloaked, ports locked! Move!'

There would be no quick getaway. The media drones swarmed around them blocking vision on all sides, and forcing the transport to reverse slowly. 'Taking control!' shouted Torsta. 'Transport! Escape protocol! Now!'

The floor of the limousine began to vibrate as if it was gathering itself for an unusual effort. 'Authority: Torsta Jai,' it replied, swinging violently on its axis to scatter the media, before launching itself backwards down the lane. It didn't pause at the junction with Carnival St. but reversed into the traffic at speed, smashing into the flank of another government vehicle, before pivoting and accelerating away. Torsta watched the chaos outside with dismay, wondering how much had been caught on record. 'What the fuck was that, man? What was going on back there?'

'I'm sorry, esteemed, I thought you would know. They've been there since that latest lynching.'

'What? It happened there, right outside the Department?'

'Yes, esteemed. A mob was protesting with a human effigy until they found two strays hiding in that doorway. You can still see the…'

'Yes, alright. I get the picture.'

Torsta sank back into her seat, furious but deciding to say nothing more. Outside, every junction was stacked three high, and police androids were checking anything they considered unusual. The human sat with its arms folded, staring ahead as the limousine edged through the traffic, using its privileged status to make steady, if slow progress. At least it wasn't making things worse by attempting to make conversation, Torsta thought. But then it turned its head and said, 'Thank you.'

'Don't speak,' said Torsta, then for a moment her curiosity got the better of her, and she found herself saying, 'For what?'

'Water. Thank you.'

Not long after, with the city centre falling behind them and the soaring architecture giving way to the softer spaces of the residential suburbs, the human spoke again. 'Where we do go?' she said.

'Doesn't matter,' said Torsta. 'It's not your concern.'

'Not trust him, that man.'

Torsta wasn't sure whether the human was saying she didn't trust Sig Norvik or presuming to offer advice. 'Why not?' she said.

'Mouth – he do this.' She licked at her lips as she spoke.

It's true. He does do that. Maybe it has some meaning for humans, insincerity perhaps.

Torsta decided not to give any advance notice of their

arrival at the Feyrsten estate; she didn't want to risk an argument with Jocasta until they were face to face. Still, there was no hesitation at the gates when their limousine drew up. An armed sentry saluted as they swept past, and two more appeared when they drew to a halt in front of the house.

'Where this?' said Kali, but then the front door opened, and Juno stepped out onto the porch. 'Jocasta,' she said quietly.

Torsta leaned over to the security officer. 'Keep the vehicle locked down until I return,' she said. 'And don't speak to the human, for any reason whatsoever.'

Torsta knew she'd be kept waiting. She made three slow circuits of the hall, examining its various vases and ornaments absent-mindedly and always under the silent gaze of the Feyrstens' pet in its braided uniform jacket. *That's it, test my patience, Jocasta. 'Lateness is the privilege of power,' you used to say.*

The swish of a door upstairs announced the imminent arrival of the Lady Consort. She appeared on the landing in a long gauzy robe that billowed around her as she made her descent. She called over the banister cheerily, 'Torsta, darling! How delightful to see you! And you're arriving in style, I see. Have events turned in your favour?'

'Perhaps, but it's not a day to be talking about favourable events.'

Jocasta paused for a moment at the foot of the stairs. 'No, of course not. That hideous explosion. I assume your expertise is being fully utilised?'

'I think the Counsellor for Human Affairs is open to my advice, which is what brings me to your door, after such a long time.'

'Goodness! Has Sig sent you in my direction? I'm flattered!

I can't imagine how I can help him, but I am definitely an admirer of his work. I gave a copy of his book to my brother-in-law just the other day.'

'To help him train his new human.'

Jocasta dropped her airy façade. 'Quite so. And I understand you might know something about that, Torsta. Yan seems to believe you've abducted his pet. Now I can't imagine…'

'He's right. I did.'

'Well, the gods' mercy, Torsta! Whatever for? You must give her back this instant! Yan's beside himself with worry!'

'Your brother-in-law made an illegal purchase and then failed to keep it under proper supervision. The Government has a clear policy on that, and after today I'm sure they will expect strict adherence.'

'No! Illegal, you say? You must tell me! Come and sit down.' She clapped her hands crisply. 'Refreshments, Juno! Quickly now!'

Jocasta led the way into an impressive atrium, where an arrangement of sumptuous white recliners stood within a circle of short marble columns, each of them crowned with a cascading plant. She took Torsta to sit on a couch, dappled with the light from an impressive verglas cupola. 'Now, do go on!' she said. 'I can't bear the suspense! How is it that Kali is illegal? I certainly hope you aren't suggesting Yan knew about this!'

Torsta had little doubt that it was exactly what Jocasta was hoping. *She forgets that I know her without the varnish.* 'Well, it was irresponsible to let a human loose on a public beach,' she said. 'But as for the purchase, I doubt he would've known. It's an obscure regulation that pertains to ferals.'

'Oh, you needn't worry about that. I've seen the little thing myself and from her grooming…'

'She's a natural.'

'Whatever is that?'

'It means she's from Earth. First generation. She wasn't born on Antaris.'

'That can't be right. I've never heard of such a thing!'

'She's the only natural *anyone* has heard of. Every other human on Antaris has been bred here, or at least within the Commonwealth.'

Jocasta's eyes widened. 'Are you saying that she's *valuable?*'

'Difficult to put a price on it, but I would say so. And your brother-in-law knows that. He's brought in Henik Varkesen to study her, because her behaviour is, well… natural for humans.'

'I knew it!' said Jocasta. 'I sensed there was insolence in that one! Most unattractive, it was. I knew straight away that she wasn't quite right.'

'Some might say it's every other human on this planet who isn't quite right. I'm sure that's what Varkesen would argue.'

Jocasta sat taller. 'That's quite absurd, a very disturbing notion. No, there's nothing about that little minx that can't be corrected with the right handling.'

'I'm glad to hear that Jocasta because she's outside in the limo. I'm sure you understand how bad it would look during a crisis like this if the Chief Counsellor's brother was found to have an illegal human, one allowed to roam and behave as it pleases.'

'Outside now? You have brought her to the right place, Torsta. Yes, absolutely, you can be confident of that! Sig Norvik may be assured that I will personally supervise her training, and Yan will be much more circumspect in future. I'll make sure he…'

'She's not going back to your brother-in-law without approval from Counsellor Norvik. Your brother-in-law cannot even know you have her here.'

'But that's ridiculous! He's asked for my help – practically begged me! I couldn't possibly keep this from him. No, Torsta. I absolutely refuse! I am sure Maarten would want no part in it.'

Torsta placed her hand on Jocasta's arm. 'I don't think it would be wise to tell your husband. It would be bad for his reputation if he was found to have covered for his brother on something so sensitive.'

Jocasta drew away abruptly and got to her feet. 'Then you shouldn't have brought her here! I'm not some temporary animal pound! How dare you, Torsta! You are compromising me. You forget that I'm the Lady Consort! Now, I expect you to…'

'Keep your secrets?'

Jocasta stood as still as the surrounding columns. Her forehead flushed, but she said nothing.

'It was a long time ago, of course,' said Torsta. 'The club.'

'You're such a prude! Do you really think Maarten doesn't know? This isn't the military, you know.'

'Foreign agents? Off-world criminals? You weren't choosy who you mind-hacked in their ecstasy, were you? Anything for information.'

'You were the one who paid me for that data, you hypocrite! You said it was in the national interest!'

'My reputation is already shot. But yours? If the media got just a sniff of it…'

Jocasta swallowed hard. 'You wouldn't!'

'I'm told that you were one of those who lobbied for me to be sent to *Bleak Penance*. A prominent voice behind the scenes, I hear.'

Jocasta sat down slowly, opened her mouth to speak, then closed it again. Eventually she said, 'That's not at all accurate. That's… that's…'

Torsta reached out and took the hem of her gown between her fingers, examined its intricate detailing. 'You've come a long way Jocasta, haven't you? You've risen right to the top of society and you play the part very well. But it's a long way to fall, and I should know.' She stood up and went to the door. 'I'll bring the human in, shall I?'

12

Fountain

MY DEAR MR. DUNSTONE… I sometimes wonder if you can read my thoughts. I do hope so, for I have no means of writing to you now. Perhaps you already know that I have got myself into some trouble. I'm in a cellar, I suppose, but I should really call it a dungeon. There are bars of static electricity, or some such thing, prickling away, but quite unseeable. I can't account for my detention. I've broken no rules, even if it was cheeky of me to spill that cup of water. You might disapprove perhaps, but I had in mind how you taught me not to give an inch to bullies. If it worked with the apprentice boys, I thought it might serve just as well here.

I don't suppose you know when it might be time for tea? Perhaps you're able to put it into someone's head to come down with something. A scone perhaps, and jam! I'll just have to be patient. 'The future comes soon enough,' you used to say.

As you can tell, I'm doing my best to be cheerful, but I'm dreadfully worried – for poor Yan as much as myself. He'll be searching high and low, no doubt. Will he think to ask Jocasta? That's the question… no, actually the question is: 'When he speaks to Jocasta, will she admit to having me in her cellar?'

I think Jocasta must know how I dislike her, for she prods and pokes at me as if she were playing with a doll, a ragged one probably, from her obvious disdain. Even when she isn't scowling at me, I see her jaw clenched. 'Must be cruel to be kind,' she'll be thinking.

I don't think there is an ounce of kindness in Juno, either. He will scarcely glance in my direction unless instructed, and he struts about in those awful jackets as if he were Lord Mountbatten of Burma. In truth, he resembles that pompous commissionaire at the Odeon! Do you recall him when we went to see The Wizard of Oz? I had to describe the film to you, and he kept coming over to shush me. Then afterwards, we walked home arm in arm, pretending that Sheep St. was the yellow brick road!

There, I'm smiling now, Mr. Dunstone! Do you see how you can still do that for me? You make me more certain than ever that there is some sense to be made of all this if only I trust myself to find it.

I hear footsteps now, so I must leave you. It's that scone, no doubt.

They came at twilight, eleven of them walking line abreast, not because it made them look impressive to advance together, Alka thought, but because it avoided an argument about the order in which they would file. She imagined the comical scenes that might have occurred on the narrow lanes along the way.

Of all the clans, only one was not represented, but it was the one that mattered most. With their territory adjacent to the financial district and their strategic position under the sky platforms, the Dockers would bear the brunt of any assault by the National Guard. They would crumble quickly, as of course everyone would, but exacting a price that left room for compromise was the thread of hope that brought the clans together, and that wouldn't be possible unless the Dockers allowed access to their territory.

Alka stood alone on the barricade, above a gap they had created to allow the clan leaders to enter. *Not side by side, but if we can't even get that far, what hope have we got?* She filled her lungs and called down to her clan to form a line.

The clan leaders came to a halt, stood shoulder to shoulder before the barricade. If their intentions had been hostile, the barricade wouldn't have held them for long, backed as they were by a small army, a clanking mass of makeshift armour that continued to file into the square. Front and centre was Chemical Mike, standing proud with the white pillowcase flying on a length of grey piping.

Alka came down off the barricade, making her descent at a measured pace, then leaping to the ground in a display of athleticism. She walked to the front of her clan, a white pennant flying from the tip of her javelin, then crouched and placed it on the ground.

'I see you!' she shouted, 'You clansfolk. You, the Unowned of our kind. We receive you here under your flag of parley!'

Chemical Mike came forward and placed a titanium staff on the ground parallel to Alka's javelin. 'I see you, Alka of the Citadel. We have come from across the zone at your invitation, to speak together of the troubles, to visit your fountain, and receive your intercession with the Redeemer.'

'It's a worthy mission,' said Alka. 'In this moment, Callista watches us. Let us not disappoint her.'

The other clan leaders began to step forward, laying down their weapons in turn, some simple industrial tools and others more elaborate instruments, brutal in appearance, if too unwieldy to concern a seasoned warrior.

The ritual completed, Alka led the eleven through the gap in the barricade. Now they were walking alone and exposed into enemy territory. *Will they hold, now? Please let them keep their nerve!*

She brought them to a halt in front of Midsummer Mall. 'Honourable leaders,' she said. 'This is a citadel and a place of worship, but it's also our home. None enters here who is unknown to us. Some of you, I have spoken with before and some of you I have fought, but I would also ask to know those of you who are from the more distant territories. I offer you each my hand, if only for the duration of this parley, and any arrangement we may forge.'

She went around the group taking their hands one by one, pausing in particular to make the acquaintance of those she didn't know. 'Mizumi of the Pharmas,' she said, grasping the forearm of a wiry woman, with short-cropped hair and painted stripes on her face. 'I have never met one of your clan before, but it is said that all who wear the white coat have great knowledge. Perhaps you might counsel me on treatments and doses.'

'I would rather counsel than fight you,' she replied, 'but if you have biofixes as I'm told, you're already doing well.'

Alka moved on to a young man in clean blue overalls. His appearance was fresh, but he hadn't been able to remove the dirt from under his fingernails. 'You must be Scrapyard Simon. Either the reputation of your trade is unfair, or I must thank you for your effort on this occasion.' She took his hand and smiled. 'Welcome.'

'Our reputation is fairly earned,' he said. 'We wear our dirt with the pride of our work, but I wouldn't dishonour the Redeemer with it.'

Alka was about to take the group into the mall when a chorus of shouting reached them from beyond the barricade. It died down as quickly as it began and a crooked figure emerged through the gap, limping heavily as he made his way towards them, a small man maimed by battle or accident. He leaned on a stick using the only arm he had, pausing to rest with each few steps he took.

'They wanted to take my stick,' he said to Alka. 'I hope you won't think it a threat. I'm late, but it's been a long walk from the docklands.'

'You represent the Dockers?' said Chemical Mike. 'I don't know you! Where's your Trajan? Is she mocking us!'

'I am Trajan,' said the little man. 'For today, I am Trajan. I haven't been sent out of disrespect, but because of the risks.' He set his gaze at his feet. 'I'm the most expendable of our warriors.'

Alka could see Chemical Mike's colour rising. He raised his chin and took a swaggering step forward. Quickly she took the man's hand. 'What I see is the bravest of the Dockers,' she said. 'If my clan caused your injuries, I regret it.'

Trajan shook his head. 'Not your clan, but it wouldn't serve any purpose to say names. It can't be undone.'

Alka looked pointedly around the group, then back at the little man. 'Your words are an example to us. You are welcome here.'

'I may see the Redeemer?'

'And she will hear you. She'll hear any who wish it. Come!'

Alka led the group into the mall, noticing how they craned their necks in wonder at its soaring architecture and abundant foliage. They walked close together, though without hesitation, and if they had any reservations, they kept them to themselves. They stopped in front of the mosaic goddess and Alka brought them close until it towered over them. She waited for them to take in its scale and splendour, the grandest representation of their species that any human might see, then she addressed them in a hushed tone. 'This is Callista, the Redeemer. She watches us in our suffering, feels our pain, and shares our humiliation. Only with her blessing can we find our gift and become worthy of our paradise home. You may place your hands on her. She receives each of you as equals and won't judge you.'

The group shuffled forward, each paying homage in their own way, some pressing their hands to the mosaic, others kissing it, and the largest and most fearsome of them, Chemical Mike, standing with his hands clasped together and his head bowed. Some were more reticent, Trajan in particular holding back, standing apart from the others. Alka approached him cautiously. 'You don't want to touch her?'

'It's enough to see her. My heart isn't ready to believe she would show me mercy. I'm sorry.'

'Honesty requires no apology,' said Alka. 'Still, I invite you to take the sacred water with us... and to hear the news.'

'What news is that?'

Alka raised her voice to address the group. 'Trajan asks me what news I have. It is this. The Time of Times is upon us!'

'You think that elemist attack signals the Time of Times?' The voice belonged to Luca, leader of the Constructors. He had said nothing up to this point, but now he made up for it. 'If that's so, it's the wrath of the People brought down on us by your clansmen, Alka. Our destruction will be your doing.'

Chemical Mike pushed forward to confront him. 'The twins were brothers only to each other. They stole the elemist from us at the Chemical Works, so you can ...'

'Callista watches!' said Alka, raising her arms. 'I hear your grievance, Luca. If I must take responsibility for the twins' actions, then I will. If there's an account to be settled, I won't go missing.'

'It won't fall to you,' said Mizumi. 'The People will blame us all, or none.'

'We'll see. The Time of Times is not foretold as a moment of annihilation, but when Callista comes to walk amongst us. And she has! I tell you that the Redeemer has come to us in flesh, at last!'

The group erupted in an outburst of shouted questions, surged forward around Alka until she had to raise her hands again to call for quiet. 'I saw her myself, here in the plaza, as did my brothers and sisters,' she said.

Mike seized her shoulder. 'When, Alka? Tell us when this was!'

'This afternoon. She arrived in human form and reached out to me in full view of my clan. But then she was taken from us.' The group began to shout their questions again. 'She's been captured by Torsta Jai,' continued Alka. 'I couldn't rescue her, and she was dragged beneath the city, even though she called out to me for help.'

Mike groaned his anguish. 'Now our despair is complete.'

'It's a test!' called a thin voice from the back. It belonged to Trajan, who was still standing apart from the group. 'If it's true that Callista has come, she will surely set us a test. For believers, this is a trial of their devotion, and for those who waver, the moment to decide where they stand.'

'That is well said!' declared Alka. She knelt in front of the mosaic and looked up at the shining face, its halo of copper hair and the swirling red of its cape. 'Hear me please, Callista! I have witnessed your arrival and I am ready to accept your command. I pledge that I will not rest until you are free from the People. Your followers are willing to prove themselves in your service. We ask for your blessing, through the sacred waters.'

With that, she stood up, bowed once, then walked away along the boulevard to where the fountain frothed in the wan light of the giant news display. Ignoring the repeating images of Maarten Feyrsten speaking to his people, she motioned for the clan leaders to gather around the pool. Slowly, she climbed over into the fountain and turned to face them, waist-deep in the water. 'I will invite each of you in turn to enter the fountain to be anointed,' she said. 'Mike of the Chemical Clan – come forward and know the Redeemer.' Chemical Mike responded without hesitation, clambering into the pool beside her. Alka took the water in her cupped hands and poured it repeatedly over his head. 'Brother human,' she said. 'Ask, and you will receive Callista's blessing.'

Mike tried to speak but he couldn't. He was crying. Alka moved closer and spoke to him gently. 'Ask her, Mike. Just ask.'

'I… I ask… for your blessing.'

Alka raised the water once again in her hands and released it over his head. 'Look at me, Mike,' she said. 'All that has gone before is washed away. Will you accept the Redeemer?'

He nodded vigorously. 'I… I will.'

Alka turned back to the waiting group. 'Next, I call Luca of the Constructors.'

Luca began to climb into the fountain, but then he stopped and frowned. 'I'm here with an open mind, Alka. I'll accept the water, but I won't make a commitment without evidence. You're asking us to take your word…'

Suddenly, there was a collective gasp. Alka turned, to find all eyes fixed on the display. It showed a human in a hooded coat being hurried down some steps and pushed into a ministerial transport. For just a moment, she looked directly at the imager and it captured her face, the hair, the crimson coat, the penetrant eyes.

A clamour erupted around the fountain, the cries of clan leaders echoing through the mall as they threw themselves into the water, splashing, and throwing it high into the air. Alka waited for the disturbance to subside. She stood under the cascading water, with her face raised to the vaulted roof, and when she could sense that attention had returned to her, she looked again at Luca.

'Are you ready now, to receive her blessing?' she said.

When they were all anointed, Alka led them out of the fountain. She had placed a pile of clean white towels on the steps to the annex and handed one to each of them. Then as they dried themselves, she went amongst them handing out boxes of biofixes. 'Let this be the first of Callista's mercies,' she said. 'It's for Clearwater Fever. We'll need to be at full strength for what lies ahead. Now, come with me to talk under the Great Tree in our transept. We must decide how to fulfil our pledge.'

The atmosphere between them had transformed. Alka was sure they could all feel it as she did. There were no longer any voices of dissent, the shared ritual and the sight of Callista, alive and at the mercy of the People had bound them together at last. Now, there was hope when before there had only been doubt, there was meaning where there had been confusion, and in place of suffering had come the prospect of deliverance.

'You interviewed well,' said Henik. 'Serious, composed, just what the situation required.' It was no idle compliment; it was what he really thought. Santi's interview was exactly what the

Progress Party needed, a new leader who was fortunate not to be amongst the dead, but was thinking of the victims, and considering the national interest.

Santi came over to him at the window and they watched the reporters walk off up the street, heads bowed to a thin rain. 'That's generous,' she said, 'It was no more than adequate, in my view.'

'Reaching out to victims' families from your home, urging people not to give in to hating, asking them to…'

'Please stop, Henik.' Santi closed her eyes and stood quite still for a moment. 'I know you mean well, but I'm not looking for reassurance. Not now, anyway. I just need to gather my thoughts.' She took his hand for a moment, then let it go. 'One practical point to start with is that you'll have to go out the back way, now that I'm leader. You can stay until they lift the security cordon at Carnival Square, but you'll have to go back to your place as soon as you can. I can't have the media figuring out we're together.'

'Are we… *together*?'

Santi shot him a glance. It felt businesslike, rather than intimate. 'Now isn't the time for anything that would be called a distraction.'

He watched her as the lights from the street shifted over the contours of her face, an advertising drone moving past the house bathing it in colour. She stared out, immediately adrift in her thoughts, breath misting the verglas. How many times had she stood there wrestling with the problems of government, choosing the comfort of her private rooms over the office. The surroundings here were hers and hers alone, but they told a story, and it wasn't an intimate one. The residence was elegant, kept to an immaculate standard, the fabrics crisp and tidy, the flowers fresh, the ornaments tasteful. It resembled a diplomatic suite, and not because Santi spent her time maintaining it, but precisely because she couldn't. A Counsellor of State had someone to manage the mundane concerns of daily life, an android service for the cleaning, probably a valet as well, certainly a provisioning manager; everything would be taken care of so that she didn't need to concern herself with mundane things. Santi didn't so much live in her house, as inhabit it.

She was right about the two of them. He would have to keep a low profile. With his radical views, he was a hazard and in times of crisis, reputations were fragile things. He wondered if this was how it would always be if they were together, whether it could be any other way. *Don't ask – just don't. Be content that you are fellow travellers again. Wherever you are going.*

'There will still be people dying in the clinics this evening,' Santi said, without turning from the window. 'For some, it will take all night.' She folded her arms as if she was suddenly cold. 'Vish is dead.'

'You don't know that.'

'He would have returned my call by now. He was sitting where we usually did, the table where you saw me the other day. No one sitting at that table could have survived.' She took a deep breath. 'I've called a meeting in the morning. I'll be allocating shadow portfolios.'

'The key one will be Human Affairs now. You'll need to choose the right person.'

'Do you want it?'

'Want what?'

'Do you want to take on Norvik on Human Affairs?'

'Seriously? We wouldn't last a day if you were my boss. No, definitely not.'

'I knew you'd say that, but I had to ask.'

'So I wouldn't be offended when you chose someone else?'

'Because I should put the interests of the Free Republic first, and you would be the best choice.'

'I would be a liability, and you know it.'

'How about Widdig Terreden? Do you know him?'

'I've had some dealings with The Human Policy Institute. He's a bit odd, but he knows the subject and understands the need for reform.'

'He was on the Georgi Factor with me the other night. I'm going to approach him tomorrow.' Santi put her hand on Henik's leg, but there was no intimacy to her touch. 'Would you at least consider working with him as an external adviser?'

It was more a statement of expectation than a question. Santi got up, straightened her tunic then moved briskly to her desk. Her hands went to work on its surface, planning, issuing communiqués, making arrangements for the morning. *Busy, focused, occupied. An island of competence.* After a while, she glanced up at him without lifting her chin, the way she might when a member of staff sat in front of her. 'I'm afraid, I won't be good company this evening,' she said, the send-off a gentle one, but a dismissal, all the same. 'In fact, I think I'll be working most of the night.'

'What about Kali?' said Henik, deciding to resist a little longer. 'Where's your thinking now on the abduction?'

There was a hint of frustration in her reply. 'I understand the importance, Henik but I have other matters on my plate as well. I've left a message for Torsta Jai, so she knows she was seen abducting Kali. That will improve Yan Feyrsten's chances of seeing her again, but he needs to…'

'You know that Kali could be useful if you want to set your own agenda. Have you thought about that? What if she could influence the feral clans?'

'Careful what you wish for.'

Henik felt a call coming through. 'Yan's here,' he said. 'You might want to hear what he has to say.' When his host materialised, there were waves crashing behind it in the twilight, and a barely visible line of foam.

'You're still at the beach house,' said Henik. 'Perhaps it would be better…'

'Where are you?' interrupted Yan. 'Have you seen the news?'

'The explosion. How could anyone miss…'

'Those bastards at the Department have got Kali! I can't believe they're trying to tie her to the terrorist attack. It's insane!'

'Just hold… Let me find it. I'm with Santi Aspil, by the way.'

'Please tell me she can help.'

Santi came out from behind her desk. 'Hello, Professor Feyrsten. I wish we could be introduced in different circumstances. Henik's explained what's happened and I'll do all I can.'

'Thank you, esteemed.'

'Santi.'

'I'm sure Henik will have said how important Kali is, but to me… well, she's become very dear to me.'

'I have the story now,' said Henik. 'Kali's been taken away in an official transport. Speculation is that she's a suspect. She was in the Department for the Interior this afternoon.'

'What's Norvik saying?' asked Santi.

'Refusing to comment. What does that mean?'

'It means they're considering their options.'

'Surely, they don't really suspect her, do they?' asked Yan.

'Well, that depends on what Torsta's told them,' Santi

said. 'If she was at the Department on a day like today it means Norvik considered it very important. There's no advantage to them if they rule Kali out of the enquiry at this stage, and it occupies the media for a while.'

Yan kicked at the sand. 'Where do you think they will take her?'

'The official limousine suggests some sort of deal with Torsta. It tells us they know Kali's value, perhaps that she's a natural. I'm speculating, of course, but I think that should keep her safe. At least for a while.'

Yan turned away from them, looked across the bay to where the Derelict Zone lay in darkness. When he spoke, his voice had become unsteady. 'On the other hand,' he said, clearing his throat, 'it could seal her fate.'

Santi recognised the view behind Sig Norvik immediately. It was familiar to her in all its detail, day or night, and whatever the weather. She could still hear the room in her head too, the furniture configuring to her command, the gentle hush of the verglas responding to the light, the hide of the chair flexing with a reassuring creak of antiquity.

'Well, this makes a change,' Norvik said. 'Late in the evening and I'm still in the office, while you're at home.'

'Still working though. I won't keep you long, Counsellor. I'm sure it's been an awful day, particularly when you're new in the role. Belated congratulations by the way.'

'Thank you, and I should also thank you for vacating so efficiently. I gather congratulations are in order on your side as well.'

'Thank you, but there can be no congratulations after an election defeat. I hope you'll find that out next time around.

In the meantime, I'm sure we'll have plenty to debate. Have you decided when to announce your new policy initiatives?'

Norvik leaned back, looking far too comfortable in her old chair. 'Soon. However, we're already one senior person down from your former team, which is unfortunate.'

'Vish. If he hadn't resigned, he'd still be alive.'

'I'm sorry, I... Don't tell me he was in the café!'

'I was there with him until shortly before the explosion.'

Norvik swivelled gently in his chair. 'I'm very sorry,' he said after a while.

'I worry there will be more casualties if you go ahead with your plans. Particularly if there isn't a proper consultation. I'm thinking major social upheaval, particularly after today's events. You're the one making the decisions now, but I'll be vocal in my opposition.'

'I'd say what happened today vindicates my position. We need to act firmly on this issue, and I'm sure the public agrees. You may be experienced in Government, but when it comes to humans, I do consider myself the expert.'

'And what was your expert opinion of Kali?'

Norvik regarded her for a while before he replied. He might not have expected to hear the name from her lips, but he didn't seem particularly surprised either. 'Quite interesting,' he said. 'So, I take it this is the reason for your call – the news report.'

'I think you know how significant that human is. I think you also know she was abducted from right outside her owner's house this morning. Professor Feyrsten was injured in the process.'

'That's not my understanding of the circumstances. And we believe there's reasonable cause for her to be held, whatever her owner might think.'

'I doubt that. But I'll be expecting to see due process followed as far as her detention is concerned, so you'll be hearing from me on that. I also saw that you reserved your position when asked if she was involved in the bombing.'

Norvik slumped further into his chair. 'Take it that way if you wish, but...'

'Counsellor, you know that's exactly what your refusal to comment was doing. You also know that Kali wasn't involved in that atrocity. We can prove she was in the custody of Torsta Jai when that bomb exploded. So, be in no doubt that we'll be watching this closely.'

'Duly noted,' said Norvik, his voice finding a harder edge. 'And that will be all you can do now you're no longer in office.'

13

Juno

KALI HAD BARELY SLEPT. It was warm enough in Jocasta's cellar, and there was a mattress, but there was no way for her mind to find rest. She couldn't determine what time of day it was, but her stomach was grumbling so she thought that morning had probably come. She permitted herself a short conversation with Mr. Dunstone, then got to her feet and did what she could to tidy herself, so she could face the day with as much composure as possible.

There were scuffing steps coming down from above. They approached along the corridor and paused. Then after a few moments, the door slid back and Juno came in with a cup and bowl. When they had met before it had felt as if he harboured some resentment towards her, but now he was on his own, it seemed even more obvious. His face was set rigid, and he had decided not to even look at her. Instead, he walked across the room sedately, knelt, and placed her breakfast on the stone floor with both hands. The bowl spoke for him, sounding hollow and cold as it came into contact with the flagstones. He stood up and edged away towards the door, not even trusting her enough to turn his back.

'Thank you, Juno,' said Kali. 'Won't you stay and talk to me?'

Juno hesitated, but still he wouldn't make eye contact. Perhaps it was the language, Kali thought, perhaps like Dill he would know something of Spanish. She tried the question again to no avail, tried a few other languages. Nothing seemed to work. Nothing brought Juno closer. At least he was no longer retreating. He stood quite still, grimaced as if her words were resonating inside his brittle shell, even if he didn't understand them.

'Won't you speak to me?' she said, returning to her own tongue. 'Or even look at me? Am I really that *offensive* to you?'

Juno's head snapped up and he stared at her. He shook his head quickly and took a step forward.

'You *do* understand! Then what is it?'

Juno dropped his chin again, glanced back at the open door.

'What is it, Juno? Please tell me. Please!'

'I… I am ashamed.'

'Ashamed? Why, for goodness' sake?'

Suddenly Juno threw himself on the floor, pressing his head to the stones. 'Forgive me, Callista! I cannot set you free or make you comfortable. I have *failed* you!'

'What? What are you saying?'

'You have come so far to show us the way home, and we have waited so long. Now I can do nothing for you, except spread the word to your followers.'

'Followers? But I don't understand! Please, Juno – get up!'

'Please take my devotion, Callista. It's all I have to give you.'

Kali was speechless. She tried to reach forward to raise Juno up, but was held back by the row of bars, immaterial but hard and cold as iron against her face 'Please, don't! Don't say...'

A shriek from the doorway broke Juno's reverence. He scrambled to his feet as Jocasta strode into the room. 'Juno! Juno! What are you doing, you little shit! You think she's something to worship, do you?' She grabbed him by the scruff of the neck and threw him against the wall. 'You give me a pathetic bow, then throw yourself at the feet of another animal? Do you think she's better than your mistress? Do you?' She slapped Juno's face, knocking him to the ground, then dragged him back to his feet and slapped him again. He didn't cry out though. Each blow he took in silence, each act of violence bringing a defiant stare in response.

Kali could bear it no longer. 'No!' she shouted. 'Stop, Jocasta! Not be hitting!'

Jocasta spun around and lunged at her. 'Give me commands, will you?' She tried to reach her through the bars then screamed her frustration. 'Torsta! Torstaaaa! Where are those fucking keys! It's time this human found out what's natural on *this* planet!'

Juno dragged himself off the floor and launched himself at Jocasta, trying to pull her away. Now her rage reached even greater heights. She seized him by the throat and ripped off his jacket, then with a flick of her hand across a panel on the wall, the bracelets around his wrists began to rise towards the ceiling, lifting him onto his toes, then higher until he was suspended by his bonds in the middle of the chamber. She seized a rod-like device from a hook behind the door and it sprung into life in her hand, beams of light curling from it like serpents. She took a whistling practice stroke as she positioned herself to deliver the beating, the light beams snaking across the room, to knock over a stool in the corner.

Juno took the first strikes with barely a whimper, but soon he began to scream pitifully when the beams cracked against his body. Jocasta wiped her forehead with her sleeve. 'You want this to stop? Oh yes, it will stop when I hear you curse this little bitch! Call her a dirty feral! Say you don't give a shit about her. Spit at her – that's what I want!' She started thrashing Juno again, grunting with the effort as she sent the beams singing through the air to carve bloody lines into his flesh.

Now Juno screamed with purpose, his voice echoing hideously around the chamber. Kali was screaming too. 'Say it, Juno! Tell her what she wants to hear! She reached out to him through the bars, clasped her hands together and begged. 'Please, Juno! I don't want this – I don't!'

'Spit on her! Curse her!' roared Jocasta, lashing at Juno with even greater venom. The beams had gouged deep channels into his back and in her frenzy, Jocasta had inflicted grisly wounds to his head as well. His voice was weakening, but still he refused to yield. 'Callista!' he gasped, 'This is for you! For you!'

Suddenly Jocasta was being pulled away. Torsta Jai had her around the waist and pulled the whip from her hand. She released Juno's bonds with a sweep of her hand and wrestled Jocasta to the door. 'Get a hold of yourself!' she shouted. 'You're drunk! You're going to kill him, if you haven't already.'

Jocasta struggled to free herself, flailing with her fists as she was dragged away. 'This is none of your affair, Torsta!' she snarled. 'The little shit was worshipping her! I'll have the hide off him. I'll beat the…' She locked her eyes on Kali as she was pulled through the door. 'This is your doing!' she shrieked. 'Do you see what you've made me do?'

The door slammed shut and the shouting died away. Kali found herself kneeling on the floor, her chest heaving. Only a few feet away Juno lay on the flagstones, blood pooling around him. From the edge of consciousness, his eyes still watched her, but there was nothing left in him. 'Oh, Juno!' she said. 'Why did you do that? Why wouldn't you save yourself?' A faint smile crept across his face, but there was no strength left to speak. *He can't die because of me – he just can't! This makes no sense at all!*

She looked at his fading eyes and struggled for something to say. Then slowly the words came to her, the words and the notes, from a happier time and from impossibly far away. She sang softly at first, hesitantly, her voice catching on every phrase, but then somehow the melody began to fortify her, and she let her voice rise and give the tune life, a sweet song from her youth, a ballad of bluebirds and rainbows.

Juno managed a faint smile, and he stared silently at Kali until the last words of the song rang out. He croaked something and she leaned forward to hear it until her face was pressed against the bars. 'You brought it,' Juno whispered. 'You brought our gift.'

Santi shrugged off her jacket and fell onto the couch beside Henik. 'Done,' she said.

'How did it go?'

'Just give me a moment.' She lay quietly for a while, her breathing slowing, until her chest rose and fell in a steady rhythm. Just when Henik thought she had fallen asleep, she spoke.

'Never easy to push people out when they've given long service.'

'You turned your feed off. You've been out of contact all day. That's not like you.'

'How would *you* know,' she said, under her breath. Henik wondered whether she would go further with her rebuke, but either she regretted it, or considered it sufficient. 'Anyway, I'm pleased with the way it went – new faces, new talent. Widdig had plenty of questions, of course. What resources he'd have to fight Norvik. Whether we're of a similar mind on humans – which we are.'

'And what *is* that exactly?'

'Hmm... good question. We won't need details for a while, but we need to know where we're headed. At the moment, it's simply opposing Norvik's reforms – the implanting programme and Torsta's task force in particular.'

'Did you see the way he made the announcement?'

'Haven't had a chance,' said Santi. She took her boots off and massaged her toes. 'I imagine he made a show of it.'

'He was out in Carnival Square talking to the forensic team at the Café Republic. He got the emergency workers together and took the opportunity to reassure them that he would be taking firm action.'

'So, the suggestion is that the reforms are a response to the explosion when they're nothing of the sort. Vish told me what he had in mind yesterday, before ...' Santi paused, closed her eyes for a moment, before continuing. 'Norvik is setting it up so the reforms are a national mission, something noble.'

'How are you going to reply?'

'Carefully. We mustn't look unpatriotic. For the most part, Norvik's appealing to those at the margins. It's the old trick of giving them people to blame.'

'People?'

'You know what I mean. In this case it's humans. Somehow, we've got to emphasise fair-mindedness as our core value.'

'When the mood on the street is justice by hovercrane?'

Santi shuddered. 'I know. How thin is the veneer of civilisation?'

'And sending a task force into the Derelict Zone will only give us more gruesome scenes. Torsta will be popular with hardliners, with her badass reputation.'

'She wasn't like that when I knew her. She was tough, but she always listened. You could reason with her.'

'You were her boss, Santi.'

'But I never sensed a preoccupation with ferals, or any particular concern she had about humans. We had other law and order issues of course, and the ferals hadn't become quite such a problem so perhaps I just didn't see it in her.'

'Times change, people change, particularly if they've lost their career. And if they've been banged up on a fifty-deck incarceration vessel. We can only imagine what...'

'I don't need to imagine, Henik. I've visited *Bleak Penance*. I had responsibility for it, all those thousands of cold metal boxes.'

'Was Torsta there at the time?'

'She'd been there a nearly a year when I went. I decided it was enough. In my experience, adversity rarely changes us for the better. Mostly, it just makes us more like we really are.'

'Interesting thought. What should that mean for the way we treat humans? What does it say about us that there are clinics about to open for implanting behaviour modules. Intelligent torture devices, would be a better description. I expect there will be a lot of demand. People will just want to ensure their human stays within the law, rather than taking responsibility for managing it themselves.'

'Perhaps, but people are genuinely worried. Some are

scared for their pets, but others scared *of* them. There's already been a spike in abandonments since the revolt in the Spice Islands, so the feral population is growing by the day.'

'You know, they tried implants in the Spice Islands last year. It was horrendous. Humans started cutting the devices from their spines themselves. Many died in the process.'

'There has to be a way to de-escalate the crisis,' said Santi. 'That has to be the policy. But it's a complex situation: revolution abroad, unrest at home, terrorism. And now there's Kali.'

'How do you think she fits into the equation?' asked Henik. It was the question that had been occupying him since the day he had met her, making him excited and concerned in the same measure. It followed him to bed each evening, then came to his mind again at daybreak, a question that lifted his spirits one moment, churned his stomach the next. And as events had unfolded the question had got no easier to fathom, the knot tighter and ever more difficult to pick apart.

Not so for Santi. Perhaps the politics focused her mind, forced her to set aside the philosophical and concentrate on what was clear and present, but when she responded, there was no hedging in her answer. 'Kali *doesn't* fit into the equation,' she said. 'She creates a new one. Depending on your perspective, she's either the most important human on the planet… or the most dangerous.'

Alka found Chemical Mike sitting in front of the mosaic. He was clutching the white pillowcase and didn't notice her until she squatted down beside him. 'Now, you feel her,' she said.

He dragged his eyes from the image of Callista, but only for a moment. 'I must go back to the chemical works,' he said.

'But I don't know if I can lead my clan anymore. Not against other humans.'

'We have a common enemy now.'

'I'm finished with killing. I can't do it anymore.'

'Is that what she says to you?'

'I'm not sure if it's Callista telling me, but it's still true. What lies ahead though… There will be blood.'

Alka sat down on the floor next to him. 'There's more than one way to fight,' she said. 'When we gathered in the transept under the Great Tree, the things you said moved hearts. Perhaps *that's* your calling now. Perhaps Callista wants you to bring others to her.'

He turned to look at her, his face open and innocent, despite its tattoos. 'Do you really think so?'

'I know there are other ways to live a life. But first, we must fight for ourselves, and for Callista. Not all of us will live, but if we hold to our plan...'

'You spoke well last night. Did Callista tell you what to say?'

'I felt her presence in the Great Tree. I saw its branches move and remembered my time in the wild places. How the strong boughs fell in the storm, but those that flexed, that dodged the wind…'

'I worry about your plan. To evade the People there must be somewhere for us all to go. We're held between the city and the sea. The People already have us in their jaws.'

'We know this place, we know how to keep moving, how to delay and frustrate them. She stared up at the haunting face of the mosaic. 'But I fear what they'll do with Callista, what use they may have for her.'

'You think the Redeemer is known to them?'

'They will know, soon enough. They are angered by the

explosion. They will say she caused it, that she has started a war.'

'Then why must we *delay*, Alka?'

'Because there are those amongst the People who will argue on our behalf.'

'The clans agreed to wait for your signal, but they won't wait for long.'

'We'll know soon enough. They will release Callista, or they'll send their army against us and find they are grasping at air.'

'But how will that be? *When* will that be?'

'We will be told. Just be patient and be ready. Take that message with you, Mike.'

They sat watching the mosaic, its expression changing subtly as clouds moved over the vaulted canopy. The water in the fountain trickled loud and hollow, and somewhere out on the distant hillside, a bushdorg howled.

'What did you think of the clans,' said Alka. Who of the leaders impressed you?'

'Trajan turned out to be wise. I misjudged him. He wasn't what I expected of a Docker.'

'I hope he's done enough for them to listen to him. I'm worried the Dockers won't follow the plan. And if they launch an attack...'

'You gave him biofixes to take back. They may give him influence.'

Alka got up, her token buzzing in her pocket as she did so. She took it out, expecting to see a pod arriving at Midsummer Station, Santi Aspil perhaps. Instead, the lights were showing something different. There was someone much closer with a token.

'I've got one of those,' said Mike as he struggled to his

feet. 'We all have them. Mine doesn't work much these days, but my brothers think they bring good luck.'

'Your whole clan have them? Where did you get them?'

'Before I went to the Chemical Works, I stayed in an abandoned pod station for a while. There was no food there so I moved on, but I found a store of those tokens so I could come and go if I needed to.'

'Your passes are still *valid?* They still let you inside a pod station?'

'You wouldn't want to go in there. They're barren places, there's nothing…'

Alka grabbed him by the shoulders. '*This* is our answer, Mike! Don't you understand? Callista is working through you! She's showing us the way!'

Kali looked at the door of the limousine as it edged away from the Feyrstens' mansion. There was a blue light embedded in the glass, and she wondered whether that meant it was unlocked. She was considering whether to attempt an escape once the transport had passed through the gates. Then beside her, Torsta made a slight sucking sound, and the light turned to orange.

Outside, the newly watered gardens were sparkling in the morning solus. There were a few humans tending the borders, picking up dead leaves with their hands. To start with they didn't seem to notice the limousine gliding by, but then as the gateway approached, they stopped working and stood to attention. A white-haired man stood shielded from the house by a tree. He looked directly at Kali's window, dropped stiffly to one knee as she passed, and held his hand to his chest.

They swept through the gate, making a turn back towards

the city, the limousine gathering speed until the countryside streaked by outside. For a while, it reminded her of England, the trees bending over the roads and the fields laden with crops. Kali turned to look at Torsta. Her expression was unreadable, but her chest was rising and falling at a rate that suggested she was anything but relaxed.

'Juno,' she said. 'He be dead?'

It seemed a very long time before Torsta answered. 'Yes,' she said simply, then looked away.

'Is not well done. Jocasta be…'

'I know. I know all about her.'

'Good we do leave. Where we go, Torsta Jai?'

Torsta drew a breath, between her teeth. There was slightly more colour to her forehead than before. She rubbed its ridges with her fingertips, as if something was stirring uncomfortably in her head. Suddenly she turned and looked at Kali directly. 'Why did Juno think you were special?' she said. 'Why did Jocasta see him on his knees?'

'Not know that.'

'And why were those humans in the garden honouring you?'

Kali shook her head. 'Not know.' The same questions were troubling her as well, the sense that she was at the centre of something, some truth that had been revealed to those around her but lay beyond her reach. Juno's words came back to her in stabbing phrases, still failing to order themselves into anything rational. *What followers? What gift? What did he mean?* The limousine had paused to hover at a control point. Outside, transports were coming and going in all directions, and giant people were strolling by, some of them accompanied by humans. Some of the humans had worn expressions, walked with their gaze fixed on the ground, but others seemed content with their place in this world, a life framed, controlled, restricted by their owner. She thought of Juno again, lying on the cellar floor, his flesh shredded and bleeding.

'Not know,' she repeated. 'I be Kali only. Friend with Yan Feyrsten.'

Torsta Jai said something to the driver in a stream of faint cranial clicks, and the limousine rose out of the traffic and onto a higher route. 'Friend,' she muttered. Then, suddenly, the frustration came bursting out of her. 'You're not his *friend!* Don't you get it? You're his human, his *property!* I don't give a shit if you're from Earth. I don't give a shit what humans might think! Just stop trying to be a *person!*'

'Why? Why be not person?'

'Oh, for fuck's sake! You can't grasp that the Free Republic could tear itself to pieces over this. I've seen it before on other worlds, what happens when things get out of hand, how everything comes crashing down.'

'You angry, Torsta. Not understand. Not understand this words.'

'No, you *don't* understand. *Of course*, you don't understand! And will you stop using my name!'

Torsta turned back to the window, and Kali found she was observing her more closely than before. She watched the way she held her limbs so they were relaxed, yet at the same time poised for action, how her face remained still, almost serene, even when her words came in a torrent. Kali reflected on what Torsta had said, the fragments she had understood and the tone. The confusion was plain; she could sense in her a collision of beliefs, a brittle desire to take refuge in accepted wisdom.

Outside, the sky was doing strange things above the city, as if it had attracted its own weather system of mountainous lilac clouds, billowing and boiling, working themselves into a frenzy. Torsta craned her neck and watched them impassively. 'It's nothing,' she said, without turning her head.

There were grand buildings rising on either side of the transport now, their architecture a confusion of lines and surfaces that appeared to flex and change as they passed. Some of them were connected to each other high in the air, and others were accepting flying craft into lofty hangars, or allowing them to pass straight through. To Kali they seemed almost alive, and some of them actually were, verdant towers of vegetation tended by a flock of hovering machines. Up ahead loomed a forbidding building with dark sides that curved and curled. Kali wondered if it had been constructed somehow from a single sheet of reflective material. There were no joins or edges and no obvious signage either, but it identified itself all the same, the word 'Police' appearing in the corner of her vision, however, she turned her head and from whatever angle she viewed it. The limousine swung onto a route that took it around the building, and by the time they had made almost a complete circuit it was clear that it was their destination, the limousine banking into a sharp turn towards one of its billowing walls. Just as it seemed that a collision was inevitable, the building parted like a drawn curtain, and they descended into its bowels.

Darkness fell upon them and Kali felt her spirits drop like a bucket in a well, a sudden sense of dread that she was entering a place from which she would never emerge, a place where there would be no light, no hope. She closed her eyes and breathed deeply, imagining herself sitting on a park bench with Mr. Dunstone, throwing bread to the sparrows. 'You do tell Yan, I not be dead?' she said. 'Please, you do tell Yan?'

Torsta looked away, sat a little more erect. 'Please, Torsta Jai,' Kali said. 'You not be bad person.'

The transport glided to a halt and Torsta opened the

door. She remained in her seat though, stared absently for a moment. 'Tell him yourself,' she said. 'You're at Police Headquarters. Make it quick. Look into my eyes, speak your message, and I will send it to him.' Then she added in a barely audible voice, 'I promise.'

Henik found Yan at the end of his garden, draping some children's clothing over the branch of a fruit tree. The bushes behind were stirring, and as he approached, he caught a glimpse of Dill's weathered face peering out between the branches.

'Clothes for Dill?' he asked.

'Well, if it made Kali happy. Dill's missing her too. I saw her on the terrace earlier, looking in at the windows.'

'That's confident.'

'She left Kali a present. Just some fruit, but she'd arranged it in a lizin's nest.' Yan spread the last piece of clothing on the ground, a bright yellow shawl, with pictures of exotic creatures. He stood back and folded his arms. 'I can't focus on anything. Kali's all I think about.'

'We'll get her back,' said Henik. 'Santi has spoken to Norvik, so he knows she's onto him. And she's looking into the legalities of it. I'm on my way to see her new appointment for Human Affairs, so I'll get his support as well. It will work out.' He reached out to place his hand on Yan's shoulder, but he stepped away, made a needless adjustment to a rainproof jacket he'd hung on a tarberry bush. 'Did you come back from the beach last night?' he asked.

Yan started to walk up towards the house. 'This morning. I arrived to find Jocasta's host exploring my kitchen.'

'Rude.'

'We argued about Kali. It wasn't a nice experience.'

'What did she say?'

'She'd seen Kali. She claimed Kali got Juno to attack her. She was drunk of course, and angry. So am I… well, not drunk.'

'Of course, you're angry. It's a ridiculous story.'

'Actually, it's you I'm annoyed with, Henik.'

'*Me?* Surely you don't blame *me* for what happened.'

'You haven't been telling me the whole truth about Kali, have you? Jocasta says the police have her in custody and that she's some sort of sorceress. She saw Juno kneeling in front of Kali, completely in her power, and then he just turned on her. She heard Kali directing him with strange noises.'

'Well, I suppose she's got both of us under her spell.'

'I'm being serious, Henik! There's something here that I don't understand, and you're an expert on humans. So, is Jocasta right? The media is already suggesting Kali had an influence on what happened yesterday at the Café Republic. Is she something different to what we think?'

'Listen to me, Yan. You're struggling to make sense of Kali's abduction, but let's not get carried away here. There's no such thing as…'

'I've heard there are species that have natural hypnotic capabilities. Just *tell* me, Henik! If you want me to think rationally about this, then you've got to tell me! Is there something else about Kali? Is there?'

'Yes. Alright – yes! I noticed something a couple of days ago, but I didn't want to worry you.'

'Shit! I just knew it!'

'There's a giant mural in Midsummer Mall. It's a mosaic of a human female, a legendary figure, called Callista.'

'I vaguely remember the fable from…'

'Well, Kali looks exactly like it. I mean *exactly*. Hair, face, eyes – it's like she was the model for the piece.'

Yan lowered himself onto the mossy steps that led up to the house, his back curving wearily. 'So, she looks like a mural. You're a scientist, but now you're going all mystic yourself.'

'Things that aren't real can still affect reality, or at least a belief in them can. The Callista legend, the prophecy, seems to be very real for feral humans. They see her as someone who will come to rescue them. And then they saw Kali being dragged into Midsummer pod station, yesterday morning.'

'Oh, that's just great – that's really going to help. So, they think Kali is their goddess.' Yan buried his face in his hands, groaned quietly. 'Do you think Kali understands any of this?'

'Why would she? It's an Antarian legend. But whether she knows it or not, she's an icon to the ferals now. And it's at a time when two of them have bombed Carnival Square, and the state seems determined to clear out the whole lot of them.'

'But it's not just the ferals,' said Yan. 'It sounds as though Juno recognised her as Callista too. That must be why he was kneeling in front of her.'

'Perhaps we could speak to him, try to understand what happened.'

'He's been destroyed.'

'Already? She wasted no time there.' Henik looked back down the garden. Dill had come out of the bushes and was creeping around the clothes, touching them delicately with her fingertips. She snatched up a purple shift and ran out of sight with it. 'You say Jocasta heard Kali making noises. I bet it wasn't any more than what we heard her doing with Dill.'

'Let's go inside', said Yan. 'I want to show you something.' He led Henik up the steps and into his study, where a recording of Juno was running on his desk. 'This is what I witnessed yesterday at my brother's house. It struck me as unusual, so I kept a record. Juno was in the garden talking to another human. Look at the language of his body. Don't you think he seems eager to convey something?'

'Such as?'

'Perhaps he overheard me talking to Jocasta about Kali's abduction. Perhaps he understood. Perhaps they all do. Juno wasn't just the docile pet that I thought. He interacted assertively with other humans. It just went unnoticed.'

Henik came closer to the desk. 'Replay it,' he said. 'Let me see the faces.' He waited until the recording caught the face of the other human in the garden. 'Look at the physical responses Juno is getting, the facial expressions. It suggests that each of them has a recognition of the independent mind of the other. I've seen this in ferals before, but I thought that breeders selected it out for domestics. This tells me that some of them, many perhaps, are disguising more advanced cognition to fit what's expected of them. Clearly, I haven't been paying enough attention to domestic humans.'

'What does this mean for Kali?'

Henik closed his eyes tightly, tried to bring the new information into some order. 'Well, it suggests that Juno may have spoken about her to other humans on your brother's estate. And presumably, they talk to their neighbours as well.'

'What about the picture of her on the news last night?' said Yan. 'There are bound to be humans who saw that and know the Callista legend. We must assume that word of her will be travelling between humans.'

Henik leaned over the desk, watched the recording of Juno again, the set of his jaw, the sharp movements of his hands. 'If the news is that their goddess has come, it won't just be travelling, it will be spreading like wildfire.'

14

Sabie

TORSTA REMEMBERED THE CELLS at the Police Headquarters all too well. She'd been held there the previous year, far removed from her office on the top floor, a situation as embarrassing for her officers as it was for her. The enclosures were only for the temporary housing of prisoners, which was just as well, considering the decrepit state of them, with the wall coating peeling off and the bedding worn and stained. And then there was the smell of disinfectant, penetrating your head, clinging to your clothes, following you even after you'd left the building.

On this occasion though, the cells seemed more than adequate; you only had to step down to the underground level, where the humans were held, to appreciate that. No natural light penetrated this dungeon, and there was no disinfectant either. Instead, the smell was of animals, the rank odour of their bodies and waste. The basement was divided into pens, stacked on top of each other and open at one end, with virtual bars that flickered enough to be more or less visible. There were both pets and ferals there, some off-world creatures Torsta couldn't name, but mostly human males. They came to the front of their pens as she led Kali past, babbling nonsensically and using their genitals to make their intentions clear. Kali seemed to shrink. She pulled up her hood and kept her eyes on the floor until they reached a pen in the far corner.

'Right, here we are!' said the keeper, a strongly built woman with a bright manner. 'I've given her a pen as far away from the others as possible. It can be disturbing for females to hear the males calling out to them like that. If she's going to be examined about the explosion, you'll need her to be calm and stable.'

She opened the front of the pen and took Kali inside. 'Well, I'm sure you have a lot to do,' she said. 'She'll be fine with me, esteemed. don't worry.'

'Why would I worry?' said Torsta. She turned on her heels and walked away without looking back. As she rounded the row of pens and headed for the door, Kali's voice rang out, cutting cleanly through the fetid air.

'Good bye, Torsta Jai!'

She stopped. A few feet from her face, a naked male was urinating in the corner of his pen. He pointed the stream at her and giggled as it fizzed against the bars. The keeper was talking to Kali now, her voice soft and low. 'Now then, let's get you settled in here,' she said. 'My, look at that hair! Now, here's the grating in the corner, and I've put down some old matting by the wall. Let's have a look at you. You're healthy enough, I'd say. Prettier than my Midge, at home. I've heard a lot about you, I have. Come on now, no tears – I'll look after you.'

For a moment, Torsta considered going back, but to what end she wasn't sure. There was nothing to say that could explain why things were as they were, and nothing that needed to be said about it to a human anyway. But still, there was the impulse to do so, if only because it would be something Jocasta wouldn't ever contemplate. She stood listening until an argument between two inmates nearby drowned out the officer's voice. Then she turned and went back up to the cells, the disinfectant now smelling fragrant when she opened the door.

She took the stairs to the top floor and was escorted by a young cadet to the office of the Chief of Police. There was no warmth in Egil Kray's greeting. The sheer size of his frame was intimidating even when he was in good spirits, but today the Feral Task Force initiative was causing everyone to stay well clear of him.

'Fuckwit idea!' he fumed. 'I decided day one, that Norvik's a bloody fool.'

'I suggested the task force,' said Torsta. 'It was my idea.'

Kray rested his giant hands across his stomach and rocked back in his chair. Somewhere underneath, its workings protested at the strain. 'Explain. You wouldn't have stood for it when you were sitting here. You'd have found someone to punch. Ah, but in the end, you did that, didn't you?'

'Cheap shot.'

Kray laughed half-heartedly. 'I suppose the idea suits your purposes, Torsta. It gets you back in, even if it screws up later. And don't try giving me some bullshit about the need for a rapid action force outside the chain of command because…'

'Neither of us would believe it.'

Kray regarded her warily. 'No, we wouldn't.'

'As you say, I wanted back in and that's what I've got. Sig Norvik liked the idea, and you won't. It is what it is.'

'And you don't give a shit.'

Torsta looked him in the eye. 'And I don't give a shit.'

'Alright then. We both know where each other stands,

and I haven't got much choice in the matter. I won't stand in your way, Torsta. We're in the middle of a major crisis and I've got better things to do than play games with you. You'll have your Task Force assembled by the end of the day. I won't give you my drop-outs, but they won't be the best I've got by any means.'

'That's fair enough.'

'Yes, it is. You go after the ferals your way if you must. But if you screw up, expect me to put the boot in. I won't have your failure sticking to my department.'

Torsta got up to leave but stopped at the doorway. 'Egil, whether you come through this crisis shining, or covered with shit is a matter of indifference to me. But if you think it's just about an elemist explosion and some hovercrane vigilantes, you have your head up your arse.' She watched Kray's ridges turn an intense shade of red, then walked away before he could bellow his response.

She found the temporary space she'd been allocated two floors down. It was in an alcove behind one of the administrative sections, data or community outreach, something undangerous. It was a corner where all manner of junk was being stored, the desk heaped with unwanted supplies and devices. The message that Torsta was unwelcome in the building couldn't have been more obvious. She swept the desk clear with a single stroke of her arm, the noise bringing officers to their feet in adjacent sections. Torsta shouted to the nearest of them and he walked over with his hands in his pockets.

'Get this lot cleared up, will you,' she said.

'Er… I don't know who you are. I work for…'

'I'm Torsta Jai. Does that mean anything to you?'

The officer shuffled uncomfortably. 'Yes, I've heard of you, esteemed.'

'Well, I'm back and you're working for me now, son. You can either do it here or get your hands dirty in the Derelict Zone. Now, I'm going to give you a list of equipment I want, and you're going to get it and make a nice neat pile of it right here. We'll see how good you are at store-mastering, shall we? But first, someone from the Security Service has messaged that they're waiting for me. Where's Convening Room F?'

'It's down the hall by...'

'Go down there and tell him to piss off. I'm not talking to him in the building.'

'But he's a security officer, esteemed. He's...'

'Then, I suggest you take your hands out of your pockets when you speak to him. Tell him I'll meet him over in the park. Tell him to wait by the memorial.'

The entrance to Constitution Park was open and welcoming, but even the fine weather couldn't draw people to the centre of Freeport on a day of mourning. No one had come to enjoy the shade of the bekan trees, their fallen blossom lay undisturbed on the lawns, and even the crested lizins perching in the branches had lost their voices. The whole park was as still and silent as the row of shrines along the Grand Avenue.

Further into the park, there were some signs of life. As usual, the Temple of the Aquatic Gods was being cleaned, an android chirping orders to a small detail of elderly humans with wire brushes. It seemed a desperate measure to Torsta, but with so few Freeporters needing the sea for a living, the Aquatic clergy looked for every possible advantage. Further along the path, the Temple of Antaris was quite the opposite. Its reposing statues looked complacent, taking the establishment's favour for granted, even if their temple was the last place anyone fashionable would worship. Then, down towards the bottom of the hill, was the Temple of the Astral Gods, the most neglected of the main structures but easily the most popular. Its spires and buttresses were streaked with algae and droppings, but neither the priests nor the worshippers ever seemed to notice. When your gods moved in the night sky, and their wonders were visible across the ocean of stars, there was no need to scour the stonework.

Torsta had never been through the doors of any of the temples. Her spiritual preferences were martial, ancestral, and the closest connection to the warriors of antiquity could be found down by the ornamental lake. A young man in a grey suit was already waiting there, standing beside the memorial to those who fell in the Third Intra-System War. Water trickled over its suspended quartz tablets, the slabs hewn from the blood-drenched battlefields and etched with images of legendary warriors and acts of valour. They turned continuously, shifting their angles so that the heroic names projected on them appeared more enduring than the rocks of the planets and moons they contested.

The man from the Security Service didn't look up as Torsta approached but stood staring at the stone tablets as if he hadn't noticed her arrival. She stopped a few steps away from him, her eyes drawn to the names on the memorial, compelled to find one in particular.

'When are you planning to go into the Derelict Zone?' asked the man, hardly even turning his head. Torsta decided not to give him an answer.

'I have information you might find useful,' he tried.

'What information is that?' asked Torsta. 'Have you got someone in there disguised as a human. Someone very small.'

'Don't joke. It's been done before. But this time we've got drones and bots crawling all over.'

'I've never detected any of them over there, and believe me, it's been my backyard recently.'

'You won't be able to these days. They're very effective.'

'Well, if the Café Republic was a demonstration of effective intelligence...'

The man glanced in Torsta's direction, his fingers playing with the cuff of his tunic. Smooth skin, unmarked by weather or duty, body thin as a green branch, he looked very young to Torsta. They all did, unmoved by fear, untouched by loss, undamaged by sacrifice. 'We have a problem interpreting data from the Derelict Zone,' he said. 'We didn't see that elemist device coming.'

'You really think feral humans were responsible, and not that there was some local or foreign agent behind it?'

'No evidence of that. Deccan hands appear to be clean. And of course, no individual or group has claimed responsibility.'

'Lone psycho, perhaps. What makes you think humans could conceive such a thing, plan it, construct it?'

'However implausible it might seem, we can't rule it out. The ferals are unpredictable. We believe they are behind the recent spate of murders, near the Derelict Zone, and we know they are responsible for much of the petty crime in adjacent neighbourhoods.'

'You don't need intelligence to work that out. But crime is driven by need. A suicide attack needs a deeper psychology.'

'We have drone recordings of suspect human interactions. It's just a shame we haven't got anyone who can interpret them.'

Torsta snorted her derision. 'You've heard about the human I've impounded. You want it.'

'In a word, "yes".'

'In two words, "fuck off".'

'What use have you got for it? It's all very well saying we screwed up, but we need to ensure it doesn't happen again. The ferals are preparing, mobilising, and we need to know what to expect.'

From a security perspective, it was a reasonable request but for a moment Torsta struggled for an answer. There was no way she was going to give Kali to the Security Service, but the reason, the real reason was something she couldn't put into words. It wasn't just about holding onto an asset, and neither was it her contempt for those who wielded authority without ever putting themselves in danger. It was something else, something more.

'Well?' said the agent. 'Surely you want to know if the feral chatter means anything.'

'I don't need to know if I move quickly enough. We're attacking, not defending.'

The agent kicked idly at the stonework. Torsta watched him hammering his toe against the monument, casual in his disrespect, oblivious to any significance. She was about to reprimand him when he stopped. 'Alright,' he said. 'If you're really going to clear the ferals out. But you better hope there isn't another terrorist attack in the meantime. If you want to know where to strike first, I can tell you that for starters.'

'You don't say. Under the sky-platforms, I suppose?'

'Midsummer Plaza.'

'No strategic value and a fucking great barricade. It would be a skirmish for the media, and that's all.' Torsta looked back across the park towards the entrance gates. Away in the distance she could just make out the white security shrouding over in Carnival Square, and the distinctive structure of the

Department for the Interior. 'I've provided enough news for them to play with already.'

'We believe Midsummer has a spiritual importance to them.'

'Oh, do me a favour!'

'Specifically, there's a mosaic in the mall. It's also the home of a dominant feral female who seems to be drawing the gangs together. Midsummer has got to be your first target. Now, I've put together a plan for you which I think will optimise the...'

'So, they like a picture, and now you think humans are religious. You're wetting yourself that some animals are planning a holy war. And "optimise"? What sort of idiot word is that?'

'Torsta, I'm only...'

'And who said you could call me that! It's bad enough coming from a human, but it sounds even worse coming out of your mouth. How old are you, sonny?'

'I don't see how...'

'Do you see those names in front of you? On that monument you've been kicking?'

'Yes, of course.'

'Look under J... Jai... Rahmat Jai. See him? He was my father, and my commanding officer. You've heard what happened in the Regis Archipelago – learned it in school? Well, we went in there on some crappy intel like yours and got ripped apart. We were outnumbered five to one. Half of them were mercenaries, disgusting fuckers they were, all slime and sinew. Drew us into an ambush in a favela, then came at us in the alleys, kept coming and coming until our weapons were expended. We were using our carbines as clubs, fighting with blades, up so close that you could smell their stinking breath.

By the end of it, my father was dead, and I was the only one in my platoon left alive. I killed more goons that morning than you've got teeth in your head. I was fifteen years old.'

'Fifteen.'

'That's right son. So, don't expect me to trust your precious data. And don't lecture me like I know fuck all, because I was doing this before you first sucked air into your lungs.'

The town of Sabie stood a thousand leagues along the coast from the capital, indifferent to the influences that shaped the Republic, let alone anything that happened off-world. It could be seen from high above the planet, strategically situated at the intersection of two timeworn transport routes, their lush verges marking it with a giant cross on the landscape. The heart of the town, with its ancient stone buildings lay amidst a patchwork of fields, where labourers gathered in the crops much as they had for a thousand generations. Some of the earliest humans on Antaris had been brought there to work the farms, and although many towns across the fertile plain had modernised their harvesting, Sabie's community was one of those that still clung to its traditions.

At mid-day, a medical transport glided into the town square, settling in the stippled shade of the gin-yin trees. Niko S'tana stepped from the rear doors and stretched his back. He pushed his hat back on his head and waited for his studio feed to configure before going through the usual sound and vision checks. He released a pair of drones, told them to collect and assemble a montage of material from around the town, then he recorded a few brief interviews with the veterinary team while they set up their field clinic.

With time to spare, he left the medics and wandered

around the square, peering into sleepy shops, finding that standing outside was enough to bring the owner scrambling to the door. Behind them, amidst the shadowed streets, there was a clock tower of crude limestone blocks, a landmark only for lack of competition. It had narrow, fortified windows and a linear analogue clock face, which must have given up on time-telling at some point in antiquity. Nico wondered whether that might have been the last real news story the town had known, the event of the year, a story to be told and retold.

He shielded his eyes to scan the fields beyond the town centre. The harvest was in progress on one of the farms, if a line of dust above the crops was anything to go by. In the other directions there was nothing, no hills to mark the horizon, no motion, not a breath of wind, and for the moment even the cikadigs in the hedgerows had stopped their clicking.

Nico had never been to this part of the Republic; there had never been a reason, never something to report. Until the opportunity had wrenched him from his sleep that morning, life beyond Freeport couldn't have been further from his mind. He had planned to spend the day on the explosion, the aftershocks, pursuing Torsta Jai in particular and the red-haired human who had caused such a stir the night before. Every fool had the image now of course, but while others had thrown themselves into the melee around the Government transport, he had focused on getting the story out first, coining the 'hooded suspect' phrase that everyone was now using. Perhaps his superintendent was right though, the competition would stick with the obvious lines of enquiry when in fact, the agenda was already moving on. Human Affairs was pushing ahead with its reforms, and the offer of an exclusive could not be ignored.

It wasn't hard to understand why Sabie had been chosen to showcase the Government's initiative. It was as predictable a town as could be found anywhere in the Republic, a place that had voted Heritage for as long as anyone could remember. The clinical team had been careful not to say anything controversial, but they had been well briefed on the implementation, speaking with apparent pride about the hundreds of other field clinics mobilising that morning.

'How have you prepared so quickly?' asked Nico. 'This is a massive programme, seemingly organised overnight.'

'It's not that difficult to co-ordinate,' said one of the nurses, buttoning the collar of her white coat. 'We're out most days anyway, on other health and maintenance initiatives. The devices we're implanting today have been used in larger livestock for some time. They'll be a bit cumbersome embedded in a small animal like a human, but better ones are on the way.'

'What about the functions, the behavioural instructions?'

'Oh, you mean the control standards. They're rules-based at the moment, but fully intelligent upgrades are coming that will be able to refine behaviour across a wide range of metrics. We understand the full behaviour protocol will be approved by the Department and operational within a few days.'

'And what difference will that make in practice?'

'Well, at the moment the controls are mainly about proximity to owner, speed of response to instructions, simple things like that. The intelligent control set goes much further: tone of voice, posture, attitude. With variable penalty and reward sensations, positive habits are established very quickly.'

Two police officers wandered out of a side street, swinging their legs slowly as if trying to make each stride take as long as possible. They came over to the clinic and stood, arms folded as they engaged in friendly conversation with the medics. Then the first of Sabie's citizens began to arrive, bringing with them a motley array of humans, some of them well-groomed domestics and others wearing the rough shifts of field workers. In most cases their reluctance was clear, some tugging at their bonds and chattering nervously to each other as they waited in line.

Nico moved to the centre of the square to begin his live reports. He positioned himself where the clock tower could be seen behind him, rising solidly above the little grove of trees and the line of people waiting in the heat.

'In this quiet little farming community,' he began, 'far from the terrible scenes in Freeport, we can see the new Government's policies already swinging into action. We have communities like Sabie to thank for much of the produce that reaches our tables, its traditional way of life meaning it has one of the highest human population ratios in the Free Republic. As you can see there's considerable demand for the new service, an implant that ensures a human's behaviour meets national standards. Clinicians say there's only a small amount of pain involved, but as you can see in the background some of the humans are making quite a fuss about it. It's this sort of mild unruliness the procedure will correct, reminding each individual with a sharp pulse, whenever they stray from acceptable behaviour. Ah! Here we have one that's just had the procedure completed. Let me see if I can have a word with the owner.'

'Esteemed, I wonder if you could spare a moment. Why did you decide to have your human fitted with a control implant?'

The woman stood stoutly, her jaw moving as if she was in the habit of chewing, even when her mouth was empty. 'Tell the truth, I was feared I would get into trouble,' she said, 'You know, fined an' all. Can't afford none of that. Didn't want my Lucy taken away neither. I ain't gonna mess about at my age.'

'And how is Lucy responding?'

'Hard to say jus' yet. Seems a mite uncomfortable wi' that thing stuck in her back. It keeps jerking her a bit, but she's walking straighter, stayin' real close and keepin' quiet. And they tol' me she'll carry things further now, without squeakin' about it.'

Nico moved over to the queue, where a farmer was standing with a young male, who was wrestling furiously with his bond. 'Central news, esteemed. You've been standing here quite a while, I see. Who's this with you?'

'This lil' fella's Jock.'

'He doesn't seem too pleased to be here. Do you think he knows what this is about?'

'Doubt it. He's just a bit of a wild one.'

'And you hope a control implant will be a solution to that?'

'Well, he's a picker and they say it'll make him more productive. An' if it calms him some, I'll not be complainin'.' He drew the human closer to him by the back of his dungarees, then pressed him into a kneeling position, held him there by the back of his neck. 'There now, fella – that's more like it.' He turned back to Nico. 'Field hands are all a bit jittery, today,' he said. 'They were lookin' at the green moon last night. Happens a bit sometimes, but they was *all* out lookin' last night. Never seen the like of it.'

'Why do they do that?'

'No one knows fer sure. Some say they think it talks to them. Jus' nature's mystery, says others. I 'spect they'll settle soon enough.'

'And beyond your own farm? Do you think this implant service will be popular in your community?'

'Don't know 'bout that. We grow up with animals round here an' we know how ter treat 'em. There's folks who are really riled at the Government's interferin'. Point of principle, an' that's no lie.'

'But not for you?'

'Got to move with the times, I reckon. So, I'll see how this works, but I know how ter raise an animal and there'll be plenty of folks who get their humans seen to, on account of bein' too idle to train 'em. There'll be trouble along the way fer sure. Not all towns are peaceable like we are, an' that's no lie neither.'

From somewhere in the distance a murmuring sound reached them in the still air. At first it was barely noticeable, but then it grew, low and rhythmic until the medics and the people waiting in line began to turn their heads towards the far side of town. Gradually the volume increased, and the sound became a chant, the words becoming clearer with each passing moment. 'No to the implants! No to the Government!'

The two policemen moved away from the clinic, and took station in the middle of the square, knees flexing, arms held loose at their sides. The protestors came into view, spilling from the streets behind the clock tower, a seething mass wielding crudely fashioned banners that decried interference by central government, laws that invaded the privacy of their homes. They fanned out around the square, to face the clinic in a wide arc, a curving wall of colour and noise. One of the police officers went forward to speak to a large man at the centre of the group, then after a brief discussion he retreated cautiously, never turning his back on the crowd.

Nico struggled to control the excitement in his voice as he reported on the turn of events. 'The tension is palpable. As you can see, the protesters hugely outnumber the police and their manner is distinctly threatening. Some are shouting abuse at the clinical team. There's a real sense that this tiny group of medics is under siege. They look bewildered. They certainly weren't expecting this.' He headed for a fierce-looking woman who was anchoring the end of the line. She had her fist raised in the air and was leading the chanting with enthusiasm. She spat on the ground as he approached.

'Day trip fer the city boy?' she snarled.

'I'm your opportunity to get your message to the Republic,' said Nico. 'Don't blow it!'

The woman turned her placard so it could be seen more clearly. 'Alright – ask away,' she said coldly.

'Here we go then... You clearly feel strongly about this issue, esteemed. Can you explain why you are here, and what you want?'

Nico swung his body as the woman spoke, so he could capture police reinforcements arriving in the background. They were piling out of transports and forming a thin cordon around the clinic. In response, the crowd began to edge forward, as if closing for battle.

'What we want is to be left alone!' said the woman. 'We're sick of bein' pushed around by the Freeport elite! We know how to raise our crops, we know how to raise our children, and we sure as heck know how to handle our animals!'

'And how is that?'

'Obvious, isn't it? Got to know when to treat them kindly and when they need a beltin'. It's jus' commonsense! We don't need no celebrity like Norvik thinkin' he knows better.'

'No, that's not it!' A young man pushed his way into the conversation from further back in the crowd. 'This isn't about local power. We just can't go on abusing humans, or we'll end up like the Spice Islands!'

'Oh, go home, you arsehole!' shouted someone else. 'You're not from round here!'

'Yeah, take your bleedin' heart crap somewhere else!' said the woman.

A tiny girl, who looked barely old enough to be out of school, tugged at Nico's arm. She spoke with a shrill voice that carried more clearly than all the others. 'I'm scared!' she said. 'I don't want a revolution, and if we carry on like this…'

'Carry on like what?' said the woman. 'We're jus' bein' normal!'

'Can't you see!' shrieked the girl. 'Can't you see them all looking at the green moon? They think Callista has come!'

Further down the line, someone threw a punch, and suddenly the crowd lurched forward. All at once what little order there had been in the crowd was lost, and they surged into Nico, terminating the interview. Now the protesters were battling each other, breaking ranks and pushing against the police cordon as they fought. The police struck back with shock-batons, while down at the other end of the square, the crowd seemed to think an assault on the police line had started and drove forward together. Then came the missiles; first it was the placard tablets, then stones launched over the police and onto the field clinic. What remained of the patients scurried for cover under trestle tables and behind trees, while the medics rushed to break camp around them.

Nico's media credentials allowed him to squeeze through the police line and retreat to the clinic. The studio in Freeport came through, asking nervously about his situation. 'Never mind that!' he shouted, 'I want a researcher on this right now. I need everything you've got about Callista.' He swung around trying to locate the young girl in the crowd. 'Yes, Callista! Yes, I know it's a bloody moon! What do we know about it and why would humans be interested? What other meanings are there to the word? Yes, of course it's urgent!'

More police were arriving to reinforce the line. They brought with them force shields, and bit by bit they managed to push the crowd back, until the missiles were falling short of their target. Nico found a refuge under the trees for his next broadcast, just as a completely new assault began. A hoverbike came in low across the fields, followed by several others in a vee formation. They came howling into the square, masked riders circling their heavily modified machines above the crowd, gunning the motors to set people running in all directions. Then they turned their attention to the clinic, breaking from their circle one by one to attack.

The lead hoverbike came through a gap in the trees and hurled a sack into the clinic. It hit a table and split open, scattering dung and offal amongst the clinical team. The others followed, some choosing the same line of attack and others coming in from different directions to hurl bags of putrid waste directly at the medics. The police responded quickly, a detachment pulling back to form a tight protective circle, only to make themselves an additional target.

Nico decided his best protection was to keep moving. He dashed from tree to tree catching as much of the action as he could yet managing to avoid being hit while he improvised his next report.

'This is a co-ordinated and determined assault… and as you can see, attackers are striking at us with impunity. The missiles seem to be bags of blood and animal tissue… police are powerless to prevent them… whoever the attackers are, their intentions are clear enough. There won't be any more implanting done today… this will generate even more controversy about the policy. Now, here they come again! Another wave of hoverbikes, this time with pillion riders.'

Nico came out from behind a tree to get a clearer view.

The second wave of attackers were riding larger machines and they carried dull metallic tins. 'Now it's smoke canisters they're throwing! You can see the crowds are running to escape from the square… it's a stampede in the far corner by the clock tower. The visibility is very poor… have to keep moving. Here comes the next attack!'

Suddenly, Nico found himself alone, standing in front of the medical transport amidst the spreading clouds of smoke. He pulled off his shirt and pressed it to his mouth as he spun around, looking for more action. A hoverbike emerged out of the smoke, turning slowly over the scattered remains of the clinic. The rider at the controls was leaning out to survey the damage, but the pillion rider saw Nico and stood up. He raised his arm with a clenched fist and pulled the mask from his bearded face, shouting in that strange babble that was unique to humans.

15

Alignment

TORSTA HADN'T EVEN LEFT the park before the call came through from Sig Norvik, his frustration spilling from the very first syllable. '*Do* you intend to make an enemy of every person in this town?' he asked, pointlessly Torsta thought, given her notoriety. 'I've just had the Security Service onto me, and apparently, you insulted their agent, when they were trying to help you.'

'They wanted the human for a spying mission in the Derelict Zone. They know fuck all about them in my experience and...'

'And you do? Been studying my books, have you?'

'You know I was right to keep Kali away from them.'

'I know you've given me another issue to deal with. Have you heard what's been happening this morning? More lynchings, and ugly scenes at implant clinics out in the provinces. I need you in here right away. The Chief Counsellor's all over me and we need to get on top of it.'

When Torsta walked into Norvik's office there was already a meeting in progress. He greeted her warmly, thanking her for coming so quickly. Either his annoyance was a fleeting thing, Torsta thought, or he needed to show a united front, a vulnerability of sorts, either way. 'Do take a seat,' he said, shuffling further around his meeting table to make space. 'I thought I should bring everyone together, to make sure we're working with a shared understanding. Introductions: you know Egil Kray, no doubt?'

Torsta glanced at the Chief of Police who was sitting on the far side of the table, looking as though he was sucking something sour. 'Reacquainted earlier,' she said.

'You won't have met my policy team. Styx Kaskai is even newer than I am. She's stepped in to cover for a colleague who, I regret to say, is still missing after the explosion. Styx is dealing with domestic and commercial humans, while Panos here has the feral brief. You'll need to work closely with him on operations in the Derelict Zone.'

Working closely with an administrator was not what Torsta had in mind. She watched Panos making careful notes on the tablescreen and decided they would get on better at a distance. She turned towards the final person at the table, an ageing man with a lazy eye and plumes of white hair obscuring his cranial ridges.

'And this is Professor Chakrat of the Commonwealth Observatory. You may have heard of his work on atypical jumpspace parallax and…'

'Perhaps a briefing afterwards if there's time,' said Torsta. 'I take it the professor is here to help us with the crisis in some way?'

Chakrat cleared his throat. 'I hope I can help with the scientific context.'

'I'll ask the Professor to explain shortly. But first, we have an escalating crisis, so let's update ourselves on the latest position.'

Styx shifted forward in her seat and manipulated the tablescreen so that it exploded with colour. 'Here's the incident map,' she said. 'You can see that new events are occurring even as we speak.'

'What's the code?' asked Egil Kray.

'Blue markers are lynchings. You'll see they're only happening in and around the capital. All using hovercranes. So…'

'Same group, or affiliates,' said Kray. 'We're already making arrests.'

'Red are protests. They're more widespread – at least twenty incidents. That's only counting those that turned violent.'

'Nothing in Freeport?' Norvik asked.

'Nothing yet,' said Kray. 'There's a major rally in Constitution Park in two days' time.'

'That's Republic Day.'

'It's organised by the Human Policy Unit. Santi Aspil's speaking in the evening, so there'll be a large crowd.'

'When was this announced?' said Norvik, his voice suddenly taught.

'This morning, following your statement.'

'Cancel it. Tell them it's off.'

'It's a legal gathering, properly organised.'

'Let them hold us in breach afterwards.'

'Aspil's a lawyer. She'd have an injunction on your desk in a blink, and that's not a distraction we need.'

'Well, if we have no alternative, you'll just have to be prepared for the worst with that event. Now, let's move on.'

'These yellows are human rebellions,' continued Styx, manipulating the image in front of her again. 'Not sure "rebellion" is the right word though. It's more that humans are participating in some of the violent protests alongside citizens. There was the attack in Sabie of course…'

'A disgrace!' said Kray. 'Never thought I'd see it.'

'And there have been at least two other incidents like it, both up in the hanging valleys.'

'Can't allow that to gather momentum,' said Torsta, an image coming to mind of the guardsmen on the Spice Islands being overwhelmed by a mob of humans.

'What worries me more is the other stuff.' said Styx, staring into the table display, stabbing at it, as if she'd forgotten everyone around her. 'We've got a lot of desertions reported in agricultural and commercial zones –and I mean a *lot*. Humans are absconding in numbers, going off to the forests. It's a pattern, a ritual.'

'What do you mean?' said Torsta. 'What ritual?'

'It starts with moon-watching, apparently. The practice looks to be spreading outwards from the capital. It's well beyond Sabie now, right up into the top country.'

Norvik swivelled his chair towards Torsta. 'It started last night. Humans have taken to standing out in fields, gardens, commercial yards, just staring at the green moon. Then, in the morning, any that aren't secured are gone.'

'It means new populations of ferals are forming,' said Panos. 'Everywhere. They're on the move, along the roads, over the fields.'

'What's the significance of the green moon?' asked Torsta.

'Have a look at this,' said Styx. She played the latest report from Nico S'tana. He was standing in a deserted farmyard, explaining an ancient legend. He had edited in a comment from a girl in Sabie, and a series of images of a mythical goddess, including a mosaic, which he identified as a mural in

Midsummer Mall. The report finished with the picture of Kali that had dominated the late-night news the day before.

There was silence around the room when the report finished. Egil Kray shifted in his seat, his ridges flaring. Torsta felt as she sometimes used to when battle order was formed, her lungs dragging thin air into her lungs. 'Shit!' she said. 'It's all making sense now.'

'Shame it made sense to Nico S'tana before any of us.' said Norvik. 'That's unacceptable to me, and I can tell you from the conversation I had a few minutes ago with the CC, it's unacceptable to him too.'

'It's more than what's in that news report,' said Torsta. 'When I brought that human in through Midsummer, one of the ferals, a tall female saw her with me and came charging at us. The Security Service believes that the mall and its mural has significance to the ferals, and the clans are uniting around a female leader.'

There was an eruption of questions around the table. Norvik stood up and called for quiet. 'Please! Let's be clear on this. Are you suggesting the Derelict Zone ferals have linked this moon legend with that copperhair human?'

'That's *exactly* what I'm saying, and I've seen domestic humans react strongly to her as well. The Derelict Zone is the extent of my brief, but I think an uprising is more likely than ever now. We can't know when it will happen, but I intend to pre-empt it.'

'I think that's where I can help,' said Professor Chakrat. 'The scientific community has known for years that a rare alignment of the Antarian satellites is coming.'

'An eclipse?' said Torsta. 'How's that rare?'

'Well, the moons often eclipse one another, as we know, but if you discount Calderon, which is big enough and close enough to eclipse something most of the time, the other moons have never aligned visibly in modern times.'

'You mean all eclipsing each other, in a straight line?' said Panos.

'Precisely, with the one in front of the others being Callista. None of the others will be visible so there will be no other reflected light in the sky. Callista's green disc will dominate.'

'Surely that can't be so unusual,' said Styx, conjuring a dance of planets to float above the table.

'One of the moons has an irregular orbital plane, so a complete alignment is extremely rare. It happened five centuries ago, but it wasn't over the Free Republic, and the weather was poor. Before that, it was in the time of the ancients, and then Calderon also aligned, so it was hidden. No, this is an extraordinary phenomenon. None of us will ever see it again.'

'Why haven't we been told about this?' growled Kray. 'Half the human population seems to know!'

'It's no secret,' said the professor, mildly. 'There's no scientific value to it, and this sort of thing isn't of much interest to the public. People see far more dramatic things occurring elsewhere in the cosmos. Compared to the birth and death of stars, this is easy to take for granted. That's not to say it won't be a spectacle, though. If it's a clear night, with Callista rising, and all the others falling into place behind, it should be quite something to behold. I'm very much looking forward to it.'

Norvik leaned towards the Chief of Police. 'To answer your point about humans Egil, I don't think we can deduce that they know about the alignment. That's way beyond their mental capacity. But they do seem to have a sense of something about to happen, much as some animals can anticipate the shifting crust of the planet. Some primitive instinct for the

Callista legend isn't surprising, but I must confess that this collective hysteria is a revelation to me. It does suggest some capacity to communicate at a conceptual level.'

'They will all recognise the alignment as something special when they see it,' said Torsta. 'Perhaps they'll take it as a signal, even a call to arms.' She expanded the incident map in front of her to a detailed layout of the Derelict Zone. 'It's just as well we have the human in custody. When exactly is the alignment, Professor?'

'The day after tomorrow, early on Republic Day. You'll need to be ready.'

Torsta got to her feet. 'I'm not waiting,' she said. 'I'm going in at dawn. I'm going to kill that feral leader.'

Nothing in Georgi's manner suggested that this show would be any more important than the hundreds of others in his long and distinguished career. He was his usual self, friendly and unassuming, greeting Henik cordially when he arrived, guiding him through a labyrinth of passages to the studio where Widdig Terreden was already waiting.

'Who's coming to put the Government side,' asked Henik. 'It's always helpful to know in advance.'

'Alas, my friends, we're at the mercy of events tonight. The Government's decided not to send a spokesperson.' He leaned towards them and lowered his voice. 'But I did get a brief interview with Counsellor Norvik, so we'll work the format around that.'

'Can we see what he's said?' asked Widdig.

'I am *so* sorry, my dears, but I think not. I want to keep this as close to a live debate as possible – in the interests of fairness, of course. I know the two of you won't be too hard on each other, so it will even things up a bit if your responses are unprepared.'

A thin girl appeared at the edge of the set, the arms of her tunic long and flapping, in the current fashion. 'We're into countdown!' she called. 'Places, please!'

'There,' said Georgi, 'no time anyway.' He sauntered over to the desk and lowered himself into his seat, before making a few adjustments to his script. 'Ready, my dears?' he said. 'Here we go.'

The programme opened with a salvo of drumbeats and three-dimensional images of the day's events. 'The Free Republic in crisis.' said Georgi, sternly. 'An unprecedented day of chaos and violence.' An image of a hoverbike soared from the backdrop, cutting between Henik and Georgi, its rider hurling his virtual bag of offal, scattering its holographic fragments around the studio and out into millions of homes. 'Police stretched to breaking point across the provinces, as protests against Government reforms gather momentum.'

A luminous sphere grew on the news desk. 'And just what is the role of the green moon in this crisis?' said Georgi. 'Tonight, we ask whether Callista is just a mythical figure from ancient times or an inspiration for revolt, and we ask the Government about its response, with Republic Day fast approaching.

'This evening, on The Georgi Factor, we have the company of Widdig Terreden who returns in his new capacity as spokesperson on human issues for the Progress Party, and also the renowned expert on feral humans, Henik Varkesen. But before we discuss today's events, I managed to catch up with the new Counsellor for Human Affairs, Sig Norvik earlier.'

Norvik's image appeared in a seat beside Georgi, and the

interrogation began without any preamble. 'On this most challenging of days, Counsellor, it seems that the public is making its feelings clear. Are you beginning to regret the announcement of such controversial reforms?'

'I think you're misinterpreting what's been happening,' said Norvik, his voice reassuringly smooth. 'There have been some incidents, as we expected, but the majority of towns haven't seen any disturbance.'

'Surely you aren't playing down what's been happening, Counsellor? We've seen protests the length and breadth of the country, some violent and with humans participating alongside people.'

'In a very small number of cases.'

'Many might say that one such incident is too many. Wouldn't it be prudent to pull back on these reforms to allow more time for consideration?'

'I think these disturbances suggest a policy of firm discipline is badly needed. I've worked with humans for many years, and trust me, this would not be happening but for an approach in the past that...'

Henik took a deliberate intake of breath at the word 'trust', hoping it wouldn't escape attention. But Georgi had already spotted Norvik's slip. '*Trust* you, Counsellor?' he interjected. 'The voters did place their trust in Heritage in the election and some may already be thinking it was misplaced, from the chaos they've witnessed in these first days of a new Government. Lynchings in the streets, protests all across the country, humans taking part in violent attacks. And all this while we mourn the worst terrorist attack in modern times.'

'I think the Chief Counsellor has already said all that is needed on yesterday's explosion,' said Norvik. 'It's an atrocity, and not something to turn into an argument at this time of grieving. We're working day and night on the investigation and I'm confident that we will very soon find who was behind it.'

It was a good recovery, thought Henik. But then Norvik's inexperience had led him into a hollow expression of assurance. 'It's good to hear that you are confident about that,' said Georgi. 'Are you also confident about this Callista situation? Can you explain what the moon-gazing is all about, why it is that large numbers of humans are running off?'

'I put that down to mass hysteria. These are simple beings, with primitive cognitive processes. We see this sort of stampeding effect in nature all the time. Rest assured, we'll be rounding up the strays and dealing with them properly.'

Now Norvik really had blundered. He had played into the hands of his most ardent critics by implying the state would use the crisis to take their pets. 'No, no, no,' muttered Henik, just loudly enough to be heard.

Georgi pounced. 'So, are you telling owners the new reforms will apply to runaway humans, and that the state will take ownership of them? Is that what you're saying, Counsellor?'

'Well, what we need to focus on first, is re-establishing order and…'

'So, you're not going to give any commitment to viewers that their companion animals won't be destroyed.'

'That's not what I'm saying,' Norvik protested. 'It's not about that. Our concern is that we believe there is a central influence behind what we're seeing and we'll need to be careful how we proceed.'

Inadvertently, Norvik had said exactly the right thing. He had hung out bait that couldn't be resisted. Georgi left the wounds that he had opened with his previous attack, to sink his teeth into less sensitive tissue.

'A central influence, you say. This copperhair human, is

it? You think this Callista…'

'That is *not* who that human is, Georgi, and I don't think it's sensible to suggest any such thing. We have an individual in custody, and it's being examined to see if anything can be learned about what's been happening. I'm sure you won't expect me to say more on the matter when it's currently under investigation.' Norvik looked away for a moment, as if someone was calling for his attention, just as he'd turned the interview in his favour. 'I'm very sorry, Georgi, but I'll need to leave you now. These are very busy times.'

'Yes, I think we've kept you long enough, Counsellor. Thank you for joining us.'

Henik felt a surge of frustration that Norvik had escaped on a positive note, leaving the impression of a responsible public servant. Georgi was taking a moment to regroup while the programme took a break. There were no pleasantries between them now. Georgi's eyes were fixed on his notes, his lips silently rehearsing a few chosen lines. It was an ominous sign. He would know that he'd let Norvik off lightly and would be anxious not to repeat that generosity with his studio guests. Now, there could be no avoiding a firm position on humans, no neutral ground on the Callista issue, nor wavering in defence of Norvik's prisoner. If Kali was to be saved, he would need to make a fight of it.

Widdig was watching him intently as if he hoped for some signal of intent, some sign that the Norvik interview hadn't disturbed their agreement to work together. Henik remembered a gesture he had seen Alka use, one which struck him as an obvious sign of strength and co-operation. He brought his hands up slowly, to where Widdig could see them, then clasped them firmly together.

***

In his brother's Check St. office, Yan waited on a sumptuous couch of fine Deccan sea silk, surrounded by portraits of famous historical figures. Under other circumstances they would have held his attention, he thought, as would the gifts from foreign dignitaries. He might have picked up the exquisite, lacquered box from the Spice Islands, or studied the crystalline duelling set from the Caris Obscura system. He might even have dared to touch the Bowl of Living Dead, its serpentine contents writhing in the gorgeous colours of their gastric juices even though they hadn't been alive for a thousand years.

Instead, he was preoccupied with a hologram of Kali, a message he had received from Torsta Jai without a word of explanation. It wasn't the first time he had viewed the recording, in fact playing it had become almost a compulsion, watching Kali sitting on his hand, earnestly explaining her predicament.

'Is not for worry, Yan. Is police, I be with. Is not danger.' The optimism was dreadfully misplaced, but Yan no longer heard the words. Instead, he saw the language of her body now, eyes round and earnest, hands moving with the cadence of her words. And he noticed that her fingers were playing with the bond bracelet on her wrist, just as he'd been doing with its pair, deciding almost subconsciously that he wouldn't remove it until she returned.

'So, it's true. She really can use our language.'

Yan turned to see Maarten standing at the door. His shirt was open at the neck, his sleeves pushed up untidily, but he still had the bearing of a great man, casual but assured, carrying the strain of responsibility lightly, as he always had.

'Yes, it's no exaggeration,' said Yan, putting Kali's image

down on the arm of the couch. 'She's why I'm here, Maarten. I'm really sorry to bother you with all that you have going on. I know this crisis must be very demanding.'

Maarten sauntered into the room. 'It's just events,' he said. 'There will always be shit happening somewhere in the Commonwealth. Without that, there would be no opportunity for achievement, would there?' He glanced at the portraits behind his desk.

'So, the explosion, the protests and all that. It isn't bothering you? You're sleeping?'

'Of course, it bothers me, but only in the compartment where I'm CC, not in the compartment where I'm a man needing a good night's sleep, or the one where I'm the brother of one of the Republic's leading social historians.'

'You're mocking me,' said Yan.

'No, I wouldn't, whatever you may think. We're different, that's all. Your human keeps you awake at night, but me... well, I've hardly thought about Juno's death.'

'Maarten, I was really sorry about that, but I just don't believe that Kali did anything to cause...'

'Of course, she didn't. Don't think I don't know when Jocasta is lying. I can guess what really happened. Juno formed an attachment to your Kali, and Jocasta lost her temper and killed him.'

'Killed him? You can't seriously think she meant to...'

'Jocasta knows how to play the dutiful partner when it suits, but she's cold to the core. Juno isn't the first pet she's beaten to death.'

Yan struggled to respond for a moment. However much he disliked Jocasta, the revelation still came as a shock. 'I... I had no idea she was like that. That's just savage! How can you stay with her?'

'I'm not really *with her* these days,' Maarten said, pushing aside the Bowl of the Living Dead, so he could sit on the edge of his desk. 'And we all know there is a lot of animal abuse around. Humans are neglected and killed all the time. It's not just Jocasta.'

'And you don't think something should be done about that?'

'Of course, something should be done! I could give you a long list of things I should do something about, and many of them affect the welfare of *people*, their rights, their safety, the quality of their lives! Don't make me out to be callous about this. I just have more pressing things to deal with. And if I'm honest, your little human is causing me more trouble than Jocasta at the moment.'

'I can assure you that Kali had nothing to do with the Café Republic bomb.'

'It does seem unlikely,' said Maarten, his eyes shifting to her hologram. 'There's no evidence, anyway.'

'So, she can be released? I can take her home?'

Maarten leaned closer to Kali's hologram. It sensed his presence and turned towards him, repeating its message. 'It's not as simple as that,' he said. 'In matters of national security, the police have seven days to collect evidence.'

'If there's probable cause.'

'Doesn't apply to animals. They aren't legally competent.'

'If you knew Kali, you would see how competent humans can be.'

Maarten picked up Kali's image and held it at arm's length. 'Oh, I can see how competent they can be. They've been so violently competent in the Spice Islands that I'm having to go out there this evening for a summit. No, the question to consider is how *civilised* humans can be, how responsible, how trustworthy.'

'I could ask that of many *people.* I would certainly ask that of Sig Norvik.'

'Come on Yan, there are laws in this country! Whatever you may want, we don't make things up as we go along. There's due process to follow.'

'I thought... I just hoped you'd agree there's nothing to connect Kali to that explosion.'

'No? The explosion can be linked forensically to humans. The humans were feral, and the ferals in the Derelict Zone are not in compliance with the Republic.'

'But Kali isn't a feral! Surely you can see that, even from the hologram!'

'But she appears to be having an influence on her species, domestic and feral alike. She may not know it, but the message the human population is taking from her is not one of compliance. That's the hard truth of the matter. So, I'm not going to overrule Human Affairs and order her release while we have an ongoing crisis. I won't put the interests of the public aside to favour one human and its owner, even if that owner is my brother.'

'Can't you make an exception,' said Yan, conscious that his voice had taken a pleading tone. 'I swear to you that I'll keep her out of trouble.'

Maarten put Kali's image back down on the arm of the couch. It turned back and forth between the two of them, confused about which should receive its message. 'I understand how important this human is to you. Believe me, I do. I've become attached to pets in the past, myself. But this matter belongs squarely in my work compartment. Surely, you can see I must act for the Republic. That's my sworn duty. And you must see that taking Kali home, when her face is known to the public and there are gangs with hovercranes on the streets, would be madness.'

'It's *all* madness to me! It's crazy to keep treating humans the way we do. From what Kali has told me about Earth, they rank as one of the more advanced species we've encountered.'

'One of the more aggressive, certainly.'

'And yet you talk about hovercrane lynchings and humans being beaten to death at home.' Maarten's forehead started to darken, and Yan sensed he had stepped over a line. 'I'm sorry,' he said quickly. 'That was unfair.'

Maarten took a deep breath. 'Not unfair, just unhelpful.'

A tall man put his head around the door and Maarten went behind his desk to take his jacket from the back of his chair. 'I've got to go, Yan. I'm sorry. Let's pick this up again after Republic Day. Things will be clearer then.' He swept his hand over his desk and stared into it. 'Kali's being held at Police Headquarters, across from Constitution Park,' he said. 'I'll tell Sig to make sure she's well-treated, and to arrange for you to see her in the morning.'

Kali got to her feet stiffly when she heard the keeper opening the door to the compound. Her legs ached, the cold reaching deep into her bones. She hadn't slept but had sat curled in the corner of her pen with as much straw as she could gather, rain hammering down outside, rattling into ducts and pipes, echoing through the dungeon like drums.

Kali trained her mind on happier times, the sunbaked farmyard at home, the smiling faces of her schoolchildren, and then sitting on the beach with Henik and Yan. She kept an image of the flickering fire in her mind through the night, the heat on her face, the sparks rising high against a dark sky. And she clung to the warmth of Yan's hand, the belief that a new day would see him come for her. But each time she opened her eyes it was as if a cloak had been thrown over the world. The darkness was so complete, so lacking in even the merest shade of grey, that when the other inmates called to her with their obscenities, it sounded as if they were just inches away. Most disturbing of all was a mocking drawl, so close and penetrating that it might even have come from inside her head. 'Save us all will you, lil' Callista, wit' your red hair? Can't even save yerself! Goddess of the cesspit, y'are, now. Picked the wrong place ya did, Red. We'll all die here. Oh yeah, we're all – gonna – die.'

When the morning came, it wasn't the gentle creeping of dawn around her bedroom curtains, but the instant arrival of artificial light as the inmates were woken for their morning feed. The keeper went around the compound, talking encouragingly to some, chastising others, and all the while bowls crackled against the bars, and water chugged into dispensers. When she came to Kali's row there was a protracted interaction with a male further down. There was no point of understanding between them; one spoke about conditions, the other about behaviour but neither of them knew what the other was saying.

Eventually, the keeper appeared outside Kali's pen. She crouched down and looked at her for a while, chewing her lip, then took a tool from her pocket and disabled the bars so she could creep inside. Kali retreated a step, pressed her back against the wall.

'Let's look at your food, shall we?' said the keeper. 'Oh dear, nothing eaten at all. And you haven't taken any liquid either.' She reached out slowly towards Kali and drew her forward by the front of her coat. She held her in a practiced grip, pinning her arms to her sides, then took a device from her belt and pressed it to her neck. 'No trace of elemist, of course,' she said under her breath, then released her. 'Terrorist, indeed.'

The keeper didn't seem in any rush to leave the pen. She knelt on the old scraps of carpet and observed her carefully, her thick arms folded across her chest. Kali didn't know what to make of her. It was clear that she was used to dealing with some very difficult individuals, having them entirely in her power, but she still seemed thoughtful about her work.

'Good morning,' offered Kali, tentatively.

'Good morning, Kali,' said the keeper. She glanced over her shoulder, then lowered her voice. 'I've heard things about you. Do you really know what I'm saying? Is it true that you understand language – understand it properly?' She started to get up, brushing the dirt from her thighs as if she was dismissing the very thing she'd asked.

'Yes,' said Kali quietly. 'Do understand some you say… officer Kanawa.'

The keeper stared for a long moment, then sank back to her knees. Kali reached forwards and touched her name badge. 'Awhi Kanawa.'

The keeper sucked in a breath. 'And you can *read*.' she said. She looked again towards the door as if she thought she might have heard someone coming. 'Can you tell me…? Do you know why you're here? Have you done something bad?'

'Not bad,' said Kali. 'I be different only.' She watched the keeper closely and found her manner was more open than other Antarians, more accepting of possibilities.

'You certainly are,' said Officer Kanawa, and knelt a little closer. 'Kali, I have a human at home…'

'Midge.'

'Yes, did I say that? She saw your face on the news, and

now she's acting very strangely. My friends say the same about their humans too. They're all looking at the sky, at the green moon. Do you understand?'

'I like green moon. Be called Callista.'

'Yes, that's right. Do you know what's happening, though? My friend says there's something very special about you. I mean… who *are* you, Kali?'

'I friend to Yan Feyrsten. I not be animal.'

Officer Kanawa stared at her again, as if trying to decode the meaning in her words. 'You do say some strange things,' she said. 'Feyrsten. That's not…?'

'Brother be Chief Counsellor.'

Kanawa wiped her forehead with the back of her hand. 'Just what is going on here?' she said. 'All this unrest, the green moon thing, and now the Chief Counsellor. I need to talk to someone.'

'Yan. Please do talk. Tell Yan.'

'You mean he doesn't know you're here?' Kanawa took out her probe again. 'Hold out your hands, Kali. Let me have a look. Here it is, an identity dot. Feyrsten. I'll reach him, today if I can.'

Kali reached out slowly and took the keeper's hand, hope giving her new energy, driving the cold from her limbs. 'Awhi Kanawa. Please, you do bring Yan.'

16

Task Force

'BETTER THAN I EXPECTED,' said Santi. She returned her flask loudly to the table and sat back, relieved at the general tone of the headlines. 'Widdig got an easy ride from Georgi.' Henik grunted in response, stayed hunched over the morning reviews. 'But he landed some good points,' she continued. 'I liked the "pause and assess" idea. It means we can slow Norvik down without appearing soft.'

'Whereas my comments did you no favours at all,' said Henik. 'If you were my boss, I'd be worrying about my job.'

'You weren't speaking on behalf of Progress, so you're not my responsibility.'

'Listen to this, though, "With his theories and philosophical questions, Varkesen treated the crisis like an intellectual playground, rather than grasping the impact on ordinary people. Instead of responding to their concerns, he would have them hugging every human they meet, inviting beasts of field and forest into their homes, and watching out for the safety of insects as they walk the pavements." Did I really seem that detached from reality?'

For once, Santi felt she was the one guiding Henik

through an alien environment, rather than the other way around. 'Look who's making the comment,' she said. 'That's from a Heritage outlet. It's an obvious tactic to misrepresent your argument. *Centrespeak* is far more reasonable: "Varkesen points to recent events as evidence of a species that is so much more than we suppose. He's right to do so. We expect from humans an authentic bond of companionship, but with these implants, we impose behaviour controls that make that impossible. Our disdain is born of fear, and our fear comes from the insecurity of a relationship with a species we can't suppress forever.' Or how about this one from *Tribute*: "Varkesen challenges us to identify a single basic capability possessed by people, that is not present to some extent in humans. It's a question that leads to profound conclusions about the way we conduct our affairs." Perhaps that one's pushing the boundaries but…'

'Well, I'm going even further in my head,' said Henik. 'I'm thinking about humans very differently these days. Kali's done that. You'll see what I mean when you meet her. You'll find yourself treating her like a person because, in every relevant sense, that's what she is.'

'I hope I do meet her, but the law decides what a person is, and it generally marks time with public opinion. Social change is something that can't be rushed.'

'Sometimes it's the only way.'

'And then the consequences can be unpredictable, brutal even. Reform will never go as far and fast as some demand, and for others, even modest change will be too much to bear.'

Santi went back to reading, shuffling a cascade of stories in front of her, disturbing them again when she reached through the images to stir her cahcana. She found herself thinking more about Henik, than the news. There was something about his ideas that still inspired her, lifted her with the idealism of their youth. But it was no longer where she was, no longer who she was. *You have a job to do, now. You have to lead in the real world, where people have everyday hopes and fears.* A headline flashed in front of her, snapping her out of her reverie: 'Republic a slave state, says renowned progressive.'

'What is it?' said Henik. 'You've coloured.'

'Henik! Oh, of all the stupid things! You've gone and used the 's' word!'

'What? I...'

'Nico S'tana got to you on the way out of the building.'

'It was just a brief conversation.'

'Are you *mad?* There's no idle chatter with these guys! We've just had human suicide bombers in the middle of Freeport, and you're calling the Republic a slave state!'

'Well, in my view that's about right.'

'You can't just throw around stuff like that! We fought wars all across the Commonwealth to eradicate slavery. You should know better! Slavery is far too sensitive to mention casually or out of context.'

'How is it out of context after what you saw at Midsummer? I thought you saw what it means for humans to live like...'

'Don't start with that, Henik! I was moved by that, but don't you dare use it against me! We're dealing in realities here. Humans can't be slaves, by definition. They're not people, whatever you might think.'

Henik dismissed his news display. 'Well, there we have it. Fundamental, isn't it? You see it one way and I see it differently. As you say, I don't speak for your party. I speak for myself.'

'But the headline calls you a renowned progressive. You're

being linked to the Progress Party whether you like it or not, and that's even without the media knowing about the two of us. I'll have to get people on this right away. We've got to clean this up before it spreads.'

Henik didn't reply. He sat staring at his hands, as he often did when they argued. Santi found herself watching him for some hint of his thought process. In fact, ever since meeting Alka, she'd found herself looking for body language in everyone around her, treating it as something of a challenge. There wasn't much of it on display, beyond the crude shifts of forehead ridges, but if she paid close attention, she did sometimes notice a subtle facial movement that could be quite revealing. *Whatever you may say, your view of humans has changed too. You won't admit it because the implications are too huge, but you do see them differently now.* She decided to change the subject and restore peace between them. 'I'm going out to the Spice Islands, today,' she said. 'There's an emergency summit.'

Henik got up from the table. 'To which you were not invited,' he said, inflicting a wound without even looking at her. 'Nose pressed to the verglas isn't a good look.'

'I need experience of what's happening there to be credible on the subject. I need ideas. And I've been invited by the opposition leader.'

'I thought he was in prison – for being the opposition leader. It's hardly getting your feet under the top table.'

'He's confined at home, allowed the occasional visitor. I know him of old and he'll give me a different perspective on the crisis. It's better than trudging behind Maarten Feyrsten, looking for crumbs.'

Henik picked up his jacket. 'I have to go,' he said.

'We shouldn't part like this, Henik. I don't want to go away when we're upset with each other.'

'You may be upset. I'm just disappointed.'

Santi couldn't ever remember Henik using that word with her before, not in all the arguments they had when they were young. Suddenly, it felt as though he was standing a long way away.

'I can't carry your expectations as a special burden,' she said. 'I can't, Henik. You know we both want to resolve the human crisis. I've seen the Derelict Zone and I get it. But I also understand how the Republic works.'

Henik got his arm caught in his jacket as he tried to put it on. He struggled with it for a moment, then tore it off in frustration and stood looking at it, as if it represented every problem he had. 'While you're in the tropics,' he said, 'Kali's being kept away from prying eyes, accused of the most serious crimes. What do you think Norvik's doing to her, while we sit talking? He may have disposed of her by the time you and Feyrsten get back from paradise.'

'I hope you aren't going to let your professional animosity towards Sig Norvik...'

'Oh, cut it out, Santi! That has nothing to do with it!'

'I've spoken to Norvik, put him on notice. I can't see him doing anything hasty.'

'You don't know that! You're assuming.'

'Look, I understand how important Kali is and...'

Henik snatched up his jacket again. 'But *do* you understand, Santi? Do you *really*? Do you see how high the stakes are, how threatening she is to them, with this Callista phenomenon spreading the way it is?'

'I'm not a fool. Of course, I bloody do!'

Henik went to the door, looked back at her for a few

taught moments. 'Then do something about it, Santi – *do* something.'

Time seemed to have moved more slowly for Yan since he'd lost Kali. Perhaps it was just that it had passed so quickly when she was about, everything seeming new and vibrant when he imagined it through her eyes, every interaction with her a surprise, something to look forward to, something to puzzle about afterwards.

Now his time was weighted with worry, each step he took to find her involved explanations, persuasion, and above all patience. He was forced to wait when he'd never found it more difficult to hold his anxiety in check, wait for others to determine Kali's innocence, to decide whether to send her back to him.

How long Yan had been standing in Sig Norvik's office he couldn't say. He'd paced around it, gazed out of the window at the cityscape, practiced in his head what he wanted to say. But Norvik had kept him waiting until his mind began to wonder if there was some design to it, some intent to wear him down.

He turned from the window and his eyes fell on Norvik's desk, the scattering of objects from his former occupation, awards he'd received for his work on the management of humans, and his research into their behaviour and instincts. He had books on his desk too, a rare enough thing in itself when people went a lifetime without reading any physical artefact.

One book caught his attention immediately. It was one of his own, something Yan had written early in his career. *Ancestral Footprints* was a dry and scholarly work about the founders of the Free Republic. He wondered what it was doing on Norvik's desk, and reached to pick it up, moving the books stacked above it. The motion sparked Norvik's desk into life, showering an array of images across its surface, violent pictures of burning buildings and rampaging humans in the Spice Islands, the horrific attacks on police, their beaten and bloodied bodies lying in the dirt, and then a close-up image of the face of one of the leading rebels, teeth bared in hatred and his eyes white and wild.

Yan recoiled from the images, tried to no avail to shut the display down. The desk kept throwing atrocities at him, until suddenly there was only one image displayed, the shadowed face of Enda Alesund, the Director of the Security Service, sitting for an interview about the carnage in the Spice Islands. 'So, what would you say we can learn from these events?' he was asked. 'What for example do they tell us about the Callista figure who's suddenly emerged in the Free Republic?'

The Director sat forward in his chair, his face cool and his eyes focused. 'We must identify any human who could become a figurehead for insurrection,' he said. 'Even if an animal appears primitive, or the belief system absurd, we must act to neutralise it. As we've seen, once these situations gather momentum, they're difficult to stop.'

'So, what steps should we take to halt the Callista hysteria?'

'You can't remove beliefs, but you can take away the figurehead. You have two choices. You turn the individual so it's co-operative…'

'Or?'

'Or you remove the threat, clinically, permanently.'

Yan's head suddenly felt light, the floor unsteady beneath his feet. When he turned to the window, the horizon had tilted, and for a moment he was out on a ledge and fighting to hold himself upright. *The most senior security officer in the Republic is thinking about killing Kali, advocating it even.* He went to sit down, tried to gather his thoughts, calm himself from the shock.

Norvik came through the door, his manner brisk, and full of energy. 'What a pleasure to meet you, Professor Feyrsten!' he said. 'Has no one offered you cahcana? I'm so sorry! What would your brother say about that if he knew?'

'Please don't worry, said Yan, trying to put what he had seen out of his mind, and focus on the matter at hand. I think my brother has more important things to concern him.'

'Yes, of course, and oh dear, I see you've caught me doing some research on you. You've found my copy of your book.'

Yan realised that he still had it in his hand. He put it down on Norvik's desk, pushed it away. 'Not my best work, I'm afraid.'

Norvik slid into his chair. 'But the subject matter is so fascinating! The Founders' achievement was just breathtaking, don't you think?'

'Well, I'm sorry to spoil it for you, but the book does expose some of them in unpleasant terms. You know, slavers, pirates.'

'True, but we shouldn't judge historical figures by modern standards. That would be unfair, surely.'

'Some say we still have slavery in our modern world. We've just imported a different species and enslaved them. We justify it by saying they're only animals.'

'Well, there will always be fringe opinions, but, as you know I've written extensively on the subject of humans, myself. I understand you've been spending some time with Henik Varkesen, so you'll know I hold different views – as does the Chief Counsellor. How is it that you and your brother find yourselves at odds on the human question? No, forgive me, that was indelicate. I shouldn't probe into family matters.'

Yan found something in Norvik's tone that prickled. It wasn't any discourtesy, any disrespect, but something insincere, as if his comment hadn't been accidental, but well-rehearsed. 'Perhaps we should talk about one particular human,' he said. 'You know that I've come about Kali. My brother said I can see her.'

'We spoke last night. I must say he does impress me, the way he's getting to grips with his office in such difficult times.'

'He's not exactly new to the subject matter, and he's well connected in the major Commonwealth systems.' Yan thought to go on, then realised that Norvik had changed course, and hadn't confirmed that arrangements would be made for him to visit Kali.

'Yes, I'm sure you are right,' said Norvik. 'He's quite a man, to be able to deal with small matters, even as he's rushing off to a conference overseas. Quite a man.'

'And Kali is quite a human,' said Yan, resisting the digression. 'My brother and I both recognise that.'

'Indeed. Kali, the natural. It's all very unfortunate if you don't mind me saying. I wonder that if my training methods had been followed, perhaps this situation would have been avoided.'

With each jab and parry, it was becoming clear to Yan that this was not a simple transaction. Norvik was trying to rattle him. Perhaps that had been his intention from the start. *Perhaps he kept me waiting deliberately. Perhaps the book, the whole desk display…*

'Professor?'

'Yes, well Counsellor, I haven't come to argue, only to gain access to Kali. So, if you'll just provide the authority, please, I'll be on my way.'

'We won't keep you much longer, Professor and I assure you I have no wish to argue either. Although, I know you'll be aware how precarious the position is around the country, and you may have thought about the crucial role your human could play.'

'She's not a terrorist or a rebel,' said Yan, feeling his patience fraying and hoping it wasn't showing. 'Kali's not looking for trouble. She isn't a threat to the Republic.'

'But you've seen the effect she's having.'

'Well, you can thank Torsta Jai and the media for that. It's not Kali's doing.'

'Yet we are where we are, Professor. Your human's mere existence inflames the situation. She could be a figurehead for a full-scale uprising if we allowed it.'

Now Yan knew. He could never prove it, but the interview with Enda Alesund was probably a fake, placed just where he would see it on Norvik's desk. *He thinks you're someone to manipulate, someone he can frighten.*

'Or she could help to defuse the situation,' continued Norvik. 'That is to say, you could make her part of the solution.'

'I'm not following. What do you mean?'

Norvik reached out and tapped the cover of Yan's book. 'Did you ever wonder as you wrote about the achievements of the Founders, what it would be like to actually *do* something like that? Not just analyse history, but *make* it?' He drew his chair closer, leaned over the desk. 'It's not often that a tipping point in history comes, but that's where we are now. Varkesen, Aspil, they don't see it. They're small-picture people, concerned with rights and injustices that can only be seen in their proper context many years from now. But I think you're different. You, with your grasp of history, are a man of perspective. You'll see no doubt, how we stand on a mountain ridge, with a catastrophe on one side that would make the Spice Islands look like a squabble between children, and on the other side peace, a return to prosperity, a continuation of the progress that raised our species up to stride across the cosmos. This moment is history in the making.'

'It's your politician's speech.'

'It's your *citizen's choice*, I would say. Your personal choice.'

'The gods' mercy! How can it be *my* choice? What could I possibly do?'

'I suspect Kali will submit to you. Get her to comply, publicly, and the heat will go out of this crisis. You can pull us away from the edge, Professor. And if you do that, you can take her home.'

Norvik had saved the words he wanted to hear, delivered them with perfect timing. Like it or not the game had brought them to a point where his hopes were soaring, his mind imagining a homecoming. *But there will be a cost. There's always a cost.*

'What does 'comply' mean?' he said. 'What do you want her to do?'

'I want her implanted, Professor. Tomorrow – before the Republic Day ceremony. I want Kali to be the prototype for my new behavioural standards.'

Officer Kanawa completed the formalities at the front desk with quiet efficiency. Yan found himself watching her as she worked. If he had met her out of uniform, he would still have guessed she was a prison guard. Her broad face suggested a spirit as immovable as the cliffs above his beach house, and her squat body stood rock solid on legs that stretched her trousers at the thigh. Yet somehow, she still moved with an athletic grace, and when she spoke her voice was as gentle as it was assertive. However intimidating her appearance, there was something about her that was instantly likeable.

For the first time since he had left Norvik's office, Yan's thoughts escaped from the conundrum of the Counsellor's proposal. He had been weighing it carefully as he walked over from Carnival Square and concluded that it was nothing less than an ultimatum. Now, he allowed himself a brief respite, focused his attention on Officer Kanawa. He watched her from the corner of his eye as she led him along a corridor from the cell block and stole glances as they waited for a lift to take them up to the interview rooms. When the lift slid into view, she touched him gently at the elbow, tipping her head in the direction of the verglas doors, with a hint of a smile. It was the third time she'd touched him, and suddenly, he understood. Whether it was from years of dealing with humans, and whether she realised it or not, she used a language of the body as naturally as Kali. And somehow, for that reason more than anything physical, she was an attractive person.

As soon as the lift doors closed, Officer Kanawa turned and looked up at him directly. 'I hope you didn't mind me contacting you this morning, esteemed. It's just that Kali wasn't sure that you knew where she was. So, I thought…'

'Thank you,' said Yan. 'It was very good of you. I only found out last night where she was being held. From my brother.'

'The Chief Counsellor.'

'He's in a difficult position on this, but that's another matter. You said in your message that you were concerned about Kali. "Confused", I think you said. I hope she's alright. I've been very worried.'

'She hasn't eaten a thing. I'm afraid the compound is a grim place and many of the inmates are ferals who won't be seeing daylight again. Kali's putting a brave face on it, but it's not an environment for a fine animal like her.'

'She doesn't think she's an animal.'

Kanawa smiled. 'I know,' she said. She brought the lift to a halt between floors, stared at her boots for a moment. 'May I speak to you in confidence, esteemed?'

'I'd be grateful if you would. I'm getting a lot of nonsense from officials at the moment, and that includes my brother.'

'I understand. Look… I'm a career police officer and I know my duty, but animals are more important to me than anything. I love working with them. I love being with them.' She examined her hands as she spoke, almost as if she was holding a living creature.

'Then I'm glad Kali's in your care.'

'I wish I could care for them better. All too often though, I have to take them for destruction.'

'That's part of your job? You have to do that?'

'Androids do the actual deed, but sadly, I have to accompany them.'

'Do they know?'

Kanawa breathed heavily. 'Some do. If it comes to it, Kali will know.'

Yan felt light-headed. He pressed his palm against the lift door to steady himself. 'You really think they will…?'

'I hope not, but hoping isn't enough. I've seen humans

destroyed for little more than being inconvenient, and Kali's certainly that. That's why I wanted to give you this reading I took from her when she arrived. I'm sending it to you now. She was clean, Professor. No elemist traces whatsoever.'

'I know she had nothing to do with the Café Republic. She was stolen from me that morning. It might suit them to make a false connection, though. Thank you, officer. I'll show this to my attorney.'

'I'm not sure how much good it'll do,' said Kanawa. 'When a destruction order comes through there isn't always time to appeal it. And with all this unrest in the Republic, they may think they need to do something about her quickly.'

'It seems to be getting worse. I can't believe they are still pushing ahead with the implants. It's madness!'

A furrow gathered above Kanawa's nose. 'I can't bear to watch an animal being implanted,' she said. 'The way they behave afterwards, with those control units on their spines. All stiff and frightened. I just don't understand why people are doing it. They might as well buy an android, as do that to a human.'

'They want me to have Kali implanted. Norvik wants to parade her in public, all meek and compliant. Then, he says I can take her home.'

'What a bastard!' said Kanawa under her breath. 'What are you going to do?'

'I don't know. It's not fair to tell her, and it's not fair not to.'

'You realise what he's up to, I suppose.'

'A public demonstration of the initiative. He wants Kali to set an example. I suppose he's hoping it will kill this whole Callista thing.'

Kanawa thought for a moment, then shook her head. 'I

think it's worse than that, Professor. They'll keep Kali's implant quiet, then make her do and say what they want. They'll try to control the human population through her. Norvik doesn't want to kill the idea of Callista. He wants to *own* it.'

Yan could feel his insides on the move again. 'I can't let that happen. I can't let them use her like that. But what can I do?'

'I bet they want an answer quickly.'

'That's right. It's Republic Day tomorrow.'

Kanawa started the lift again. She stood with her hands on her hips watching the struts moving past outside as it took a turn and ascended diagonally through the building. It wasn't until the doors had opened and she had begun to lead the way along a long white corridor that she spoke again. She glanced behind them and reverted to headspeak. 'Haven't you seen the news, Professor. It's not just Republic Day they're worried about, it's that lunar phenomenon that's happening tonight. It's the Callista Alignment.'

The people of the Marsh Estate came flocking from their houses to watch the spectacle. They stood huddled in the thin dawn light, watching the Feral Task Force assemble. Some of them were fresh from their beds, and others had brought food and chairs, everything they needed for the day's entertainment.

The Feral Task Force arrived in a convoy of transports and hoverbikes, settling in an orderly line across an expanse of rough ground. They dismounted and stood to attention beside their machines, the androids because they knew only order, and the rest because they knew the reputation of their commander.

Torsta Jai stood in her saddle, waiting for the last of the transports to make their way up the hillside from the city, the dust hanging behind them, red and thick in the still air. She was wearing her black combat armour for the first time in years, not just the chest plates and helmet, but the whole ensemble, scarred impressively from years of colonial service. It felt as comfortable on her body as it always had, causing her to stand a fraction taller, setting the adrenaline surging through her system.

But the engagement would be different this time. Taking the Derelict Zone wouldn't be a violent firefight, but a mission of subtle dangers, conducted in full public view and under intense scrutiny. Torsta knew what was at stake. This was the day when she would be forgiven, when her honour would be reclaimed, her place in society restored.

The troops were a mixed bunch, not what she would have selected herself, but still better than she'd feared. The cohort of androids was from storage and had seen better times, but they would do a job. Some she would hold in reserve, and others would drive the primary assault, where their lack of fear would speed the advance. The rest of the force had been drawn from the ranks of the riot police and would be waiting with dry throats. Most had seen only civil action, but nothing that placed their life at risk. There wasn't one amongst them who'd ever killed, let alone done it eye to eye, weapon to flesh. In all, they numbered two hundred, divided into units of twenty, each commanded by someone Torsta knew. That didn't mean she trusted them, any of them, but they were all she had. 'Don't look for perfect,' her father would say. 'Better the bastards you know than the freshers, you don't.'

Torsta's father was never far from her mind on occasions like this. He would make sure his troops saw him before a battle, and Torsta had always followed his example. She wanted them to know she'd be fighting with them, not standing in a control room, playing with schematics. So, she left her hoverbike and walked along the ranks making a few comments on their preparation, stopping now and then to engage in good-humoured banter. Then she called the commanders together and took them to a patch of high ground, where a children's play area offered a commanding view of the Derelict Zone.

'You all know your objectives,' she said, 'but be clear about this: if some of your troops are afraid, that's a good thing. Make sure they all are, because the greatest risk you face today is complacency. This isn't the first time I've gone up against a much inferior force and sometimes they can offer stubborn resistance, even knock you backwards. So, expect the unexpected, and don't let your guard down. Remember what they have to their advantage. They know this place, every alley, every drain hole, every place you can shit. They know where to defend and where to counter-attack, where they can move quickly, set up traps, where they can get up close with blades, points, projectiles. I even have experience of a human using an elemist pistol. So, whatever you think about humans, assume on this occasion that they're as capable as you are. You'll be safer that way.'

Torsta turned to look across the Derelict Zone, over to where the roof of Midsummer Mall was catching the first of the morning solus. 'The ferals have been active in the last few days building a barricade at the mall, and we've found other places they've fortified as well: the terminal building under the sky platforms, the chemical plant, the sewage works. Don't be drawn into pitched battles at those points, just seal them off if they prove difficult to take under control. At the moment, the level of feral activity is very low. Consider that ominous. It's likely that they're expecting an assault and have taken concealed positions. We'll need to root them out patiently. But not *too* patiently – this operation must meet its objectives by nightfall. The alignment of the moons isn't until later in the evening, but if they look at the sky when it gets darker, they might just understand what's going to happen. One last thing. I've said it before, and I am going to say it again, that this operation is major news. The Republic is watching you, the media will get into our comms, so mind what you say. There'll be little credit for getting this right, but serious shit if there are examples of indiscipline. So, you capture rather than harm, wherever you can. Particularly the weak and vulnerable. Stun ferals that resist, and only kill those who are on the list of leaders and agitators. They are our high-value targets and I want to see their bodies lined up for the media this afternoon. Keep your heads, use sound judgment, and be professional.'

Torsta gave the order to start the operation, then withdrew to her hoverbike to check the latest drone feeds. In many parts of the Derelict Zone, there was hardly a feral to be seen, but there were still a few scurrying through the Docklands. She decided to go there first, to ensure the overland link from the sky platforms to the city centre was secured.

A barricade had been raised around the terminal building at the base of the platforms, not as imposing as the one at Midsummer, but still a strong and defendable position. Torsta watched a platoon working its way around the obstacle, moving methodically, covering each other doorway to doorway. She raised her eyes above the barricade, craning her neck to follow the towers up to the lilac sky, where she could make out an ethereal shape between the drifting clouds, a bulk transporter coming into position with a barely audible murmur of docking drives. From over at the sewage works came an occasional crackle of shooting, but the docklands were quiet. Too quiet. She decided to take a unit and attempt to get to the ground terminal herself, pushing through the cargo compound to get behind the barricade on its dockside flank.

For a while they made good progress, advancing half a league through the docklands without opposition. But then they ran into a canyon of containers, a place that couldn't have been better designed if its purpose was to allow a determined group to hold a stronger force at bay. Torsta called a halt and watched for telltale signs, irregular sounds, flashes of solus on unshielded weapons. She called two androids forward and ordered them into the metal valley. They looked at her as androids always did, their black eyes reflecting her own image, pupils constantly adjusting to the ambient light. Then, without question or complaint, they turned and advanced into the killing zone, legs flexed, carbines held ready at the shoulder. Halfway down, they turned in unison and began to climb the containers, presenting an obvious threat to the flank of the barricaded compound behind, as well as an easy target for its defenders.

The counterattack didn't come. The battlement remained still and unoccupied, the morning solus spearing between the containers now, making a stark silhouette of the androids when they reached the crest. They stood there, fully exposed and awaiting further instructions, twitching slightly as their risk programmes battled against a combat override. Torsta gave them a new goal, sending them along the top of the containers to reach the barricade at its end, while she watched for insurgent activity through their eyes. Again, the objective was achieved without resistance, and they were able to climb over the barricade, then drop down onto the forecourt of the terminal complex. Torsta ordered them to scan for human life in the buildings. She took a status update from the unit on the opposite flank while she waited.

'No contact, esteemed,' reported the commander. 'Clear on this side and ready to move in. We have company though. News drone swarm.'

'Ignore it, and move in,' said Torsta. 'We'll be coming in on the opposite flank, so proceed with caution. Weapons to stun.'

She led her unit up from the cargo compound, checking carefully for wire traps as they climbed over the barricade. When they reached the androids, they were crouching close to the terminal wall in an identical posture. They sent Torsta a schematic, showing a cluster of nine humans on the upper floor, and two moving quickly around the lobby. Beyond the building, on the far side of the terminal, the other unit was coming down from the barricade and taking positions behind a row of abandoned transports.

Suddenly, one of the terminal doors burst open and two humans came running out, youngsters so absorbed in a chasing game that they didn't see Torsta until she had moved behind them to block their retreat. They came skidding to a halt and stood staring at her. One began to back away, but the other stood its ground, picked up a piece of stone, and wielded it threateningly.

'Take them,' said Torsta, then turned and went into the building. At the foot of the steps to the upper floor, the schematic sounded a soft alert. The humans above hadn't moved, but now there were only eight readings. The reason became apparent soon enough. Huddled in a corner of the transit lounge the group made a pathetic sight, elderly and weak, holding hands around the body of a withered female. 'Contact made,' she said. 'Secure the rest of the complex.'

An elderly human stood up shakily and walked towards her. There was little flesh on his bones, and what strength that was left in his body seemed to be concentrated in his eyes. He stopped a few feet short of her and pulled open his overalls, thrusting his ribs forward defiantly. Torsta lowered her weapon. 'Where is everyone?' she said. 'Where?'

The man gave no indication that he understood, he just pulled his overalls back further from his chest, his lips drawing a smile across dark and crooked teeth. Torsta turned back towards the steps but was halted by his high-pitched voice behind her.

'Gone!' shouted the old man, 'Gone!'

17

The Trouble Bird

KALI LAUNCHED HERSELF ACROSS the room when she saw Yan. She bowled into him, throwing her arms around his thighs. 'You do come, Yan! Well done! Is for going home, yes?'

Yan lifted her and held her close, pressed his face into her hair. 'Kali,' was all he seemed able to say, but his forehead was working a sequence of shades. Behind him, Awhi Kanawa was standing at the door, arms folded.

'Awhi be good police,' Kali said. 'You do trust.' But when she looked over at her, Awhi glanced away.

Yan took her to sit on a simple bench in the middle of the room. He swallowed before he spoke, and then she knew disappointment was coming. 'Everything's going to be alright,' he said. 'You can't come home just yet, though. I'm sorry, Kali. I'm still talking to the Government about releasing you.'

Kali pushed away the prickling feeling behind her eyes and grasped for a question to ask. 'Maarten,' she said. 'You do talk to brother?'

'Yes, I have. For the moment though, I've brought you some things.' He looked towards Awhi as if seeking permission, then took out a bag. 'I've tried to prepare food like you do. You must eat this, Kali. Officer Kanawa says you haven't been eating.'

'Is for animal food here,' she said. 'I do need people food.' She took the container from his hands. It released a strong aroma as she removed the lid. She sucked its sweetness into her lungs, let it transport her somewhere else for a few moments.

'I've brought some things so you can keep yourself clean as well, and some clothes. I've given clothes to Dill too. She says your name now. I hear her call…' Yan coughed, then looked into the bag. 'Here,' he said.

'Dill be more happy with clothes,' said Kali. She pulled a colourful set of pyjamas from the bag. A picture of Juno in his pantomime outfit came into her head. 'Juno is dead,' she said.

'I know. Jocasta said he attacked her. Do you remember what happened?'

'Always for remember that. Jocasta be very angry. She hit Juno many.'

'But why? Why was Jocasta angry with him?'

'Juno, be strangely.'

Yan took her by the hand. 'Did Juno think you were special, Kali? Do you know the story of Callista?'

Over Yan's shoulder, Kali could see Awhi standing straighter now, paying close attention to the conversation. 'Is green moon. Juno do call me "Callista" and Jocasta be angry.'

'As I thought,' said Yan. He sat taller as if gathering himself to lift something. 'People have seen your picture on the newsfeeds, Kali. They know your face.'

'Is well done, yes?'

'No, it isn't. Many humans have seen you as well. They think you're Callista, the spirit of the green moon. Just like Juno did. Do you understand? They think you've come to help them.'

Instinctively, Kali saw the opportunity before the risk, a chance to bridge a gap in language and understanding. 'I do help!' she said. She stood up and smoothed out her coat. 'I do help.' There was a soft vibration in the air, and Awhi took a step towards Yan. He responded in their impenetrable head language.

'What you do say? Yan? Awhi?'

Pulses were coursing across Yan's forehead now as if his brain was working hard on something. He thrust his hands into his pockets. 'You can't help them, Kali. Humans think you've come from the green moon. They think you're a god. They think you will take them all back to Earth.'

Kali suppressed a sudden urge to laugh. She looked from Yan to Awhi hoping to see some vague sign that they weren't serious. Yan's face kept its own counsel, as it usually did and Awhi seemed to have retreated behind a professional front. She came forward and crouched to look her in the eye. 'It's true Kali,' she said. 'I think that's why my Midge is looking at the moon.'

Kali's eyes suddenly refused to focus. Awhi's face was distorting in front of her, smearing in a carousel of colour. The implications needed no explanation, they were galloping around her head so fast that she found herself gripping the edge of the bench, 'Is danger now!' she said. 'Earth? How I do take to Earth? You do tell is not truth!'

'They know that. My brother, Torsta Jai, all of them know that. But humans don't understand. Tonight, there will be an eclipse. You know we talked about...'

'Yes, understand eclipse.'

'There's a special eclipse of all the moons tonight. All behind the green moon. Humans may think that Callista...

that *you* will help them soon. And it's Republic Day tomorrow I'm worried a lot of humans will be hurt.'

Kali shook her head. 'I not want hurt! What we do? Must think! She walked as far away from them as the room would allow. 'Think!'

'You've met Counsellor Norvik,' said Yan.

'Is not trust, Sig Norvik.'

'You mean you don't trust him?'

'Is what I say – not trust him!' Kali could feel her hands starting to shake. She balled them into fists until she could feel her nails biting into her palms.'

'He wants your help.'

Kali drew a finger across her throat. 'He do want my head. Is bastard!' She heard the air crackle again and looked over at Awhi. 'Is what you do say, yes?'

'Sometimes you have to work with bastards.' said Awhi. 'You've no choice.'

Kali folded her arms and held Awhi in her gaze. '*Always* there be choice,' she said.

Santi Aspil caught her first glimpse of the whitewashed house through a grove of soldier palms, the tropical light flickering through their ranks as her open-topped taxi plunged intermittently from solus to shade. She closed her eyes and allowed the low whine of its drives to tell her when the ride was coming to an end. It was her third visit to the Spice Islands, but the first time she had ventured away from the capital to the other side of the mountain. Here, far from the government offices in Nabrone, the bustle of the markets, and the traffic stacked five-high, nature had fashioned a perfect retreat.

The transport banked into a curving avenue of ferns and

drew up sedately in front of the house. Santi stepped down and waited for the driver to wrestle her bag from behind his seat, before following him up to the porch. From the top step, she could see a curl of smoke drifting across the sea from another of the islands, where the chaos of rebellion was in full flood. She thought of the burning buildings, and the battered corpses and couldn't make up her mind which was more surreal, this island jewel, or the carnage across the water.

The front door opened behind her and a tiny human stepped out. She wore a headdress of bright fabric and a wide smile. 'Welcome, E'Santi,' she said, placing her palms on her knees in the traditional island greeting. She pointed to a little path that wound its way up the wooded hill behind the house.

'Doctor high,' she said.

Santi lifted her eyes towards the summit and hoped the comment was meant literally, given Dr. Bewelna-Todi's notorious penchant for hallucinogens. She thanked the little human and received an even broader smile in return. It retreated through the door dragging her bag and making a clicking sound with its tongue.

Santi followed the path up through the tiered gardens and into the woods, brushing aside the branches of plants outlawed in the Free Republic for their psychoactive properties, and stopping occasionally on the damp steps to allow iridescent beetles to scuttle out of her way. Soon the house had disappeared from view and the canopy was so thick that only occasional shafts of light reached the forest floor, creating pools of brightness in which all manner of tiny insects floated and danced. On she went, over moss-covered roots and the damp mulch of generations, until eventually, as her breath was beginning to shorten, the path broke free of the foliage into an open meadow. From a branch overhead, a bird with exuberant plumage rose with an angry screech to announce her presence on the hilltop.

A wooden folly stood at the summit, a round tower of overlapping boards, rising above a shaded porch and encircled by well-kept lawns. Dr. Bewelna-Todi sat in a rocking chair, something fragrant smouldering in his pipe. He struggled to his feet as Santi came up the steps, then embraced her for slightly longer than she found comfortable. 'Thank you for coming,' he said. 'I don't get many visitors these days.'

'How long has it been? Seven years, at least, I would think.'

'Since my government fell, six, but only three under these intolerable restrictions. As you can see, my life's a harsh one.'

'Brutal,' said Santi, shielding her eyes to survey the hilltop, then turning her gaze out along the coast, where an arc of white sand separated the forest from an azure bay. 'You seem to be bearing up though. You don't look much different from when you taught me at law school.'

'Then I was a failure. I thought I was teaching you objectivity.' He tugged a chair into position for her, then lowered himself back into his rocker.

She turned to the neighbouring island, with its curling plume of smoke. 'And objectively, how would you appraise this situation?'

'Troublesome,' he said.

'That's rather mild.'

The bird that had taken exception to Santi was settling in a tree on the edge of the forest, creating a showy disturbance in the branches. 'Do you know what they're called?' said the doctor.

'No, but I suppose I should. It's your national symbol.'

'The name's practically unpronounceable, so the islanders just call them trouble birds. They shriek whenever they think there's danger.'

'That's your appraisal then? The Spice Islands serve as a warning to other places with human populations?'

'Why else would leaders gather here at such short notice? Of course, they say they want to help us, but mainly they want to prevent contagion.'

'And do you think this rising *will* be contagious? How much do the conditions here translate to other countries?'

'What other country is there but the Free Republic? Oh, don't protest out of politeness, Santi. You dominate Antaris – it's yours. The rest of us exist in your shadow, like so many other worlds out there in your Commonwealth. All of us depend on your approval and tolerance.'

'Alright. How does this crisis translate to the Free Republic, in your view?'

'Your problem is much worse, just at an earlier stage. We can contain ours geographically, while yours will spread across the surface of the planet, then jump to the Home Systems, the Inner Sequence, and beyond. Once this gets going…'

'So, your message is "beware".'

'Well, more constructively, we're inviting people like you to come here and learn. I'll give my opponents credit for that if nothing else. You can fly over the affected areas too, if you wish. You won't see anything you haven't already, but I'm told that first-hand, the scale of it is shocking.'

'I haven't come to be a voyeur. I've come here because I'm already on an accelerated learning curve as far as humans are concerned.'

'It was part of your brief in government,' said the doctor. 'Shouldn't you be an expert already?' He paused as if he expected a sharp reply but Santi just kept her eyes on the horizon and waited for him to continue. 'Don't worry,' he said. 'I'm not judging you any more than myself. In government, you're drawn to immediate priorities, not what might occur in the longer term. And now, out of power, we're reduced to criticising from the sidelines.'

'Perhaps so, but I don't want to do that blindly. I've spent some time with feral humans in Freeport recently and I've started to perceive things differently. I'm trying to imagine a different way forward. That's why I've come. But I'm still not sure why you invited me. You're a traditionalist while my outlook is progressive.'

'Labels, Santi. I'm not sure they have much bearing on the human question if you consider it across worlds. All that matters, is what will work. We have to be pragmatic. We've created this situation over many centuries, and we aren't going to fix it with some riot shields and stun sticks.'

'But those were the tactics you used in power. You had an incident with humans, I recall. Minor perhaps in comparison, but you used force. You crushed it, killed everyone involved.'

Santi wondered whether she'd strayed into unwelcome territory, but the doctor just took another draw on his pipe, blew a steady stream of smoke through his nostrils. 'Now you are judging *me*, Santi. This isn't the Free Republic. You have to adopt policies that will work in their own context.'

'I do know that,' said Santi, suddenly feeling naïve. 'But you were always so considered. Yet still you tried to mould the situation forcibly to meet your perspective, rather than…'

'Moulding my perspective to meet the situation?' The doctor leaned back and looked up at the sky for a few moments while the wooden boards creaked beneath the rockers of his chair, their rhythm marking how the pace of his life had changed. 'Up there,' he said. 'You nearly had a serious collision in your solus yacht a few years ago. Someone cut across your bow.'

'How in all the gods' names do you know that?'

'I was the other yacht. I tacked out of turn – a novice error.'

'You're joking! That was *you*?'

'Fortunately, you're an advanced sailor. You went into a gravity spin and had to take in sail, but it was impressive the way you handled it. I messaged an apology, but I was always a bit nervous at the helm, and after that, I lost my appetite for the sport. So, at least on that matter, I moulded my perspective. I was never going to be able to handle my yacht like you could. So, I traded it for a timeshare in a telescope – the Orbital Array, actually.'

'You're into astronomy?' said Santi. 'I never would have guessed.'

The doctor patted the folly's clapboard side. 'What do you think this is?'

'Don't tell me you've got a telescope in there.'

'Nothing so mundane,' he said, rising unsteadily from his chair again. 'Come and have a look.' He led her through a door into the dark interior of the tower, then up an open staircase to the narrower floor above, where he opened a louvred hatch in the wall to let in some light. However primitive the tower's construction, the technology it held went far beyond Santi's comprehension, a jumble of panels and floating displays around a giant scope that moved with a subtle wave of the hand. The doctor turned it so that it angled through the hatch, a faint whirring starting up inside as it began to track its celestial targets. 'I can access historical feeds from the Orbital Array for free,' said the doctor. 'In fact, from any array in the

Inner Sequence. What costs most of the credits, is the licence to focus the Orbital Array where I want during my time slot. For that brief period it sends everything through this capture point exclusively and in real time. Today, as you might expect, I've been looking at our local phenomenon unfolding.'

'The Callista Alignment. I'm ashamed to say I wasn't aware of it until the news coverage.'

'And it complicates your human issue.'

'Considerably – your point being?'

The doctor offered Santi no more than a glance in response, and she took it as a reproach for her impatience. After a moment, he continued. 'I can't show you what's happening up there right at the moment. Accessing the array this afternoon and tonight is way out of my league, but I have got some material from this morning.' The doctor closed the shutters and as blackness returned to the tower, it was suddenly filled with spheres, moving around and through them with crystal clarity.

'Our moons,' said Santi.

'It's difficult to see the pattern emerging quite yet, but you can see two of the slower ones almost lining up, over there at the edge. The rest are playing out the final movements that will bring them into full alignment tonight, beautiful Callista rising first and closest to us, and fiery Calderon right behind us over here, so it doesn't interfere with the view.'

'It's remarkable.'

'Let me show you something else.' The moons disappeared and were replaced by much smaller objects that hung motionless around the tower, tiny bulbs of light that became even more intense when the doctor shut down the control panels. They stood in the blackness now, the doctor's voice a disembodied presence in the virtual cosmos. 'We're looking across the vastness of interstellar space,' he said. 'The distances are not to scale, of course, but there are sixty-three star systems represented here, some of them part of the Deccan Dominion, but most of them members and vassals of the Commonwealth.'

'I've been to a few of them. The nearer ones were within my remit. But why only sixty-three – the Commonwealth alone has hundreds.'

'These are just the systems of the *advanced* civilisations we've encountered, which I concede is a judgment based on my own criteria. All of the systems are on our spur of the galaxy, and we know them well, those of the Inner Sequence very well indeed.' The doctor went to the edge of the room, to a point of light close to the tower's curving wall. 'This system way out here is different though. It's far beyond the Commonwealth, out of bounds you might say, in disputed spacetime. It has one inhabited planet, which we know surprisingly little about. But it's home to an advanced life form, paradoxically, one we think we know intimately.'

'Humans,' said Santi.

'It's Sun 3, otherwise known as Earth. Of all of the worlds, scattered across these other systems, Earth is perhaps the most similar to Antaris. It was discovered by privateer traders at least half a millennium ago, but it's been off-limits for much of the intervening period. It's never been properly explored, or even visited officially, certainly not in modern times. It's slightly larger than our own world and a smaller proportion of it is covered by water. It revolves a little more slowly, but not much. And it takes roughly the same time to orbit its star. Sun has a slightly different colour to our Solus. It's also younger by perhaps as much as half a billion years than any other star represented here.'

Santi went over to the tiny sphere of light and peered at

it closely, expanded it with her fingers until she could see a tiny grain of reflected light nearby, a brilliant point of blue. 'I see where you're going with this,' she said. 'When you consider how young their system is, the human species is extremely advanced.'

'Well, when our system was that age, none of the complex species had begun to emerge. We've been very slow developers by comparison. I don't know what stage they've reached there now. There's only so much we can understand from a distance, but there's some evidence of increasing energy output and some interesting shifts in atmospheric composition.'

'Rapid development?'

'Hypothetically, but quite likely in my opinion. I suspect that one day humans will join the ranks of the interstellar species.'

Santi stared at the blue spec, a tiny and vulnerable dot in all the blackness. 'Time. I've never thought about it that way,' she said. 'Perhaps we're lucky that time hasn't made Antarians into labourers on Earth.'

The doctor opened the shutters again and led Santi back down the stairs. He squinted at the solus as they emerged onto the decking outside. 'So, what does all that tell you about our human situation?' he asked.

'It gives me more respect for them. We should probably view our human population as an advanced species in the making, one of significant potential and capability. Or depending on your perspective of time, one that's not so far behind us.'

The doctor leaned against the tower, the tropical breeze billowing his shirt. Santi noticed for the first time that he was barefoot. Somehow, he was more a philosopher now, than the ambitious leader she once knew.

'I can respect them,' he said, but I'm still uncomfortable about having a human population amongst us. We've interfered with the development of their species, and in turn, we've become dependent on them. It blunts the pace of our own development, makes us lazy. We need to decouple.'

'What does that mean?' asked Santi, hearing an edge coming to her voice. 'I hope you're not going to suggest…'

'Look up there!' said the doctor, suddenly. 'Can you see it, Santi? It's faint, but even at this time of day you can just about see Callista. I've been there, you know.'

'Have you? How did you get permission to do that?'

'Bluffed my way onto a scientific team, bribed a few people of influence. Oh, don't stare at me like that – I'd do it again in an instant. It's a wonderful place, lush, cool… utterly beautiful.'

'Which is why it's protected, if you're about to suggest what I think.'

The doctor curled his toes over the edge of the decking. 'I'm suggesting a new future for humans,' he said, his voice quietening as he watched the moon. 'A future untainted by our influence, developing close by at their own pace, with pride and autonomy. Callista's protected status was provided by treaty. It can be changed by treaty too.'

'A new home?' said Santi, 'Or just another once-beautiful island with smoke hanging over it.'

'We must make it the former,' said the doctor. He placed his hand on Santi's shoulder. 'I'm going to build an international coalition to campaign for a human homeworld. I can think of nothing more important we can do for our civilisation. That's why I invited you here, Santi. I want you at the forefront.'

***

Sig Norvik stood waiting at his office door when Yan arrived. The Counsellor greeted him courteously, asked about his journey, whether the gods favoured him with good health. His civility wasn't extended to Awhi Kanawa, whom he told to wait outside, and he made no attempt to acknowledge Kali's presence at all. She didn't appear to notice though, trailing behind, the language of her body unusually quiet.

'Please, do take a seat,' said Norvik. 'And if Kali could stand alongside you, she might get some impression of our discussion.'

Kali fixed Norvik with a stare. 'Stand?' she said, then clambered onto a chair between them.

Yan felt the moisture leaving his mouth. Despite what he'd said to her on the way over from Police Headquarters, Kali was already provoking the Counsellor. Norvik glared back at her as he took his seat and all Yan's mental preparation began to dissolve. Suddenly he felt exposed, foolish. He realised with nauseating certainty that his role would be to mediate a high-stakes contest, between one of the most powerful men in the Republic and the little human that only a few days ago he'd bought as a pet.

Norvik sighed heavily. 'I had hoped you would agree to what I proposed Professor Feyrsten, but it appears you won't even bring her to heel in my own office.'

Yan glanced at Kali. He wasn't sure how to read her expression but staring at the Counsellor with her arms folded didn't look particularly submissive. 'Counsellor, I won't have Kali implanted,' he said, 'not when the programme is so contentious and subject to legal challenge.'

'That's precisely why it would be so helpful if you did. It would set such an example.'

'I'm sorry, but it isn't my responsibility to help you. I'd be happy to do so if I thought it would also be helping the Republic...'

'It most certainly would be doing that.'

'If I may finish, please. I haven't even asked Kali about having a behaviour implant. I thought...'

'Ask? You shouldn't have to ask!' Norvik stood up. 'Oh, for goodness' sake!' He turned to Kali. 'Do you want to go home, Kali?' He took an implant from his desk and held it up for her to see. 'Go home?' he repeated, then reached forward and pressed the device between her shoulder blades. Immediately she recoiled, shrugging away his arm, but her eyes never left his face.

'Stop that, Counsellor!' said Yan. 'You can't have this both ways. If you want her to be a compliant animal, then don't think you can negotiate with her directly.'

'I not be *animal*,' said Kali, her voice a low growl.

'Look... I think there's a middle way here,' said Yan.

'I can't wait to hear it, Professor, because time is running out, as is my patience. I must have this situation under control by tomorrow. I need to know very clearly whether you and your human are with me in my efforts to restore order, or whether you are part of this uprising.'

'That really isn't a fair way to...'

'I don't care how fair it is. I only care about ensuring that the public remains secure in a time of crisis. Believe me, if this was about anything less important, we wouldn't be having this conversation – even if you were the Chief Counsellor's *mother*!'

'She's dead. Our mother went to the gods earlier this year.'

'And your human will be dead tomorrow if you don't co-operate!'

A silence descended on the room. Yan felt as if Norvik's words were reverberating inside his body, shaking his blood to foam. Kali's face had darkened. Her eyes were narrower now, and a muscle was twitching in her jaw.

'I shouldn't have said that,' Norvik said eventually.

'No, it's good to know what's in your mind, Counsellor. If we're being threatened, there's no point pretending otherwise.'

'Professor Feyrsten...'

'Actually, I was going to suggest that Kali appears with me on Republic Day and behaves impeccably, follows your standards, but without an implant. And you could stand alongside us and say for the media that she wants humans to be peaceful and obedient.'

'No, Yan,' said Kali quietly.

'You can say she thinks they should return to their owners,' Yan continued, noticing that Norvik's ridges were softening. 'You can say... we can say this green moon thing is nonsense. We can say she isn't Callista and...'

'No, Yan! I not do that!'

Yan had never heard Kali shout before, but now her voice echoed around the room. It felt as if it was sucking the life from his proposal, just as surely as if he was at the beach with the surf tugging the sand beneath his feet. 'Please, Kali!' he said, hearing desperation in his tone. 'Please just do this, and then you can come home. We must stop this Callista uprising, before it's too late!'

Kali shook her head. 'He do say I die tomorrow. Is truth.'

'But Kali, listen to me, please! You don't understand!'

'No, be *you* don't understand! I do *tell* you I not be animal! *Human* not be animal. I do *tell* you!'

Norvik got to his feet, scooping up the implant in his hand, his ridges now vivid. 'I'll tell you what you are! You're…'

'Callista!' screamed Kali. She slammed her fist down on Norvik's table. 'Ca-li-staa! I *do* be Callista!'

18

Warriors

IN THE POD STATION down at the Chemical Works, Alka stood mesmerised by a display of the network, the myriad threads pulsing with traffic, changing colour with its ebb and flow. 'There's so much of it!' she said. 'Where are we, Mike? Show me.'

'There are five stations near here,' said Chemical Mike, pointing at the tangle of filaments at the edge of the metropolis. 'Apart from this station, which is just here, and the one at Midsummer, there's one here, on the far side, by the Pharmas, and on the Dockers' territory, there are two stations, one for the water port, and the other for the sky platforms.'

'And they're all connected.'

'But Midsummer's the only place in our territories where the pods still stop.'

Alka nodded, but her attention had shifted elsewhere. 'Look at all this over here. Hundreds of stations, right across the city!' She pointed at a swirling symbol on the other side of Freeport. 'This must be the port for when they go up to the stars, and up there, where there's tree pictures, must be what they call the Green Zone. And here, right in the centre, there are at least ten stations almost on top of each other! Why do they need them all?'

Abruptly, the display reverted to its default setting of the news, two people arguing about something. Mike touched it with his knuckle to bring the map back into view. 'That central area is all treasure,' said Mike. 'Fancy things for fancy people. They have two stations in this street alone, and another two in this great square next to it, just where the explosion was.'

'How do you know all this? Have you been there?'

'When I lived in here. I spent a lot of time playing with this, figuring the system out. What you see here is just the start of it. Just watch this.' Mike made a few rapid selections from a menu and brought up a labyrinth of tunnels and pipes that made the pod network look simple by comparison.

'What the…? What's all *that?*'

'All the hidden stuff: service tunnels, ventilation ducts, storm drains, sewers. We've got plenty of it underneath the chemical works, but here it's like a city under a city. If there was enough food, the clans could live down here without anyone knowing.'

Alka shook her head. 'Hiding isn't living. Anyway, what about all those moving lights? They must be able to detect what's in the system. Can they show life signals too? Can they see us?'

'In some places. They can only see living beings in the pod network itself, not the other tunnels.' He waved a dirty finger at the screen and brought up a different image, thousands of red dots gathered in clusters around the pod stations. 'People and humans.'

'Then, they'll find us,' said Alka. 'It's just a matter of time before they realise where we are, and then they'll hunt us down dot by dot. The display reverted again to the news, but this time, when Mike went to reactivate the map, Alka blocked his hand. 'Hold on!' she said. 'Hold!'

The display was showing a schematic of the Solus and its planets, then it focused in on Antaris with its eight moons, each orbiting at different speeds, until suddenly they lined up behind the green sphere of Callista. The news report kept repeating the schematic, while a reporter stood outside on a rooftop with a group of people, all looking up at the sky. 'Do you understand what that people is saying?' asked Mike.

'Just odd words,' said Alka. She's saying "Callista" a lot. Wait... do you know what? I think he's saying that all of the moons are going to line up behind Callista! That's the *signal*, Mike! It's the Redeemer! She's moving the heavens for us!'

'But *when?* When is the alignment going to happen?'

The image changed. Now, on one side the schematic continued to play, and on the other a small army was shown assembling above the Derelict Zone, the skyplatforms dominating the horizon behind them. There were armoured hoverbikes parked in a line and troops were climbing into transports. There were androids too, soulless things that Alka remembered from her time working in the forests.

'It's begun,' she said. 'The Time of Times is here at last. There's no time to lose, Mike. We must send word. You go to the Dockers' stations, if you can still get there and I'll go to the Pharmas, then over to Midsummer. Tell them to stay in the service tunnels where they can't be seen. Tell them to assemble at daybreak at that place where the stations are clustered, under that great square in the centre of the city. We're going to make the People release the Redeemer.'

'But... but how can we do that?'

'She will show us. With her help, we'll take that square and make them listen.' Alka turned and started to run towards the station entrance. 'I must tell her our plan, Mike! I must go to the fountain and ask Callista for her help one last time!'

It wasn't the argument that bothered Henik. He'd quarrelled with Santi on plenty of occasions in the past, and he saw it as nothing more than the way they were together. There would never be anyone else for him, of that he was certain and if they were to make their relationship work a second time around, they would need to take the odd disagreement in their stride.

No, it was more than that, he realised as he wandered the old city, his path aimless, but drawing him towards the Commonwealth quarter. There in the bustling alleyways, and ancient courtyards he could lose himself. There the noise and colour swirled around him like a blanket, freeing his mind with its chaos, allowing his thoughts to crystalise more easily than any quiet bar in the centre of town.

Their roles had changed, that much was clear, but that wasn't what he found troubling either. He knew it would be like this. Santi was at her peak, and she'd got there without his help, rung by rung, through her talent and sheer hard work. If his carelessness caused her problems, it was hardly surprising that she would take him to task about it. He would get over it, and so would she. *But it will be fine only until my next indiscretion. Then we'll have it all over again.*

Halfway down the street. the crowd thickened, and the sound of drums and horns came pulsing through the thick air. People began to draw aside and suddenly, a parade swung out of a side street and began to make its way up the corridor of people, all swirling capes, banners, and resounding volleys of chanting that were taken up and thrown back by the crowd. It was the first time that Henik had seen the procession since he was a child, the celebration of the Commonwealth's diversity on the eve of Republic Day. It marked the beginning of the festivities, gloriously defiant in its pageantry, centuries after the conquest of the last civilisations of the Inner Sequence.

Henik backed himself into a stone alcove and stood shoulder to shoulder with a rosy-cheeked Chotai matron, who took his hand in hers without eye contact or introduction. 'Svezia! Svezia!' she shouted and threw a handful of dried flowers over the procession as it passed. Henik tried to identify each of the peoples as they went by. There were Hela tribesfolk, with their flat features and piercings, Icefolk from the frozen worlds in the Telar system, their faces covered by hair, and their eyes a piercing blue. And there were little Sand people whose planet had a long name that no one could ever remember, but didn't need to, since it translated as 'the planet where the Sand people come from.' They sat high on their indigo Dor birds, controlling them with high-pitched 'Yip, Yip' sounds, and the motions of finely curved canes. Each were exotic to the Antarian eye, proud citizens of the Commonwealth, though different enough in physiology to qualify as separate species.

It occurred to Henik that one species was not on parade though. It was found throughout the Commonwealth, yet was unrecognised due to its lack of a home, any place where it was dominant, where it thrived. Humans had no culture, no artifacts, or ancient traditions. Instead, they belonged with the lower order of beings, weaker physically, disadvantaged in intellect it was supposed, a species of mere pets and chattels. They were like the dorgs that bounded beside the procession, and the pogs clinging to the sides of wealthy off-world merchants. They were lower even than that, Henik thought, the sheer number of them diluting their value or significance.

But there were still humans at the parade, even if they

weren't represented. He could see a group of them around a bin in an adjacent alley, and up on a roof, a juvenile was cleaning the gutters. Then a flax-haired young male came by, naked but for a thin strip of cloth and a feathered hat. He was ignored even though he danced with bells on his clogs, stepping lively to the encouragement of a whip, which snicked the air above him. A jowly Murthian street trader was tugging him by a bond collar and collecting credits from anyone he deemed to have been entertained. He stopped and looked threateningly at Henik, while the human quick-stepped in front of him.

'Credie!' he whined, his hands moving in a hypnotic flourish.

Henik drew his jacket closer. 'Not a chance,' he said and moved aside to let him pass. The Murthian, held him by the arm. 'You want this one give you service?' he said and pulled the human to his side, gripping his face to open his mouth. 'See, no teeth!'

Henik wrenched himself free and walked away. He didn't look back. His thoughts were solidifying, now. His argument with Santi was bound to fester. She was pragmatic about the human issue, moved and sympathetic, but still navigating by her political instincts. For him though, everything was changing. It was Alka. It was Kali. It was the boy with bells on his toes. They *were* slaves, people of a different species, ripped from their roots and spread carelessly across an ocean of stars. There could be no turning away from the truth, no arguments of convenience, no compromising an honourable cause. *Not even for Santi's sake.*

Henik had no recollection of his walk back through the streets. The entrance to his building was suddenly there, in front of him. Then, he was sitting in his reclining room, staring into space. A flask of cahcana had somehow appeared in his hand and the pot was chirping merrily in the kitchen. He decided he would stay inside for Republic Day, do nothing but watch the events on his feed, with the windows shaded. And wait for Santi to return.

Out in the provinces, the disturbances were continuing. Sabie had been in the spotlight again as a place of unrest, but it was now just one of many towns where protests had taken root. Public concern had spread to the mountains and beyond, where village communities were reporting a steady stream of humans migrating to unknown destinations. In several regional cities, there had been clashes between protestors and police. The coverage focused on one town, Jelkavik, where the authorities were struggling to disperse a crowd that comprised not only disaffected citizens but humans too, some unaccompanied yet still accepted among the protestors. It was easy to understand why the media was focusing on these images; they were immensely powerful, not just raising the prospect of a full-scale uprising, but presenting it as an alliance against the government. *Is this a turning point? Is this the moment when everything changes for the better… or gets much worse?*

Sig Norvik appeared regularly, repeating his comments from the Georgi Factor. He was well-briefed now, managing to appear calm but not complacent, outlining the actions he was taking with confidence. It was his references to the Carnival Square explosion that Henik found most annoying. He was exploiting it shamelessly to justify a policy position he'd decided beforehand, calling it 'a declaration of war on our society', and steering interviewers towards the 'fightback' in the Derelict Zone.

Norvik's tactics might have worked better if the action against the ferals had more to show for it. The longer the operation went on though, the more it looked as though Torsta Jai was hunting shadows. The news drones had no pictures of snarling humans being rounded up, let alone the barricade assaults that had been predicted. Instead, the force was moving unopposed through the Derelict Zone, finding nothing more than small pockets of vulnerable humans, cowering in corners.

As the day progressed, Henik saw the tone of the coverage shifting. The Chief Counsellor was attracting criticism for being out of the Republic at a time of crisis, and Widdig Terreden had to deal with persistent questions on Santi's whereabouts too. But the main story had become the Callista Alignment, which was being run side by side with coverage of the 'moon-watching hysteria' gripping the human population.

They were showing the schematic of the alignment again when Henik's door announced an unexpected visitor. Yan didn't wait until he was inside, before he launched into his story, the words erupting from him in a monologue of panic so that a neighbour opened a door opposite to see what was going on. Henik drew Yan inside and listened without comment while he paced around the kitchen, explaining what had happened.

'Why did she do it Henik? What possessed her to behave like that? I told her what she needed to do if she wanted to come home, and now she's given Norvik the perfect excuse to send her to the elemist chamber! I thought I had a chance to get her out of there. She even said she was Callista!'

'Well, let's just think about this,' said Henik. 'Let's just...'

'She *shouted* it at him, Henik. "I am Callista!" she said. Why would she do that?'

'A few days ago, I would have said that humans work in packs and they follow strong leadership. She sensed you weren't taking a position of strength, so she went her own way. It's the law of nature. Fear is the weakest signal to give, and you were afraid.'

'Oh, well thanks for that! What else could I do, but try to negotiate? Her life is at stake!'

Henik poured him a stiff shot of mead. 'Well, as I said, that *would* have been my view a few days ago, when we were still thinking of Kali as a creature driven largely by instinct. But we're way past that now, and that makes it more complicated.'

'What do you mean?'

'I mean that we should assume she was thinking about the situation rationally. She told you she didn't trust Norvik. I can't argue with that. And you tell me that he'd just threatened to have her destroyed. Summarily executed, would be a better description.'

'Then, why would it be rational to provoke him?'

'Not provocation, she just reached her limit in the negotiation, her limit in *your* negotiation. She's told us very clearly, Yan. She doesn't expect to be treated as an animal. Hasn't that been her message from the beginning?'

'But it's self-destructive!'

'If you think you're probably dead anyway, maybe you take the risk. And she's just raised the stakes for Norvik too by adopting the Callista persona.'

'Oh, come on, Henik! I'm as impressed by Kali as anyone, but do you really think this was calculated? She was really angry, with me I think, as much as anyone else. You could feel the force behind her eyes, the intensity. I don't think I'll ever forget it.' Yan's shoulders sagged. He looked defeated, drained of energy. 'I've let her down,' he said. 'I've lost her trust. She thinks I took Norvik's side, against her. She was shouting at me as well, even when the police officer was dragging her away.'

'Was she? What was she saying?'

'Just what she said to Norvik. She was staring at me and shouting that she was Callista.'

Henik took a gulp from his flask. 'And so she is,' he said. 'Yan, my friend, you can be slow on the uptake sometimes.'

'What? I don't...'

'Don't you see? We aren't the only ones who've changed our perspective in the last few days. Kali has seen the brutal way humans are treated – experienced it first-hand now. And now she's told you she won't play the role expected of her, not for people she doesn't trust or a state of affairs she doesn't accept. Being Callista might just protect her, but not if she's only declaring it in private. It's a risk Yan, a huge risk, but...'

Yan put his cup down hard, sending the mead jumping over the rim. 'She's telling me to go public,' he said. 'She wants me to *announce* her!'

The Feral Task Force had occupied the whole of the Derelict Zone's central valley without resistance. They had set up control points, removed street barriers, and occupied key buildings and facilities, checking them carefully for traps and taking up sniping positions. By late afternoon, the units were spreading right down to the coast, mopping up the occasional small groups of humans, the elderly and infirm mainly. But as for the main body of the feral population, the hunt went on without success. The platoon commanders' determination turned gradually to frustration, and then as shadows lengthened, a desperate race against the failing light.

From her vantage point on a hill above the chemical works, Torsta Jai could see the mission unravelling, the metrics of her failure projected all too clearly on her schematics. The sky was darkening, and already some of the moons were showing themselves. *Nothing to show for the day, but territory. Not a single active feral... not one. Where the fuck are they?*

She stepped up onto the saddle of her hoverbike to scan the horizon and noticed one of the commanders trudging up the hill from the coast road. She pulled the bike into a steep turn went down to meet him.

'You're out of shape, Commander,' she said, drawing up beside him. She waited as the man struggled to catch his breath, the colour high in his cheeks. 'A change from desk work, is it?'

'Sorry, esteemed... I didn't want... I didn't want to risk this intel on the comms. We've found elemist traces in the chemical works. It matches the Carnival Square signature.'

'Good work, Commander. Is there a trail to follow?'

'We're on it, esteemed. We're into the pod system, tracking in the direction of the city centre.'

'What? The system's closed! There's been no breach. All the security doors are intact.'

'No break in, esteemed, but it looks like those feral twins took their device in that way.'

'Shit! They have access! That's where the fuckers are! How is it they aren't showing up on the system maps?'

'We don't know yet, esteemed. The pod stations and platforms are all visible, but I don't know about the tunnels. And then there's the service pipes and utilities.'

'I want the plans and routines for the whole system, Commander. I want every channel and gutter searched, every pipe and shaft, right across the Derelict Zone. We're finishing up out here and shifting the focus underground.' Torsta turned her bike to project a map of the Derelict Zone onto the road. 'Five stations. Entry points at the docks and... What?

What's that?' A flickering signal was shining through the canopy of Midsummer Mall. 'It's saying there's a human in there. I thought that area had been cleared.'

'Yes, esteemed. Apart from the barricade.'

Torsta located a nearby drone and directed it to investigate. It took a few moments for it to find the human but when it did, the picture came through clearly. Torsta felt her throat tighten as she recognised the face of the feral leader. 'Can't believe it,' she said. 'It's standing by the fountain, bold as anything!'

'Esteemed?'

'That's the one, Commander! That feral's right at the top of our kill list. And it's mine.'

It took Alka most of the day to reach the Pharmas on the far side of the Derelict Zone, then return to Midsummer. She wouldn't have attempted it before, walking alone through the territories of several rival clans, but now things were different. Now the danger was coming from the People, and it came in the form of machinery and elemist weapons, and implacable metal warriors. This danger couldn't be fought and could barely be resisted; it had to be evaded. And so, she moved only as quickly as caution allowed, listening for sounds of the approaching army and staying away from major routes and open spaces.

The discussion with the clan leaders assembled in the Pharmas' pod station had taken longer than she'd hoped. Mizumi was a formidable leader, quick-witted, and persuasive. Alka knew that she would need her support to convince the others and so she spoke to her first on her own. She knew that an assault on the Derelict Zone had started but she was sceptical about an underground march to the centre of Freeport, and she didn't share Alka's conviction that Callista would provide a solution when they got there. In the end, it was Mizumi's own logic that swayed her mind, knowing that the forces sent to attack them expected to find them in the Derelict Zone, and the centre of their shining city was the last place they would look.

'Alright,' she said. 'We'll follow you. We'll go where we're least expected, and hope Callista makes her presence felt. And if she doesn't, then at least it's better to be exiled from our home, than exterminated.'

The daylight was waning by the time Alka got back to Midsummer Plaza. The People had already been there and punched a broad gap through the barricade, but now they had gone. They would have found they were grasping at shadows, hunting for an enemy they had underestimated. Alka studied the open space, watched for movement in the hidden places and on the rooftops. Then, when she went forward, she kept to the arcades and skirted blind corners. Still, her eyes wandered, drawn to the sky where the coming wonder would unfold. With the exception of the angry one, all the moons were now visible, each moving steadily along paths that would bring them into alignment, a single glorious moment when Callista would embrace them within her green aura. With each step Alka felt herself being drawn upwards, lifted by her ribs until she realised she was walking on her toes, and the dangers of the square had slipped to the edge of her mind.

The mall was quieter than she'd ever known, so still that the fountain could be heard as far away as the entrance, and by the time she'd reached it, the rushing of the water sounded almost deafening. She put her javelin down and scooped the water into her hands, bringing it slowly to her lips to drink. Then she took hold of the fountain's edge and plunged her head into it.

The bottom of the fountain was dressed in its familiar colours, alternating green and silver tiles, set in a pattern that tricked the eye. The twisting light fairies had taken their leave for the day and the water greeted Alka in sombre folds. She released some of the air in her lungs, the bubbles rattling past her ears as she began her prayer. *Sweet Redeemer, I'm here again to beg your blessing at the Time of Times. Tonight, you are calling the moons into order and we will rise to make ourselves heard in your name. Show us the way, Callista. Guide us with your gift!*

Alka sensed a change in the water. It began to move to a different rhythm, not the soft rush of the fountain, but something else, the stirring of a celestial voice perhaps, a sacred message. *No, it can't be. The sound has no beauty. It's harsh it's...* She jerked her head out of the water, spun towards the source of the noise. Up at the rear entrance, a hoverbike had entered the mall. The rider had dismounted and stood looking down the boulevard to the fountain, rotating her shoulders and flexing her knees as if preparing for combat.

It's Torsta Jai. You've sent her, Callista. You've sent me a test! Alka began to back away from the fountain, picked up her javelin as she went, and the enemy responded, started forward at a run.

Alka turned and sprinted for the entrance to the mall, glancing at the mosaic as she passed. Then she was out onto the plaza, running under the dusky sky, scanning it for a hint of divine intervention. She reached the barricade and began to climb, just as Torsta Jai burst through the doors behind her. She watched her over her shoulder, while she picked her way up through the precarious tangle of furniture, appliances, and building materials to her defensive position at the top. There she stopped and readied herself for the attack.

The enemy slowed to a walk as she approached the barricade. She halted at its base and studied it, hands on her hips, then pulled a pistol from her thigh holster. Alka ducked behind the leg of a thick wooden trestle, but then to her surprise, the enemy threw the pistol aside and stood there in a silent challenge. *A warrior. She wants this hand to hand.*

Alka was under no illusion that she could defeat Torsta Jai without some advantage; the disparity in their size was too great. But she had no intention of running to the pod network and giving away their plan. Somehow, she had to buy the clans more time to get through the drainage channels, to escape beneath the city. *This is where I stand, and where it must end.*

She raised her head cautiously, looking for the pistol. It lay on the ground, well out of Torsta's reach. Slowly she stood up, raised her javelin above her head, and hurled it into the plaza behind her. 'Are you coming?' she shouted. 'If you want me, you'll have to climb! Come on then – climb!'

As if she'd understood, Torsta bounded onto the barricade, scrambling first over the burned-out transports and containers at its base, then moving up through a jumble of packing cases. Alka picked up a short baton of piping, brandishing it as she moved along the battlement to a position directly above Torsta's line of ascent. It was enough to cause the enemy to pause, choose a different route, traversing into a prickly mass of canteen furniture at one end of the barricade. It flexed and creaked with her weight, and her progress slowed, but still, she came on undeterred, her face showing no sign of her murderous intent.

It wasn't until the enemy had closed to just a few units

that Alka began her defence. It wasn't the noble hand-to-hand combat she would have preferred, but it was the only tactic that made sense. She started to wrench pieces of furniture from the structure and hurl them down at the attacker. First, it was a stool and a garden chair, then some small domestic appliances. Torsta ducked them easily enough or deflected them with her armoured gauntlets, but her advance had halted, and she was forced to focus her attention on avoiding the missiles.

Alka paused for a breath and their eyes met. There was no anger or fear in Torsta's stare, just the resolve she often saw in herself when she looked at her reflection in the fountain. *It's who we are and we have this, only this in common.*

Now Alka began on the larger objects in the barricade, prising them loose as best she could, raising them above her head to launch them down the barricade, so they would dislodge other objects as they went. A table took with it a heavy stack of pots as it fell, forcing Torsta to take cover as they crashed past. Next it was a docking drive, which she dislodged with a few heavy kicks. Then suddenly, as she'd hoped, the top of the barricade started to lose its stability, began to shift and moan like an injured monster.

Alka found another large transport component that was anchoring much of the structure around it. She pushed at it with her feet, bracing her back and using all the strength of her legs to break it free. It was stubborn to begin with, but when it came loose, it happened abruptly, setting the whole section of the barricade into motion. Suddenly Alka's handhold came free as well, and she began to slide herself, scrambling and kicking frantically against the current of debris. She could see Torsta Jai struggling to hold her position too, stabbing at the moving material around her with a hunting knife, though watching all the while as her quarry was drawn towards her.

Alka could see what was going to happen and she was powerless to stop herself slipping towards Torsta Jai's blade. Another moment, another desperate stab, and the knife would anchor itself in her leg. Instinctively she rolled, forgetting the need for something to grip, rolled and fell, plunged past her enemy, and felt the point of the knife graze her shoulder. And then the barricade lost the last of its cohesion.

Alka hit the ground hard and lay with her face to the heavens. The barricade swung into view as it broke above her, curling like a wave, gathering momentum, collecting larger objects further down until the whole tangled bank was tumbling. She scrambled backwards, straining to catch a glimpse of Torsta amid the squealing chaos. For an instant she came into view, still stabbing with her knife, and then she was swept away.

Alka waited for the avalanche to subside. Then, when at last the barricade lay still, she got to her feet carefully and checked herself for injuries. She felt no elation, not even relief to be alive, just the urge to finish the contest, to know that the test had been passed. The last threads of light were leaving Midsummer Plaza now, the multitude of shapes at the base of the barricade almost indistinguishable in the gloom. At first, there was no sign of Torsta's body, then as she picked her way further around the debris field, she spotted a gloved hand, still gripping a hunting knife. The point began to move as she came close, the fingers flexing on the handle.

Torsta's grip was strong and Alka struggled to prise the knife from her. Then she set about moving the debris, throwing it aside until the enemy's head and torso were clear. Something was trapping one of Torsta's legs, but her body armour had done its job well enough. Her face had taken a beating, but she was breathing steadily, staring up blankly, as if resigned to her fate.

It wasn't the first time that Alka had dispatched a fallen enemy and she remembered each one, from her first skirmish in the clan wars to the vicious culmination of the conflict with the Squalids, that winter past. It was the way of warriors, the way they lived, the accepted way of passing from mortality into memory. Yet somehow, this time it was different. Now the moment had come, Alka found her will to take another life faltering as it never had before. The enemy seemed to sense her hesitation and muttered something. There was no understanding the words, but Alka knew in the tilt of her chin that they were not an appeal for mercy.

She straddled Torsta's chest, pinning her shoulders, then drew the knife and said the only words they would both understand. 'Torsta Jai,' she said, then pointed to herself. 'Alka.'

'Alka,' murmured the fallen soldier, completing the introduction. She could see what was coming and waited silently for it, her eyes following the knife as it rose above her head.

Suddenly the blade shifted in Alka's vision, twisting with reflections of the night sky, its colour turning from silver white to jade. She lifted her head to look at the moons, the furthest now in partial eclipse and the others converging to make their divine appointment. The green moon looked to Alka just as it had done that first time in the forest when she lay pinned herself, and the wollven were circling. *Am I the wollven, this time, Callista? Is this the real test?* Slowly she lowered the knife and slid it back into the sheath on Torsta's thigh.

'Your life is not mine to take, Torsta Jai,' she said. 'You belong to Callista now.'

***

'No. I have no comment to make on Professor Feyrsten's claim,' said Sig Norvik. He spoke slowly, determined not to let his composure slip in front of Nico S'tana. 'You'll be aware we have plenty to occupy us at the moment, and the public may be assured that my attention is focused on higher priorities than any individual animal.' He squashed the hologram with the palm of his hand, terminating the call. 'Shit!' he said. 'Shit!'

Across the office, Styx Kaskai stood watching. 'We'll have to issue a formal response,' she said. 'How long have we got, Counsellor?'

'No time at all. They're going live now. Pull it up, will you.'

Panos appeared in the doorway. 'Report from the Derelict Zone,' he said.

'Well, it'd better be positive, because if I get any more bad news today...'

'It's not, Counsellor, but you'd better hear it.'

Norvik slumped back in his chair. 'What's Torsta done? Amaze me.'

'She's missing. She went to engage a feral leader on her own, and she's been out of contact ever since. They're trying to locate her, but her comms are out.'

'The commander of the operation going rogue – just what we need! Anything else?'

'She gave orders for the task force to move into the pod system. She thinks that's where they've all gone.'

'There's never been a breach of the system before, has there? How could they have broken in?'

'Legitimate access, it seems.'

'And I suppose they've no idea where in the system

they've all gone. How did we not know they had access? The Security Service in this town is a joke! They could be heading for the city centre as we speak!'

'Here comes the news report,' said Styx. 'It's S'tana again, Counsellor.'

The wall of Norvik's office burst into life, Nico S'tana's image stepping out into the room from a background graphic of the Callista Alignment. He was dressed more formally than usual, in a well-cut grey tunic with black detailing.

'The Callista affair gathers momentum,' he announced. 'In sensational breaking news, we've learned that the object of human devotion is a unique *natural* specimen, stolen from the beach house of the Chief Counsellor's brother, Professor Yan Feyrsten.'

'Oh, for fuck's sake!' shouted Norvik. 'Look at him! He's loving every moment! Why didn't we have a plan for this, Styx?'

The image of Kali being taken from the ministry by Torsta Jai, appeared behind S'tana, alongside one of Yan Feyrsten standing at the gates of the National Academy. 'A statement from Professor Feyrsten claims that the human female in police custody is the spiritual leader of the human population. He is demanding her immediate release. Extraordinarily, he states that the human was sourced from a planet in the distant Sun system. The planet, Earth, will be known to some as the ancient origin of the human species. Certainly, the striking resemblance of this human to the storybook image of Callista only adds to the mystery of the moon-watching epidemic. So far, the Government has declined to comment, but with increasing unrest around the country, and tonight's unprecedented alignment approaching, the emergence of such a compelling figure for the human population is a critical development in this crisis.'

'Turn it off,' said Norvik. He stood up and went to the window, the panorama now threatening to engulf him. He felt unsteady on his feet as if he was about to plummet from the window. He closed his eyes, and tried to pull his thoughts into order.'

Alid's reflection appeared in the window. The android was holding a folded document with a traditional legal seal. 'What is it now?' said Norvik. 'A physical message. Never known a good one of those.'

Panos took the document from Alid and broke the seal. He scanned the message inside and snorted. 'It's a Writ of Deliverance,' he said. 'From Santi Aspil. It's a sharp move.'

'Just bloody explain it to me, will you?'

'It's one of the most time-honoured legal devices. It requires us to produce a prisoner for due legal process.'

'Prisoner? It's just a human!'

'It's true that this law is only for people. What Aspil's doing is questioning whether, in this instance, a human should be considered a person.'

'But that's just ridiculous! How does she think she can make that stick?'

'She probably doesn't. But the argument will need to be heard, and that can't happen until after the holiday. Santi Aspil is trying to slow us down, to stop us from destroying the animal, if that's what you decide to do.'

'And does this writ achieve that?'

'Yes. I guess it does.'

'Guess? I don't want guessing! Does it, or doesn't it?'

'We could get a waiver in extraordinary circumstances. But that might be seen as a tacit acceptance that the writ can be applied to a human.'

'We can deal with that if we have to. What would constitute extraordinary circumstances?'

'National Emergency – an immediate threat to the Republic.'

Norvik sat down at his desk, rocked back in his chair. 'Interesting,' he muttered. He looked up at Styx. 'First things first.' he said. 'Statement: the human isn't some figure of children's imagination. She isn't even from Earth.'

'But that's not true, Counsellor. The CC's brother has shown that...'

'That's *our* truth, Styx! You find the right words, but we do *not* concede that she's from Earth. We are simply holding her while we follow up on intelligence regarding the explosion.'

'And Yan Feyrsten?'

'We treat all citizens fairly, regardless of family connections. All that sort of thing. Then follow with some patriotic stuff.'

'I'm going to have to put something out on the task force as well,' said Panos. Without causing alarm that we have a feral population invading the pod system.'

'Talk it down. Part of an ongoing operation.'

'And that's just the message. There's also the actual situation to deal with.'

'Alright, Panos – I know! I'm not some village idiot!'

Styx was working head down to the tabletop, her fingers rattling furiously across the verglas. 'Almost there with the statement,' she said. 'Ah! Terreden has just issued the Progress response.'

'Quick off the mark,' said Panos. 'Must have had prior notice from Feyrsten.'

'They're welcoming the announcement, saying Callista could be the way to restore stability. The statement says that if the Government can't get hold of the situation, maybe a human role model would be helpful.'

'That piece of shit! Get something into our statement about this, Styx. Say something about not using a national crisis to play games.'

'And where does this leave us with Feyrsten?' said Panos. 'And his human?'

'You just focus on your brief. I want those ferals out of the pod system, do you understand? Mobilise the National Guard if you have to, orders to shoot any animal that resists arrest, including any trying to avoid capture.'

Norvik brought up an image of Kali over his desk. 'Absurd that one little animal can cause so much trouble. We're going to cut Feyrsten out of this now. I'll deal with her directly.'

'You're going to *negotiate* with a human?' said Panos. 'Doesn't that go against everything you've said about their capability?'

'It won't be negotiating. An animal can't consider the mind of an opponent. It can't form a counter-strategy. With humans, you simply start from a position of strength, incentivise positive behaviour, threaten punishment for the opposite. It's a one-way process.'

'Isn't that what you've already tried?'

'I should've realised that a human wouldn't fully appreciate its own mortality. That takes an advanced level of self-awareness. But they're instinctively tribal and I think we can use that to our advantage. Let's see how the goddess Callista finds the burden of leadership when the fate of her followers depends on her.'

'What are you suggesting, Counsellor?'

Norvik turned back to the window, the lights of the city

spreading below like a carpet of luminous thread, filaments of knowledge and development that placed Antarians above all other peoples, and people far above the crude impulses of creatures.

'Out of adversity…' he mumbled. 'I think this might still come together very nicely. Get that officer from the animal pound over here, Styx. I want to make sure this is understood. That human has a decision to make: whether to comply or to make herself and all her followers a threat to national security. We'll give her a choice. One way we win, and the other, she loses.'

19

Redemption

KALI DIDN'T WANT AWHI KANAWA to see she'd been crying. She hugged her knees to her chest and pretended to be sleeping when she heard her coming, letting her hair fall forward to hide her face.

Awhi didn't speak. There was just the sound of food containers being opened and pieces of matting being rearranged. Then it was quiet, or what passed for quietness in a place where there was always something unpleasant reaching the ears. After a while, Kali's curiosity got the better of her, and she raised her head to peer through a gap in her hair. Awhi was also sitting, head back against the wall of the pen, hands hanging loose over her knees. 'Hate night shifts,' she said. 'Mind if I join you?'

'I give you this space,' said Kali. 'When I die.'

Awhi closed her eyes. She breathed slowly through her mouth, exhaling each time with a soft hushing sound. 'You're not going to die,' she said. 'I'm staying right here tonight.'

'Norvik. He do say…'

'I know what he said, and I know what you said too. "Callista." Why did you say a crazy thing like that?'

Perhaps she was right, Kali thought; perhaps it was crazy. She'd been asking herself why she did it, ever since she was dragged from Norvik's office. The anger had been building inside her for days, the feeling that she was being pressed into a smaller and smaller space, until she could do nothing but explode. But it had been a calculation as well. She'd felt it, her brain going through the gears, not front of mind, but still working the situation, knowing there was more safety in the bright light of publicity than making a deal with a man like Norvik. *And then there was Yan…*

'Yan is not well done. Not tell Norvik I not be animal.'

'He was only trying to protect you. He was scared for you, Kali. Don't be angry with him.'

'Must be scared for *all* human.'

Awhi opened her eyes and handed her a blanket. 'You look cold without your coat,' she said, changing the subject rather too obviously. 'I'm sorry I had to take it from you. You can have it back tomorrow.'

The blanket smelled of disinfectant. Kali wrapped it around herself and stood up to stretch her legs. 'Why tomorrow?'

Awhi exhaled very slowly. It seemed to take forever for the breath to leave her lungs, 'I have a message for you from Counsellor Norvik. He told me I must make you understand.'

'What he do say?'

Awhi turned to look around her at the other pens. 'He reminded me I have a duty. I must explain the choice to you, so you will do the right thing.'

'For who the right thing? What choice he do say?'

'He wants me to make sure you understand, but I'll give you his message exactly as he spoke it. He started by conveying his greetings to Callista.'

'Callista?'

'I'm addressing you by your new name because it has now been announced to the public. Your species has a new leader and unfortunately, it will force me to end the lives of a great many humans who are outlaws by your inspiration. I understand that you set little value on your own life, but your followers don't have the immortality of a god. So, I invite you to speak to them tomorrow, on Republic Day. Tell them to return home and submit to their owners and the laws on the conduct of animals. Otherwise, the responsibility for their deaths will be yours.'

Awhi finished with a long sigh. 'Did you understand that?' she said.

'Understand enough. Is not "right thing" he do ask, Awhi.'

'Can't you ask humans to go home? Surely that's reasonable, isn't it?' Awhi's tone lacked conviction. Whatever her words, it was clear she found nothing reasonable in Norvik's proposal either. 'All you need to tell them is...'

'You think I do say they be animal?' Kali said. 'Be like lizin and fish? Say implant be well done? Say be trusting Norvik?'

Awhi rubbed her forehead with her hands. 'What are you going to do?'

'Not know. I do thinking.'

Awhi picked up a container of food and handed it to her, along with a spoon-shaped implement. 'Well, while you're doing that, at least have something to eat.' she said.

Kali scooped the mixture of egg and cereal into her mouth. There was something very solid about Awhi Kanawa, she thought, something dependable. She had none of the vulnerability she found endearing in Yan. She appeared very comfortable in her area of expertise, even in such an awful workplace. The grim surroundings hadn't hardened her though. The long days spent with human inmates seemed to have forged a bond of understanding, so much so that when she spoke, it was almost as if she was a human herself.

'Awhi, why you do work so many?' she said.

'Why I work so much. That's a good question.'

'You not have someone?'

Awhi's mouth curled into a smile. 'That would be nice! I'm not what most people look for though.'

'You be good person.'

Awhi blinked, and her eyes held more moisture than before. 'Thank you,' she said. 'Yan Feyrsten is a good person too, Kali. Please don't be too harsh with him. You need him. You're a stranger in this world, and he knows you better than anyone.'

Kali thought of all the other times she'd felt like a stranger. Everywhere she'd been, it had been a struggle. Time after time she'd had to prove herself, to raise herself up and walk into a gusting wind. 'He not know all of me,' she said.

She finished eating her meal, then tried to think about Norvik's message. Instead, her mind wandered. She found herself playing with her bond bracelet, thinking about her time with Yan on the beach. It had been brief but she couldn't remember an occasion when she had been more content. Whatever tomorrow held, she thought, it was unlikely such a time would come again, or that she'd be allowed to go home with Yan, whatever she agreed to say. She would stay in prison, or worse. And Yan's house would have its silence back.

'Yes, is good man,' she said, after a while. 'He be alonely, and you be alonely.' She winked. 'Is what I do think.'

Awhi stared at her for a moment, then laughed. 'The Chief Counsellor's brother, and *me*? You really *are* crazy.'

The adjournment hadn't come soon enough, for Maarten Feyrsten. He pushed his chair back from the conference table and made for the door, brushing aside his aides and looking for a way out to the garden. His head was throbbing, and a stream of distorted data points flickered in his vision. It was as if he had just stepped off an interstellar shuttle, somehow separated from the world by a membrane that made colours clash and sounds resonate in his skull.

The summit negotiations had continued through the night with barely a break, and dawn had brought only modest progress. The heads of state had reached an agreement of sorts, but inevitably it was achieved at the expense of a fully effective solution. At least there would be an international force sent to the Spice Islands but lightly armed and with a peacekeeping mandate. The bare bones of a reconstruction package had been agreed to, but the amount was still to be settled, and in all probability, it would never materialise. As ever, it would be left to the Free Republic to act in the end, but the minor states still expected to have their say first, to go through the motions of being relevant to the outcome.

Feyrsten wandered down through the verdant tiers of the President's garden until he found a secluded pool, edged with polished stone blocks. As he stood at its edge, he noticed a vague disturbance beneath the surface and crouched to observe it more closely. A cloud of minute fish was moving as a single fluorescent entity, folding over on itself and spinning in a helix formation. It appeared both ordered and random at the same time. Just like his state of mind he thought, restless but craving equilibrium. But his presence in the Spice Islands was itself a contradiction. If he chose, he could use the dominance of the Free Republic to impose his will, but history was littered with such acts of force and they never ended well in the long term.

So here he was, treating mere statelets as equals and wrestling with their leaders over a simple matter of emergency assistance, when over the horizon in his own country he could act decisively if only the situation was straightforward enough to allow it.

A shadow on the water interrupted his thoughts. He turned to see President Abewaelo approaching the pool, his drifting gait barely stirring the silken folds of his robe.

'Beautiful, aren't they?' he said.

'Yes, they're fascinating.'

'Watch this.' The President squatted and touched the surface of the water with his finger. The cloud of fish reacted immediately, darted away as a single body then returned almost as quickly, settling back into its original pattern. 'It happens so quickly that you can't see what occurs, but it all starts with a single fish, a leader who can take the whole mass in a different direction.'

'But which direction is best, Ebele?'

'I wanted to talk to you about that, and I'm glad to have the opportunity. Thank you for coming here to the Spice Islands, and for staying at my home.'

Maarten couldn't help but admire the President's manner. He was as serene as he'd been throughout the conference, incongruously so, when his regime's reputation was anything but gentle. 'It's for me to thank you for your hospitality,' he said.

'I know you will be criticised for it at home. I'm an authoritarian ruler, a dictator. I curtail the liberties of my opponents. I dispose of those who stand against me.'

Maarten was taken off guard by the President's candour. There was regret in his tone, but he wasn't going to let that draw him into indiscretion. 'That's for you to say, Ebele. I'm not here to talk about the differences in the way we run our countries. That's for another time, perhaps.'

'Although it's relevant to the human issue.'

Maarten turned away from the pool, looked at him directly. 'How so?'

'The authority of the people is a fine thing,' said the President. 'When it reaches maturity, it provides the stability your citizens take for granted. But it responds sluggishly to changing times. It's more like the rock-fruit tree than these cloudfish. It develops more slowly than the lifetime of individual citizens, demands more patience than they possess in a young country like this.'

'So, you as the ruler are creating the conditions for...'

'I am the stake of authority that must hold the tree firm until it has sunk its roots deep into the cultural soil. It isn't pleasant, but it's necessary. I like to think we've been making progress. The people are learning the benefits of the rule of law, and that's more important for the general good than individual freedoms.'

'They aren't mutually exclusive,' said Maarten.

'Not once the sapling has become a tree.'

'Forgive me Ebele, but you're talking about social progress while part of your country is ungovernable. You have one island ablaze, and others about to catch fire too.'

'It's my fault. To you, I'll confess it. I was managing the temperature of my people and failed to see the animal population coming to the boil. We've been talking all night about how to handle the uprising, and let's be honest, it won't be peacekeeping. In practice, it will be a brutal suppression. But it's what we must do to restore order. That doesn't mean I wouldn't prefer reform.'

'That really isn't a word I expected you to use.'

'Well, it's too late for a reforming solution when bodies are rotting in the streets. But it's not too late for you. If you learn from what's happened here.'

'And what lesson would you have me take?'

'That if the ruler of a small island nation couldn't control a human population by force, why should it be possible in your giant republic, the hub of a diverse commonwealth of star systems?'

'I know I haven't slept much, but it seems rather surreal to have you of all people recommending a more liberal position on the human issue.'

'Not liberal. Realistic. You have to seize your opportunity in adverse situations, ride your luck.'

'What opportunity is that? What luck?'

President Abewaelo touched the water again, watched the disturbance beneath the surface. 'Your Earth human, Maarten. Your shining little fish.'

Are you still there, Mr. Dunstone? Sometimes, I think I can see you in the darkness, and you can see me. I hope so, for I need you now more than ever.

I can no longer write but perhaps that's no loss. There are times to write, and times to speak. Tomorrow I must speak, though goodness knows what I'll say, for my courage is all set to desert me.

'There's always a choice,' you used to say, but sometimes it isn't much of a choice. I must decide between doing the right thing, even though it pains my conscience, and doing the wrong thing, though my heart calls it decent. My mind would prefer to take me back to the farm, or your study with its leather volumes and squeaky floor, but I know it's this decision that my whole life has brought me to make, and I can't shrink from it.

I feel so awfully alone. I do wish you were here to help me, though I fear even you would be confounded by the trap Counsellor Norvik has set for me. I'm sure he knows that whether I decide to encourage these humans to rise or beg them to accept their lot, my own fate will be assured.

Perhaps it wouldn't be much of a downfall though, for I'm already as low as I could be, fallen from the stars into this wretched place. But if I sit here tomorrow, it'll either be with blood on my hands, or I'll have betrayed the hopes of everyone who believed in me. My following will be lost to slaughter or disappointment, and Norvik will then do with me what he pleases. However much Yan and Awhi might come to my defence, I fear that in the end they will have to do without me. Some things are written in the stars.

There now, it's done. With your help, Mr. Dunstone, my decision is made and I feel better for it. You've done as much for me as you can, and tomorrow I must go forward on my own. This perhaps is my purpose at last… to find something to give all the poor humans of this world.

Torsta Jai had lost track of time. Her comms had not reset after the fall, and all she had was what could be done in each moment, an endless succession of them spent cutting at the wreckage of the barricade, the passing time measured in pain and effort, and the steady movement of the night sky. Sooner or later, a search party would come, but the chances were that a stray feral would find her first, one of those who had been left behind. For whatever reason, she'd been spared once, but it was too much to expect that act of mercy to be repeated.

Mercy. It's what people show, only people. Was it that? What other explanation is there? There had been something else, the change that had happened when the feral leader noticed the green moon. The tension went from her body and she'd sat more heavily, handled the knife as if it had become a burden. Absurd as it seemed, it was almost as if she'd made a moral decision, based on some spiritual conviction.

Something had shifted in Torsta's thinking too. Perhaps it had been there all along, Perhaps Kali had just forced it to the front of her consciousness, got into her head with those eyes, the curious, knowing things she said. And now this feral. When Torsta formed a mental picture of a human now, she couldn't help seeing something more than she had before, something… some*one* capable of arguing with her, outwitting her, overcoming her in combat. *And then showing mercy.*

Torsta changed her grip on the knife and continued to hack at the objects that held her legs trapped. There was pain in the right knee, a fierce stabbing that went right through the joint. There wasn't any qualifying data coming through from the injury, but it felt like more than a flesh wound. Something had ruptured, or perhaps there was a break. She could still feel her feet though, so there was at least a possibility that she could reach safety. But only if she could free herself.

The knife had made light work of the softer objects, but the resistant materials were proving much more difficult. Torsta worked with the blade where she could and used any other object she could reach, to lever the more solid debris away from her legs. Every so often she would stop to regain her breath. Then, she would lie back and suck the night air into her lungs, crane her neck to search the buildings around the square for signs of movement. She found herself looking at the sky as well, and quite inexplicably, drawing courage from the presence of the green moon.

At last, it was only her right knee that remained trapped, and it became clear why it hurt so much. The mounting bracket of a long shelf had pierced the joint from the side, and then the shelf had wedged itself at the other end, between two heavy appliances. She tried to carve into it, but the knife could make no impression. Then she tried lifting it, but the pain was too great, her consciousness ebbing with each attempt.

The green moon pulled at her attention again. Its companions were sliding in behind it now, as if driven by some immense celestial clock, programmed in the origins of time to bring them on this particular night, into perfect formation. She looked back at the debris field and saw that it too had been arranged. It was no random product of gravity but had been placed, designed by an unseen hand to torment her, to trap and injure, and then, when the precarious balance of its components shifted, to crush the person who was sent against the disciples of Callista.

The instrument of her death was positioned further up the tangled bank. Torsta could see it, a silicate lintel, poised on the lip of a container, and rocking alarmingly with each breath of wind. Sooner or later, a stronger movement of the air would push it beyond its balancing point and send it crashing down.

There was a scraping sound somewhere behind her. Torsta shifted her body to view the building opposite the entrance to the mall. Somewhere in one of the lower units there was movement, then vague shapes appeared, humans creeping slowly around the perimeter of the square, perhaps aged and infirm like the ferals in the terminal building, but still more than capable of taking the life of a defenceless enemy. She began to imagine the manner of her death at their hands, the torments they might devise to make her passing a long one. The decision was easy to make. Somehow, she had to disturb the lintel before the ferals overcame their fear and came at her.

Further along the barricade, a scaffolding pole protruded

from the debris. Torsta had already tried to reach it and failed, but now she raised herself onto one knee and lunged at it, shrieking with the pain as each attempt twisted the bracket in her joint. At the third attempt, she got her fingers to it and drew it close. As expected, her cries had emboldened the ferals. They were out on the square now, at least five of them, shifting like phantoms, their eyes catching the moonlight as they closed in around her. She flashed her knife at them to buy more time, then set about her final task.

The pole was just long enough to reach the lintel. Torsta propped it into a position where she could topple the block with one quick thrust, then steeled herself to do it. She lay still for a moment, conjuring in her mind all the experiences that had brought her to the end of her life, surprised at how forgotten moments leapt unbidden into her thoughts, how things she'd worked to achieve were suddenly without meaning. And then, for a moment she was a youth again, sent to a foreign war and less afraid of death, than failing in her father's eyes. So it was now, as it always had been, the same battle to be fought over and over, that same contest between fear and courage. She looked once more to the night sky, then thrust the pole forward.

The lintel came loose with a jarring screech, tipped onto its end, and for a moment stood perfectly erect and still, toying with her life, everything it had been or could ever be. And then it toppled, came ploughing down through the debris to complete its allotted task.

But that wasn't what happened. The silicate block didn't crush Torsta's skull, didn't even compound her injuries. Instead by some wondrous working of weight and leverage it was deflected by the corner of an industrial fabricator, triggering a complex sequence of movements across the debris field. The final lever in the mechanism was the shelf, anchored to Torsta's knee by its bracket, and in one excruciating moment, it was wrenched from her flesh. The opportunity occupied the merest sliver of time, but she seized it without hesitation, clawed and scrambled on a surge of pain-fuelled adrenaline before the lintel came sliding to a halt where she'd been lying.

She used the scaffold pole to push herself upright, balanced on one leg as she searched the square for danger. The ferals had gone, and the world was silent. The debris monster was at rest once more, and she was alone. Even the breeze had dropped, leaving the air still and warm and fragrant. Only the heavens still moved, making final adjustments to their dance of moons, so that now only Callista remained visible. It glowed more brightly than ever, greening every surface around the plaza as she'd never seen before, and wouldn't ever again.

Torsta stared at the phenomenon. And suddenly, she found she was laughing. Laughing and then crying at the same time. The tears welled in her eyes, drawn from the cauterised wounds of the child warrior, the frustrated ambitions of the adult achiever. She cried freely, for the first time she could remember, her body shaking as she watched the spectacle overhead.

Five years had passed since Santi had travelled with ordinary people, and it wasn't an experience she was enjoying. She stood sweating in the embarkation area, her jacket over her arm, and her eyes closed, her mind conjuring the planets and moons floating in the cool interior of the doctor's folly.

Five full orbits around the Solus had been her time in government, countless transport boardings attended by the full retinue of a Counsellor of State, though never believing she was more than the citizens she served. Now she waited with all the other travellers again, people whose interests she considered her calling in life, but whose chatter she now found alien.

It was bad enough to be kept waiting for their transport to drop from its holding pattern, but the reason for the delay added humiliation to the discomfort. At the dock opposite, sitting smugly on its haunches, the blue and gold-liveried transport of the Free Republic's Chief Counsellor was occupying the berth of the much larger craft it was delaying. Santi reminded herself that the protocol for state visits had been no different when she'd been in government, but still, she found reasons to blame Maarten Feyrsten for the way her shift was clinging to her back. It wasn't even as if the great man had been delayed at the conference; his limousine was parked in front of the transport and he had already boarded. *Security check complete, drinks cabinet full, pillows properly plumped. And the most attractive cabin staff… Oh, stop it, Santi!*

Whatever flirtations she imagined of the Chief Counsellor, her own relationship was far more problematic. It would become common knowledge in due course, but somehow, she would need to fence it off from her public life, even though she'd already used Henik as an adviser, and it would be nigh impossible to restrain his pronouncements. He hadn't changed. He was the most honourable man she knew, the most principled, and that reminded her of the reasons she went into politics in the first place. But he was frustratingly naïve at times and with that came considerable risk. *"Human slavery." How did he think that was going to be helpful?* And yet his passion had pushed her to greater effort, inspired her idea to issue a Writ of Deliverance. He was someone who would always be honest, always remind her who she was. And for that, she was prepared to make the odd policy detour, show him she wasn't just another suit, that she stood on principle even when it made the path more difficult.

A call from Widdig Terreden came as a welcome distraction. Santi took herself as far away from the other travellers as the lines on the ground permitted and listened to his take on the overnight events.

'So, things have deteriorated as a result of the Callista Alignment,' she said.

'Mainly protests against the implanting, although on the other side of the equation, there are still some lynchings occurring. Freeport is quieter, but the disappearance of pets and commercial workers has become an epidemic. It still isn't clear where they're all going but it appears that Torsta Jai's task force has gone into the pod system, so that tells us something.'

'It tells us we've now got a population of humans swelling under the city. Everything interconnects down there, Widdig. The services are just part of it. There are natural watercourses, ancient canals, and almost as many disused transport tunnels as there are modern podways. It could swallow the whole human population of the city without a trace. Is there any sense that the Government understands the seriousness of this?'

'Well, the implanting has been paused, but only for Republic Day. I think they're struggling to contain the crisis and just hoping it has peaked. The police haven't been getting much sleep. Amazingly, they've managed to re-open Carnival Square though. I saw a rehearsal for the ceremonials there this morning. I got some intel that their focus is simply to get through the day without a major incident. They plan to deploy the National Guard around the country afterwards. They're also considering an emergency processing centre.'

'Processing what?'

'Strays, ferals that are redeemable, the ones that are passive or responsive. They'll check ownership on each. Any that are identifiable will be fitted with an implant and returned,'

'And the others destroyed, presumably. I want you to look at the legality of it, Widdig. I want this made as difficult as possible for them. Are they still holding Kali, or has Yan Feyrsten got her back?'

'They still have her. Our legal counsel is talking to theirs. At first, they weren't taking your Writ of Deliverance seriously, but now they're trying to hide behind emergency powers. If they can show Kali is an immediate threat to national security, they could take action without a hearing.'

'Understood, but they'll be treading more carefully now, particularly with the CC out of the country, and the family connection. What's the reaction been to Yan Feyrsten's announcement?'

'That she's a goddess? The media are in love with the idea, of course. The Callista name has stuck, and her picture is just everywhere. I've lost count of the number of times I've seen it this morning. Most people hadn't heard of Earth yesterday and now you'd think it was the most famous planet in the cosmos. One enterprising operator is already talking about an expedition to the Sun system.'

'Just an attention seeker. That whole quadrant is off-limits. But are you telling me that the crowd is more for her, than against?'

'Difficult to say what the balance of opinion is, but there are people outside Police Headquarters shouting for her release. It's wishful thinking if the Government believes the unrest will go away anytime soon.'

Santi finished the call and stood staring at the ground, while she considered the implications. She noticed she had wandered outside the designated security area while she was talking, and when she looked up a stone-faced young man was striding towards her. She had been in the company of enough Security Service officers to recognise one at a distance, and she backed away quickly, resumed her position among her fellow travellers. 'Sorry!' she called.

The man continued to approach, stopped in front of her with shoulders set, as if he thought himself a living shield against the misdemeanours of tired travellers. 'I'm sorry,' she said again. 'I was making a call and forgot where I was.'

'May I ask you to step away from this group, esteemed,' said the security officer. 'A word, if you please.'

Santi glanced around her. The other travellers were already starting to distance themselves as if they thought she might be carrying an infection. The man had moved away a few paces, and she walked over to him feeling as if she was being told off at school. 'I know I shouldn't have strayed,' she said. 'I do understand. Look, it's very hot and...'

'That's what the Chief Counsellor said, esteemed. He saw you waiting out here and he's asking if you would join him for the journey back to Freeport.'

'Oh!' said Santi, suddenly at a loss for words. 'Oh!'

'He thought you would be more comfortable and...'

'That's very kind of the Chief Counsellor, but I'm not sure it would be wise. We're not exactly...'

'The Chief Counsellor anticipated your concern, esteemed. He said you don't have to speak to him, but...' The security officer stood slightly taller, drew a breath. 'He was insistent.'

'He told you not to come back without me, didn't he?' Santi looked the young man in the eye, but he was giving nothing away. 'Sometimes silence is the most eloquent response,' she said. 'Come on then, I won't make you drag me.' She started to walk towards the Chief Counsellor's transport, the security officer falling in beside her, scanning the terminal buildings around them as he assumed a brief responsibility for her safety. After a few steps, she stopped and looked back pointedly to where her bag was straining in its attempt to cross the painted line and follow her. 'I think I can look after myself,' she said, 'as long as you don't lose my luggage.'

The Chief Counsellor's transport felt like a different world, an oasis where officials whispered in corners and ice rattled enticingly in tall flasks. It wasn't the first time that Santi had travelled in the vessel and some of the staff were the same as they had been under the last administration. One of them greeted her warmly and guided her up a spiral ramp to the upper deck where an immense curved window wrapped around the bows. Maarten Feyrsten was sitting in the corner, his bare feet propped up on the bulkhead, and his fingertips pressed together as he concentrated on a call. He got up from his seat as Santi approached, but continued his discussion. The steward escorted her to a reclining chair on the other side of the cabin, where her favourite cocktail was waiting. With its vivid turquoise colour and fat beads of condensation, it was the most exquisite sight of the day.

Outside, the view began to shift, the queue of travellers sliding by as the transport drifted away from the dock. Santi sipped her drink, impressed to find it was made exactly as she requested when she last travelled as a Counsellor of State.

Maarten Feyrsten didn't look in her direction until the Spice Islands were distant specs in the sea beneath them. Then he got up and came over, his sleeves rolled to the elbow. 'They mix a good cocktail, don't they?' he said.

'Chief Counsellor,' said Santi, rising to press his palm.

'This is very kind of you. I wasn't sure whether to accept, but your man was quite persuasive.'

Feyrsten slid into a chair opposite. 'Let's drop the formality, shall we, Santi? We've known each other a long time.'

'We have indeed. And I appreciated your token of congratulations on my appointment.'

He regarded her for a moment, then laughed. 'You've got me already. I'm sorry, I don't know what I sent you. If it was pleasing, I take no credit, and if it wasn't, then I'm even more at fault. But I do congratulate you. You've earned your shot as party leader and you'll be a trickier opponent than I was hoping for.'

'You can count on that,' said Santi. 'But in the meantime, this beats standing in the heat. Thank you.'

'I'm sure you would have done the same – at least I hope you would have.'

'Well, perhaps if there was something I wanted to discuss.'

Feyrsten turned towards the window. If there was something on his mind, it seemed he would take his time coming to it. They watched the sky darken outside, the transport climbing above a curved horizon to its sub-orbital trajectory. Feyrsten leaned his head towards the verglas. 'I always hope to see the magnetic fields,' he said. 'I never tire of them.'

'And they're more beautiful here than on any other planet I've visited.'

'Are you well-travelled?'

'A few systems in the inner sequence. You've been much further than that, I expect.'

'Only when business has demanded, but on those occasions, you pay less attention to nature than you should. Did you see the alignment last night?'

'I made a point of it. I thought I should if millions of humans are so taken with it.'

Feyrsten grunted, stared at the bubbles rising in his drink. Whether he agreed with the sentiment or not was unclear and his ridges gave no indication. 'I'm going to stop the implant programme,' he said, suddenly. 'I'm going to announce it later today.'

Santi decided to respond coolly. 'I see. Is that what you wanted to discuss, to gauge my reaction perhaps? What did Norvik say?'

'Haven't told him yet. I've just decided.'

'So, why tell me? If you think I won't take advantage Maarten, you're presuming a lot.'

'That's a matter for you,' said Feyrsten. He took a sip of his cocktail and drew his finger over the condensation on the glass. 'I've spent the night in that conference, immersed in the consequences of the Spice Islands' failure with humans. We must learn from it because now it's our problem too, arguably the most challenging issue we've faced in our times. You can sit there and tell me my new policies are the problem, if you like, Santi…'

'The thought had occurred to me.'

'Then I can counter that you allowed the conditions to brew for years.'

'And I can point out that those conditions were caused by the previous Heritage administration's economic strategy.'

'To which I say that strategy was needed to fix… blah blah, on and on. And where does it take us? We point fingers at each other while the world burns.'

Santi knew he was right, however much she disliked being admonished by her opponent. She prodded the islands of ice in her drink. 'You know why I was over there, I suppose.'

'Of course. Did he recruit you to his grand scheme, or did you point out the most obvious obstacle to a lunar homeland?'

'The need for an international agreement, to overturn an international agreement. I see huge problems with the idea. On the other hand, repression is only a short-term solution. Probably, not even that.'

'They're under the city, you know,' said Feyrsten. 'They're migrating into the whole infrastructure of the capital, numbers growing as each day goes by. We haven't got the luxury of time.' He sighed. 'Anyway, the doctor is wrong.'

'Because?'

'Because he has a small island perspective. When he thinks big, he's still only thinking about Antaris. He's never been further than the home planets except through his telescope. Out in the Commonwealth, there are any number of worlds watching events in the mother system, and many of them have sizeable human populations.'

Santi sipped at her cocktail. The wider issues had occurred to her, but her instinct had always been to focus more on immediate and local concerns. *That will have to change if I want to compete with him. I'll need to lift my head and think more strategically.* 'The treatment of humans is often worse on those worlds than it is here,' she said.

Feyrsten looked at her in silence for a moment or two. 'If we keep the lid too firmly on humans, it will encourage more extreme policies elsewhere in the Commonwealth. Look, Santi, I know that's already how you view what I'm doing, but I do understand that if control isn't exercised with sensitivity, we're asking for trouble. More than that, I know that if revolution happens in one system, it will spread to others.'

Santi wasn't sure how to respond. The point was one Feyrsten would never have made in public. It might even have cost him the election. 'But humans are used more extensively in some Commonwealth systems than they are here,' she said. 'Reform too quickly, and some may see their interests threatened. They might turn to the Deccans, who have fewer qualms about how humans are treated.'

Maarten was staring at the palms of his hands now, weighing them like the scales of the ancients. 'So, we each see the other's side of the debate. But you can be sure that Decca will exploit the human crisis if we let them, stir revolution if we hold firm, encourage systems to secede to them if we reform too fast.'

'And yet they were allowed to attend the conference.'

'A diplomatic courtesy, and only to observe. Like it or not, we share the same star, and our economies are intertwined.'

'Did they say anything interesting at the margins, if you don't mind me asking?'

Feyrsten's mouth lifted very slightly at its corner. 'You never get the true position from them,' he said. 'Gengathna Kobt never attends anything, and however elegantly his emissaries talk, you can only ever guess what the Overlord really wants.'

'He's over a hundred years old, apparently.'

'And still sharp, they say. But who knows? Regime change could occur at any time, and that's always a dangerous business on Decca. Whoever leads them, they'll only ever do what's in their interests. But we are where we are… and where we are isn't sustainable.'

'The human situation, or our relationship with the Deccan Dominion?'

'Right now, the former, but we can't ignore Decca.' Feyrsten appeared to retreat into his thoughts for a few moments, staring at his reflection in the blackness of the window. He didn't seem to notice when a stewardess arrived with a delicate selection of *appetisers*. Santi decided not to intrude on whatever was occupying the Chief Counsellor's thinking. She reached forward and chose a sculpture of cold-water truffles.

'What do you make of this Callista figure,' Feyrsten said after a while. 'The human we're holding.'

'I know she belongs to your brother. I knew that before he went public, actually.'

'And I'm sure you'll also know they've been working with Henik Varkesen.'

Santi's skin prickled at Henik's name. She wasn't going to ask for clarification, but if Feyrsten was firing a warning shot, it was right on target. 'Yes,' she said. 'I haven't met the human, but I hear she's quite exceptional. She has Sig Norvik rattled anyway.'

Feyrsten didn't take the bait. He took a mouthful of his drink, then leant forward and placed the glass very deliberately on the table, as if to signify that he had reached a conclusion. 'We're in the first days of our new jobs, Santi. My policy hasn't got off to a good start, and you haven't even got one yet. Standing between us is this little human.'

'As an obstacle or a bridge?'

'Both. Or perhaps she's better thought of as an opportunity. I think the chance to engage her in a solution must be explored.'

Finally, it seemed that Feyrsten was reaching the subject he wanted to discuss. *Where is he going with this? What does he want?*

'The problem is that both of us have our hooks into her,' he continued. 'I have her in custody, and ultimately, I can decide her fate. But you, or rather my brother and Varkesen are the people she trusts.'

'So, you're suggesting we need each other. Is that what this conversation is about?'

Feyrsten looked at her directly now. 'I'm saying we both need that human to co-operate. If there's any chance that a solution can be built around her, neither of us can do it without the help of the other.'

Santi suddenly realised she was looking at Feyrsten through Kali's eyes, in fact she'd been doing so for much of the discussion, trying to see his face as a human might, searching for any slight shift of expression or posture that might signal his intentions. She saw his hands resting easily on the arms of his chair, his chest rising and falling with a gentle rhythm, his eyes fatigued rather than calculating.

'Alright, Maarten,' she said after several long moments had passed. 'I've accepted your hospitality, so let's play this out. Let's say we were co-operating. What's your Calista solution?'

20

Republic Day

IT WASN'T THE FIRST time Henik had gone to watch the Republic Day ceremonies, just the first time it had really meant something to him. In part, it was the extraordinary way Freeport had recovered from the explosion that made this time feel different, the way the people of the capital had put the horror aside, determined to make Carnival Square ready for the annual celebration of their story.

Theirs was a civilisation raised from primitive beginnings, growing according to legend from a simple fishing settlement, then rising in knowledge, power, and technology to lead the Antarian species as it reached out across interstellar space. Yet for all the pride he felt in its achievements, Henik couldn't help but notice, on this day in particular, the complete lack of recognition for humans, the absence of any acknowledgement of their contribution over the centuries.

The morning was still fresh, but already the crowds were flocking around him in the square, noisy and light-hearted, enjoying a seemingly endless procession of costume and revelry. The shops and bars around the perimeter were doing a brisk trade, customers appearing to hardly notice the shrouding around the ruins of the Café Republic. People ambled beneath the galleries at the perimeter, without even breaking their conversation at the place where so many had died. Henik observed them and wondered whether the atrocity was even crossing their minds.

Perhaps it was the National Guard that was putting the crowds at ease, their presence providing an illusory sense of security. The centre of the city was bristling with arms and armour, guards clustered on every street corner, lining the parade route on the ground, on the rooflines, and deployed with particular density around the pod stations. In the middle of the square, a ring of police officers guarded a giant circle of darkly polished tiles, beneath which lay the colossal Monument of National Destiny, ready to rise from its resting place on the stroke of mid-day and take its annual position as the centre of attention for the people of the Free Republic. For Henik, its message of pride and achievement had always felt hubristic, even embarrassing. This year he felt it even more strongly and had no shortage of words to express the hollowness of the ceremony. *Pride without conscience, chauvinism without imagination.* It was a day for looking backwards, for conceit and complacency.

Santi would be there in spirit if not in person. She was bound to the proceedings as all establishment figures were. She wasn't the type to tear things down, she was a person of compromise. She dealt in diplomacy, listened and spoke patiently, whilst his approach was bolder, unwise sometimes, and unfettered by responsibility. Theirs was an alliance, a loose and fragile one. It could never be comfortable.

The crowd was swelling now, pushing Henik on towards the great circle, where a lattice barrier had risen to secure the circumference. He resisted the tide; there was no need to move closer when the ceremonials would be projected around the plaza, and the speeches would be sent ringing through millions of skulls, Usually the first speech would be the Chief Counsellor or his representative, then the High Priests of Aquatic and Astral deities, flanked by their respective soapstone icons. And finally, the Archpriestess of the Antarian Divinities would step forward to give her annual blessing.

Only it might just be different this year, this might be an occasion that broke with tradition in a way that would create news across the Commonwealth. If Yan was successful in his efforts to persuade Kali, she would be the first human ever to appear on the monument's high platform. It would be a landmark moment, though not in a good way, not in any respect an acknowledgment of her species. *Controlled, humiliated, the first human to appear, and quite possibly the last.*

A call alert came, and Henik retreated to the shade of the galleries to take it. Yan looked as though he hadn't slept much, but he moved with a nervous energy, and when he spoke his voice held a cautious optimism.

'She's going to do it, Henik! She'll speak. I just hope it will be enough, and I'll be able to bring her home afterwards.'

'What changed her mind? I'm a bit surprised that she's given in to Norvik. She was so set on her position, so determined.'

'Well, Norvik withdrew his requirement for her to have an implant, so that probably had a lot to do with it.'

'I don't want to dampen your enthusiasm, but he could go back on that, after the ceremony. I don't trust him any more than Kali does. How was she this morning?'

'Subdued and serious, not at all herself. I think she still feels betrayed. Hopefully, that will pass though, and she'll cheer up when she's out in the solus.'

Henik tried to imagine the situation from Kali's perspective, wondered how her rational processes would operate, whether she'd worked through the decision as he might have. There was something about Yan's optimism, and Kali's seriousness, that made him think she was the one with the better grasp of her position.

'I suppose it's natural for her to be apprehensive,' continued Yan. 'Most of us would be if we were about to speak to the nation. Imagine what it must be like for her, having to face that crowd. I hear that many people have brought their humans with them.'

'That's true,' said Henik. 'I can see almost as many humans here, as people. Perhaps the news about Kali has leaked already. We just have to hope she can handle the occasion, particularly after a couple of nights in the cells.'

'If only it were the cells. She's been in a cage, Henik, in a stinking *pen!* I couldn't have imagined it, if I hadn't seen it this morning myself. It was all straw and piss. Anyway, she's getting cleaned up. Awhi's taken her…'

'Awhi?'

'The guard, the keeper. I've been impressed by her. She's been very kind to Kali.'

'And what about the big question? Do you know what she's going to say?'

'She won't tell me. Which makes me nervous, of course. Awhi showed me a message Norvik sent to Kali, last night. He's told her that as Callista, she'll be responsible for a lot of humans being killed if she doesn't speak against the uprising.'

'So, he's called our bluff. He can look like he's being reasonable, but if Kali… if Callista encourages humans to resist the Government's policy, she'll strengthen his hand. And if she takes the Government's side, the human population may turn on her. Do you think she has any understanding of that?'

'Awhi thinks so, but who knows? I tried to give her advice, but she wasn't listening. I just want her home, Henik. That's all I want.'

'And do you think that's what *she* wants? Is that still *her* objective?'

Yan took a long time to answer. The question seemed to have punctured his mood. 'Depends who will speak today,' he said eventually, 'If it's Kali, then yes, definitely. But I'm afraid Callista may have other ideas.'

A boy in short trousers spotted Alka through the kerbside grating and began tugging at his father's hand. She ducked out of sight and slipped back down the drain to where the other feral leaders were waiting.

'Square's filling up,' she said. 'There's lots of humans out there too, so that will help.'

'What about soldiers?' asked Chemical Mike.

'All around the square, but not in the middle. The sky's buzzing with metal things too. After what the twins did, they'll be looking for humans with bags. So, we'll go out empty-handed.'

'What, you mean no weapons?' said Kit. 'Are you serious? How can we defend ourselves?'

Alka rolled her javelin slowly between her hands. She stood a little taller, raised her voice. 'Brothers and sisters of the Unowned, I ask you to hear me on this. We cannot fight the People and win. There are too many of them. They're heavily armed and they are ready to crush an uprising. That's the plain truth of it. This is a different kind of war now. It's a war of ideas, above all, the idea of our liberation, as it has been foretold. We must trust in Callista to bring our gift… and we must go out *unarmed*.'

'Then they will take us,' said Mike. 'We won't make it out of the square.'

'That's right,' said Alka. 'Some of us won't be coming back. Some of us must continue the struggle in captivity, as Callista does. But those who attack the people with weapons, those who draw blood, they won't be taken. They will die this afternoon with a gut full of elemist.'

'Then, what can we do?' said Kit. 'What are we here for?'

Alka looked at the faces around her. They were all waiting for inspiration. They needed more than a vague notion that Callista would provide a miracle. She placed one hand on Mike's shoulder and the other on Kit's.

'I will tell you why we're here,' she began. *We are here* to make our presence felt so powerfully that it shakes the soul of every people in this land. *We are here* because we can't go on at the margins of their society, barely clinging to life. *We are here* because we have no other option, but to bring our cause to their door!'

She paused, her voice still echoing through the underground pipes and chambers. She saw that bodies were turning more squarely to face her now and chins were lifting. She stepped forward to walk among them, greeting each of the clan leaders as she went. '*We are here* to assert our right to a place amongst the People on the day they praise themselves for what they did with our labour! *We are here* to say that we are not their tools, we are the humans of this land and we demand that they accept us!'

There were murmured voices of agreement now, lifting her, spurring her on. 'I will raise my voice and I will be heard!

And those who are with me will raise their voices too, until we cannot be ignored. And if they capture me, I will go shouting, '*I am here!*' If they shoot me, I will die shouting it, and after I have gone, others will shout in Callista's name, until those shouts fill the ears of the People wherever they go in this land! *We are here! We are here!* And then my brothers and sisters, they will not be able to hold us back any more than the waves of the sea, nor ignore us any more than they could ignore Callista's great spectacle last night! Did you see it? Did you see the way she placed her light on all things and how worlds moved at her command? Did you witness the arrival of the Time of Times? She has matched us with this moment of redemption. *Our – destiny – is – why – we – are – here!*'

Alka gave no opportunity for debate. She threw her javelin aside, then scrambled back up the drainage pipe, a wave of cheering following her. They had broken the latches on the drain covers all around the square and in a few moments, she had slipped through from the underworld and was standing for the first time in the heart of the capital. The buildings rose around her, grand, gleaming, and at her shoulders the bodies of giant people pressed thicker than a forest. *No fear, Alka! It's your city too and you're here to claim it!*

Behind her Kit was struggling through the drain opening and no one had noticed. She helped him to his feet, then turned away and set off into the crowd, sliding between bodies and ducking under elbows and arms. There were more humans than she'd expected, most standing beside their owners, compliant and unable to see anything beyond the body in front of them, but some were taking turns to sit on each other's shoulders for a better view. They were all better dressed than Alka, with clothes that fitted them, even if some looked uncomfortable or outlandish. *How long before you're noticed? How long... and then what?*

She paused for a moment, her progress blocked by a particularly dense knot of people. She felt a gentle tug at her overalls. It was an elderly man, with bright eyes that shone from beneath the brim of his cap. 'Are you here for Callista?' he asked.

She nodded. 'I'm hers to command, brother. Do you think they will speak of her, show her image?'

The old man grinned, his tongue showing pink through the gap in his teeth. 'Haven't you heard? They say she'll be here. They say she'll speak to us herself!'

'What? Are you sure, brother? Aren't they afraid of her – of her authority?'

'They've had her for days. I'm worried for her. I worry that they may have her in their power.'

Alka took the old man by the shoulders. 'Have faith,' she said. 'This is the Time of Times. I will raise my voice for Callista, and for all humans. Will you join me?'

'At my age, what's there to lose?' he said, and grinned.

'Then pass the word!'

Alka moved forward again, following the daylight that stabbed at her through the crowd, until she could see the front rank. From beyond it, out on the open space of the great circle, there came the rumble and grind of machinery. The ground started to shake, and the crowd hushed for the beginning of the proceedings. In front of them, the stones of the square began to slide back in a complex folding and gathering movement, to reveal a chasm, from which the Monument of National Destiny began to rise. Its pointed summit appeared first, sculpted with representations of the stars, the interstellar transports of

Antaris spearing amongst them in curving trajectories. Then the carved landmarks of the Freeport cityscape rose into view, interspersed with snow-capped mountains, glaciated valleys, and rugged forests of stone.

The conical tower continued to rise and turn, the machinery squealing intermittently beneath it, until Alka could see the speaking platform. Below it, were the carved figures of some of the great people in Antarian history. Alka didn't know the names of any of them, but there were some she'd seen depicted before. One was a chemist who was always pictured holding a glowing substance, and there was another whose image was associated with exploration of the planets. Lower still, the stone tableau became more confusing still, depicting conflicts amongst Antarians, glorifying it seemed, the destruction and bloodshed of wars. Then finally, at the base of the monument, was a tableau that told the story of the founding of the Free Republic, a chaotic scene of people in flowing garments, wielding spears, cutting crops, riding on the backs of giant beasts or pushed by the wind in vessels upon curling stone waves.

The monument's rotation slowed and finally, it ground to a halt, its summit now high above Carnival Square. The crowd hushed, as thousands of eyes explored the detail of the edifice, carvings so intricate and so finely observed that they tricked the mind, drawing observers into the alleys of ancient towns, and amongst the hooves of war steeds, along winding wilderness trails, and up to the exotic colonies of distant systems. Together, the sculptures portrayed the myriad events that comprised the triumph of the People over all they had encountered in this world and on others. It asserted their destiny, favoured by the gods to extend their influence across the cosmos.

Alka could only see the monument in shifting fragments, gaps opening and closing between the giant bodies that moved around her. She was still coming to terms with the close presence of people, their towering bulk, and their deep musky scent, the way their hands flexed on the shoulders of their humans, all bony knuckles and fine nails. She craned her neck to see the face of the giant beside her and recognised him immediately. For a moment, she wondered whether to keep her distance, but then, as if he sensed he was being watched, he turned and looked down at her, his mouth lifting into a lopsided smile.

'Alka!'

'Plain,' she said and pointed at the monument. 'Callista?'

High above them a horn sounded, and there was a flurry of movement on the speaking platform. A group of people emerged from inside and came forward to stand at the stone parapet.

'We're about to find out,' said Henik.

Kali arranged the folds of her coat as she waited inside the Monument of National Destiny. It gave her something to do with her hands. And to occupy her mind, she imagined the coat had magical powers. She pretended it could give her voice an irresistible force, that it would stiffen her nerve, prevent her from shrinking from the decision she'd made.

She could feel Awhi's presence behind her, calm despite the argument she'd had with Sig Norvik at the police headquarters. Kali had insisted that Awhi should accompany her to the monument, and it was only after a tense stand-off with the Counsellor, that he relented. Yan was also standing with her, his hands turning his bracelet round and around, as if he found comfort in it, just as she did. But his skin had lost its colour, and he kept swallowing. She decided not to look at him, however much she wanted to. It made her feel weak to indulge her affections and every time he placed a reassuring hand on her back, she felt her resolve melting away. She pulled her hood further forward and decided to concentrate on the coming test, just one brief ordeal amongst all the injustices this world held for humans, from the petty indignities of their daily life to the most awful cruelty. *You're not Emily anymore, and you're not Miss Coppen, of the Berseba mission school, either. You're not Kali, companion of Professor Yan Feyrsten. Not now. Now, you are the goddess mother of your species, and you are here to give them hope. You are Callista!*

She found Juno pulling at her thoughts as he had throughout the long night, how she had misjudged him when just like Dill, he had looked to her for comfort. He had been driven by hope, he'd placed his faith in her, and she'd not been able to save him. Now he was no more, but Jocasta stood nearby, serene in a flowing turquoise gown and not giving so much as a glance in her direction. Kali closed her eyes and held the image of Juno in her mind, remembering the way he had refused to yield as the whip tore into him, how he lay on the flagstones, believing she had brought him something to cherish even in his dying moments.

And with that, a new thought burst into her head, sharp and clear, as if her mind had held it in reserve for this very moment. She gasped, and Yan reacted with a hand on her shoulder, his face coming into view around the edge of her hood. In front of her, Sig Norvik heard it as well. He turned and stared at her now, his face as rigid as the sculptures that lined the monument's inner chambers. In that moment, she felt her power and relished it, knowing at last what her words would be, while he could only place his confidence in theories and manipulation.

Norvik sidled closer to them, leaned towards Yan, so they stood eye to eye. 'Let me just remind you before we start, Professor,' he said, his tone low, but sharp-edged. 'The stakes here could not be higher. There are a large number of humans down there and I've received word that hidden amongst them are a significant number of feral infiltrators, renegades who have escaped from the Derelict Zone. There are armed police and National Guard all around, and if it looks to me that either you or your human are encouraging disorder rather than compliance, I will give the word for them to move in and eradicate all feral humans in the interests of national security. There will be very substantial loss of animal life. So be warned, Professor Feyrsten, and ensure your *fucking goddess* understands...'

Kali didn't see the actual moment that it happened, the instant when Yan's mild nature lost its battle with pent-up frustration. There was a blur of motion at the corner of her eye and then Yan's hand was around Norvik's throat. He propelled him backwards into the wall and held him there, with his eyes bulging, and his feet thrashing desperately. Yan's forehead was a blaze of red, and the air around him pulsed with his anger, a cranial outpouring so intense that Kali had to pinch her nose as a painful wave of pressure swept through her sinuses.

The storm passed as quickly as it occurred. Yan's self-control reasserted itself, and he let go of Norvik's throat. He stepped back, and the Counsellor crumpled to the floor, surrounded immediately by a cluster of novices of the Aquatic order, who helped him to his feet. He brushed at his tunic with his hands and tugged it back into shape, shrugging away assistance, as if it was heightening his embarrassment. He stood there preening in front of them, without passing another glance at Yan, but once he considered his dignity restored, he turned to Kali and glared at her, as if the incident had been her doing. She met his eyes with a steady gaze, then just as she felt she couldn't remain silent for a moment longer, there came the sonorous blast of a horn, and they were all suddenly in motion. They went forward as a group, leaving the cool interior chamber of the monument, and shuffling out onto its platform. Out they went into the harsh white solus, and the dizzying embrace of the crowd.

The cheering was unlike anything Kali had ever experienced, a thunderous explosion of voice, reverberating on and on, around the square. If anything, the greeting rose to greater heights when she stepped into view. Whether the reception was positive, she couldn't tell, but she decided to treat it that way, to receive it as she imagined a goddess might. She held her hands loose at her sides and lifted her chin.

It appeared that the ceremony would begin with a message from one of the priests. A tall figure in a white robe and headdress moved forward and stepped up onto a dais, where a verglas lectern awaited. He began a rambling incantation, stretching out his arms and looking narrow-eyed into the mid-day sky. There was not a word of the address that Kali understood. It had a different accent and cadence to the language she was learning as if it was some archaic dialect. Still, the priest delivered the words as if they came to his mouth without thought, the familiar habit of a clergyman. The delivery was faultless, but it did nothing to move the people in the square, leaving them silent at its conclusion, either out of respect or indifference.

When Sig Norvik stepped forward, it was with less flamboyance. Kali wondered whether he was nervous to be the

Government's spokesman on such a grand occasion, with his image everywhere around the square on giant displays, but then her stomach jolted as it had every time she thought of what lay before her, and it brought her attention back to keeping her own emotions in check.

Norvik spoke with assurance. Kali could only understand the gist of his speech, but his delivery was controlled and purposeful. He talked of the honour of speaking for the Government as hundreds had before him and of the meaning of Republic Day. Then he spoke of the explosion at the Cafe Republic and praised the citizens of the capital for returning to the square so soon, for showing their patriotism and defiance. More worryingly, he used the word 'human' all too often, in connection with the atrocity. Perhaps there was a nuance that Kali couldn't grasp, but she was left with the distinct impression her species was being cast as the enemy.

Suddenly, the Counsellor stopped and turned towards her, and the crowd erupted to welcome her to the platform. She started forward, knees wobbling for a moment, then stepped up onto the dais. And then she was alone, the acclaim assaulting her ears, pounding at her body, echoing on and on, as if nothing would make it subside. She saw her face looming large around the square, composed somehow, even as her thoughts faded into nothingness. She pushed the hood back from her head and sucked air into her lungs, desperate to recover her senses. Her hair fell free onto her shoulders, and the crowd responded instantly, the noise rising to a rapturous crescendo. And then suddenly, inexplicably, she felt the force of its support, a multitude of humans, as well as citizens, sensing a moment of change was upon them.

Now Kali waited, not because she had no words, but because with every passing moment of anticipation, the crowd was becoming her instrument, her means of confounding the Counsellor for Human Affairs. She let the noise come at her in volleys, bounding around the square like cannon fire. Then, after what felt like an eternity the cheering eased, the noise reducing steadily, until soon it was no more than a murmur. Still, Kali waited. She waited until the square fell still and quiet, the silence broken only by an occasional cough, or the cry of a baby.

'Citizens,' she said, beginning in the native language. 'People of the Freeport city. Companions. Please you do forgive my speaking not well. I do be asked to say to humans for peace. I know you do all very worry. All Republic be worry – is truth. What I do say? I say, be good heart and not fear with companions. Be trust with them, and they be peace. All be well done.'

The cheering started up again, but it dwindled as soon as she began to speak in her own tongue. 'My fellow humans,' she said. 'You've watched the moons last night, and now you look to me with hope in your hearts. It's true that I come to you from very far away, from the place you know as "Terra". And I know it's foretold, that through me you will find your way home.'

The cheering took a different tone now. The citizens of Freeport stood in silent incomprehension, while their human companions responded with wild adulation. Kali raised her hands to quell the noise. 'There are some who ask me to send you away quietly and some amongst you who expect me to lead you into battle. I will tell you this: we must struggle for what is right, but endurance is more noble than the shedding of blood. But how do you endure, how can you sustain yourself in your struggle for justice? It's a question we humans have always asked ourselves, and I will now give you the only answer I know. It is your gift.'

Again, the crowd responded with rapturous cheering, but this time, when the noise abated, Kali's voice changed. It lifted and transformed into a tapestry of tones, and her words were lyrical, a swelling hymn of lost souls and redemption, of all that it meant to be human.

Now, there was no cheering and not the slightest movement in the crowd. Every head was turned to her, every sense attuned to the rise and fall of her voice, the cadence of the lyrics, the beautiful conjuring of a lost vocal tradition. Kali forged ahead, raising her voice to new heights, repeated the verse so that it soared with even greater fervour than before.

Down in the square, human voices were beginning to respond, first a hesitant murmur, then a hum, which swelled to anchor Kali's song. She looked at Yan over her shoulder. He was smiling, not a forced expression, but one of genuine delight, perhaps even pride. There was no such response from Norvik though. He was whispering angrily to his aides, debating perhaps whether they could risk dragging her away from the platform. But there would be no stopping her now. She lifted her voice and her arms, and summoned all the strength inside her to send the anthem out to each corner of the square, to all the human hearts it contained, every being great and small.

There was a scuffle behind her, and she glanced back as she completed the final ringing words of the hymn, seeing Yan holding someone back by the sleeve, guarding the approach to the dais.

'That, dear friends, is all I can give you,' she said. 'It is all I have to lift your spirits, to bind you together in just and peaceful cause.' Her voice felt unsteady in her throat now, and she gripped the side of the lectern as a spasm of nausea threatened to overwhelm her. 'And with it, I must leave you. Before the spirit of Callista is brought to ashes.'

She turned to look at Yan, her fingers finding the bracelet on her wrist, and she saw the realisation fire in his eyes, the flash of clarity about what she was about to do. He started forward, reached for her, but she spun away from the lectern, her mind empty as she scrambled onto the parapet and launched herself into the void.

Yan had found himself revelling in Kali's triumph. It came as an unexpected release from the guilt that had tormented him ever since Kali had been dragged from Norvik's office. Yet again, she'd pushed the boundaries of his perspective, caused him to reassess things he'd taken for granted.

He had thought it a straightforward arrangement at first, compliance in return for Kali's freedom, a demonstration of quiet acceptance. Just a few words to encourage observance of the law, and they could walk away from the whole nightmare. He had arrived at Police Headquarters that morning, elated to hear that Kali had agreed to Norvik's demand and that it no longer included the requirement for her to receive an implant.

His optimism evaporated as soon as he saw her curled in the corner of her pen. This time she didn't throw herself at him when he came in. Instead, she stood up slowly, held herself straight and proud. He found himself going to her, crouching to her level, taking her hands, and doing all the talking.

'Do you know what you will say?' he asked. 'What will your message be?'

'I do say for people be patient with humans.'

'But it's your own species you must tell, Kali. That's what's important. What are you going to say to *humans*?'

'Callista do tell it first to humans,' she said stiffly. 'You do be a *people*.'

He had turned to Awhi Kanawa in bemusement, unsure how to react to being treated merely as an example of his species.

'She's been like this since she woke up,' said Awhi. 'It's not just you – she's been this way with me too. I thought she'd be a wreck this morning, but she seems cold and distant.'

'But why? She knows we want to help her, doesn't she?'

'She knows today is a trap. She understands that if she complies with Norvik, her following will disappear. And then, as soon as the crisis is over, he'll act against stray and feral humans anyway.'

'But she'll be able to come home.'

'It's no longer just about her interests. That's my reading of it. Callista isn't just a name anymore, it's a responsibility.'

'But what should we do?'

'I can only give you my opinion.'

'I suppose she thinks I've let her down. Well, perhaps I have, but I just don't understand what to do!'

'Choose, Professor. Norvik has forced Kali to make a choice, and you mustn't suppose she doesn't feel the weight of it. I think she wants you to make a choice too. She wants us both to decide whether we stand with Norvik, or on the side of humans. Not just her though, *all* of them.'

Awhi had made her decision before they left for the ceremony. Kali forced it upon her by refusing to speak to the crowd without her there. She'd waited until Norvik was at Police Headquarters, before making her demand. In the exchange that followed she watched impassively as tempers flared until eventually Awhi put her job on the line and refused to relinquish custody. They left for the monument together, and somehow even to Yan's untrained eye, it seemed that the language of bodies had become easier between them.

Crowded into the internal passages and chambers of the monument, there was no respite from the tension and guilt. With Kali standing beside him, Yan felt even more alone than before she'd arrived in his life. He knew that Awhi was right, but was still unable to understand what Kali expected, how he could restore himself in her eyes.

There was no explaining his attack on Norvik. It came as much as a surprise to him as to the Counsellor. In all likelihood it had done more harm than good, allowing anger to override sound judgment. But maybe, that was the answer. The impulse to throw caution aside in defence of what was right. Perhaps it was the reason why Kali's hand found his for a moment afterwards, why she had looked at him directly for the first time that morning. Perhaps she saw in his loss of control, the recognition that all beings retain a vestige of their ancient selves, and that the superiority of one species over another is only a matter of perspective.

Out on the platform, Yan was glad about what he'd done. He saw Kali's fear fall away as she addressed her audience, witnessed her beguile the crowd with the same force and charm that he'd found so irresistible. He'd underestimated her again, and more importantly, Norvik had too. He had no idea what she'd said in her own language, but with the magic of her voice, Kali had lifted everyone in the square, human and Antarian alike. Somehow, she'd used it to steer a course around Norvik's strategy.

But then in an instant, it all changed. He saw it first in the movement of her face, the moistening sheen of her eyes. She knew that Norvik would never allow her victory to stand, that there was only one way to preserve it, undiminished in the minds of her followers. His realisation came without deduction, a rush of intuition stirred by his new awareness of human expressions. But as usual, she was quicker than him. And so it was, that he was left grasping the air behind her as she threw herself from the parapet. Whether he screamed aloud, or whether it was the collective voice of the crowd, a dizzying noise exploded in his head, his mind registering, but not accepting the sight of Kali falling, arms outstretched, her coat filling and flapping behind her.

Then followed the moment when he knew she'd gone, that his Kali had turned to nothing more than a falling object, mass subject to the force of gravity. And in that moment, he mourned, he felt the loss of her as if his whole world had tilted irretrievably, and what he'd found with her had gone forever.

But then came the wonder. In fragments of shattered time, he watched his hands setting about their work, moving without conscious instruction, the fingers of one going to the wrist of the other, first as an act of grief as they found his bracelet, then turning it, triggering the bond. It happened slowly at first, Kali's body continuing its plunge into the yawning well beneath the monument. Then her arm turned, dragged behind her, pulled her body around as the black cavern approached. Finally, her fall was arrested, and she was left bobbing and swinging over the crowd.

Now Kali looked up. Held by her wrist, and knowing the means of her rescue, she gazed up at the platform, perhaps more in relief than shock. Whatever she was thinking though, she was smiling, and her smile was only for him.

In the square beneath her, the crowd had become a boiling mass of bodies, the National Guard closing in, tightening the cordon around it. Yan began shortening the bond to haul Kali up again. Further along the parapet, he could see Norvik flushed scarlet and barking orders at his aides. Jocasta had slipped away, and Awhi Kanawa was fixing a bond around her waist as if she intended to climb down to help Kali.

And now, the mood of the crowd shifted again. It surged and fractured, its roar turning to shrieking fear as blue flashes prickled around the square. Out at the edges of the crowd, the National Guard had set up a killing zone. They stood waiting for ferals to break cover and flee and were picking them off with clinical precision.

The crowd pressed at Henik from all sides. Only seconds before it had been united in wonder at the sound of Kali's voice, but now it had become a disorderly mob. It didn't seem to be Kali's brush with death that had changed the mood, it was something else, something that was causing alarm and confusion as people struggled to see what was happening at the fringes.

A call sounded in Henik's head, and Yan's name appeared. He looked up at the speakers' platform, where Kali was still hanging on her bond, a uniformed officer now climbing over the parapet to help her.

'It's crazy down here!' he shouted. 'Can you see what's…?'

'Norvik's ordered the National Guard to exterminate ferals! It's going to be a massacre!'

The crowd gave another lurch, and from the corner of his eye, Henik saw a flash of elemist. Someone was shoved into his ribs and he turned to see Alka, fighting for a way out. She looked up at him, and he saw in her expression, the horror of someone who could neither flee nor defend herself. Instinctively, he stooped and grabbed her around the waist, lifting her away from the trampling feet. For a moment she struggled, then as Henik raised her higher, her expression changed, and she began to search the crowd from her new vantage point. Henik took her hand; he raised it above his head and shouted at the top of his voice.

'They're killing the ferals! Quick – pick them up! He grasped at a shoulder next to him. 'Behind you! Pick that feral up now, or he's as good as dead! Already Henik could see humans being taken into arms all around, some domestic, and others feral, shielded despite the wildness in their eyes, and the grime on their bodies and clothes. Alka had grasped what was happening. She began calling to the other ferals, her voice carrying clear and shrill and answered by other human voices repeating her message. Now humans were throwing themselves into waiting arms, and the crush of bodies began to ease. The crowd stood its ground, gradually forming itself into a tight phalanx, shouting its defiance as it sheltered the ferals within its ranks.

Faced with a battle formation of the citizens they were assigned to protect, the National Guard stood in indecision. Riot shields were rumbling into position on the front line, but the guards were beginning to lower their carbines. Henik could see their commander, walking along his lines with his fingers pressed to his face. He was looking up at the Statue of National Destiny and speaking in short bursts as if arguing with someone further up the chain of command.

The screens around the square were occupied with Kali's rescue on the face of the monument, a drama being seen across the Republic, but now they cut to a report on the massacre in the square. The familiar figure of Nico S'tana appeared on the screens, holding a feral as he spoke, a young male with matted hair and a scar on his cheek. Henik hadn't realised S'tana was in the crowd, but when he looked along the phalanx, he could see him standing tall at the corner of the formation, the feral gripping his shirt at the collar. His report would be going out live to the nation, a powerful message of co-operation between the species.

Now the image on the screens changed again, dissolving and re-forming into the seal of the Office of the Chief Counsellor, spinning in its familiar gyroscopic movement to herald a live statement from Maarten Feyrsten. The crowd began to settle in anticipation, and a few moments later he appeared in front of the panoramic window of his transport, his face looking weary against the brightness of the sky.

'Esteemed citizens,' he began, his voice smooth and controlled. 'Few of us would have imagined that such events could happen in the heart of our capital and around the Republic as we have seen these past days, and now our day of national celebration has been marred by further loss of life. It's the Government's job to act assertively in a crisis and be assured that we will do that. Order must be restored, but we must also apply the greatest diligence to the challenges that confront us. In affirming the special destiny of the Free Republic, we must recognise our reliance on our companion species, the duty of care we owe to the humans in our midst. I have heard the words, and the extraordinary voice of the one who is being called 'Callista' and I'm sure many of you will also be asking whether she may be the example we need to find a better path.'

Somewhere behind the Government buildings, Henik could hear the distinctive sound of a sub-orbital transport. It came into view, threading its way between the towers and spires, the livery of the Free Republic instantly recognisable. Henik turned to watch it approach, noticing the National Guard doing the same. He'd almost forgotten that he was still holding Alka until she stretched out her arm and pointed at the transport. 'Chief Counsellor,' he told her.

'I have issued an Administrative Order,' Feyrsten went on. 'The new laws pertaining to humans will be suspended to allow time for reflection, and behavioural implanting will be cancelled with immediate effect. Military operations in the so-called Derelict Zone will cease.'

The crowd responded with raucous approval, drowning the speech for a moment. Henik enhanced the volume of the message in his head but still strained to hear Feyrsten's words. 'I have consulted with the Leader of the Opposition, Congressioner Aspil,' he said. 'Based on those discussions an independent commission will be formed to consider our relationship with the human species. Congressioner Aspil will make her own address later, and a chair for the commission will be appointed before the end of the day. I can't give specifics just yet, except to say that we are agreed that whilst there must be clear public order requirements, there must also be representation for the interests of humans and consideration of their rights. But now, citizens and fellow travellers, I request from you a gesture of goodwill. The National Guard will stand down, and I ask you to give this new initiative a chance, by halting your protests. Please enjoy the rest of the day peacefully, and may the gods sustain you.'

The Chief Counsellor's transport came to a halt above the square, turned on its axis, then slowly entered the vast skydock high on the flank of the Department for the Interior. Henik watched it for a few moments as he considered what he'd just heard. The crowd was already starting to disperse around him, and the National Guard was marching away. Alka had gone. He couldn't remember putting her down, but as he looked around the square, he saw that the other ferals had disappeared as well. He caught Nico S'tana's eye, and they stood together as the phalanx dissolved. At its centre there was a large grating set in the tiles. He knelt beside it and found it was loose. From far below came the echo of footsteps, hurrying away in the darkness.

When Henik stood up, he found that even Nico S'tana had left. The Republic Day celebrations continued in the surrounding streets, but a faint echo of what they had been before. The moment for revolution had come, and it had passed them by, granted them an opportunity to avoid its carnage.

A call from Santi came through and he took it as he made his way back to his quarters. 'How did you manage to pull that one off?'

'I have my powers of persuasion, you know. Sometimes it's amazing what you can achieve over lunch.'

'You've been dining with Feyrsten?'

'Still with him. He's just been called away for a moment.'

'Sounds like he's the one who's been doing the persuading.' Henik could feel resentment waking in his head, pulling on its boots to kick at any rational assessment of the situation. He reminded himself of Feyrsten's announcement, its effect on the crowd, the lives it had saved.

'I'll admit it,' said Santi. 'I couldn't bear queuing in that heat, so I accepted his hospitality. I don't regret it.'

'No, of course not,' said Henik, trying to sound reasonable, but his voice finding an ironic tone anyway.

'Look, I think we've got something we can work with here. He knows he's in the shit, and who's got him into it. But I think the Spice Islands affected him. He's looking for a solution that...'

'Will get him out of trouble. I bet he is.'

Santi sighed. 'I don't blame you for being sceptical, but I

won't win public support by putting my party before the Republic. There are tangible results in this. Norvik will go, if he hasn't already, the implanting ends, the Feral Task Force demobilises.'

'But it gets him off the hook for a policy disaster of his own making, and a failed operation in the Derelict Zone. You can't criticise while this Commission is doing its work, and if it fails, you'll get your share of the blame.'

'That's true but…'

'How do you know he won't just load the Commission with his Heritage cronies?'

'Well, I'm pretty confident on that point actually…'

Santi's voice faded, inviting Henik to draw his own conclusion. 'Because?' He waited for her to elaborate, but she remained silent. 'Alright, I'm being slow here so… Oh no! Don't tell me…!'

'Why not? I can appoint the Chair. Why not you? You'd be independent. I wouldn't be your boss, and neither would Maarten Feyrsten.'

'But what about *us*? It's a conflict of interests. He'd find out – *everyone* would.'

'He knows already. I'm sure of it. And the public will judge on results. It won't be an obstacle.'

'It's an obstacle for me. It doesn't look right. It isn't right.'

'I know you have your principles Henik, but sometimes you have to be pragmatic. If you were me, you'd still be waiting for your transport in the Spice Islands, and there might well have been a full-scale uprising in the middle of Freeport.'

'This is different. This would be an ongoing conflict between an independent role, and a personal relationship.'

'You're the right person for the job.'

'In your not-so-unbiased view. Remember that headline before you left? You thought it tied my unhelpful views to your party.'

'Please, Henik. I need your support on this.'

'I need you too. I don't want to lose you.' He had said it. His mouth had spoken the words that his mind had refused to compose, that the consequence of their differences was to be living alone again.

Santi's image flickered for a moment. She hung her head, and her ridges lifted through the fine ranks of her hair. 'You don't have to, Henik,' she said quietly. 'There is no dishonour in this. Really, there isn't.'

'This proposal, this Commission, is where my path has been leading me. You're right – I can't ignore it. But we can't have it both ways. We just can't. So…'

'Don't, Henik. *Please* don't do this!'

'Somehow, I knew this would happen.' Henik's breath was coming ragged through his words now, his voice failing. 'The heavens may align for some,' he said. 'But for others, they just never do.'

21

Home

ALKA FOUND THE OTHER clan leaders congregating in an immense underground cistern a short distance from Carnival Square. She climbed down from an access pipe and walked to the centre of the cavern.

'Who have we lost?'

No one answered. No one wanted to meet her eyes either. 'Four that we know,' someone said, eventually. 'And others missing.'

'Where's Chemical Mike?'

Kit pushed through to the front of the group. 'He took a hit, Chief.' He pointed towards one of the tunnels that fed the cistern. 'There's an old watercourse below. We've taken him there with the others. Three of the Dockers got it too. It's bad.'

Mike had been placed on a makeshift stretcher, a rough board between two lengths of piping. Behind him, on the mossy bank of an underground river, three bodies lay in a line, their heads covered by scraps of sacking. Mike would be joining them soon. He was breathing heavily, a wound in his chest bubbling with blue froth, and his teeth chattering as the elemist chilled his circulation. Alka knelt and took his hand.

She could see how the toxin had already worked its way into his tissues, swelling the skin, distorting the tattoos around his knuckles. 'I'll get you something for the pain,' she said.

He shook his head. 'It won't be long… and I must speak to my clan. Bring… let me see them.'

Alka stood aside to let the Chemicals come forward. They crouched around the stretcher, some showing their distress openly, groaning at the back of their throats and beating their fists against their chests. Others remained still and sombre, muttering incantations in an unfamiliar dialect. Mike's body gave a sudden lurch and began to shake, his heels rattling against the board beneath him, hands fluttering.

'I'm leaving you, brothers, sisters.' he said. 'This… is my last command. You will follow Alka now, as your leader. She has wisdom. What she foretold has come to pass.'

'We will avenge you.' said one of them, a hollow-cheeked girl, who had been casting a wary eye at Alka.

'No… there's been enough killing. I saw… people holding your hands. That's the way… the hope Callista has shown us.'

Alka saw him trying to turn his head in her direction. She moved back into his view. 'Do you know what happened?' he said. Did you… hear the words?'

She could see how the colour was ebbing from his face now, the flesh drawing back from the bones. 'I didn't understand the leader of the People,' she said, 'but his words brought peace. It was Callista's doing. He must have understood her message. He saw the sacrifice she was prepared to make and the miracle that saved her.'

Mike's body convulsed for a moment. 'The colours are brighter close to death,' he said.

Alka knelt close. 'She's coming for you, Mike. It's your redemption.'

'She saw me. I felt it… her voice, her gift. It told me I was going home.' He smiled through gritted teeth and gripped Alka's arm tightly. 'You brought me to her… and now I'm going home to Terra.'

A voice came to them from one of the tunnels, and Mike turned his head to listen. It started as a low humming, alone at first, then joined with faltering words by another voice, and another again. It swelled and filled the caverns, steadying into a mournful reprise of Callista's anthem.

Kali stood at her bedroom window squinting into the morning light as she watched the Chief Counsellor's limousine settle outside. Yan was at the kerb, even before the transport had come to a halt. The brothers greeted each other with locked forearms, stood that way for a brief conversation, then walked away together. They crossed into the woodland opposite and disappeared from view, followed at a respectful distance by a brace of security guards.

She went back to sit on her bed, fingers settling briefly on the sleeve of the new coat Yan had laid out for her homecoming. Then she drew her magic desk onto her lap. Her face was everywhere, the news focusing inevitably on her leap from the Monument of National Destiny. It was playing on a repeating loop, the closer images capturing her expression as she fell. She tried to recall what was in her mind at that moment and found only the sound of the wind and the dark chasm below.

She examined the abrasion on her knee where it had grazed against the monument, wondered whether it was her imagination, or whether it was healing much faster than it would on Earth. Her wrist was much better too, no longer swollen where the bond bracelet had arrested her fall. Yan had taken her for treatment at a mobile veterinary unit, a sleek white transport where she sat on a bench, opposite a dog-like animal that looked to be suffering from the heat. The vets had tried to remove her bracelet, but she had insisted on keeping it, a gesture which seemed to affect Yan, caused him to colour and turn away from her sight.

Kali was pleased to see that there was coverage of her speech, at least what she had said in their language, and there was a picture of her singing which she liked more than the others. Best of all though, was a report from Nico S'tana, who had been made into something of a hero. National News featured a giant image of him holding a wide-eyed boy, as they faced a row of guardsmen. Kali was just beginning to read a commentary under the headline 'Callista Inspires,' when she heard a distant announcement from the front door.

There were footsteps on the stairs, but when the door opened, it wasn't Yan who stood there, but Jocasta. She leaned heavily on the frame, a flask held lightly between thumb and finger and her mouth stretched into an unnatural imitation of a smile.

'Hellooo again, my dear!' she said. 'I thought I would stop by to offer my congrat… congrat-u-lashuns on your performance. And to say I have no hard feelings about…' She tossed her head, so the rows of hair along her ridges moved like the plumes of a circus horse. 'Well… you know.'

She took a gulp of her drink and wandered into the room, looking around as if she was planning to have it re-decorated. After their last encounter, Kali decided it would be best to remain silent. Jocasta had probably been told to stay in the limousine, but here she was nevertheless, towering unsteadily in front of her, and just as capable of violence as generosity.

'I'm sure it's been quite a day for you. Nearly died, didn't you? But no! How forshunate. How very, very… You'll need someone to guide you now. A new wardrobe! Yes, I shall shoose it for you. Green – a moon theme.' She stumbled slightly and steadied herself against the wall. 'And animal prints… the animal goddess.'

'I not be…' Kali caught herself. *Don't provoke her. Stay calm.*

'Come on, Callista. Didn't I say that should be your name? Didn't I shay that? Come on. I'll take you shopping. I'll make you look as you should!'

She reached out towards Kali and she shied away instinctively. 'I do wait for Yan,' she said. 'Is not for go shopping now.'

'No shopping?' said Jocasta, her voice thinning. 'But I've come to take you to the boutiques, and thash where we're going!'

'I do wait for Yan.'

Jocasta's demeanour changed in an instant. Kali ducked as her flask shattered against the wall beside her. 'You ungrateful little shit!' she hissed. 'You think you can shange everything, don't you? Think you're so superior! So loved!'

'Please. Is good for shopping with Yan, too. Please, we …'

Jocasta's anger had sobered her, sharpened her tongue. 'You'll be in the news for a few moments,' she said. 'Soon you'll be forgotten. And then where will you be, you grubby little creature? You'll crawl back asking for help! Well, you can fucking crawl now! Go on – crawl!'

Kali slid off the bed and edged towards the door, but with a motion of Jocasta's hand she could feel her bond bracelet tugging, hauling her back.

'I'm going to teash you how to behave!' Jocasta snarled. She grabbed a fistful of Kali's hair and held her down on the mattress. 'You need something to remind you what you are!'

Jocasta took a silver tool from her pocket. It looked like a pen at first glance, but when she pressed it with her thumb a piercing blue light appeared. 'Know what this is? Of course not! It's an elemist knife – really good for marking possessions! It'll hurt of course, but humans are such little squealers! I don't want to hear a sound from you about it!'

Kali bucked and squirmed as the elemist knife hovered over her face. 'No, Jocasta! No! Stop!' Jocasta tightened her grip, holding her closer to the bed until Kali thought her hair would rip from her scalp. Somehow, she managed to get her hand to Jocasta's wrist, exert enough force to deflect the path of the knife and hold it away from her face. 'Please, Jocasta! Please stop!'

'Hold still!' shrieked Jocasta, and she bore down on Kali again, the knife's blue point aimed at the centre of her forehead. Kali spluttered and fought, twisting her body under Jocasta's weight but resistance was futile. The blue light was blurring close and Jocasta's eyes stared down with a crazed fervour. Then suddenly something moved in them, just a flicker of surprise as if a switch had been triggered. Jocasta released her grip. Her mouth dropped open and she sucked a great gulp of air, her hand reaching behind her neck as she turned away. The cause and effect came into view at the same moment. Blood was pumping from a wound behind Jocasta's neck, coursing between her fingers and down her back. And standing behind her with a pointed garden implement, was Dill.

The cry that erupted from Jocasta's throat was as loud and primal as anything Kali had heard on the plains of Africa. Dill stood transfixed as if she couldn't fathom what she'd just done.

Kali screamed her name and her senses returned just in time to duck a ferocious sweep of Jocasta's arm. The elemist knife carved a blue trail through Dill's hair. She dropped the garden tool and threw herself in front of Kali, cowering from the attack, but using her body as a shield all the same.

Jocasta had no words to express her rage. Any remnant of self-control had left her, and she thrashed wildly at them with the knife. Her first stroke scored the wall above their heads, but her second was shaping up to be a vertical strike, the piercing blue light rising high over their heads.

The knife was just beginning its downward stroke when Jocasta's life ended. A searing bolt of elemist caught her full in the face, her eyes instantly bluing, and the blood vessels in her cheeks raising like roots in a parched forest. She was dead before her knife clattered on the floor, and if she knew in her final moment that she'd been shot, there was no sign that she'd seen her nemesis standing in the doorway, or the weapon still levelled at her head.

Torsta Jai waited for Jocasta to fall before she came into the room. She stood over the body, rolled it onto its back with the side of her foot.

Kali struggled to her feet and backed away, holding Dill close to her side. Her mind was struggling to absorb the shock, racing to assess the new threat.

'Torsta Jai,' she gasped, 'I do thank you.'

Torsta slid her pistol into a holster and limped to the window. She stood with her hands on her hips, looking in the direction of the woods for several moments, then turned her head in Kali's direction.

'She wasn't breaking the law,' she said. 'I've murdered her.'

However welcome the intervention, the word 'murder'

still felt like a physical blow. It told Kali that the danger was far from over, reminded her that violent crimes often led to further desperate acts. Whatever was in Torsta's mind though, the only option that made sense was to engage her in conversation, to get her talking.

'Is well done,' she said. 'For save me, and Dill.'

Torsta's gaze settled on Dill for the first time. 'Makes no difference to the law, however many of you there are,' she said.

'Your leg is having injury, Torsta.'

Torsta's fingers found a groove on the forearm of her body armour. There was a subtle shifting of its contours, from the shoulders right down to the greaves, as if the whole outfit had softened. Immediately, Torsta seemed to relax. 'Something happened in the Derelict Zone,' she said. 'I almost died – I should have.' She saw the elemist knife on the floor and limped over to crush it under her heel, extinguishing the blue light. 'I was wrong to do what I did Kali, taking you from your home. I can't say how everything is different now, but it is.' The arrogance seemed to have left Torsta, her brittle defences easing with the rest of her armour. For someone who had just killed so clinically, her manner was curiously subdued.

'What you do now?' said Kali.

'I'll have to live as a fugitive. And... I'll atone.'

'Atone. Not understand this word.'

'Do good things to pay for the bad. There are difficult times ahead and there may be occasions when I can help you.' Torsta's eyes went to Dill's garden tool lying on the floor. She picked it up, then pushed it inside her armour. 'You will be questioned. You must say this was my doing. Mine alone.'

'Is bad for you, Torsta.'

'It's not something I'll regret.'

'I tell Yan you did save...'

'You're not out of danger, Kali. Everyone in the Republic knows you now, and there are some who would do you harm. Norvik would...'

'Norvik is gone away now.'

'You haven't heard the last of him. He craves attention and he has a loyal following, So, there may be a time when you will need my help.'

'How I do find you?'

Torsta turned to look up at the corner of the ceiling, where two tiny spiders with red eyes were peering from a crack. 'Come to this room and call for me.'

Deep in the woods a giant bekan tree stood in a clearing, the ground beneath it a combustion of colour and dappled light. It was a place where the air was alive with floating seeds and tiny resin bubbles, the chattering of small creatures, and the memories of past times.

'I still come here sometimes,' said Yan. He watched his brother scanning the majestic spread of the branches above them. The tree would be awakening Maarten's childhood memories, he thought. It was a good place to talk.

'Our special tree,' Maarten said. 'I knew we'd end up here.' He turned to survey the clearing, while his security detail probed the bushes around the perimeter.

Yan placed his fingers on the trunk, rehearsing the handholds that had so often taken them to their favourite vantage points. 'Tempted?' he asked.

'You'll have to do it on your own this time, brother. I can't stay long – Jocasta's in a foul mood. She's looking for people to blame, as usual.'

'Blame for what?'

'For things not being as they should. It's her default position. She's very set in her thinking – hates change.'

'And change is coming.'

'Yes, and your Kali is at the centre of it. Jocasta knows that, but she can't accept it, can't bring herself to get out of the limo and be polite. She's drunk, of course.'

'I'm sorry.'

Maarten pushed his hands into his pockets, poked at the forest floor with his shoe, no longer seeming the important man that he was. 'Don't be,' he said. 'I've known for a long time that I'd have to put an end to it. It's been poor judgment on my part, from the moment I met her. But there's always been something about Jocasta that's fascinated me, how she tramples everyone as if they are lesser beings, the way she thinks rules don't apply to her. She's just so brazen, so reckless. In a way, I find it exciting.'

'I would never have thought that of you. You're always so cool-headed, so rational.'

'Well, there you are. No one's perfect.'

'With a job like yours, I can't believe you need more excitement.'

'But it's not good to be alone, either. We're a fine pair, you and I, neither of us with a special person in our lives. Although, you've got Kali now, and she'll be good for you.' Maarten leant against the tree and gazed up into its branches. 'Do you know how much the neighbours disapproved of us playing in these trees? They thought we were wild, whispered that we'd turn out badly.'

'Probably still think they were right about that, at least as far as you're concerned!'

'Well, this isn't a Heritage neighbourhood.'

'Surely it didn't bother you what people said back then, did it?'

'No, because I always knew where I wanted to go and what I wanted to be.'

'And now you've achieved it. Are you happy?'

'Not really. Becoming Chief Counsellor only gave me a fleeting satisfaction. I already want more.'

'More? Come on Maarten, how could you possibly want *more*? You govern the whole Commonwealth!'

'A legacy depends on the scale of the challenge. Not just managing a steady vessel but piloting it through uncharted spacetime.'

'So, you don't mind that…'

'That I have in front of me the challenge of a generation? That's the way I want it. Kali may have ignited a forest, but it was dry and waiting for lightning to strike. How is she, by the way, shaken I'd imagine, coming back from the dead like that.'

'Quite calm, believe it or not. When you think what she's been through, it's quite extraordinary how resilient she is, how adaptable. Actually, she's got quite a lot in common with you.'

'I've been compared to a lot of things in my time, but not to a human.'

'Well, perhaps you'll need to start thinking more like one. Henik says Santi Aspil is coming to the conclusion that we must bridge the gap.'

'Henik Varkesen and Santi Aspil. Who would have thought? You knew about that, I suppose.'

'I guessed. Did she tell you?'

'I didn't need her to. I'm Chief Counsellor.' Maarten looked pointedly at his security detail.

'So, this challenge of a generation. Where do you think it's going?'

Maarten wandered a few steps, head down and scuffing the ground. 'What would you say is the main weakness of our civilisation?'

'Difficult one. Complacency?'

'Arguably. For all the wars we've had in this star system, none has been decisive enough to create a single dominant state.'

'How's that a weakness?'

'When you start to reach out across the cosmos, you find that other interstellar civilisations you encounter, the Gilessians, the Croesans, are based on a single state. They can move decisively, without debate and negotiation, while we struggle to deal with a small revolt on a tropical island. And even if the Free Republic dominates Antaris, there are still two competing interstellar powers in our system, the Deccans autocratic, whilst we supposedly are an enlightened community of peoples. Our species is split between two adjacent planets, arguing and fighting down the millennia. It must amuse alien civilisations to see it.'

'You don't think we're respected?'

'Not enough to be safe. And we'll be respected less if the Commonwealth starts prickling with revolutions over the human issue, if our systems start defecting to the Deccan Dominion, if the Deccans encourage those defections. We'll end up fighting each other again. And meanwhile all the spacetime we consider to be ours will be ripe for the taking.'

Yan knew Maarten would expect a considered response, but his mind was struggling with the sheer scale of the implications. 'Presumably, you think Santi Aspil can be persuaded to work with you on this,' he said. 'You need consensus.'

Maarten sucked in a breath. 'I need more than that. I need you, brother.'

'You've never needed me in your life.'

'Not so, and less true now than ever.' Maarten stepped closer. 'Actually, Kali needs you… and I need Kali.'

Yan's stomach lurched. 'But you've only just released her! After all I've been through with Norvik. I won't let you…'

'Norvik's gone, and his policy has gone with him. Maarten looked back in the direction of the house. 'Look, I get it that you want Kali at home, but things can't be as they were. You do understand that, don't you? She's a celebrity now, an idol. Whether she asked for it or not, she's part of the solution to the human question, and there's no bigger issue for our civilisation than that. A lot will depend on her involvement. In a very real sense, she is Callista.'

'I can't just tell her to co-operate, Maarten. As you've seen, she makes up her own mind. And she doesn't trust politicians.'

'But still, will she help?'

'Perhaps. If I approach her in the right way. But don't take her for granted, and don't take me for granted either. If I find you're using Kali for your own benefit, we'll fall out in a very public way.' Yan knew how much his warning would have annoyed his brother, but for once he was in the stronger position.

'How much does she understand about our civilisation?' Maarten said, moving the discussion on to practicalities, as if the point of principle had been agreed and Yan's warning needed no acknowledgment.

'She's learning fast. She wants to know everything about the Republic, about Antaris.'

'Just Antaris?'

Suddenly Yan understood. 'You're kidding!' he said. 'Surely you don't think she can help you hold the Commonwealth together?'

'In time, yes. What happened yesterday is already travelling to the furthest colonies and protectorates. Just think about it. Kali's face, what she does with that voice of hers. She'll soon be known in every system where there are humans. Do you imagine we can keep the peace without her support?'

'But she barely even knows about the Commonwealth. She's not ready to…' Yan could feel his breath shortening, his blood pumping more fiercely. He was succumbing to his brother's will and ambition as he always had, following his lead up through the high branches of the wood to look across a vista, far beyond their childhood world. 'Admit it,' he said bitterly. 'You've got people in Check St. already making plans for her, haven't you?'

'It's their job to think ahead,' said Maarten. 'As for me, I'm certainly hoping Kali is all you say – for the sake of the Republic, I'm counting on it.' He put his hand on Yan's shoulder. 'Think about it. Please.'

Yan watched his brother's bodyguards pacing the perimeter of the clearing, their presence suddenly more relevant and more intrusive. 'I expect we'll have to tolerate all this crap in future, as well.'

Maarten didn't answer, he didn't need to. 'Alright, I'll speak to her,' Yan said, 'but don't think either of us will be rushed, however much is at stake.'

'Thank you,' said Maarten, and he had the sense to pause and let his appreciation stand for something in itself. 'You'll have to pick your moment of course,' he said, 'but sooner or later, she'll need to know the truth about her species.'

'The truth. You mean, that humans exist on other planets too.'

Maarten looked up beyond the wood to the cloudless sky

above. He spoke softly. 'That her species has been scattered across the cosmos for longer than anyone knows.'

'I was just thinking,' said Henik. 'I don't know your real name. I've never thought to ask. What do they call you on Earth?'

For a moment, Kali didn't register the question. She stood looking up at the mosaic in the middle of Midsummer Mall, absorbed by her likeness. It made her shiver to imagine that some influence might have brought her together with the mural, across the unfathomable vastness of space. She heard Henik clear his throat and went to sit with him on the edge of the fountain. 'Emily,' she said. 'My name was Emily Coppen.'

'You had two names?' said Henik. Then he caught himself, looked away. 'Yes, of course, you did. Why wouldn't you?'

'Now, you do try say it.'

'Eym… Emeeylj Cohprn,' tried Henik, his tongue wrestling with his first words in a human language.

She smiled. 'I be… I am Kali now.'

'Not Callista?'

She glanced up at the news display, which was showing an image of Jocasta Feyrsten, and the police transport that had been stationed outside Yan's house for more than a day. 'Is not name. "Callista" is like "Counsellor." Is a thing.'

'A title.'

She nodded. 'Like clothes you do carry.'

'Clothes you wear. Until one day maybe, if you can go home to Earth. Then you can take off those clothes.'

Kali laughed. 'I do wear clothes in Earth! You know I not be animal!'

'I meant that...'

She smiled again and touched his arm. 'I do be funny with you, Henik.'

They sat together watching the display, while the fountain trickled behind them. 'There is much need to do here,' Kali said after a while. 'Is home now.'

'Can you really think of Antaris as home, after all you've been through here?'

Kali remembered the farm by the sea, lying in the corn under an English sky, the geese calling for her in the distance. Then another memory came to her, closer and more vivid, the sea hurling itself on the sand in front of Yan's beach house, the surf flashing in the firelight, and all three of them merry. 'Home is friends,' she said, and took his hand.

'Well, maybe you'll make another friend today.'

'You think Alka do come?'

'I don't know, but I can't go searching under the whole city. This is a special place for her. But you know that if she does come, you'll have to be Callista for her.'

Kali nodded. 'You like Alka, I do think.'

'She's taught me a lot. You know, I always thought I was learning about humans, but now…'

'You be learning about people too. About self.'

Henik shifted his weight slightly. Are you going to tell me what really happened up on that monument? Why didn't you tell Yan what you had in mind? Why did you take the risk?'

Kali found the question strangely empowering. For the first time, an Antarian was assuming that her actions were considered, that she had a strategy. 'Norvik,' she said. 'He must see Yan be shocking.'

'Seriously? You took a chance that Yan would know what to do, just so it wouldn't look planned? You were just expecting Yan to save you?'

Kali folded her arms, the sound of the water suddenly chilling her backbone. 'Not be expecting. Be hoping.' She could feel Henik looking at her, peeling away her layers, and she decided not to return his gaze, not to concede a further explanation.

The screen shifted to a view of the interstellar terminal, a crowd following Sig Norvik across a busy concourse. The sight of him made Kali shudder, but still she watched, listened to what he said to reporters. He was suggesting his dismissal was something temporary, launched into lurid predictions, all blood and violence.

'No honour, no shame,' said Henik, turning away from the screen. Then suddenly he gripped Kali's arm and his gaze went to the entrance of the mall. Out in the blazing light of the plaza a silhouette was approaching, running with an easy stride, and holding a javelin. 'She's here,' he said.

Alka didn't see them to start with; her attention was taken by the mosaic. Then she stopped in her tracks, and the mall echoed with the sound of her javelin falling on the tiles. Kali got to her feet, motioned for Henik to stay back, then approached sedately. Alka appeared to stumble, as if her body was caught between an urge to go forward and a reflex to run away. Then she dropped to one knee and bowed her head.

Kali continued forward, maintained her silence until she was standing right in front of her. 'Hello, at last,' she said, trying her native tongue.

Alka raised her head slowly. Her lips began to move, but it seemed that she couldn't bring herself to speak. Kali stooped and took her by the elbows, raised her to her feet. They stood face to face, Alka taller by some margin, but flexing her knees as if embarrassed by her superior height.

'Alka,' said Kali quietly. 'You do me honour.'

There were tears on Alka's cheeks now. 'Callista,' she whispered, the name catching slightly in her throat.

'You've led your clan with courage. I know the burden you have carried.'

Alka's shoulders slumped, as if the words had finally given her permission to put down her load. She bowed her head again and sniffed. 'It's been so hard,' she said. Then, regaining her composure she straightened her back. 'But now you are here, and I am glad to do your bidding.'

'Then come and sit with me,' said Kali. 'I'll need your counsel. There's work for us to do.' She led her back to the fountain, and Alka perched on the very edge, as if she would have preferred to be kneeling on the tiled floor. Kali decided to give her time to find her voice, and sat very still until eventually she was able to speak.

'I know there have been times when I've disappointed you,' Alka said, her accent strange to Kali's ears, and the dialect forcing Kali to pluck words from other languages to make sense of it. 'There have been times when I have failed to follow your path.'

'The greatest struggle is always with yourself,' said Kali. 'But each day is a chance to start afresh.' She took Alka's hands and placed them into the water of the fountain, rubbing them gently with her own. 'You were in Carnival Square and heard what I said?'

'I will never forget it. I will take your gift to my heart, and hope to learn it, as some of my brothers and sisters already have. What is it called, Callista – your gift?'

'Singing is a simple pleasure, but it will strengthen you, hold you together on the difficult path ahead.'

'The path that will take us home?'

'Perhaps one day that's where it will lead. But it's preparing yourselves in this world, that will make you complete.'

'Forgive me, Callista. I don't understand.'

'And I cannot explain, except to say that the more you strive in this world, the closer Terra will come. You've already taken the first steps on that journey.' She turned and beckoned to Henik. 'I am heartened that you placed your trust in my friend.'

Henik had been keeping his distance, as they spoke. Now he came forward, and Alka registered his presence for the first time. She looked from one of them to the other. 'You know Plain?'

'You were stronger on Republic Day when you were together. So, I'm asking you now, to help him.'

Alka's forehead creased into a frown. 'I will do whatever you command, Callista, but I don't understand.'

'The Chief Counsellor of the People has agreed there will be a Commission, a great council, to decide how humans and people can live together better.'

'But they already have a council in their city. Its laws have always oppressed us.'

'Change will come slowly, but surely if you persist. This new Commission is not a place for politicians. They've asked Henik to lead it.'

Alka looked up at him. A muscle moved in her jaw, and her temple pulsed. 'He's strange,' she said, 'but he means us well.'

'He must appoint members to the Commission, and he wants there to be human voices amongst them.'

'This is good. You are our voice, Callista. This is very good.'

'I'm here to guide you, and I can speak the language of the People. But the humans of this land must stand for themselves if they are to win respect. Will you sit beside Henik on this Commission? As the leader of free humans?'

Alka's eyes flew open. 'Callista, please do not ask this – I beg you! I am nothing! I don't know letters. I don't know the ways of the People!'

Kali held her by the shoulders. 'Listen to me, Alka. I know what I'm asking of you is a great responsibility. I understand you're afraid, but you won't be alone. You can help Henik to choose others to give voice to human interests as well, and I'll be there to advise you. It's time for humans to raise themselves up in this world.'

Henik edged closer and Kali translated as he spoke. 'I've seen your skills as a leader, and I know this is your calling.'

Kali knew how much she'd added to Alka's burden. She had the power to lead her into the fire, and there could be no refusal. She was confident that Alka would rise to the challenge, but it felt a cruel assignment all the same.

'How will the clans survive under the city?' asked Kali. 'Do you have a plan?'

She lowered her eyes, then shook her head. 'I'm sorry, Callista. I presumed too much of you.'

'Henik has a proposal. He says it will be safe for you to bring the clans back to live here in Midsummer, as long as they leave the docks and other facilities. He has the authority to make the buildings around the plaza suitable for you to live in, and to ensure you have all that you need. He will make this work for the clans, so that they will be safe, and you'll be able to give your attention to the Commission.'

Alka sighed. 'He gives us life, and I thank him for it. I know I must accept the task you are giving me. It's a great privilege, and I know you won't desert me, but I cannot hide my fear. Must I go to the great building of the People? Is that where you are sending me, Callista?' She turned to watch the bubbling water of the fountain as if she found in it a comforting familiarity.

A thought occurred to Kali. 'Haven't you spoken with other clan leaders before? Was it here, under this roof?

Alka nodded. 'We've fought too much. It's better to talk.'

'Then talk to Henik about this, now. Talk to him as a leader of free humans. Kali got up and stood between them. 'How do you want this Commission to be, Alka? And *where* do you want it to meet?'

For the third evening in a row, Yan arrived home to Kali's cooking, the house filled with the aroma of herbs she had foraged from the garden. He called to her from the hallway, then wandered into the kitchen. She was busy stirring a colourful mixture in a bowl, whipping at it vigorously with a wooden tool that looked as though it had come from Dill's shed.

'I'm getting used to this.' he said.

She glanced up at him, and grinned. 'It not be heart that do miss me in prison – it be stomach.' She poured some more ingredients into the bowl and stirred them again.

'Steady there! I don't think my stomach needs as much as that!'

Kali stood upright, brushing a strand of hair away from her cheek with the back of her hand. 'Is not you only. There be guest I do invite!' She pointed in the direction of the reclining room.

Yan spun around to see Awhi Kanawa getting to her feet. He almost didn't recognise her out of uniform, her proportions more appealing in casual robes. 'I'm so sorry Professor,' she said. 'Kali said you had invited me. She *assured* me. I only wanted to see if she was alright, after what happened with… I should go.'

'No, please don't,' said Yan. 'Kali's quite right – I did mean to invite you. Had I known you were coming today… Well, I did want to thank you for... I mean, of course, it would be nice to see you, anyway. I didn't mean to say that it wasn't…'

Kali left her cooking to rescue Yan from his awkwardness. 'I do take my pet away now,' she said. 'He do need a washing.' She tugged him by his tunic and led him to the stairs.

'I'm sorry!' he called, as he was dragged away. 'I put it down to poor training!'

'It looks like she's trying to correct that!'

When they got to the top of the stairs, Kali pushed him into the washroom. 'Just what do you think you're doing?' he hissed, closing the door behind them. 'You should at least have told me!'

'You want Awhi be going now? Is alright. I do tell her.' Kali turned back to the door.

'No! No, that's not what I meant!'

Kali gave him one of her one-eyed expressions, a sort of humorous knowingness, he thought. She took a fine-grained washing block from the sink and handed it to him with a towel. 'Is well done. You do be washing self now. Trust?'

'Wait! Kali!' But before he could protest any further, she was gone, the door closing firmly behind her.

Yan thought about his guest sitting downstairs. Awhi definitely wasn't his type, but there was something very pleasant about her, something attractive. And they shared a common interest, obviously. *Not your type? Who are you kidding? When were you last with anyone at all?*

When he had finished, he found Kali in his room, going through his clothes. She had opened up the storage compartments and spread various garments on his bed. He stood watching her for a few moments, struggling to comprehend how so much had happened in such a short space of time. Only a few days before, he'd been sure of his domain, even if his existence was a dull and solitary one. Now his life had been turned upside down, and he felt powerless to resist. He didn't *want* to resist. There was no denying that he was happier than he'd been in a very long time, but it was still disorientating to find his home changing around him so quickly. When he woke that morning, the voice of Nico S'tana was already reporting from downstairs, and he had to wait to wash while Kali warbled one of her songs in the shower. Then when he went outside, he nearly tripped over Dill, who was sitting on the back doorstep munching something Kali had cooked for her. It was almost as if he was the one who'd just arrived on an alien planet.

Kali looked up and flashed her smile when she saw him standing there. 'I like this shirt,' she said. 'This trouser be well done with.'

'These trousers go well with it,' he corrected.

'Yes. Is good you do agreement!'

'Kali, it's just a casual meal!'

'Awhi do look very nice, yes?' Kali picked up the shirt and handed it to him. 'Be quickly please, Yan.' She unclipped his tunic and tried to take it from him, but he stepped back and pulled it from her grasp.

'Wait. Is it really necessary that I…?'

Now, Kali looked at him severely. A cleft appeared in the middle of her forehead, and her brow dropped. She held out her hand resolutely for his tunic. 'Yan…' she said, 'Give!'

Acknowledgments

I owe thanks to a many people for their support in the writing of this novel. Some have given generously of their time as beta readers, others have provided their opinions by the scene or chapter and will only now get to read the whole story. There are all the friends I have turned to for their views on everything from characters to cover designs, those who have listened politely to my dinner table groaning, and all those near and dear who have been both kind and brutal when I have needed it. Thank you to you all.

About the Author

Steve Gay is a writer of science fiction, historical fiction and short stories. He grew up in central England, and in Connecticut, and gained his first degree in History and Politics from the University of Southampton. It wasn't until relatively late in life that he wrote his first novel, completing it on the train as he commuted to London. He left his career to focus on his writing, and completed a masters degree at the University of Warwick. His first published novel, *The Birds that do not Sing* was the product of those studies, a historical novel set during the Second World War. *The Callista Alignment* is Steve's first science fiction novel, the beginning of an ongoing series. Steve lives in the Midlands and is never happier than when he is ski-ing with his wife and adult children, or touring in his campervan. His laptop is a constant companion.

More information at:
www.rookabbeypress.com

If you enjoyed reading The Callista Alignment, don't forget to leave a review!

KALI WILL BE BACK SOON IN

THE CALLISTA ASCENDANCY

NOTHING MADE TALITH VA Kablaithan's skin crawl like the sight of a feral human. It was the furtive scurrying of the things she found so repulsive, the unpredictability of movement, the filth and disorder of them. Yet here in this great Antarian metropolis, this shining place of commerce, the creatures were tolerated on the streets, indulged with scraps, counted as individuals. Only her cultivated mind saw it for the disgrace that it was, only her foreign eye saw its dangers.

She had the comfort of distance, but Talith could see the creature clearly enough from the embassy balcony. It was crouching beside a market stall, gnawing at a piece of fruit without a care in the world. It could see her too; it glanced up at her now and again and its eyes shone in the lamplight. It had no fear, no sense of the proper order of things, and why should it when everyone moved around it unconcerned, carried on with their business as if it wasn't there?

There had been another time, long ago, when Talith had encountered a human in the kitchen of Decca's Imperial Palace. She'd been playing there with Prince Temurbek and it had scuttled in front of them with a jar of preserves from the pantry. Temurbek had sent her after it with a whip, bullied and threatened her as she'd moved furniture and forced it into the open.

'Kill it, cousin!' he'd said, and she'd let the whip fly, seen the creature's blood fleck the walls, heard its yelps. She'd chased it around the kitchen, thrashing it until they were both exhausted, until it cowered and whimpered in a corner. 'Don't stop!' Temurbek said. 'One day I'll be Overlord, and you'll be no service to me if you're weak.'

'I'm not weak! I've whipped it bloody!'

'Finish it then, or I'll tell everyone you're not strong enough. You'll never lead House Kablaithan if your weakness brings it dishonour!'

The human chose that moment to run. It got by her, made her shriek. Then it was over the window sill and into the bushes. And Temurbek had laughed at her. He'd kept that moment as their secret, taunted her with it, kept its memory alive in her mind.

But now she was a great lady and had control of her house from top to bottom. Its affairs were run to her direction, its estates were managed by her bidding, its goods moved at her command between distant worlds. She was not weak, but a formidable adversary, whether in business or politics. She had climbed the ladder of state as well, become an architect of foreign policy and now, Decca's ambassador in the Free Republic of Antaris, the fulcrum of its influence in its neighbouring world. The embassy here was hers to govern, its staff, its resources, its diplomatic team. She listened to them of course, she accepted their counsel when it was wise, but she had her own way of doing things too, her own skills, and they owed as much to resolve as diplomacy.

Still, there was the inescapable human factor. That Decca's commercial partner, its planetary neighbour, should see no disgrace in the permissive treatment of humans was perplexing enough, but its drift towards the granting of rights was a catastrophe waiting to happen. They didn't see it, these pampered gentlefolk, they didn't fear these little creatures, the sheer number of them, the ease with which they bred, and their wild and wicked nature. They didn't understand how pandering to humans would suck at the foundations of their republic, undermine their whole commonwealth.

Down in the street, the feral human had moved from under the market stall. It was sitting on a kerb, its body draped with a crude shift, its hair long and matted. It still had the piece of fruit, still held it tight as it eyed the street for its next mischief. And then those greedy human eyes came to her balcony once again and settled on her. It stared, then opened its mouth, poked out its tongue.

Printed in Dunstable, United Kingdom

82373121R00241